MOONSINGER'S FRIENDS

An anthology in honor of Andre Norton

Edited by Susan Shwartz

BLUEJAY BOOKS INC.

SC
M

Library of Congress Cataloging in Publication Data
Main entry under title:

Moonsinger's friends.

1. Fantastic fiction, American. I. Shwartz, Susan.
PS648.F3M66 1985   813'.0876'08   85-6201
ISBN 0-312-94325-3
ISBN 0-312-94326-1 (pbk.)

HS41192

To Andre Norton
Master storyteller, mentor, and friend

CONTENTS

INTRODUCTION

ANDRE NORTON: BEYOND THE SIEGE PERILOUS

IN *Witch World,* THE MODERN-DAY MERLIN, JORGE PETRO-
nius, describes the purpose of the Siege Perilous. "One takes
his seat upon the Siege and before him opens that existence
in which his spirit, his mind—his soul, if you wish to call it
that—is at home. And he goes forth to his future there."

Simon Tregarth, soon to find a home and a destiny in the
Witch World, comments wryly, "Some odd worlds your
stone must have opened if your tale is true."

Some odd worlds indeed. And some very wonderful ones.

Like the Siege Perilous of the Arthurian myths Andre
Norton loves, she too is an opener of Gates—from the Witch
World to burnt-out Dis and isolated Beltane, from Arzor to
Zacan, and throughout Earth's past and its many possible
futures. Andre Norton has spent over fifty years opening
Gate after Gate to legions of readers and writers. As you read
this, she is probably sitting in her study at her typewriter,
companioned by her cats and her honors—the Gandalf award
for life achievement in fantasy, the Balrog, and the first
Grand Mastership that the Science Fiction Writers of America ever awarded to a woman.

These are the obvious honors. The others are subtler—the
reams of correspondence, pen-friendships that have matured
over years, the stack of manuscripts, frequently first or second novels sent her by publishers who trust her to give a
newcomer a break, the published books dedicated to her or

1

inscribed to her by their authors, the animals of glass and china, the ornaments, and the embroideries painstakingly created and offered by their makers who want not to repay her—for that is impossible—but to try to make her a gift in return for the great gift she has made to them and millions like them. And is busily working on right now.

Moonsinger's Friends, named in tribute to Andre Norton's persona in the Sword and Sorcerers' Guild of America—Moonsinger of Nine-lived Bast—is another one of those gifts. In it, some of the finest writers of fantasy and science fiction have combined their talents and dreams to produce stories that Andre Norton might enjoy. There are only fifteen stories here, for if every writer who was influenced by Andre Norton had contributed a story, you wouldn't be reading an anthology. You'd be holding in your hands the first volume of what could easily grow into a library.

The idea for *Moonsinger's Friends* was born at a Philcon several years ago, following a discussion of "critical recognition"—such as it is—for fantasy and science fiction writers. Andre Norton's name came up, and, as Donald Wollheim has remarked in his Introduction to the 1974 *Book of Andre Norton:*

> In lists of leading science fiction writers such as might be compiled by academics and fan experts, it is probable that the name of Andre Norton would be missing, whereas such writers as Robert Heinlein, Poul Anderson, Arthur C. Clarke, John Brunner, and others would certainly be present.
>
> The world of science fiction and fantasy readers, the same people who devour Anderson and Simak and Farmer and Niven, also buy and read everything by Andre Norton they can get their hands on.
>
> While they spend a lot of time discussing the sociology and speculations of the other writers, Andre Norton they read for pleasure.

And yet, because—also, as Donald Wollheim says, "you will not find her at conventions or bumbling around at literary gatherings, nor expounding any special theories at academic halls," she receives less notice than one would expect. This "relative critical neglect is regrettable," observes *The Science Fiction Encyclopedia.*

While it doesn't necessarily seem regrettable to Andre Norton, who is a storyteller in a tradition thousands of years old, it bothered the crowd of us who lingered after that 1981 Philcon panel. Clearly something had to be done about this, and we were the ones who were going to do it. Ironically, the idea for *Moonsinger's Friends* arose from precisely the sort of academic halls in which Andre Norton does *not* bumble about, as well as from fantasy writers in general. The senior statesmen (and women) of universities, in the fullness of their careers, are often honored by their colleagues and former students, who present them with a book. Such a book is called a *Festschrift* (since universities go in for Anglo-German rituals), literally, a text that celebrates something: in this case, an eminent career and an outstanding individual. The academic *Festschrift* usually consists of essays and articles written within the honoree's field, though poems (usually learned translations) are occasionally allowed. I remembered one such book compiled in honor of scholar and fantasist J. R. R. Tolkien, and suddenly decided that such a volume— but one of stories like the ones Andre Norton has made a career of telling—would be the very thing. Several authors present agreed with me. One of them, Diane Duane, is a contributor to this book.

And so, here it is . . . a collection of short stories and novelettes written to honor the woman who opened Gates to many of us and who, as writer, mentor, and friend, has *been* (to borrow another contributor, C. J. Cherryh's, phrase) "the gateway through which so, so many of us have come into this field in the first place." Usually books like this include biography, bibliography, and an attempt by the general editor to come to grips with what's all too frequently termed in academic circles the "achievement" of the person to whom the book is presented.

I'm not going to try that. Andre Norton's "achievement," so to speak, is all around us, not just in the shelves of bookstores, libraries, and readers, but in the lives of the men and women who, in many cases, have grown up reading her novels.

As Joan D. Vinge remarks in her Afterword, Andre Norton has helped us to grow up. Many of her books are the first science fiction a lot of readers encounter. The experience is always the same. Something about that particular novel strikes a chord in the young reader, who suddenly feels at home and knows that he or she has to find more of these books. Ask any Norton reader. Chances are, any one can tell you which Norton book opened the Gate to wonder—and will probably urge you to reread it before you do anything else.

We are, of course, lucky that we had someone like Andre Norton to open Gates for us when we were children and teenagers, because the impressions that are made then are lasting ones. Opening Gates for young people is a tremendous responsibility that Andre Norton has borne lightly and joyfully, and for which frequently she has not gotten the credit she deserves. As Ursula K. LeGuin (no mean opener of Gates herself) remarks in "Dreams Must Explain Themselves," "Sure it's simple, writing for kids. Just as simple as bringing them up."

In the same essay, LeGuin points out:

> The British seem not to believe publishers' categorizations of "juvenile," "teen-age," "young adult, etc." so devoutly as we do. It's interesting that, for instance, Andre Norton is often reviewed with complete respect by English papers, including the *Times Literary Supplement* . . . They seem to be aware that fantasy is the great age-equalizer; if it's good when you're twelve, it's quite likely to be just as good, or better, when you're thirty-six.

This is true of the worlds that Andre Norton's Gates have opened to us. We don't just read her new books and then add them to the collection on the shelves to gather dust; we reread the old ones. Any new Witch World novel is a perfect invitation to sit down and reread all the others. Norton's books don't just show us wonders that don't dim as the years pass and, presumably, we enter the "real world," they show us wonders in such a way that we see ourselves in them. We participate, we share, and, if we happen to be in need of it, we are healed just as surely as if we'd stumbled upon one of those pools of red mud that you find in Escore if you're very, very lucky. It isn't just that we can "relate"—in some cloying pop-psychology sense—to a renegade like Simon Tregarth, or a displaced person like Troy Horan, or veterans like Ranger Kartr mourning burnt-off worlds, or Beastmaster Hosteen Storm, but in a more personal and immediate sense.

Like the Gates that the Siege Perilous unlocks, the Gates created by Andre Norton let us into places where our spirits find homes, where we're not strange, where there are people who are like us, who want what we do. They heal our loneliness, at least while we're reading. And goodness knows that for most of us who regard castles, starships, wizards, and aliens as desirable mental furniture, we need that. Adolescents spend plenty of time wondering if they'll ever find a place where they fit in, where they could be accepted *precisely* for the qualities that make them feel like outskirters in our schools, our shopping malls—in the "real world."

Here was a real live published author (and if that's not an authority figure, what is?) showing us wonders. The existence of her books implied that there might be more writers who told such stories.

For those of us who are female, there was a special shock of recognition, usually expressed as, "You mean Andre Norton's really a woman?" That was almost as much a delight as finding out she existed in the first place. Not only did *she* do things—she wrote books, which is what a lot of us wanted to do—she wrote books about characters we might, if we were very, very lucky, be able to match. After all, very few of us are likely to grow up into Jirel of Joiry or Red Sonya. But a bookish girl, given a star-faring society, might grow into a Roane Hume or a Charis Nordholm; a sensitive one might become a Kaththea or Jaelithe Tregarth, a resourceful one Joisan, or Gillan in *The Crystal Gryphon* and *Gryphon in Glory* and *Year of the Unicorn*. That was a relief for me, at least. While I had no trouble identifying with the promising young cadets of Robert Heinlein's *Space Cadet* (probably because I assumed that the female cadets were too busy studying astrogation to come forward and tell their stories), it *was* much, much easier to put myself in the slippers or spaceboots of another girl—and it still is. And seeing such people actually doing things that counted made it easier for me, and women like me, to try for lives of our own. Not that we wouldn't have, in any case. But just by being there and telling her stories, Andre Norton made it easier for all of us.

For many of us, male *and* female, those of us who weren't content just to read but who tried to figure out what Kaththea and her Hilarion might do *next,* or what Nik Kolherne did with his new face and new family, another, greater Gate opened up: we discovered to our great joy that we too could be openers of Gates. If we did a good job, then people would go through our Gates too, perhaps, in the process of creating Gates—and stories—of their own; and no one would ever run out of Gates or things to read.

This is what the writers in *Moonsinger's Friends* have in common with the readers: they travel through Gate after Gate like C. J. Cherryh's Morgaine, but with one important difference. No one gets hurt or stays lonely.

Still, Andre Norton isn't just one Gatekeeper out of many; she remains quintessentially *the* Gatekeeper, the first one, the one we return to.

There's always a special quality to Andre Norton's stories. If you read her as an adult, you once again become the wise child or adolescent or whatever that you were when you discovered her books. Who says you can't go home again? And who says that you can only have one home? You can find a home in any one of Norton's books and, better yet, you can take from them the very things that delighted and impressed you at any point in your life. Best of all, once you put the book down and reenter daily life and the all-too-familiar round of teachers, classmates, and later, jobs, bills, and other obligations, you can use what you gained in her books to help you function . . . better than before. This is due to the very special insight all of Andre Norton's books contain, an insight that makes them simultaneously exotic and familiar.

Most of Andre Norton's characters are young. Through no fault of their own—there's been a war, a plague, their parents have been killed or called away—these people find themselves alone like the children in *Dragon Magic*. Some are actual exiles or refugees, like Rahotep, nomarch-in-exile, or Troy Horan and Niall Renfro, who drift in the shadow world of the Dipple, where the luxuries of exotic Tikil serve as a frustrating reminder of what they can't have, what they might have lost, what others have, but aren't sharing. For some, it's even worse than that: they've lost their parents, or like Nik Kolherne, been disfigured, wounded like Kemoc Tregarth, or tested to the limits of their endurance like Kaththea, his sister. And then there are the others, like Roane Hume in *Ice Crown*, who have never been loved, or who, like Ross Murdock, turn feral because no one cared whether they lived or died.

If these were actual flesh-and-bloods, social workers would make gloomy observations in casebooks, and the rest of us might look away. That's because what these characters face are the very things that we all fear: loss, exile, loneliness, pain . . . and they face it under stark circumstances.

Then it usually gets worse. Even as the protagonists cope with their initial grief or trouble, the writer pits them against an overwhelming problem. To quote a maxim of fan writers: "First you chase your hero up a tree. Then you throw rocks at him." The Tregarths must first rescue Kaththea from hostile Witches, then help purify all Escore. Charis Nordholm is sold by enemies to a free-trader and runs into Jacks and Wyverns almost simultaneously. Troy Horan falls afoul of the Hunters, a time trap, and postwar intrigues, while Kana Karr, Kade Whitehawk, and Travis Fox encounter bigotry, manipulative governments, violence, and a chance to make a better future . . . assuming they can survive the present.

And the wonderful thing is that they make it! Each one of Norton's characters faces a test in direct proportion to his or her abilities to cope—and succeeds. This is profoundly satisfying to read. We know that at the end of a Norton novel, a sympathetic character will win through to what he or she most wants. So what if Roane Hume's uncle and cousin take off and leave her on Clio? She has good friends and a sure place in Reveny. Troy Horan will never see his range again, but he'll hunt the wilds with Rerne and his fur friends. Ross Murdock may never have known his own parents, but he finds a father-substitute and friend in Gordon Ash.

If the worlds Norton's characters live in really offer them no future, if they're totally barren, then her heroes and heroines find worlds in which they *can* be at home. Niall Renfro in *Judgment on Janus* and *Victory on Janus* becomes Ayyar of the Iftin, and is probably hunting in his deep, leafy forests now. At this very moment, Diskan Fentress of *The X Factor* may be dancing thal patterns with the brothers-in-fur in the magic city of Xcothal. And Dane Thorson is checking his cargo lists, content with the ship that has become family and hearth for him. We wish them well. And, just a little, we envy them. By the end of the book, each has found a sure place; found friends, love, an end to loneliness, and a purpose within their power to achieve.

That last point is very important. Note that with all these characters, their struggles fall into a larger pattern. This is especially true for characters in a series such as Witch World, in which the black/white opposition found in all high fantasy forces everyone not just to take sides but to take up arms. There is no such thing as simply going off and living your life. You either share the common war, or you die in it.

Mind you, none of Norton's characters is asked to solve the whole problem. You can imagine Shann Lantee giving a helping hand to a youngster who needs it; but you can't see him lobbying for better orphanages on Tyr, his homeworld. Troy Horan will probably be content to protect the wilds of Korwar, but I doubt he'll stand for election to the very political bodies that forced him from his first home. Characters like Kade Whitehawk or Kana Karr, who find themselves forced to become revolutionaries, know that they'll have only their own, individual guerrilla actions to worry about. No one's asking them to take up the One Ring, blast the Death

Star, single-handedly maintain Equilibrium, or even pull a sword out of a stone. If their tasks are less lofty, that just makes their success more believable—and themselves more approachable. The sum of their lives seems to outweigh any theories about life that a lesser writer might impose.

But the sum of Norton's characters' lives includes a subtle and far-reaching moral code that permeates her books and impresses readers more surely than a thousand lectures or incendiary pamphlets. No one, reading of the adventures of the *Solar Queen*, can fail to note how well the crew members from all races get along . . . at least some of the time. And in *Star Rangers* (now retitled *The Last Planet*), we can see how the rangers of all races and species work together to survive. And just in case we miss it, we have contrasting characters: the settlers of Khatka who created a reverse apartheid, the people who denied Travis Fox a scholarship, Joyd Cummi, who dies partially because of his own hatred of people he considers barbarians. This isn't just restricted to Norton's science fiction. The Witch World is peopled not just with humans but with the Thas, the Krogan, the Flannan, the elven-seeming People of the Green Silences, and the Renthan, to name a few. If they are considered good or evil, it's because of the side they choose, not their physical form. The Renthan might be grotesque on first glance; but they are wise, even majestic in council. Dinzil, on the other hand, was a handsome man, and totally corrupt.

Norton's—and her characters'—respect for otherness extends not just to "intelligent life forms" but to animals, especially to cats. At times, the distinction between "people" and "animals" blurs, as in *Catseye*, where Troy Horan becomes one equal in a team of cats, foxes, and kinkajou. Hosteen Storm has an eagle, a dunecat, and meerkats to assist him. On Warlock, Shann Lantee teams up with wolverines, while Charis Nordholm is adopted by a curl-cat. And if anyone thinks that these animals are subordinate or cute little pets, they'd better think again, and reread the books in which they appear.

Another value Norton insists on, in that unobtrusive, matter-of-fact way of hers, is egalitarianism. Nowhere is this more apparent than in the Witch World books. Koris of Gorm is despised by his father's people for his mixed blood—and those people fall prey to Kolder, while the Torfolk too are punished. Simon Tregarth, of unknown race, is welcomed into Estcarp, which finds him a strong shield against the Dark. Loyse of Verlaine stands with hereditary enemies against the Shadow and against Kolder. Again, what matters is the side they're on, not their race.

But even on the "right" side, Norton shows situations that clearly cannot be allowed to go on. For example, the Matriarchate of Estcarp's witches causes population decline and makes women with Power regard men (who are thought to lack it) with disdain, a situation that occasionally has explosive consequences, as when a Witch is raped in order to take away her power and, not so incidentally, humiliate her, and all other witches. This situation cannot endure. Into it walk Simon Tregarth, with his Cornish second sight, and his wife, Jaelithe, who surrenders her virginity, but not her magic. Into it walk the triplets, their children, who can link together. And into it also come later pairs of people who have overcome prejudices to be together: Tanree of the Sulcars and the Falconer Rivery, who has seen the curse that turned the Falconers into misogynists broken in "Falcon Blood"; Tirtha and the Falconer Nirel in *Ware Hawk;* Dairine, who escapes the horrific female chauvinism of the weaving spiders, to renew the spirit of another exile in "Spider Silk."

Nor does Norton tolerate vindictiveness. In "Toads of Grimmerdale," Hertha seeks to destroy a man she believes is her rapist, but must ultimately fight to save him because there are things no human may be tossed to. And turning to her science fiction novels, we see Hosteen Storm of the Beastmaster books planning to avenge himself, his father, and his grandfather upon Brad Quade, who ultimately becomes a father-figure for him. Nik Kolherne has been used and manipulated in "Night of Masks," but when he is critically injured, he still tries to save the man who exploited him from an alien terror. Andre Norton insists that we see straight. Certainly, people have legitimate grievances. But there are things greater than grievances, and we'd best remember it.

It's a critical commonplace to observe that throughout the past decade, at least, Andre Norton's books have "darkened" greatly. And yet, even in dark stories like *Dread Companion* and *Dark Piper*, during which we see star-spanning civilizations collapse past the power of individual people to restore, there is still hope, a chance for a new start, a fresh beginning that may take the descendants of Norton's characters back to the stars and maybe beyond this time . . . if they do it right. Barbara Tuchman once wrote of humanity's capability to "muddle through" as the thing that might save it. Norton's characters raise that to a moral imperative and show us how, too.

In their low-key, unobtrusive ways, Norton's characters are both fine and tough. If we wish them well—and we usually do—we also feel that they're good people to introduce our friends to. As C. J. Cherryh points out in her introduction to *Lore of the Witch World:*

> Andre's books are the ones they're going to put into the hands of their own sons and daughters and say with that special, waited-for hope: "I think you might like this. It's good."

We can trust them to get people started off into the right Gates: to dream without giving up the capacity for action, to be strong but not brutal, to plan but to be realistic, to be kind, to love, and never to give up hope. Something, some solution, some act, is always possible throughout her work; Andre Norton raises the level of what is possible to a gentle art.

This art is what is good to remember when we close the book, turning back through whatever Gate we've entered to our ordinary lives.

As a writer, too, Andre Norton is a mistress of the possible. She does not attempt to overwhelm readers with polemics or special pleadings, and therefore her own strong views on the treatment of animals, on warfare, on feminism, and other issues pass almost unnoticed. Nor does she seek to impress readers by deliberately abstruse reasoning or by cooking up odd theories. Why should she? Her characters already have a universe to travel in and magic to learn. Her style doesn't incline to pyrotechnics, but instead to spare, eloquent narrative that conveys mood and character without demanding the reader's applause at every neatly turned epigram.

Her skills as a writer have special meaning to those of us who read her and decided that we too wished to open Gates. Her spare, elegant simplicity in storytelling made us believe that writing *was* a possible goal . . . until we tried it and learned that while it was still possible, it wasn't nearly as easy as it looked. Still, what we'd learned from Andre Norton's books made it unlikely that we would give up. So we tried again, painfully, and worked on it—sometimes with her encouragement—until we started to get it right. All of the writers in this book are working on "getting it right" and have been doing so all their lives. Just like Norton characters.

Ultimately, Andre Norton's "achievement" may be even more a triumph of character than of narrative alone. After all, her stories exist because she decided that they were going to exist, that she had something to say that people needed to hear—and then she wrote them and kept on writing. Like her characters, Andre Norton cares, and out of caring, has made us all a great gift.

It is only natural that people who have passed through Gates—hers or their own—need to return to their own world and time, bringing gifts that will enable all of us to thrive and repay some old obligations. Here, then, are stories of forests and of hunts, of young children and wise animals and wizards, of love, law, and magic, of healing and laughter and tears . . . in short, about all the things that Andre Norton has spent so many years writing.

The participants in *Moonsinger's Friends* want to thank Andre Norton in their own words for all of us. It's proper that they do so. But as befits people who have guested in *her* worlds, they had also best thank her in her own words, by the very customs she has created. And so:

To the giver of the feast, thanks, fair thanks. For the welcome of the gate, gratitude. To the rulers of this house, fair fortune and bright sun on the morrow.

Accept our thanks, Andre, and the welcome of these gates.

THE SEA AND THE SORCERESS

Full fathom five thy father lies.
  Of his bones are coral made;
Those are pearls that were his eyes:
  Nothing of him that doth fade,
But doth suffer a sea-change
Into something rich and strange. (*Tempest*, I, ii. ll. 397–402)

Though Andre Norton is a landswoman, sea changes have always fascinated her. In her Witch World novels, Sulcar and Falconers flee across the sea to Estcarp. But strangeness also crosses the seas to menace Estcarp and the Dales, or glides beneath them into Tormarsh. Similarly, rescuers cross the sea, braving the Lost Trace, questing after marvels. In Norton's work, the sea is often the gateway to wonder.

Sea changes fascinate Marion Zimmer Bradley, Diane Duane, and Tanith Lee, too. Marion is perhaps best known as the creator of Darkover, where the sea is mentioned only as a far-off wonder. In "Sea Wrack," she turns to another of her popular characters, this one out of the Thieves' World stories: Lythande the Pilgrim Adept. Mage, minstrel, and, beneath the Blue Star and concealing robes, possessed of an all-too-tender heart, Lythande is drawn to the sea whose mystery and vastness complement her own loneliness.

But the sea is changeful, treacherous. Some of what it casts up, or the beings who live by it, can imperil even an

Adept of the Blue Star, who doesn't need to wait for the final battle against Chaos to find mortal danger.

A member of the most recent generation of fantasy and science fiction writers, Diane Duane is almost as well known for her Star Trek novels and sense of humor as she is for her chronicles of the magic kingdoms of Arlen and Darthen as they appear (so far) in *The Door into Fire* and *The Door into Shadow*. Like Bradley's Lythande and Norton's witches, Diane Duane's Rodmistresses and sorcerers battle Chaos, or entropy, as Diane prefers to call it, holding back the final Darkness as long as possible so that life may be lived and praised over and over again.

Unlike Lythande, Diane Duane's magicians like to stay where they're put. Unless they're on quest, they're homebodies. Usually, her Rodmistresses, who train in the deep forest, are associated with the woods. Indeed most of Diane's stories take place . . . one cannot say "safely on dry land," but in the hills and forests of the Two Kingdoms.

But the sea has a special place in her books; it's what you reach when you pass the final gate of all—as any Rodmistress (or any child in the Two Kingdoms) will tell you.

Lior, the heroine of Duane's story, lives on the shore. Much like LeGuin's wizard of Earthsea, she specializes in sea lore, and finds in the sea a livelihood, education, entertainment, companionship, and perhaps more.

Winner of the 1984 World Fantasy Award for her redaction of the Snow White legend, "Red as Blood," Tanith Lee is mistress of one of the greatest ranges of style currently gracing the field. Her stories can skulk through a vampire's catacomb, explode from a volcano, riot under a domed city, or live along the shore in this, any other—or even the next—world. Saddest and wisest of her stories are her fables in which a demon sacrifices his immortal life for the world he loves, or a sorceress's fierce magic is tamed, or any cold heart warmed and healed.

Like Diane Duane's Lior, Tanith's witch girl lives by the sea. And no one ever had a more compassionate or powerful matchmaker.

SEA WRACK

Marion Zimmer Bradly

THE CRIMSON EYE OF KETH HOVERED NEAR THE HORIZON, with the smaller sun of Reth less than an hour behind. At this hour, the fishing fleet should have been sailing into the harbor. But there was no sign of any fleet; only a single boat, far out, struggling against the tide.

Lythande had walked far that day along the shore, enjoying the solitude and singing old soft sea songs to the sounds of the surf. *Tonight, surely,* the Pilgrim Adept thought, *supper must be earned by singing to the lute, for in a simple place like this there would be none to need the services of a mercenary magician, no need for spells or magicks, only simple folk, living simply to the rhythms of sea and tides.*

Perhaps it was a holiday; all the boats lay drawn up along the shore. But there was no holiday feel in the single street: angry knots of men sat clumped together scowling and talking in low voices, while a little group of women were staring out to sea, watching the single boat struggling against the tide.

"Women! By the blinded eyes of Keth-Ketha, how are women to handle a boat?" one of the men snarled. "How are they to handle fishing nets? Curse that—"

"Keep your voice down," admonished a second. "That— that thing might hear, and wake!"

Lythande looked out into the bay and saw what had not been apparent before; the approaching boat was crewed not

16

by men, but by four hearty half-grown girls in their teens.
Their muscular arms were bare to the shoulder, their skirts
tucked up to the knee, their feet clumsy in seaboots. They
seemed to be handling the nets competently enough, and
were evidently enormously strong; the kind of women who,
if they had been milking a cow, could sling the beast over
their shoulder and fetch it home out of a bog. And the men
were watching them with a jealous fury poorly concealed.

"Tomorrow I take my own boat out and the lasses stay
home and bake bread where they belong!"

"Thass' what Leukas did, and you know what happened to
him—his whole crew wrecked on the rocks, and—and something, some *thing* out there ate boat and all! All they ever
found was his hat and his fishing net chewed half through!
An' seven sons for the village to feed till they're big enough
to go out to the fishing—that's supposing we ever have any
more fishing around here and that whatever-it-is out there
ever goes away again!"

Lythande raised a questioning eyebrow. Some menace to
the village. But not the kind that would provide work for a
mercenary magician. Though Lythande bore two swords gir-
dled at the narrow waist of the mage-robe, the right-hand
sword for the everyday menace of threatening humankind or
natural beast, the left-hand sword to slay ghost or ghast or
ghoul or any manner of supernatural menace, the Adept had
no intention of here joining battle against some sea monster.
For that the village must await some hero or fighting man.
Lythande was magician and minstrel, and though the sword
was for hire where there was need, the Adept had no love for
ordinary warfare and less for fighting some menacing thing
needing only brute strength and not craft.

There was but one inn in the village; Lythande made for it,
ordered a pot of ale, and sat in the corner, not touching it.
One of the vows fencing the power of an Adept of the Blue
Star was that they might never be seen to eat or drink before
men, but the price of a drink gave the mage a seat at the
center of the action where all the news of the village could be
heard. They were still grousing about the fear which kept
them out of the water. One man complained that already the

ribs of his boat were cracking and drying and would need mending before he could put it back into the water.

"If there's ever to be any fishing here again . . ."

"Ye could send the wife and daughters out in the boat like Lubert—"

"Better we all starve or eat porridge for all our lives!"

"If we ha' no fish to trade for bread or porridge, what then?"

"Forgive my curiosity," Lythande said in the mellow, neutral voice that marked a trained minstrel, "but if a sea monster is threatening the shore, why should women be safe in a boat when men are not?"

It was the wife of the innkeeper who answered her. "If it was a sea monster we could go out there, all of us, even with fish spears, and kill it like the plainsmen do with the tusk-beasts. It's a mermaid, an' she sits and sings and lures our menfolk to the rocks—look yonder at my goodman," she said in a lowered voice, pointing to a man who sat apart before the fire, back turned to the company, clothing all unkempt, shirt half buttoned, staring into the fire. His fingers fiddled nervously with the lacings of his clothing, snarling them into loops.

"He heard her," she said in a tone of such horror that hearing, the little hairs rose and tingled on Lythande's arms and the Blue Star between the magician's brows began to crackle and send forth lightnings. "He *heard* her, and his men dragged him away from the rocks. And there he sits from that day to this—him that was the jolliest man in all this town, staring and weeping, and I have to feed him like a little child, and never take my eyes off him for half a minute or he'll walk out into the sea and drown, and there are times"—her voice sank in despair—"I'm minded to let him go, for he'll never have his wits again—I even have to guide him out to the privy, for he's forgotten even that!" And indeed, Lythande could see a moist, spreading stain on the man's trousers, while the woman hastened, embarrassed, to lead her husband outside.

Lythande had seen the man's eyes: empty, lost, not seeing his wife, staring at something beyond the room.

Far from the sea Lythande had heard tales of mermaids, of their enchantments and their songs. The minstrel in Lythande had half desired to hear those songs, to walk on the rocks and listen to the singing which could, it was said, make the hearer forget all the troubles and joys of the world. But after seeing the man's empty eyes, Lythande decided to forgo the experience.

"And that is why some of the women have gone in the boats?"

"Not women," said the innkeeper's potboy, stopping with a tray of tankards to speak to the stranger. "Girls too young for men. For they say that to women, it calls in the voice of their lovers—Natzer's wife went out last full moon, swearing she'd bring in fish for her children at least, and no one ever saw her again; but a hank of her hair, all torn and bloody, came in on the tide."

"I never heard that a mermaid was a flesh eater," Lythande observed.

"Nor I. But I think she sings and lures 'em on the rocks where the fishes eat them. . . ."

"There is the old stratagem," Lythande suggested. "Put cotton or wax plugs in your ears—"

"Say, stranger," said a man belligerently, "you think we're all fools out here? We tried that; but she sits on the rocks and she's so beautiful . . . the men went mad, just seeing her, threw me overboard—you can't blindfold yourself, not on the sea with the rocks and all—there's never been a blind fisherman and never will. I swam ashore, and they drove the boat on the rocks. And only the blinded eyes of Keth-Ketha know where they've gone, but no doubt somewhere in the Sea God's lockup." As Lythande turned to face the man, he saw the Blue Star shining out from under the mage-robe and demanded, "Are you a spell-speaker?"

"I am a Pilgrim Adept of the Blue Star," Lythande said gravely, "and while all mankind awaits the final battle of Law and Chaos, I wander the world seeking what may come."

"I ha' heard of the Temple of the Blue Star," said one

woman fearfully. "Could you free us of this mermaid wi' your magic?"

"I do not know. I have never seen a mermaid," said Lythande, "and I have no great desire for the experience."

Yet why not? Under the world of the Twin Suns, in a life lasting more than most people's imaginations could believe, the Pilgrim Adept had seen most things, and the mermaid was new. Lythande pondered how one would attack a creature whose only harm seemed to be that it gave forth beautiful music—so beautiful that the hearer forgot home and family, loved ones, wife or child—if the hearer escaped. Lythande shuddered. It was not a fate to be desired: sitting day after day staring into the fire, longing only to hear again that song.

Yet whatever magic could make, could be unmade again by magic. And Lythande held all the magic of the Temple of the Blue Star, having paid a price more terrifying than any other Adept in the history of the Pilgrim Adepts. Should that magic now be tried against the unfamiliar magic of a mermaid?

"We are dying and hungering," said the woman. "Isn't that enough? I believed wizards were sworn to free the world from evil—"

"How many wizards have you known?" asked Lythande.

"None, though my mother said her granny told her, once a wizard came and done away wi' a sea monster on them same rocks."

"Time is a great artificer," said Lythande, "for even wizards must live, my good woman. The price of magic, while a suitable diversion while we all await the burning out of the Twin Suns and the final battle between Law and Chaos, puts no beans on the table. I have no great desire to test my powers against your mermaid, and I'll wager you anything you like that yonder old wizard charged your town a pretty penny for ridding the world of that sea monster."

"We have nothing to give," said the innkeeper's wife, "but if you can restore my man, I'll give you my gold ring that he gave me when we were wedded. And since he's been enchanted, what kind of man are you if you can't take away one magic with another?" She tugged at her fat finger, and

held out the ring, thin and worn, in the palm of her hand. Her
fingers clung to it, and there were tears in her eyes, but she
held it out valiantly.

"What kind of man am I?" Lythande asked with an ironic
smile. "Like none you will ever see. I have no need of gold.
But give me tonight's lodging, and I will do what I can."

The woman slid the ring back on her finger with shaking
hands. "My best chamber. But oh, restore him! Or would ye
have some supper first?"

"Work first, then pay," said Lythande. The man was
sitting again in the corner by the fire, staring into the flames,
and from his lips came a small tuneless humming. Lythande
unslung the lute in its bag and took it out, bending over the
strings. Long thin fingers strayed over the keys, head bent
close as Lythande listened for the sound, tuning and twisting
the pegs which held the strings.

At last, touching the strings, Lythande began to play. As
the sound of the lute stole through the big common room, it
was as if the chinks letting in the late sun had widened, and
the light spread in the room. Lythande played sunlight and
the happy breeze on the shore. Softly, on tiptoe, not wanting
to let any random sound interrupt the music, the people in the
inn stole nearer to listen to the soft notes. Sunlight, the shore
winds, the sounds of the soft splashing waves. Then Lythande
began to sing.

Afterward—and for years all those who heard often spoke
of it—no one could remember what song was sung, though to
everyone it sounded familiar, so that every hearer was sure it
was a song they had heard at their mother's knee. To everyone it called in the voice of husband or lover or child or wife,
the voice of the one most loved. One old man said with tears
in his eyes that he had heard his mother singing him to sleep
with an old lullabye he had not heard in more than half a
century. And at last even the man who sat by the fire, clothes
unkempt and stinking, hair rough and tangled, his eyes lost in
another world, slowly raised his head and turned to listen to
the voice of Lythande, soft contralto or tenor; neutral, sexless, yet holding all the sweetness of either sex. Lythande
sang of the simple things of the world, of sunlight and rain

and wind, of the voices of children, of grass and wind and harvest and the silences of dawn and twilight. Then, the tempo quickening a little, the Adept sang of home and fireside where the children gathered in the evening, calling to their fathers to come home from the sea. And at last, the soft voice deepening and growing quieter so that the listeners had to lean forward to hear it, yet every whispered note clearly audible even to the rafters of the inn, Lythande sang of love.

And the eyes of every man widened, and the cheek of every woman reddened to a blush, yet to the innocent children there every word was innocent as a mother's kiss on their cheek.

And when the song fell silent, the man by the fireside raised his head and brushed the tears from his eyes.

"Mhari, lass," he said hoarsely, "where are ye—ye and the babes? Why, ha' I been sittin' here the day long and not out to the fishing? Why, lass, you're crying. What ails the girl?" And he drew her to his knee and kissed her, and his face changed, and he shook his head, bewildered.

"Why, I dreamed—I dreamed—" His face contorted, but the woman drew his head down on her breast and she too was weeping.

"Don't think of it, goodman. Ye' were enchanted, but by the mercy of the gods and this good wizard here, ye're safe home and yourself again. . . ."

He rose, his hands straying to his uncombed hair and unshaven chin. "How long? Aye, what devil's magick kept me here? And—" he looked round, seeing Lythande laying the lute in the case "—what brought me back? I owe ye gratitude, Lord Wizard," he said. "All my poor house may offer is at your command." His voice held the dignity of a poor workingman, and Lythande bent graciously to acknowledge it.

"I will take a lodging for the night and a meal served in private in my room, no more." And though both the fisherman and his wife pressed Lythande to accept the ring and other gifts, even to the profits of a year's fishing, the wizard would accept nothing more.

But the others in the room crowded near, clamoring.

"No such magic has ever been seen in these parts! Surely you can free us with your magic from this evil wizardry! We beg you, we are at your mercy—we have nothing worthy of you, but such as we can, we will give. . . ."

Lythande listened, impassive, to the pleading. It was to be expected; magic had been demonstrated, and knowing what it could do, they were greedy for more. Yet it was not greed alone. Their lives and their livelihood were at stake. These poor folk could not continue to live by fishing if the mermaid continued to lure them onto the rocks to be wrecked or eaten by sea monsters, or, if they came safe and alive to their homes, to live on rapt away by the memory.

Yet what reason could this mermaid have for her evildoing? Lythande was well acquainted with the laws of magic, and magical things did not exercise their powers only out of a desire to make mischief among men. Why, after all, had this mermaid come to sing and enchant these simple shore folk? What could her purpose be?

"I will have a meal served in private, that I may consider this," the magician said, "and tomorrow I will speak with everyone in the village who has heard this creature's song or looked upon her. And then I will decide whether my magic can do anything for you. Further than that I will not go."

When the woman had departed, leaving the tray of food, Lythande locked and double-locked the door of the room behind her. A fine baked fish lay on a clean white napkin. Lythande suspected it was the best of the meager catch brought in by the young girls, which alone kept the village from starving. The fish was seasoned with fragrant herbs, and there was a hot coarse loaf of maize bread with butter and cream, and a dish of sweet boiled seaweed on the tray.

First Lythande cast about the room, the Blue Star blazing between the narrow brows, seeking hidden spy-holes or magical traps. Eternal vigilance was the price of safety for any Adept of the Blue Star, even in a village as isolated as this one. It was not likely that some enemy had trailed Lythande here, nor prearranged a trap, but stranger things had happened in the Adept's long life.

But the room was nowhere overlooked and seemed impregnable, so that at last Lythande was free to take off the voluminous mage-robe and even to ungird the belt with the two swords and draw off the soft dyed leather boots. So revealed, Lythande presented still the outward appearance of a slender, beardless man, tall and strongly framed and sexless; yet, free of observation, Lythande was revealed as what she was: a woman. Yet a woman who might never be known to be so in the sight of any living man.

A masquerade which had become truth; for in the Temple of the Pilgrim Adepts, Lythande alone in all their long history had successfully penetrated that Sanctuary in male disguise. Not till the Blue Star already shone between her brows, symbol and sign of Adepthood, had she been discovered and exposed; and by then she was sacrosanct, bearing their innermost secrets. And then the Master of the Pilgrim Adepts had laid on her the doom she still bore.

"So be it; be then in truth what you have chosen to seem. Till Law and Chaos meet in that final battle where all things must die, be what you have pretended; for on that day when any Pilgrim Adept save myself shall proclaim your true sex, on that day is your power forfeit and you may be slain."

So together with all the vows which fenced about the power of a Pilgrim Adept, Lythande bore this burden as well: that of concealing her true sex to the end of the world.

She was not, of course, the only Adept heavily burdened with a *geas;* every Adept of the Blue Star bore some such Secret in whose concealment, even from other Adepts of the Order, lay all his magic and all his strength. Lythande might even have a woman confidante, if she could find one she could trust with her life and her powers.

The minstrel-Adept ate the fish and nibbled at the boiled seaweed, which was not to her taste. The maize bread, well wrapped against grease, found its way into the pockets of the mage-robe against some time when she might not be able to manage privacy for a meal and must snatch a concealed bite as she travelled.

This done, she drew from a small pouch at her waist a quantity of herbs which had no magical properties whatever (unless the property of bringing relaxation and peace to the weary can be counted magical), rolled them into a narrow tube, and set them alight with a spark blazing from the ring she bore. She inhaled deeply, leaned back with her narrow feet stretched out to the fire, for the sea wind was damp and cold, and considered.

Did she wish, for the prestige of the Order and the pride of a Pilgrim Adept, to go out against a mermaid?

Powerful as was the magic of the Blue Star, Lythande knew that somewhere beneath the world of the Twin Suns a magick might lie next to which a Pilgrim Adept's powers were mere hearth magic and trumperies. There were moments when she wearied, indeed, of her long life of concealment and felt she would welcome death, especially if it came in honorable battle. But these were brief moods of the night and always when day came, she wakened with renewed curiosity about all the new adventures which might lie around the next bend in the road. She had no wish to cut it short in futile striving against an unknown enemy.

Her music had indeed recalled the enchanted man to himself. Did this mean her magic was stronger than that of the mermaid? Probably not; she had needed only to break through the magical focus of his attention, to remind him of the beauty of the world he had forgotten. Then, hearing again, his mind had chosen that real beauty over the false beauty of the enchantment; for beneath the magic which held him entranced, the mind of the man must have been already in despair, struggling to break free. A simple magic and nothing to give overconfidence in her strength against the unknown magic of mermaids.

She wrapped herself in the mage-robe and laid herself down to sleep, halfway inclined to rise before dawn and be far away before anyone in the village was astir. What were the troubles of a fishing village to her? Already she had given them a gift of magic, restoring the innkeeper's husband to himself. What else did she owe them?

Yet a few minutes before the rising of the pale face of Keth, she woke knowing she would remain. Was it only the challenge of testing an unknown magic against her own? Or had the helplessness of these people touched her heart?

Most likely, Lythande thought with a cynical smile, it was her own wish to see a new magic. In the years she had wandered under the eyes of Keth and Reth, she had seen many magics, and most were simple and almost mechanical, set once in motion and kept going by something not much better than inertia.

Once, she remembered, she had encountered a haunted oak grove with a legend of a dryad who seduced all male passersby. It had proven to be no more than an echo of a dryad's wrath when spurned by a man she had tried and failed to seduce. Her rage and counterspell had persisted more than forty seasons, even when the dryad's tree had fallen, lightning-struck, and withered. The remnants of the spell had lingered till it was no more than an empty grove where women took their reluctant lovers, that the leftover powers of the angry dryad might arouse at least a little lust. Lythande, despite the pleas of the women fearing to lose their husbands to the power of the spell, had not chosen to meddle. The last she heard, the place had acquired a pleasant reputation for restoring potency, at least for a night, to any man who slept there.

The village was already astir. Lythande went out into the reddening sunrise, where the fishermen gathered from habit, though they were not dragging their boats to the edge of the tide. Seeing Lythande, they left the boats and crowded around.

"Say, wizard, will you help us or no?"

"I have not yet decided," said Lythande. "First I must speak with everyone in the village who has encountered the creature."

"Ye can't do that," said one old man with a fierce grin. "Less ye can walk down into the Sea God's lockup an' question them down there! Or maybe wizards can do that too?"

Rebuked, Lythande wondered if she were taking their predicament too lightly. To her, perhaps, it was challenge and curiosity; to these folk it was their lives and their livelihood, their very survival at stake.

"I am sorry; I should have said, of course, those who have

encountered the creature and lived.'' There were not, she supposed, too many of those.

She spoke first to the fisherman she had recalled with her magick. He spoke with a certain self-consciousness, his eyes fixed on the ground away from her.

"I heard her singing—that's all I can remember—and it seemed there was nothing in the world but only that song. Mad, it is, I don't care all that much for music—savin' your presence, minstrel,'' he added sheepishly. "Only I heard that song, somehow it was different; I wanted no more than just to listen to it forever. . . .'' He stood silent, thoughtful. "For all that, I wish I could remember . . .'' His eyes sought the distant horizon.

"Be grateful you cannot,'' Lythande said crisply, "or you would still be sitting by your fire without wit to feed or clean yourself. If you wish my advice, never let yourself think of it again for more than a moment.''

"Oh, ye're right, I know that, but still an' all, it was beautiful—'' He sighed, shook himself like a great dog, and looked up at Lythande. "I suppose my mates must ha' dragged me away an' back to the shore; next I knew I was sitting by my fireplace listening to your music, minstrel, an' Mhari cryin' and all.''

She turned away; from him she had learned no more than she had known before. "Is there anyone else who met the beast—the mermaid—and survived the meeting?''

It seemed there were none; for the young girls who had taken out the boat either had not encountered the mermaid or it had not chosen to show itself to them. At last one of the women of the village said hesitantly, "When first it came, and the men were hearin' it and never coming back—there was Lulie. She went out with some of the women. She didna' hear anything, they say. She can't hear anything; she's been deaf these thirty years. And she says she saw it, but she wouldna' think about it. Maybe, knowin' what you're intending to do, she'll tell you, magician.''

A deaf woman. Surely there was logic to this, as there was logic to all the things of magic if you could only find out the underlying pattern. The deaf woman had survived the mermaid because she could not hear the song. Then why had the men of the village been unable to conquer it by the old ruse of plugging their ears with wax?

It attacked the eyes too, apparently, for one of them had spoken of it as "so beautiful." This man said he had leaped from the boat and tried to swim ashore. Ashore—or on the rocks toward the creature? She should try to speak with him, too, if she could find him. Why was he not here among the men? Well, first, Lythande decided, she would speak with the deaf woman.

She found her in the village bake shop, supervising a single crooked-bodied apprentice in unloading two or three limp-looking sacks of poor-quality flour, mixed with husks and straw. The village's business, then, was so much with the fishing that only those who were physically unable to go into the boats found it permissible to follow any other trade.

She glowered at Lythande, set her lips tight, and gestured to the cripple to go on with what he was doing, bustling about her ovens. The doings of a magician, said her every truculent look, were no business of hers and she wanted nothing to do with them.

Lythande went to the apprentice and stood over him. She was a very tall woman and he was a wee small withered fellow; as he looked up he had to tilt his head back. The deaf woman scowled, but Lythande deliberately ignored her.

"I will talk with you," she said deliberately, "since your mistress is too deaf and perhaps too stupid to hear what I have to say."

The little apprentice was shaking in his shoes.

"Oh, no, Lord Magician . . . I can't . . . she knows every word we say—she reads lips and I swear she knows what I say even before I say it. . . ."

"Does she indeed," Lythande said. "So now I know." She went and stood over the deaf woman until she raised her sullen face. "You are Lulie, and they tell me that you met the sea beast, the mermaid, whatever it is, and that it did not kill you. Why?"

"How should I know?" The woman's voice was rusty as if from long disuse; it grated on Lythande's musical ear.

It was unfair to think ill of a woman because of her misfortune; yet Lythande found herself disliking this woman very much. Distaste made her voice harsh.

"You have heard that I have committed myself to rid the village of this creature that is preying on it." Lythande did not realize that she had, in fact, committed herself until she heard herself say so. "In order to do this I must know what it is that I face. Tell me all you know of this thing, whatever it may be."

"Why do you think I know anything at all?"

"You survived." *And,* thought Lythande, *I would like to know why; for when I know why it spared this very unprepossessing woman, perhaps I will know what I must do to kill it—if it must be killed, after all. Or would it be enough to drive it away from here?*

Lulie stared at the floor. Lythande knew she was at an impasse; the woman could not hear and she, Lythande, could not command her with her eyes and presence or even with her magic, as long as the woman would not meet her eyes. Anger flared in her; she could feel, between her brows, the crackling blaze of the Blue Star; her anger and the blaze of magic reached the baker woman and she looked up.

Lythande said angrily "Tell me what you know of this creature! How did you survive the mermaid?"

"How am I to know that? I survived. Why? You are the magician, not I; let you tell me that, wizard."

With an effort Lythande moderated her anger. "Yet I implore you, for the safety of all these people, tell me what you know, however little."

"What do I care for the folk of this village?"

Lythande wondered what her grudge was that her voice should be so filled with wrath and contempt. It was probably useless to try and find out; grudges were often quite irrational. Perhaps she blamed them for her loss of hearing, perhaps for the isolation which had descended on her when, as with many deaf people, she had withdrawn into a world of her own, cut off from friends and kin.

"Nevertheless you are the only one who has survived a

meeting with this thing," Lythande said, "and if you will tell me your secret I will not tell them."

After a long time the woman said, "It—called to me. It called in the last voice I heard: my child's, him that died o' the same fever that lost me my hearing; crying and calling out to me. And so for a time I thought they'd lied to me when they said my boy was dead of the fever, that somehow he lived, out there on the wild shores. I spent the night seeking him. And when the morning came, I came to my senses, and knew if he had lived, he would'na call me in that baby voice. He died thirty years ago, by now he'd be a man grown, and how could he have lived all this time alone?" She stared at the floor again, stubbornly.

There was nothing Lythande could say. She could hardly thank the woman for a story Lythande had wrenched from her, if not by force, so near it as not to matter.

So I was on the wrong track, Lythande thought. The deaf woman had not been keeping from Lythande some secret which could have helped to deal with the menace to this village. She was only concealing what would have made her feel a fool.

And who am I to judge her, I who hold a secret deeper and darker than hers?

She had been wrong and must begin again. But the time had not been wasted, not quite, for now she knew that whereas it called to men in the voices of the ones they loved, it was not wholly a sexual enticement, as she had heard some mermaids were. It called to men in the voice of a loved woman; to at least one woman it had called in the voice of her dead child. Was it, then, that it called to everyone in the voice of what they loved best?

This then would explain why the young girls were at least partly immune. Before the power of love came into a life, a young boy or girl loved his parents, yes, but because of the lack of experience, the parents were still seen as someone who could protect and care for the child, not be selflessly cared for.

Love alone could create that selflessness.

Then, thought Lythande, *it will be safe for me to go out*

*against the monster. For there is, now, no one and nothing I
love. Never have I loved any man. Such women as I have
loved are separated from me by more than a lifetime, and I
know enough to be wary if any should call to me in the voice
of the dead. No lover, no child—if this thing calls in the
voice of the heart's desire, then I am safe from it. For I love
no one, and my heart, if indeed I still have a heart, desires
nothing.*

*I will go and tell them that I am ready to rid the village of
their curse.*

They gave her their best boat, and would have given her
one of the half-grown girls to row it out for her, but Lythande
declined. How could she be sure the girl was too young to
have loved, and thus become vulnerable to the call of the
sea creature? Also, for safety, Lythande left her lute on the
shore, partly because she wished to show them that she
trusted them with it, but mostly because she feared what the
damp in the boat might do to the fragile and cherished
instrument. More, if it came to a fight, she might step on it
or break it in the small boat.

It was a clear and brilliant day, and Lythande, who was
physically stronger than most men, sculled the boat briskly
into the strong offshore wind. Small clouds scudded along the
edge of the horizon, and each breaking wave folded over and
collapsed with a soft musical splashing. The noise of the
breakers was strong in her ear, and it seemed to Lythande
that under the sound of the waves there was a faraway song
like the song of a shell held to the ear. For a few minutes she
sang to herself in an undertone, listening to the sound of her
own voice against the voice of the sea's breaking; an illusion, she knew, but one she found pleasurable. She thought if
only she had her lute, she would enjoy improvising harmonies to this curious blending. The words she sang against the
waves were nonsense syllables, but they seemed to take on an
obscure and magical meaning as she sang.

She was never sure, afterward, how long this lasted. After
a time, though she believed at first that it was simply another
pleasant illusion like the shell held to the ear, she heard a

soft voice inserting itself into the harmonies she was creating with the wave song and her own voice. Somewhere there was a third voice, wordless and incredibly sweet. Lythande went on singing, but something inside her pricked up its ears. Or was it the tingling of the Blue Star which sensed the working of magic somewhere close to her?

The song, then, of the mermaid. Sweet as it was, there were no words. *As I thought, then. The creature works upon the heart's desire. I am desireless, therefore immune to the call. It cannot harm me.*

She raised her eyes. For a moment she saw only the great mass of rocks of which they had warned her, and against its mass a dark and featureless shadow. As she looked at the shadow, the Blue Star on her brow tingling, she willed to see more clearly. Then she saw—

What was it? Mermaid, they had said. Creature. Could they possibly call it evil?

In form, it was no more than a young girl, naked but for a necklace of small rare glimmering shells, the shells which had a crease running down the center, so that they looked like a woman's private parts. Her hair was dark with the glisten of water on the smooth globes of bladder wrack lying on the sand at high tide. The face was smooth and young with regular features. And the eyes . . .

Lythande could never remember anything about the eyes, though at the time she must have had some impression about the color. Perhaps they were the same color of the sea where it rolled and rippled smooth beyond the white breakers. She had no attention to spare for the eyes, for she was listening to the voice. Yet she knew she must be cautious; if she were vulnerable at all to this thing it would be through the voice, she to whom music had been friend and lover and solace for more than a lifetime.

Now she was close enough to see. How like a young girl the mermaid looked, young and vulnerable, with a soft, childish mouth. One of the small teeth, teeth like irregular pearls, was chipped out of line, and it made her look very childish. A soft mouth. *A mouth too young for kissing,* Lythande thought, and wondered what she had meant by it.

Once I, even I, was as young as that, Lythande thought, her mind straying among perilous ways of memory; a time—how many lifetimes ago?—when she had been a young girl already restless at the life of the women's quarters, dreaming of magic and adventure; a time when she had borne another name, a name she had vowed never to remember. But already, though she had not yet glimpsed the steep road that was to lead her at last to the Temple of the Blue Star and to the great renunciations which lay ahead of her as a Pilgrim Adept, she knew her path did not lie among young girls like these, with soft vulnerable mouths and soft vulnerable dreams—lovers and husbands and babies clinging around their necks as the necklace of little female shells clung to the neck of the mermaid. Her world was already too wide to be narrowed so far.

Never vulnerable like that, so that this creature should call to me in the voice of a dead and beloved child. . . .

And as if in answer, suddenly there were words in the mermaid's song, and a voice Lythande had not remembered for a lifetime. She had forgotten his face and his name; but her memory was the memory of a trained minstrel, a musician's memory. A man, a name, a life might be forgotten; a song or a voice—no, never.

My princess and my beloved, forget these dreams of magic and adventure; together we will sing such songs of love that life need hold no more for either of us.

A swift glance at the rocks told her he sat there, the face she had forgotten; in another moment she would remember his name. . . . *No! This was illusion. He was dead; he had been dead for more years than she could imagine. . . . Go away,* she said to the illusion. *You are dead and I am not to be deceived that way, not yet.*

They had told her the vision could call in the voice of the dead. But it could not trick her, not that way. As the illusion vanished, Lythande sensed a little ripple of laughter, like the breaking of a tiny wave against the rocks where the mermaid sat. Her laugh was delicious. Was that illusion too?

To a woman, then, it calls in the voice of a lover. But
never had Lythande been vulnerable to that call. He had not
been the only one; only the one to whom Lythande had come
the closest to yielding. She had almost remembered his name;
for a moment her mind lingered, floating, seeking a name, a
name . . . then, deliberately, but almost with merriment,
Lythande turned her mind willfully away from the tensed
fascination of the search.

She need not try to remember. That had been long, long
ago, in a country so far from here that no living man within a
ten-day's journey knew so much as the name of that country.
So why remember? She knew the answer to that; this sea
creature, this mermaid, defended itself this way, reaching
into her mind and memory, as it had reached into the mind
and memory of the fishermen who sought to pass by it,
losing them in a labyrinth of the past, of old loves, heart's
desires. Lythande repressed a shudder, remembering the man
seated by the fire, lost in his endless dream. How narrowly
had she escaped that? And there would have been none to
rescue her.

But a Pilgrim Adept was not to be caught so simply. The
creature was simple, using on her its only defense: forcing
the mind and memory; and she had escaped. Desireless,
Lythande was immune to that call of desire.

Young girl as she looked, that at least must be illusion; the
mermaid was an ageless creature . . . like herself, Lythande
thought.

For the creature had tried for a moment to show herself to
Lythande in that illusory form of a past lover—no, he had
never been Lythande's lover—but in the form of an old
memory to trap her in the illusory country of heart's desire.
But Lythande had never been vulnerable in that way to the
heart's desire.

Never?

*Never, creature of dreams. Not even when I was younger
than you appear now to be.*

But was this the mermaid's true form or something like it?
The momentary illusion vanished. The mermaid had returned
to the semblance of the young girl, touchingly young. There

must then be some truth to the appearance of the childish mouth, the eyes that were full of dreams, the vulnerable smile. The mermaid was protecting itself in the best way it could; for certainly a sea maiden so frail and defenseless, seeming so young and fair, would be at the mercy of the men of the fisherfolk, men who would see only a maiden to be preyed upon.

There were many such tales along these shores, still told around the hearth fires, of mermaids and of men who had loved them. Men who had taken them home as wives, bringing a free sea maiden to live in the smoke of the hearth fire, to cook and spin, servant to man, a mockery of the free creature she should be. Often the story ended when the imprisoned sea maiden found her dress of fishscales and seaweed and plunged into the sea again to find her freedom, leaving the fisherman to mourn his lost love.

Or the loss of his prisoner? In this case Lythande's sympathy was with the mermaid.

Yet she had pledged herself to free the village of this danger. And surely it was a danger, if only of a beauty more terrible than they dared to know and understand: a fragile and fleeting beauty like the echo of a song, or like the sea wrack in the ebb and flow of the tide. For with illusion gone the mermaid was only this frail-looking creature, ageless but with the eternal illusion of youth. *We are alike,* thought Lythande. *In that sense we are sisters, but I am more free than she is.*

She was beginning to be aware of the mermaid's song again, and knew it was dangerous to listen. She sang to herself to try to block it away from her awareness. But she felt an enormous sympathy for the creature, here at the mercy of a crude fishing village, protecting herself as best she could, and cursed for her beauty.

She looked so like one of the young girls Lythande had known in that faraway country. They had made music together on the harp and the lute and the bamboo flute. Her name had been . . . Lythande found the name in her mind without a search . . . her name had been Riella, and it seemed to her that the mermaid sang in Riella's voice.

Not of love—for already at that time Lythande had known that such love as the other young girls dreamed of was not for her—but there had been an awareness between them. Never acknowledged, but Lythande had begun to know that even for a woman who cared nothing for man's desire, life need not be altogether empty. There were dreams and desires which had nothing to do with those simpler dreams of the other women, dreams of husband or lover or child.

And then Lythande heard the first syllable of a name, a name she had vowed to forget, a name once her own, a name she would not—no. No. A name she *could* not remember. Sweating, the Blue Star blazing with her anger, she looked at the rocks. Riella's form there wavered and was gone.

Again the creature had attempted to call to her in the voice of the dead. There was no longer the least trace of amusement in Lythande's mind. Once again she had almost fatally underestimated the sea creature because it looked so young and childlike, because it reminded her of Riella and of the other young girls she had loved in a world—and a life—long lost to her. She would not be caught that way again. Lythande gripped the hilt of the left-hand dagger, warded against magic, as she felt the boat beneath her scrape on the rocks.

She stepped out onto the surface of the small rocky holt, wrinkling her nose at the rankness of dead fish and sea wrack left by the tide, a carrion smell. How could so young and fair a creature live in this stench?

The mermaid said in the small voice of a very young girl, "Did they send you to kill me, Lythande?"

Lythande gripped the handle of her left-hand dagger. She had no wish to engage in conversation with the creature; she had vowed to rid the village of this thing, and rid it she would. Yet even as she raised the dagger she hesitated.

The mermaid, still in that timid little-girl voice, said, "I admit that I tried to ensnare you. You must be a great magician to escape from me so easily. My poor magic could not hold you at all!"

Lythande said, "I am an Adept of the Blue Star."

"I do not know of the Blue Star. Yet I can feel its power," said the sea maiden. "Your magic is very great—"

"And yours is to flatter me," said Lythande carefully, and the mermaid gave a delicious, childish giggle.

"You see what I mean? I can't deceive you at all, can I, Lythande? But why did you come here to kill me, when I can't harm you in any way? And why are you holding that horrible dagger?"

Why, indeed? Lythande wondered, and slid it back into its sheath. This creature could not hurt her. Yet surely she had come here for some reason, and she groped for it. She said at last, "The folk of the village cannot fish for their livelihood and they will all starve. Why do you want to do this?"

"Why not?" asked the mermaid innocently.

That made Lythande think a little. She had listened to the villagers and their story; she had not stopped to consider the mermaid's side of the business. The sea did not belong, after all, to the fishermen. It belonged to the fish and to the creatures of the sea: birds and fish and waves, shellfish of the deep, seals and dolphins and great whales who had nothing to do with humankind at all, and, yes, to the mermaids and stranger sea creatures as well.

Yet Lythande was vowed to fight on the side of the Law against Chaos till the final battle should come. And if humankind could not get its living as did the other creatures inhabiting the world, what would become of them?

"Why should they live by killing the fish in the sea?" the mermaid asked. "Have they any better right to survive than the fish?"

That was a question not all that easily answered. Yet as she glanced about the shore, smelling the rankness of the tide, Lythande knew what she should say next.

"You live upon the fish, do you not? There are enough fish in the sea for all the people of the shore, as well as for your kind. And if the fishermen do not kill the fish and eat them, the fish will only be eaten by other fish. Why not leave the fisherfolk in peace, to take what they need?"

"Well, perhaps I will," said the mermaid, giggling again, so that Lythande was again astonished; what a childish crea-

ture this was, after all. Did she even know what harm she
had done?

"Perhaps I can find another place to go. Perhaps you could
help me?" She raised her large and luminous eyes to Lythande.
"I heard you singing. Do you know any new songs, magician? And will you sing them to me?"

*Why, the poor creature is like a child; lonely, and even
restless, all alone here on the rocks. How like a child she
was when she said it. Do you know any new songs?* Lythande
wished for a moment that she had not left her lute on the
shore. "Do you want me to sing to you?"

"I heard you singing and it sounded so sweet across the
water, my sister. I am sure we have songs and magics to
teach one another."

Lythande said gently, "I will sing to you."

First she sang, letting her mind stay in the mists of time
past, a song she had sung to the sound of the bamboo reed
flute, more than a lifetime ago. It seemed for a moment that
Riella sat beside her on the rocks. Only an illusion created by
the mermaid, of course. But surely a harmless one! Still,
perhaps it was not wise to allow the illusion to continue;
Lythande wrenched her mind from the past and sang the sea
song that she had composed yesterday as she walked along
the shore to this village.

"Beautiful, my sister," murmured the mermaid, smiling
so that the charming little gap in her pearly teeth showed.
"Such a musician I have never heard. Do all the people who
live on land sing so beautifully?"

"Very few of them," said Lythande. "Not for many years
have I heard such sweet music as yours."

"Sing again, sister," said the mermaid, smiling. "Come
closer to me and sing again. And then I shall sing to you."

"And you will come away and let the fisherfolk live in
peace?" Lythande asked craftily.

"Of course I will, if you ask it, sister," the mermaid said.
It had been so many years since anyone had spoken to
Lythande, woman to woman, without fear. It was death for
her to allow any man to know that she was a woman; and the

women in whom she dared confide were so few. It was soothing balm to her heart.

Why, after all, should she go back to the land again? Why not stay here in the quiet peace of the sea, sharing songs and magical spells with her sister the mermaid? There were greater magics here than she had ever known, yes, and sweeter music too.

She sang, hearing her voice ring out across the water. The mermaid sat quietly, her head a little turned to the side, listening as if in utter enchantment, and Lythande felt she had never sung so sweetly. For a moment she wondered if, hearing her song echoing from the ocean, any passerby would think that he heard the true song of a mermaid. For surely she too, Lythande, could enchant with her song. Should she stay here, cease denying her true sex, where she could be at once woman and magician and minstrel? She too could sit on the rocks, enchanting with her music, letting time and sea roll over her, forgetting the struggle of her life as Pilgrim Adept, being only what she was in herself. She was a great magician; she could feel the very tingle of her magic in the Blue Star on her brow, crackling lightnings . . .

"Come nearer to me, sister, that I can hear the sweetness of your song," murmured the mermaid. "Truly, it is you who have enchanted me, magician—"

As if in a dream, Lythande took a step further up the beach. A shell crunched hard under her foot. Or was it a bone?

She never knew what made her look down to see that her foot had turned on a skull.

Lythande felt ice run through her veins. This was no illusion. Quickly she gripped the left-hand dagger and whispered a spell which would clear the air of illusion and void all magic, including her own. She should have done it before.

The mermaid gave a despairing cry. "No, no, my sister, my sister musician, stay with me . . . Now you will hate me too. . . ." But even as the words died out, like the fading sound of a lute's broken string, the mermaid was gone, and Lythande stared in horror at what sat on the rocks.

It was not remotely human in form. It was three or four

times the size of the largest sea beast she had ever seen, crouching huge and greenish, the color of seaweed and sea wrack. All she could see of the head was rows and rows of teeth, huge teeth, gaping before her. And the true horror was that one of the great fangs had a chip knocked from it.

Little pearly teeth with a little chip . . .

Gods of Chaos! I almost walked down that thing's throat!

Retching, Lythande swung the dagger. Almost at once she whipped out the right-hand knife which was effective against material menace, struck toward the heart of the thing. An eerie howl went up as blackish green blood, smelling of sea wrack and carrion, spurted over the Pilgrim Adept. Lythande, shuddering, struck again and again until the cries were silent. She looked down at the dead thing, the rows of teeth, the tentacles and squirming suckers. Before her eyes was a childish face, a voice whose memory would never leave her.

And I called the thing sister . . .

It had even been easy to kill. It had no weapons, no defenses except its song and its illusions. Lythande had been so proud of her ability to escape the illusions, proud that she was not vulnerable to the call of lover or of memory.

Yet it had called, after all, to the heart's desire . . . for music. For magic. For the illusion of a moment where something that never existed, never could exist, had called her sister, speaking to a womanhood renounced forever. She looked at the dead thing on the beach, and knew she was weeping as she had not wept for three ordinary lifetimes.

The mermaid had called her sister, and she had killed it.

She told herself, even as her body shook with sobs, that her tears were mad. If she had not killed it, she would have died in those great and dreadful rows of teeth, and it would not have been a pleasant death.

Yet for that illusion, I would have been ready to die . . .

She was crying for something that had never existed.

She was crying *because* it had never existed, and because, for her, it would never exist, not even in memory. After a long time she stooped down and from the mass that was melting like decaying seaweed she picked up a fang with a chip out of it. She stood looking at it for a long time. Then, her lips tightening grimly, she flung it out to sea, and clambered back into the boat. As she sculled back to shore, she found she was listening to the sound in the waves, like a shell held to the ear. And when she realized that she was listening again for another voice, she began to sing the rowdiest drinking song she knew.

LIOR AND THE SEA

Diane Duane

Love enters in nowhere so readily as through the
door of the already-broken heart.

(Gnomics, 412)

THERE IS A STRETCH OF THE NORTH DARTHENE COASTLINE
where the cliffs turn abruptly from brown granite to black
basalt, the remains of some ancient lava flow. The beaches
along this part of the Darthene Gulf are dark as night, starred
with semiprecious stones carried from the gem-bearing head-
lands of Mimis by the westerly Gulf current. Perched on a
bluff behind one of those beaches, two hundred feet above
the semicircular cove that harbored its fishing vessels, was a
little town called Daike. The huddle of slate-roofed houses
was home to forty-eight fisherfolk, assorted dogs, cats, goats
and chickens, and the town's Rodmistress, Lior.

On the face of it, it might seem odd that a twelve-house
town, two hundred miles from anywhere, would have a
resident Rodmistress. But Lior had been born in Daike, and
fostered by the other fisherfolk there when her parents died of
lunglock fever in her early childhood. She had grown up to
be a quiet, self-sufficient little girl, her only notable charac-
teristics a preference for her own company and a close-
mouthed, matter-of-fact bravery which no one in Daike
recognized for the resigned desperation of someone who has

already lost everything there is to lose. But the circuit Rodmistress who came through Daike once a year caught the scent of the blue Fire in Lior, then twelve years old, and took the girl away to the Silent Precincts for training. Six years later, and standing high in Power among her yearsmates, Lior won her Rod, and was offered her choice of several prestigious practices. Instead, she went home.

For all the tininess of the town, and all her Power, Lior was as busy in Daike as she might have been in any city. After the daily business of using her Fire to read the weather for the imminence of squalls or the troublesome Gulf waterspouts, there was the Sea itself to be read for the movements of silverspine or hack or brownbait, depending on the season. Once that was done, and her advice given to the boat crews, Lior would climb the winding trail back up the cliff and take the measure of her people with the same affectionate efficiency. There were ills to be treated, pains to be talked out, children to be held; cats to converse with, dogs to tell where to dig for bones. In between she usually found time to indulge her love of cooking—drowning in Lior's soup kettle was widely considered to be the second best death available—so that a long morning of working on a child's polio might be followed by an afternoon spent helping one of the neighbors find something different to do with brownbait. A touch of the hand here, a pinch of saffron there, a flicker of the Fire somewhere else—that was the way Lior's days went.

Her evenings, though, were normally her own, and she spent them by herself. If asked why she so rarely attended the village's social gathering she would only smile and say that she liked to be alone. No one pressed the point. The older villagers felt that a woman who could tell three days in advance where the hack would be running, talk a boat's wood into patching its own holes, and bring the rain down when fresh water ran short, was entitled to a few quirks. Some of the young men and women she had grown up with would gaze after Lior's solitary figure and sigh to themselves. But if Lior noticed this, she gave no sign of it.

In the Precincts she had usually spent her evenings outside, meditating under the open sky; for Lior was one of those who had a particular love for the Goddess in Her aspect as Queen of Night, Mother of stars and dreams and moonlight. But since she had come home and started going down to the beach to meditate in the starlight, she had found another delight—the Sea itself. All through her childhood it had simply been a place to work, a dangerous environment as likely to give death without warning as life. But the many new senses that had come with Lior's mastery of her inner Fire, the heightening of her old senses, were changing her mind, showing her that she had never really *seen* the Sea at all. The long nights she came to spend on the beach in moonlight or moondark, watching the ceaseless curl and roll of the water as one watches the light shift on a sculpture or the breathing of one's sleeping love, taught Lior the Sea's whims more surely than the oldest sailor in Daike could have.

Most evenings, then, when Lior was free, she would leave the tiny cottage where she lived alone and take the path down the cliff. She would sit for hours on the jewelled black beach, feeling the soft shift of sand still warm from the day, tasting the savor of the salt wind. Slowly Lior began to perceive what lay behind the idioms of speech that portray the Sea as a living thing with moods; and as this perception grew in her, she began to listen to what the Sea had to say in its huge voice, and to tell it in return the things she could not share with anyone else.

Some nights there was nothing much to say on either side, and Lior and the Sea would listen quietly to the sound of one another breathing, needing nothing more for their mutual peace. Some nights the Sea would toss wildly about on its shore, leaping up in foam and hissing; Lior would reach out with her Power and listen until the anger seemed spent and the Sea rested quietly again, stroking the beach in long curved apologetic gestures. Some nights Lior would rage silently over some death she couldn't stop, or ought not, or over some village couple who were out of love with each other and intent on staying that way. The Sea would listen patiently, and eventually its immense soft voice whispering the same word again and again would remind Lior that no

death is final, and no love the last love; that in life and love
as in all else the Goddess endlessly and shamelessly repeats
Herself. The Sea was good for her, Lior thought; and the
merry way it would push a wave silently up the beach and
pour it on her, after she had listened it out of a storm, made
her think that she was probably good for the Sea too. It was a
most satisfactory relationship.

Three years into her practice, there came a day when a
wild spring storm began to brew off the coast. It was a bad
time for a nor'easter—the winter stores of dried fish were
almost gone and the fleet needed to be out after the run of
silverspine that would keep Daike in oil and food until the
"Maiden's Madness," the unpredictable late spring weather,
was fully broken. Lior began to smell the extraordinary
violence of the impending storm in late afternoon and realized that it could go on for days if it went unchecked.
Thinking to listen the Sea out of the storm, Lior went down
to the dark shore. She flung an unseen net of her Power out
through water and air and sandy bottom—seining, as it were,
for some way to divert the growing wildness of ocean and
sky. She found no adjustment within her ability to make—the
storm had come up too fast. And talking to the Sea helped no
more than listening had; all Lior got for her coaxing and
cajoling was a growing feeling of destruction-to-be, far past
her ability to handle.

She went back up the cliff trail and met the townspeople at
the boulder-flanked spot where it came out on top, wearing a
grimmer face than anyone there had ever seen on her. The
rising wind whipped Lior's long dark hair about, and her
brown cloak leaped and writhed like a live thing; her blue
Rodmistress's robe was plastered to her. The Flame streamed
blinding blue-white down her Rod, visible indication of Power
building to some purpose.

"Get everyone inside and keep them there," Lior said to
the village elders. "I'm going to try something. If it doesn't
work, there'll probably be storm for a tenday or more—so be
ready to ration what food's left. If this does work, though,
we can have the fleet out tomorrow." And, frowning, down
she went to the beach again.

She walked a couple of miles west of Daike's cliff, listening with ears and underhearing to the rumbling threat of the rising storm. At last Lior picked a spot, stopped there, and peeled off her sodden cloak and her robe, draping them over a boulder far up on the beach. For a moment she stood and weighed her aspen Rod in her hand, considering—then shook her head and thrust it narrow-end-down into the sand, like a sword.

Small and taut and naked, her hair whipping around her in the howling wind, Lior strode down to the surf line. For a few long minutes she paused there, listening hard in the storm-green dusk as the waves plunged and hammered around her. Nothing was listening back.

"All right!" she cried into the gathering storm, and at her cry the clouds above her curdled and the wind began to scream, and the beach shuddered beneath the battering of the waves. "You're going to have a tantrum, and you won't let me stop it? Fine! But leave the boats and the town alone, and get it over with now! Do it all tonight, and do it *here!*"

Faintly Lior sensed a wavering of purpose out there. She thought one last time of going back for her Rod, her Power's focus. Empty-handed, she was greatly weakened. With the Rod to channel and direct her considerable Fire, she would have some slight advantage. . . . But no. The Sea faced her with nothing that was not part of itself. She would be fair to her friend, her adversary.

The wind seemed to be dropping off a bit now, moaning with uncertainty, but Lior didn't trust the shift in mood. So much potential force couldn't be built up without discharging, and her challenge might make the storm-blow fall harder on some other innocent village. "Come on!" she yelled scornfully. "Me against you! Just the two of us! *Or are you afraid?*"

The wind spat spray in Lior's eyes, and the salt stung them half blind. But Lior stood there with her fists clenched and her head high, watching the first terrible wave rise up and impossibly up before her, leaning, towering; the sudden slicing rain whipping its crest gray-white—until, drowning the windroar in the crash of its own uncontrollable anger, tremendously it fell . . . and Lior beneath it.

All that night the townspeople of Daike peered out their doors in unease at the wild weather. Though the boats in the deepwater cove rocked and groaned in churning water, the disturbance seemed only backwash spreading from a place some miles upcoast. There lightnings struck and thunder tore across a tattering sky, and the maddened Sea beat itself against the cliffs until their cracked faces wept brine in rivers and the wind howled in pain.

That same mourning wind drove the clouds away around daybreak, and then fell silent under a clear sky. When the villagers went down to look for Lior, they found her tossed wet and limp as a wrung-out rag on the black beach—pale with shock, blue with bruises, gasping shallowly from two broken ribs, her left forearm greenstick-snapped and lying wrong like the arm of a broken doll. But she opened her eyes and greeted her people as they lifted her to take her back to Daike. Hoarsely but politely Lior asked them to first carry her up the beach a ways, and from the litter made of their linked arms and clasped wrists she reached out with her good hand to pluck her white Rod from the sand. All the way home Lior gripped it tight, smiling with closed eyes what seemed a smile of relief and pride.

And all that week, until her fever broke and her arm and ribs began to mend, the wind spoke no louder than a whisper around Daike, and beneath unclouded sunlight the Sea was still as a pond.

Everybody knows what terrible convalescents Rodmistresses make, and Lior was no exception. There was no keeping her in bed for more than a day or so. By the end of the week, when her Power was approaching normal levels again, she had begun to force her own healing with the same cold-eyed professionalism she had used on goats and crying children so many times before. Seven days after the storm, bones knit and bruises gone, Lior was busy around the village, tending to her people—though their attitude toward her wasn't what it had been. Before, she had just been Lior, who despite her solitary nature and her training in the Precincts was, after all, just another villager. Now, at least behind her back, she was "the woman who fought with the Sea, and won." Since turned back and whispers mean nothing to a Rodmistress's underhearing, Lior heard that remark more than once and went away smiling, for they had it all wrong. She didn't bother to argue the point. Sooner or later the awe would wear off and life would go back to normal.

In the meantime she went back to spending her evenings by the Sea. The odd stillness of the water ceased when Lior started coming down the cliff again, and the waves were behaving normally once more, bubbling and sighing and stretching toward her. Yet at the same time Lior began to wonder if her brief illness had somehow made her more observant, for the Sea seemed to be bringing her gifts more frequently than before. Often enough in the past something had been pushed up to her feet or poured playfully into her lap by an unexpected wave: a bright shell, a gracefully curved piece of driftwood, a very surprised fish. She had always accepted these gifts with thanks and taken them home (except for the fish, which she would slide into the next wave before it overstayed its welcome in the air).

But now hardly an evening went by without a flattened, creeping wave nudging something up against her knee, and the gifts were stranger. One night it was the hugest piece of Dragon's-eye opal she had ever seen, a stone round and smooth as skua's egg. She spent all that evening turning it over in her hands, contemplating its fires, like a crystallized sunset, which shifted with every movement. Other gifts were less collectible. Another evening's meditation was interrupted by a high-running breaker that soaked Lior to the waist. This by itself wasn't unusual, but when she looked down at her lap she found it occupied by eight or nine blueback crabs, all of which stared at Lior with stalky obsidian eyes and waved their claws testily at her. Lior broke down in uncontrollable laughter, and the crabs one by one clambered over her knees and sidled off down the beach, looking offended.

The night after that, something came which was not precisely a gift.

The water was restless that night, and so was Lior. She went walking, aimlessly she thought, up the coast in the moonlight, while beside her the Sea shifted and tossed in its bed like someone trapped in uneasy dreams. Lior moved at a gentle, half-aware stroll among half-buried boulders and across packed sand, until something in the feel of the place to which she had come stopped her. She looked around with eyes and Fire, and realized that this was the place where she had fought the Sea. Lior stood there on the moon-silvered beach, smelling the spray and remembering: that first awful wave that fell on her with a sound like all dooms—and the next, and the next. . . .

But there was a scentless flavor on the wind tonight that hadn't been there, that other evening. Lior breathed it deep and frowned. Fear? At least it would have meant that if she had sensed it in a person—but the *Sea* afraid?

"What's the matter?" she said to the roiling water. "What could make *you* afraid?"

The answer didn't come in words. Down close to the water, one of the big black rocks *moved*—shifted, and was still again.

Lior had not been much afraid of anything since she was little; fear had just made life hurt worse than it already did, and so she had broken herself of the habit. A moving rock merely surprised her. She pulled her Rod out of her belt and went straight over to the big dark shape. It turned out not to be a boulder at all. It was a seahorse.

Lior knelt beside the creature, too concerned with the bizarre angle at which one of its forefeet lay to worry much about the prospect of working on a mythical beast. The seahorse was darker than the beach or the cliffs, but its eyes were pale; one of them rolled silverly at her in the moonlight, its depths vague with pain. The seahorse's nostrils shuddered and flared as the breath went in and out. Lior put her hands on the twisted leg, and kept them there though the seahorse grunted and tried to kick away from her. Her other senses showed her, through the touch, feelings like a simple fracture of the main bone below the knee, a dislocated knee joint, and some twisted ligaments and nerves.

Lior tucked her Rod out of the way between her arm and her side while she pushed her Fire out of her, into the seahorse, and down into the leg nerves to block them. That done, she held the seahorse's leg bones together with her hands while forcing the odd dense marrow to knit through itself again, and making new bone grow over the break. Probably, Lior thought, the creature had been racing along the seashore as the undersea horses were supposed to love to do on moonlit nights, and had put its foot in a hole. The idea was odd. It had never occurred to her that one of these creatures might be able to hurt itself, to fall or get a stone in its foot like any unicorn or yale.

Lior unpinched and repositioned one nerve which she judged otherwise undamaged, relocated the knee joint, restrung its ligaments, and tightened the muscles back into place. Then she sat back on her heels to think, for normally the next step would be to send the injured person to sleep. But the seahorse took that problem out of her hands. A heave, a shudder, and it was on its feet again—and Lior came fully to herself and realized that she was looking up at a legend. The seahorse's mane and tail would have reached almost to the sand, had they not been curling and swirling about it as if caught in some unseen ocean current. Mane and tail and coat were all black as a secret thought, yet the seahorse gleamed with moonlight and some other faint brilliance not as identifiable, and it looked too graceful for dry land to bear its presence long. Here it was, right in front of her, one of the creatures that dance on the waves in the midnights of deep summer and come out of the Sea on nights of moon to sire wonderful foals on the mares of men: a legend. . . .

The legend danced back a step, testing the healed leg, and hesitated, looking down at Lior. She gazed up enchanted into the silvershot eyes, not daring to reach out and break the dream. But the dream put its head down, slowly, tentatively, and touched *her*—a cool velvet brushing of cheek and nose against her bare neck and shoulder, and the touch spoke. *Thank you,* it said—and the seahorse wheeled and fled toward the Sea. Its hooves made no mark on the sand, its passing made no sound. In the time Lior could draw breath and whisper "Wait!" it was in the Sea, and part of the Sea, and gone.

After a long time Lior got up, trembling with wonder and confusion. The speech she'd heard through the seahorse's touch had been cool as water, emotionless—yet there had been a look in its eyes that had stopped Lior's breath somewhere south of her heart. Her uncertainty of what the look might mean bled her composure away until she was as weak as if wounded again.

Eventually Lior started for home. The flavor of fear was gone from the air, and beside her the waves slid up and down with seeming nonchalance from a quieter Sea. But inside Lior there was no quiet at all.

She was back at that spot the next night, and the next, and each time was greeted by sea breeze and tide's turn, but nothing else . . . not even a seagift. All her listening revealed nothing but a Sea that no more noticed Lior than it would notice one particular pebble among the millions it rolled up and down the beach. So, early on in the third night, Lior came to her senses. She laughed at herself in good-natured scorn and went up the cliff to her house and her bed, schooling herself to an indifference like the Sea's. It was just water and sand, after all, she told herself; just a beach, like any other. She fell asleep, a few hours later, almost believing it.

Much later, after Moonrise, someone knocked on Lior's door. She rubbed her eyes, muttering at herself for not anticipating one of old Rai's ulcer attacks, and climbed out of bed, fumbled about for her Rod, made her way to the door, and swung it open.

The seahorse filled the whole doorway, gleaming in the moonlight like a statue of polished onyx. Its silvery eyes, looking down into hers, caught the Fire streaming about Lior's Rod and revealed a blue haze like that of morning coming up over the water. Lior reached out slowly, still afraid of breaking the dream, and slid her fingers through the waving mane, down the silken neck. At her touch she felt the

seahorse greet her inwardly, a cool and almost toneless thought;
yet at the same time its eyes half-closed as if in pleasure, and
Lior felt the sudden reopening of that wound of uncertainty.
The contradiction . . .

The seahorse dropped gracefully to its knees on the flag-
ging of her doorstep, looking up sidewise at Lior, and leaned
its head against her. The touch said, *Will you ride?*

Without hesitation Lior knotted up her shift, slipping the
Rod through the knot, and slid onto the seahorse's back. It
stood up, and wheeled about, and they rode.

Only the starlight and the flying Moon could have paced
them on that first wild ride over a dark Sea slicked with
liquid brilliance like silver oil. The water sang beneath the
seahorse's hooves, and Lior held her seat with one hand well
wrapped in the satiny mane, scrubbing spray out of her eyes
with the other. Out past three miles or so the waves grew
huge, and the seahorse would throw its head back and charge
up the sheer black slopes like the enchanted steeds of old
tales, which could climb mountains of glass without a slip.
Sometimes they would not reach the top of the wave before it
broke, and the seahorse would plunge straight through the
wave just under the down-curling crest. After the first time,
Lior learned to enjoy this, for whenever they did it she came
out dry.

Then for a while they went more slowly, and Lior gazed
down from the seahorse's back at water that boiled with pale
green luminescence. Through the light slid graceful dark
shapes, the fish that fed on the glowing algae; and as the
seahorse paced across the rocking water, a shape at first
vague and then less so rose toward the surface near them,
blocking away the brightness, swelling, until with a great
rushing of water the golden whale broke surface. Waves
churned around them as it rolled hugely over and blew. One
small dark eye gazed at Lior and regarded her, mild and
inscrutable. Another leisurely roll, and the whale sank away
except for one languorous fluke forgotten in the air as it
sounded; then that too slid beneath the surface.

It was all like that, all salt dark and wonder and whispering night, until Lior felt likely to fall off the seahorse's back from both fatigue and the sheer marvelousness of what was happening. It seemed only a few breaths later that she found herself standing on the beach, gazing in the morning twilight at the creature which had just risen from its knees beside her. Out of its darkness, the seahorse's silvery eyes gazed back at her, and still in them was that curious look—longing, Lior thought now—that she wanted to understand better. She reached out to touch the seahorse one last time, but it danced away from her hand and melted away into the surf, swift and traceless as a retreating breaker.

Lior went home to Daike. She did her work well enough that day, but the townspeople noticed that she seemed preoccupied, and all the young men and women looked at one another sidewise, wondering which of them had inspired such a fulfilled expression in their Rodmistress. Lior went musing about her work and noticed nothing of this at all.

That twilight she hurried down to the beach, and about the time the twelfth star came out, the seahorse came sliding out of the water to her. It bent down its head to breathe its silent greeting into her hair. Lior stroked it hesitantly on the softest place, the one just under the jawbone.

No Rod? the seahorse said, its inner speech cool as always.

"No," Lior said. "It isn't necessary." She met its eyes. "My name is Lior, by the way."

She had hoped it would share a name with her in return, but the seahorse only bowed its head in grave acknowledgment and dropped to its knees. Without pressing the subject Lior mounted again, and again they rode.

So matters went for many nights, as Lior was borne through wonders she had never dreamed of, marvels even to one who has passed through the mysteries of the Silent Precincts and so seen the Sun rise at midnight. Together she and the seahorse climbed high promontories to watch the beleaguered fleets of kings tack their way through the wild winds of the Darthene Gulf on their errantry. They stood off the Eorlhowe in the whispering water and caught the burnt-stone smell of Dragonfire blowing from the Howe peak in the wet breeze; they saw the air and land around the Howe fill with the huge black-winged shapes of thousands of Dragons assembled in Convocation, and heard their vast voices murmuring all through one long night, an incomprehensible music of breath and fire. Together Lior and the seahorse soft-footed it around the Isles of the North, skirting those shores where none of woman born may ever walk, so that Lior first of all humankind glimpsed through the mist the diamond spires of Entellen and heard across the water the music of crystal bells. The two of them were welcome in the dolphin haunts off Teberkh, where the delphine poets made joking songs about the seahorse's sudden tameness, and brought Lior schools of mackerel as presents. Together she and the seahorse climbed the cliffs of Eie, and there Lior was taught the word which prevents Eie's Indweller from invoking the Untoward Circumstance—persuading it to show the beginning of the world rather than causing its end.

Nor were their journeys limited to the surface. Lior, with the seahorse peering over her shoulder and a couple of lanternfish hanging by for light, would sift through drifted sand for the scattered cargo of some anciently sunken carrack— the dull glint of obsolete coinages, the gleam of jewels like dimmed eyes. The two of them visited drowned Sonacharre together and walked through its silent streets, noting how fish had nested in the coral-crusted trees and swaying weed had choked the chimes in the town's gilded bell tower; they passed by the place where the Inhospitable lay bound for his wickedness, and Lior saw how his hating eyes followed her and the seahorse as they went away. Once the seahorse even leaped with Lior into the icy darkness of the Ureistine Trench, and together they fell like a dark star until the water was no longer icy, but almost too hot to bear. There Lior made the acquaintance of those who do not understand light, but are to earth and water as Dragons are to air and fire. Lior came away staggered, her mind seared by the shadowy intelligences of the utter depths, her heart both darkened and delighted by perception of what she could not possibly understand.

Through all this wild procession of wonders, the seahorse's inward speech drifted into Lior's mind now and again, dispassionately telling her the story of this wreck or that haunted cave; but its eyes were always lively with delight, and never more so than when she was delighted too. The difference between eyes and mind, the contradiction, puzzled Lior mightily. Her underhearing was no help to her, for all she could hear was a far-off rushing of feelings in the seahorse's heart, discomfort and joy ebbing and flowing like the tide. She tried to conceal how this disturbed her, and suspected she was not doing too well, for over a number of journeys the seahorse began to acquire a look of sorrow that would not come out of its eyes.

A night came, as others had, when Lior was too tired to wander. She sat in her usual place on the beach instead, with the seahorse beside her, its legs folded under it like a foal's. Lior leaned on her companion, one arm around its neck, resting in its warmth and nearness.

"There must be some reason I can't hear your thoughts directly," she said, stroking its neck and gazing into the darkness. "It doesn't feel like a self-imposed block. Are you under a spell, I wonder?" She looked down; the seahorse met her eyes with that look of mute pain. "You are . . . ? Well, there has to be a way to break it. There's always a way, every spell has its loophole. . . . When it's broken, I imagine your friends and relatives will be glad to have you back again. Or your loved . . . do you have a loved, I wonder?"

This time the seahorse would not meet her eyes at all. Suspicion flared in Lior, for most well-wrought spells have inhibitors set in them to keep the victim from revealing the breaker, if he knows it, or from thinking much about the problem if he doesn't. Lior reached around, turning the seahorse's warm face toward her so that she could read its silvery eyes. "Yes," she said. "There *is* someone—"

Then she saw the answer, and the old wound of uncertainty tore wide and deep, leaving her momentarily speechless with consternation and pain. The seahorse gave a great shudder and scrambled to its feet. Lior did too, and as she reached for it again, her companion lowered its beautiful head and shocked her still by speaking. *"Lior,"* it croaked, just one painful word in a voice that went into Lior like a knife, for she *knew* it from somewhere. The agony in its eyes blurred her own with tears as the seahorse leaned its head against her arm. *I must go,* it said through its touch, its voice unmoved; but oh, its eyes— *I cannot come again.*

And it turned and fled into the water. Lior's own anguish and confusion left her no strength to do more than watch the seahorse melt into the breakers and vanish.

She stood on the beach for a long time, listening to the waves. Slowly the sky started to lighten, the Sea turned all one color of pewter gray, and still Lior stood there, alone.

"I don't even know your name," she whispered to the wind and the waves, and finally turned away toward home, confused again, for she could not remember the last time she had cried.

She walked through the weeks that followed with such an air of bewildered desolation and anger about her that the villagers drew away from Lior and left her lonelier still. More than anything she wanted to go off searching for the seahorse; but she had responsibilities here, and could go nowhere. Lior was furious with herself for having driven the seahorse away; and the near-familiarity of its voice nagged at her until she couldn't sleep nights. Not that she could have slept anyway, for her mind was going around in circles. Who ever heard of a woman having a seahorse for a loved? Even if it came back, what could she do? Heart's love she could give it, certainly, but no more. Her own ideas of a loved did not exactly include a horse. Yet how could she refuse anything to the soul behind those silver eyes? It was all hopeless, useless, mad—

She did not spend her time on the beach meditating anymore. Lior began pushing her Fire harder than she had ever dared, threading it tenuously through air and earth and water and stretching her othersenses out along the strands of the web until she was tempting extrasensory collapse. With all her Power she listened and felt for anything that seemed like the seahorse. Lior knew she was unlikely to find it without even an outer name to go on, and of its feelings nothing but that dim internal tumult. Nevertheless she kept trying, using what perceptions she had, incomplete though they were. Lior found nothing, but she would not give up. Night after night the rough gems and wet stones of the beach glistened blue in the light from her blazing Rod; and when the fog came in the people looking curiously down from the cliff could see the Fire blooming through the mist, like a strayed star washed up on the beach.

Then came one early evening when the watchers saw the light blaze suddenly brighter than usual, and from the bottom of the cliff Lior shouted at them, "Get a boat, get a boat, there's someone drowning out there!" One villager ran to pound on the sailing-master's door, and the men and women who were skippers and crew ran down the trail to the cove. Shipwreck was common enough in those waters, where unwary ships sometimes drove onto the Seafangs to the east. The westerly Gulf current frequently bore the flotsam past Daike, and the villagers had a sharp eye for floating timbers and the people who might be clinging to them. So they found the survivor of this particular wreck, stark naked and blue as a salmon with cold, clasping half a splintered mast close as a lover. The fisherfolk pried him loose, wrapped him in a blanket, and brought him home to the cove and Lior.

They laid him on the shelf bed in her cottage, and Lior changed the boat's blanket for one of her own and shooed the fishers out. When she got a fire started and saw that he was young, she was relieved, for he was in bad shape.

She had no sooner touched him with hands and Fire to check his life level than she discovered there was more to this man's unconsciousness than simple exposure. Her othersenses told her that his body's internal balances and functions were fluctuating insanely; and when she tried to hear what his undermind was doing, all she could make out was a confused babble, no one image clearer than any other. This was probably a result of the high fever the man immediately began to run, but there was no clear cause for the rest of his problem. Lior set her body to making soup, while with mind and Fire she began working on the body itself.

With hours' passage the man only got worse. He tossed and moaned in the grip of the fever, which refused to break

despite much fish broth poured down him and the hundreds
of delicate adjustments Lior made in his blood and tissues
with the Fire. Then he began to convulse, and the seizures
led in turn to his heart stopping three times in an hour. Lior
began to despair of keeping him alive. "Mother and Queen,"
she muttered in desperate annoyance as his heart stopped the
fourth time, "only save me this man's life and I will give
You what You most desire from me!" She pounded on the
man's breastbone again, fisting the bolt of blue Fire straight
into the tiny nerve-node that regulates heartbeat, and this
time felt the heart rhythm jitter abruptly back to normal. The
man's body arched on the bed and then settled back again,
and Lior swallowed dryly, realizing that she had been heard.
It was an uncomfortable realization. The Goddess does not
waste energy and never fails to call in Her debts.

Lior sat down by the man to watch him, and as the night
slid by, the adjustments she had made in his blood and his
lungs gradually began to maintain themselves. Gradually the
twitching of muscles overloaded with their own wastes began
to decrease, and nerves stopped misfiring. Lior noticed that
the man's color seemed to be improving, and then realized
that the house was filling with dawn, and things were acquir-
ing shapes and shadows.

She had been so preoccupied by her client's internal work-
ings that she had given his outsides no more than passing
notice. Now, as light grew and his breathing deepened, Lior
relaxed and regarded him with weary interest. He seemed
young—no more than her own age, surely—well-muscled,
built strong and compact: dark haired, with the beginnings of
a beard. A seaman, perhaps; or if he had been a passenger on
the wrecked ship, then possibly an athlete of some kind. Eyes
downturned at the corners, a sweet-looking mouth with a
wisp of smile about it even in sleep. His family would be
glad to have him back home safe. . . . The man made a
small sound, and as Lior looked down at him, his eyes
opened.

Silver-gray eyes with a hazy blue note exactly that of
morning coming up over the water. As her own eyes widened
in astonishment, he spoke one word. "Lior," he said—his

voice more a croak than proper speech, but still the same as the seahorse's voice, half-familiar, longed for. No longer half-familiar, though . . . for hearing it through a human throat, Lior knew it at last. It was the voice of the Sea.

Her name was the only word he knew. She couldn't hear his thoughts at all for the rushing, unceasing tumult that filled his undermind; but Lior understood now what that sound was. She took to pointing at objects in her house and naming them, and when she ran out of inside words, she turned her guest over to the village's children. They were fascinated by the prospect of an adult who couldn't speak Darthene, and would crowd around him for hours as he sat on Lior's doorstep in his baggy borrowed clothes. He would listen with grave courtesy to everything they told him, useful or not, and he never needed more than one try to get a word or phrase right.

Lior called him Aren, that being an old Darthene word for something the waves have washed up, and she gave out that he would be staying with her until he was fully recovered. When he could walk easily, she took Aren around the village, introducing him to the elders, and after that began taking him along on her rounds too. For some days he watched and listened to everything intently, but said almost nothing. Lior did not press him. She went about her business, cooking and talking and healing and maintaining, every day more aware of the silent presence behind her which seemed to be waiting until it had enough words.

It was at the end of their fourth day together that Lior was too tired to walk straight home from the sailing-master's house and her latest battle with the woman's slowly remitting stomach cancer. Almost blind with fatigue, she walked over to the edge of the cliff and sat on one of the big boulders that flanked the trail down to the beach. Aren came to stand silently beside her, looking at the water; and Lior wondered wearily whether she had forgotten to tell him *that* word, perhaps the most important of all. She waved a hand down at the shoreline, as she had waved at so many other things lately. "The Sea," she said.

Aren gazed at it with the expression of someone who has
been away from home too long and finds all the familiar
things turned strange. "I know," he said, and looked over at
her. "Aren," he said, waving down at the water.

"I know," Lior said. Even through her weariness, the
wonder touched her deep. "Aren," she said on impulse.
"*why?* Why did you . . . why me?"

He looked sorrowful. "The words . . ."

"Ahh, no," Lior said, regretting. "I'm sorry. It can wait.
When you have more words—"

"No." He sighed. He had needed no teaching to do that;
the sound was the same as that of the waves beneath them,
sliding into the Gulf. "No. You—" Aren slowly smiled; for
the first time the warmth in his eyes was in his voice too.
"You fought. The children say it: 'I dare you.' You dared.
Dared *me*."

"Challenged," Lior whispered.

"Challenged, yes. You challenged me. The first one. 'Me
against you. Just the two of us.' "

"But I lost," Lior said, wondering.

"You *dared*," the Sea said.

Lior was silent while the two of them looked westward,
toward where the Sun was going down into a burning bed of
feathery clouds. "Aren," Lior said at last, "this . . ." She
reached out to touch his arm; he almost shied from her, then
held still, endured the touch. "How? How did you do this?"

He looked around him helplessly, as if searching for some
one thing to point at, then gave that up; tried a few times to
say something, and gave that up too. Finally he spread out
his arms and looked out into endless air, like a man trying to
embrace everything at once. He let his arms fall. "I asked,"
he said. "Asked. . . ."

"The Goddess," Lior whispered.

"The One Who Is," Aren said.

Lior put her face down into her hands, caught between awe
and an unclassifiable unease at something that seemed to be
happening. "O my Mother," she said, and breathed out, not
knowing what to think. The gentle fingers beneath her chin,
touching the softest place just under the jawbone, brought her

head up again. Aren looked at her out of silvershot eyes, and the wind of approaching evening stirred his dark hair as the seahorse's mane had once stirred of itself. "I need more words," he said.

Lior shook her head. For the first time since her childhood, she was beginning to be afraid. "So do I," she said, and took Aren's hand, and took him home.

They were rarely apart, the Rodmistress and the man saved from the Sea. By day he was her shadow, always just behind or alongside her; by night he would go down with Lior to her accustomed place on the beach, and there they would stay until far into the night, doing no one knew what. The only certainty was that Lior never took her Rod with her anymore. The two of them would go to communal suppers and business meetings together, and Aren was still usually silent, except for one supper that turned first into a drinking match and then into a songfest. Lior watched and listened in a warm haze of wine as her townspeople sang one raunchy sea chantey after another, and she smiled when the inebriated sailing-master pushed the lute into Aren's hands. He didn't know what to do with it, but the look in his eyes drew a silence about him; and when it was fullest he raised his voice and began to sing, unaccompanied, in a raspy, warm-timbred tenor. His singing was a wordless music, and one the towns-people had never heard. But Lior saw tears brightening in their eyes just as they did in hers—the bells of Entellen sang as poignantly through Aren's throat as they had across the water. She heard the waves shifting under the seahorse's feet again, saw the moonlight on the glittering spires . . . and his voice dwindled and faded and the dream was gone. So was Aren, through a door left standing open. Lior went after him.

She found him on the beach, sitting with his back against a boulder. Lior sat down beside him, and waited, as she had waited on so many other nights.

"Entellen," he said after a long while, his hushed voice running together with the waves' whisper. "Did you like it?"

"*Like* it?" Lior tried to find words and finally shook her head. The light, the sound, the stolen glimpse of an ethereal otherness that no one of her world was really ever supposed to see . . . "It was beautiful," she said finally, though the word was pitifully inadequate.

"It was hard knowing if you liked it," Aren said, speaking slowly to be sure of getting the words right. "The *anye,* the seahorse—"

"You were beautiful too."

Aren looked at her with grave wonderment. "*I* was? . . . I meant to say that that body—well, yes, I wanted—for it to be beautiful, so that you would—" He faltered. "To please you. And that form had power. I could show you my world. But the—the brain of the seahorse does not hear feelings or make them. They are—were inside but could not come out. And in another, I could not tell—not know—"

"I could tell, a little," Lior said. "Your eyes, they—" Now it was her turn to falter. "I saw."

Aren put his head down on his drawn-up knees. "So . . . another answer was needed. I found it by accident. Sometimes people go up onto high places and cast themselves down into my waters to die. I have never understood it. But this one . . . had just slipped out of what I wear now when I found it, and saved it." He breathed a long breath out, closed his eyes. "There is no power in this form, not as I had before. There are words, the names, the feelings . . . but still this is hard. She told me it would be."

"*She* . . ."

He nodded. "She said She does it all the time. The everything—infinity?—poured into one place, one thing, closed up. Finite. And not eternal, but in flesh that can die. She said that infinity is not interesting unless it is—enclosed. I did not know 'interesting'—but I knew, knew what I wanted—and so She taught me. But She is infinite, and though I am very big, I am still only finite. This makes it harder, She said. I was sick; there was too much of me."

"But you're—you're out *there*—"

Aren lifted his head, reached out to touch her arm. "You are there sitting, but *you* are more than this, the—enclosure. Where is what makes Lior *Lior*? Destroy the enclosure, and Lior endures. The inner—the—"

"The soul—"

"The soul." Aren nodded. "Men's souls walk my waters, I see them sometimes in the night; but their bodies are elsewhere, they work by themselves until their souls return to them again. My—body works, the same way. My soul—" He looked at his two hands, slid them down his shins, and rested his head on his knees once more. "It is hard. We can talk, but it is hard. . . ."

More strongly than ever Lior felt that combination of awed wonder and discomfort at being swept up by something beyond her control. But her friend's pain hurt her too. "What's hard?" she said, afraid but unable *not* to ask the question. "Aren, let me help. . . ."

He made a sound so perfectly balanced between a laugh and a sob that Lior couldn't tell what to do. "Just that. Who asks the waves what troubles them, who asks the Sea to let them help? You only—ever thought yourself my equal, without threatening . . . I heard the children say the words, but they were—practicing, they played . . . and now I must say them and without the practice." He lifted his head. "O Lior," he whispered "come be with me, be my loved. . . ."

There it was, what Lior had been dreading, and nonetheless it took her completely by surprise. Eventually the tumult died down in her head, and she found enough breath and composure to speak. "If—if two people live together as lovers," she said, retreating desperately into theory, "they usually give one another something, and take something from each other. What would I have to give you?"

"An equal," Aren said, his voice full of longing. "One who dares."

"And what would you give me?"

He reached out to take her hands in his, a child's gesture, shy and fragile. "Some of it you have seen," he said, so quietly that she could hardly hear him over the waves. "The rest—I think I can show you, but—but you would have to come into me, far in, all the way—and for that I think you would have to give me your inner Name."

Lior was surprised not to feel herself go pale with shock at the very suggestion. Too much was happening, too fast.

"For me to come that far in," she said, "I think you would have to give me yours."

He hesitated no more than a heartbeat. He gave her his Name; and for as long as it took him to say it, the air went silent as the waves stopped in mid-motion. When he was done, the breakers finished falling and crept up the beach again, but to Lior they sounded terribly subdued.

"I could never have hurt you again anyway," Aren said, sounding subdued himself. "But now you know it."

Lior trembled. She did not have to go through with this. She could back out. And she now had such power as no one had ever had. She knew the inner Name of the Sea. She could bind it, control it—

I had power already.

But there's more to life than power.

Oh Goddess, have I gone mad?

Her world was shattering around her under the onslaught of Aren's terrifying trust. Suddenly she had everything to lose, and nothing was safe. The image of that first wave rose up in her mind, towering, leaning, about to fall—

She met the silvery eyes with her own, and gave Aren her Name; and her terror, hearing itself named at last, rose up and blinded her.

Aren bowed his head into her hands and showed her what he would give.

It started as a silence that began to reach all through Lior, like some dark new blood. Sinuous and gentle, it sighed through her thought, darkening it like smoke, drowning the light of her self. Black, all black; like the seahorse, like the depths of the Ureistine, unrelieved darkness.

And suddenly, light above the darkness, as in the vision of worldbirth that the Indweller had shown them; silver light, of starlight and moonlight, of bright day on beaches that shone. There was always light above, so that the darkness came in shades: the drowned dusk-green of Sonacharre, or the lucent crystal blue of water in places where summer never left the shores; golden and crimson evening seas ablaze with wildfire sunsets; glass-brown waters, glowing green, burning silver,

white; she was all of them at once. Lior stretched languidly
into the colors that were her, shone under the Sun, shrugged
spray-borne rainbows about her shoulders. The Moon pulled
at her back; she arched like a cat under its caress, let it stroke
her toward it—the Goddess's hand, touching her in the softest place . . . constant lover, never quite in reach but never
out of sight.

Feelings. Touching everything, everywhere. Sand smooth
as skin, modeling itself silkily to her whim everywhere she
brushed it; the bright razors of coral, dividing herself from
herself a million million times, the sensation both exquisitely
painful and fascinating; cracked rocks, blunt boulders, sunk
deep and motionless as buried memories. Ages of silent
gliding about sunken isles and those not raised yet, threading
herself through wreck and undersea cave and sliding, stroking weed. Crushed in her own depths, weightless in her own
shallows; outflung forever, meeting herself and embracing
everything—coastlines, continents, the hot heart of the world—
all within her, covered, encompassed, surrounded. Hers.

And life, all the lives, *her* lives—from the tiniest mindless
light-eaters of the upper waters to the great complex minds of
whales and the unfathomable beings of the boiling dark . . .
all open to her to share, to be, to be *within*. Quick bright
schools of silver fish, zigzagging like random thoughts: the
long leisurely dances of the great whales, arguments in a stately
philosophy of doctrine and doubt; dolphin song, tender and
fiery, and the unceasing bass mantra of giant kelp; death-
wishes sliding through her on silent sharkfins, dreaming in a
dim mist of blood all their lives. A huge millionfold consciousness that never really changed, though birth and death
made it new every second. . . .

And him, of course. Oh, not a "him" truly, but the Sea's
own self, its soul and being. Intelligent, as any life will
become with time when so many pathways for thought are
bound together by one shared system—and until now, despite
the hugeness and complexity of that system, all alone. But no
more, if she would become part of it. Nor would *she* ever be
alone again, ever lack for another who touched, cherished,
loved. He would always be there; the vast eternal self that

had poured itself into this little shape, crippled, finite. For her.

For her.

She found herself staring dumbly down at his head, still bowed into her hands. She was still trembling. So was he. "All that," he said. "And more. This shape—some of the thoughts still will not come through. But more. And forever; for as long as there is a Sea. While I am, you would be too."

She struggled for breath. It seemed odd, not breathing water—not *being* water. "My Name," Lior said, "my heart— you know mine, now, as I know yours. My faults, my failings. But you would, would still—"

"Forever," he said.

Some fire that was not blue ran under her skin, yet cold sweat stood out on her, and she felt pale and frail as grass withered in the blast of day. Surely this was what death was like—

"I would even—There is a sharing," Aren said very low, and then had to swallow and start again. "The children— they said there was a special sharing; one person with another. They did not know much about it yet. They said I would find out when I grew up."

For the first time in her life, Lior felt herself begin to fill with tears that were not of sorrow. It hurt incredibly, as the first use of her Fire had hurt; and she would not have traded the sweet pain for all the comforts of the world. Very gently she turned Aren's face up toward hers. Tears were running from the silvery eyes. Slowly and carefully she touched them away, one by one, blind to the blurring of her own vision; and at last, "I think," she said, "I can help you with that."

"Tell me something."

"Anything."

"Why did you run away that last time you were the seahorse?"

"Well . . . as I told you, that body was not well suited to why I wanted to be with you. It could not well share your joy—or tell you mine. That was a pain to you; so it had to stop. And besides, you were thinking that night of spells and their breaking. And if by some wild chance you had broken it, then I would have had all that work to do again—getting all of me into so small a space from full size. But tell *me* something.''

''Anything.''

''Why were you so eager to break my spell?''

''Huh? That's what Rodmistresses do. Free the bound—''

''So I hear. But if I had been some poor enchanted person, and you had set me free, soon enough you would have been alone again.''

''Uh . . .''

''Is it that you would rather be alone?''

''It would have been the right thing to do.''

''The Inhospitable, down in Sonacharre, bound to that stone . . . doubtless he brought that on himself, and the sentence passed on him was just: the right thing to do. But still sometimes I feel sorry for him. Has no one ever felt sorry for Lior? Not even herself? Who breaks *your* spells, dear heart?''

No answer.

''Now I think I see what you saw in me before. Your voice has gone dumb, but your eyes speak. Lior . . . Loved, let me help. . . .''

The sound of sobbing, a soul's veil tearing from top to bottom. ''Aren—no one ever, ever said that to *me*—''

''Here, then. Here. No, don't turn away. Goddess and Mother, look at her; she doesn't want to get me *wet!* Little one, it's all right, I'm here. She only knows what kept me so long. . . . If I'd known about *this*, I might have been here sooner. . . .''

''Aren!''

''What? Am I not supposed to do that when you're crying? How about this?''

A brief silence. ''No . . . I suppose I'll let you do that.''

''So you said the last time.''

''Mmm . . . how many times is that?''

''Crying? Six.'' And sudden laughter.

''What's funny?''

"I have just figured it out. You know what you look like?"

"Huh?"

"When you're crying. A blowfish. You go this way—"

"Why, you—!"

Much more strangled laughter, tussling and rustling and an abrupt *thump*.

• "Aren? *Aren?* You all right?"

"Uh, yes. The floor—is a bit harder than I am, that's all."

"Revenge! But I bet that's a problem you never had before."

"What? Revenge?"

"No, falling out of your bed."

"Mph—" More rustling. "It's dangerous business to mock me, mortal woman."

"Oh? And what are you going to do about it?"

"This."

No answer, at least none in words.

"Revenge is a two-handed game . . . my loved."

"Aren."

They began again to weave that sweetest stillness, the one wrought of swift breath and silence and closed eyes and one another's Names; and outside, at the bottom of the cliff, the tide ran high.

They walked through their days and spent their nights with their arms about each other, no longer the shadow and the shadowed, but shining in each other's light like Sea and sky. Aren learned about sunburn, and why it's wise to use a blanket when making love on the beach, and about the grateful, not-quite-believing way Lior's lips would curve when he told her she was beautiful. Lior learned another reason to love the Goddess as Queen of Night, discovering that night is mother not only of dreams but of desire. She learned that there was no need anymore for her mind to fill frantically with thoughts when a silence fell, and her meditations became such in truth rather than distractions to keep herself from noticing how alone she was. In her heart the silver day danced with Aren's warm darkness that underlay it, parting never—but sometimes she would stop that thought, not knowing why. Her life seemed to have flowered into the climax of a fairy tale, prince and princess in each other's arms at last, surrounded by a bright haze of rejoicing. If there was something Lior had chosen to forget, it was that the only thing surely meant by "happily ever after" is that the storyteller is about to go home.

"I'm going to have to leave soon," Aren said.

"Leave?" Startled, Lior opened her eyes and looked up at Aren from his lap. He looked down at her, and Lior saw in his eyes again the seahorse's look, irremediable sorrow. Her heart seized.

Aren gazed out at the Sea. "How long can you stay out of your body?" he asked.

"A day, maybe two—Aren, do you mean that—" Lior began to sit up, but Aren held her gently down; much against her will she settled back.

"Very soon now," he said, "unless I go back, I will not be able to—and that is contrary to my agreement."

"With Her?"

Aren nodded. "When I was new here, and struggling for the words, you waited. You were so patient. Loved, I can wait for your answer." He took a long breath. "But I will miss you. . . ."

Lior closed her eyes, unable to think.

"Is it so hard to decide?" he whispered.

She buried her face against his middle. "No, Aren, I love you, but—"

He waited.

"Aren—*will I be me?*"

He stroked her dark hair. "Do you mean, will you lose your knowledge of yourself, swallowed up in me? Of course not. Why ask you to share with me if I would be as alone in the sharing as before it?" He smiled down at her. But Lior did not move and was not reassured. "What more, then?" Aren said.

"It's—it's only—Aren, I was myself enough before, but only because there was nothing much better to do, no one to be myself *for*. I guess I was afraid to let my body love people, because when you love people, they die—my parents did—''

"Until the world ends," Aren said, "I do not die."

"—but instead I let my body love things, feelings and tastes, light and dark, the Fire—and that way having a body was at least bearable. But now, now there's the touching, and the nights, the days, you here holding me, and inside and all around me when we share—and now I love being me, and I love having a body, and I don't, don't—''

"—want to give them up," he said. "You said there would be giving and taking—''

"And besides, what about the town? If I go away, who'll take care of the people?''

"And this is what I am taking from you," Aren said, more to himself than to her. "Maybe the price *is* too high. I am no judge. Lior," he said, and taking her by the shoulders, helped her straighten up and sit beside him. "Little one. I can't stay. I could push my time a few days more, but it would be dangerous, and I would be returning Her evil for all Her good. I should go back to my right body tomorrow. I don't want to go without you; your Name is part of mine now and the Sea won't truly be the Sea unless you're there—''

So much use of human language, perhaps, had done it, or the pain of the moment, but Lior looked into Aren's eyes and for the first time saw his thoughts there while he spoke. *Unless you come with me when I go,* he was thinking through the great clenching pain of loneliness-to-be, *you will never come. You know it. I know it. I offered you too great a dare, and we both know that this is where it will end, untaken—*

"—but I can wait." He smiled. "Even if you never come, still for a while someone loved the *me* that is. That will last me a long time." *O Goddess, the thousands of years piling on one another till there is no end to them, and alone, having just once known what it was like not to be—*

Lior put her arms around him. *Even though it was the courage he loved, he sees that I, that I just can't, and he still, still—* "You'll stay the night?" she whispered.

"Certainly," he said, "if you promise not to knock me out of the bed again."

She held him close and tried hard not to think of what she must be taking from *him*.

The night was all that Lior had known it would be, and worse; his darkness shut the starry dark away, and left *it* lonely—poor abandoned night, crying outside the circle of their arms to be let in. Held in his warmth, she wept, and he did too, till like a thief the dawn crept in the window. . . .

"I'll go and see you off," she said.

They went together down the cliff trail in the growing light, and once on the beach Lior gathered Aren close and put her face down against his shoulder, shaking with the attempt to just this once find her old habit again and hold in the tears.

"Oh, please be careful," she whispered.

"In the Sea," he said, "what can hurt the Sea? I'll be all right."

But she did not let go of him. "Aren," she said, fighting the words out past something in her throat that was trying to keep them in, "I don't—I want—"

He waited.

"You were—you were right—*Aren, break my spell!*"

She felt his arms tighten around her. "You of all people should know better," he said, his voice thick with his own weeping. "Why do you think I left last time, rather than let you waste your effort on me? No spell can be made to break unless the person under it wants to break it from their side too. . . ."

He kissed her one last time on the lips and once very tenderly on the forehead, and held her away. "I'll wait," he said. "Fare well, loved." He turned and began to walk down to the shore. The waves reached up toward him.

She stood and watched, as if watching a shrouded body borne up onto the pyre at a funeral, and knew that *everything* was going away with him—light, love, joy, the newest things in her life and the dearest. She was *sending* them away, willingly, where she knew she would never dare follow. And as an exchange she was taking empty arms, empty nights, welcoming back the old familiar loneliness, the narrow bed where there would once again be enough room, the days in which there would once again be enough time to get everything done, and then to sit on the shore and wonder why she felt something was missing—and would be missing forever—

"*Aren!*" she cried after him.

Just at water's edge, where the breakers teased and curled, he stopped, turned—held out a hand.

"Come on, Lior," he said. "Just the two of us. Or are you afraid?"

She felt herself being held still, felt her lungs seize and her throat choke closed over the words—and by that knew that the spell was of her own weaving, and that fear was the warp and the woof. Pull one thread and the whole thing begins to unravel. One thread—

—just one—

"Yes," she said, pushing the word out of her frozen throat, a faint cracked squeak. And "Yes!" louder, and "*Yes!*"

Aren dropped his hand.

"—but I'm going with you," she said.

He was holding her again, and she was no less terrified of the loss of her body, perhaps of her humanity, but it was better to be afraid within his arms than without them. She held Aren to her and they rocked each other like children for a long time, until Lior raised her head, sniffling, and said, "Just one more thing."

"What?"

Lior let go of him and turned away. There was of course no one direction to look in, but she held herself straight as befit a liegewoman of the Queen above all kings and queens, and closed her eyes to shut out, for this last moment, the sweet terror of life to which she was about to surrender herself. "Mother," she said, very low, "I don't know if I should go. There is our agreement outstanding. I haven't given You the thing You most desire of me—"

The wind fell to a whisper.

Haven't you? the answer came back.

Lior bowed; then, quick as a child going swimming, peeled

her Rodmistress's robe off over her head, tossed it over a boulder, and turned to reach out to Aren.

Solemnly, hands joined, the bride and the groom walked down into the water, out past the breakers, until the silver-gray morning Sea closed over their heads.

The people in Daike were only confused about the disappearance of Lior and the shipwrecked man until they found Lior's robe, which the high-running tide had taken to play with. They knew then that the bodies would likely not be found; the undertow off Daike is fierce. Any question of survivors was settled by Lior's Rod, found shattered on her bed, sure sign of a Rodmistress's death. They mourned her, but otherwise did well enough with just the circuit Rodmistress, who came through three times a year now. And certainly no one could fault the fishing, which became the best within memory; or the weather, which seemed to push storms just east of the town or west of it, but never straight in.

Daike prospers still, but the place is no longer quite ordinary. Always around Opening Night, when the walls between worlds grow thin and familiar things turn strange, there falls a night of Moon on which the waves run with the blue Fire, as if that Sea of which the starlight is a faint intimation were breaking on the North Darthene coast instead of the shadowy shorelines of the Dead. Unearthly musics then are heard, and the burning waves have a voice. Some say it is the voice of Lior, crying out for revenge on the jealous Sea that slew her and her lover long ago. But few who say so have stood on that jewelled beach by night and heard the Sea whisper again and again, as if to another self:

"You dared. . . ."

THE PALE GIRL, THE DARK MAGE, AND THE GREEN SEA

Tanith Lee

THERE WAS A WITCH GIRL LIVED ON A SEASHORE. HER HAIR was pale, her eyes were clear, her thought was sheer—but oh, her heart was sold. She loved with a rage a mage, who dwelled nearby upon a hill in a tower of old chill stone. Hour by hour she thought of him, there in the tower, and of how the dark hair hung like sea wrack down his back, blacker than night. But he paid her no heed; indeed, less than none, do what she might. This, her plight.

One day she called upon him, in the way of a sorceress, dressed in her best. Such magnificence, the wind itself did not dare to breathe upon a tress of hair. Pearls she wore, green gems, clean as her eyes. The mage was courteous, and cool. Still, he took her about the house, up and down the stairs, to north and south, everywhere, and showed her the skulls and gloves and magic lamps and chemic probes, and amphorae of banes, and psychic chains, and boons in bottles, imps and astrolabes, and last a glass whereby the stars might be seen as thick as eyes of grass, if seldom green. She showed him too she was most wise in each, though living on a beach. He gave her wine and kind unkindnesses. She went away and wept with pain. For then he had not said to her—Oh, call again, dear girl. Each tear, a pearl, fell in the sea. The sea said *Listen*. But the witch girl heard no sound save the waves' soft fall, and that was all.

Year ended. Sendings sent the witch in her peeve to break

74

the windows, nets of fishermen, or next to loose the fish in them. The fishers said, Drat that witch with a sleeve of spells. And hitched their nets together with regrets. But well, she was sorry, but the worry of love tormented her, for sure. She took her courage in her pale slim hands, and put on rings and things of wealth, and in the guise of an empress—yes! —she went to call on him again, that mage, her black-haired storm-eyed lord, in the stony bone of a tower. Like a flower trying to seed of need in sand. That was her. So grand she was this time, the very air and the earth's rime swooned, and the wintry birds croaked out of tune. He opened his door like the winter, and he frowned. It killed her, that. Unkind cold mage, the ice of his eyes could have locked the bay for a year and a day. He did not ask her in—surprise! Despite her glamorous panoply, she must then pretend, in all that empty land with miles between each cot and manse, she had by chance knocked on the wrong door. And so she had, for sure. Home then she went, once more, and once more wept, and slept no moment of the night. Such slights and sorrows, slings and arrows. The marrow of her heart, she would have said, seemed dead.

But the sea, at dawn, swarmed to her sill, and whispered *Listen.* Unsleeping now, she heard the sea say this: If you would seek a kiss, do not go wooing in your armour with a sword. Naked is love, a child, a sigh, a muted word. Both sorceress and empress have their place, which is not here— hear me and know. See how I am, vast as a sky, yet I upon my endless breadth and deep lure men to sleep with my soft smiles. But I will aid you, for it is my whim.

And then the sea swept in, like all the tears unshed, which overbrimmed. No hope to swim, or save. The ocean's architrave wide-opened and flung free the house, the shingle, and the girl and all her arts, into the sea. It raised her and it cast her up, and in her shift and hair alone, upon the stone step of the towering tower's bleak bone, and laid her there, not quite aware. And as the sea sank down, the moon flew up and on the step was thrown the mage's shadow as he leaned to look. What hapless helpless victim lay in need of care? He saw, and took her in. Not winter, then. He warmed her at a fire, and gave her sweeter wine, and held her to assuage the fear of water and its cryptic charge. So lost the game this mage. For love comes wending helpless, mild, a blinded child, the sheath of barbs it hides against its side—Beware an act of love, which lets love in. Beware the dream, the autumn tide, the sea change and the charm and foam. For long before the sea-moist seasoned night was done, there in the stone the flower put down its root, and grew. Before the night was through, all through the stone was warm.

The moral:

> That which you wish the most to take,
> That thirst the most you needs must slake,
> To take be taken, fly to pursue,
> The cup to your lip—
> But let the wine drink you.

> (And yet I must, and will, append,
> It helps to have a powerful friend.)

THE HUNT

Any heroic quest is best described as a hunt. A unicorn leaps into a clearing and draws men and maidens out from a well-known court into a forest—or onto the great Unicorn Tapestries; a white hart darts in front of Arthur's knights and drives them out of Camelot into Broceliande. "Whoso list to hunt, I know where is an hind,"Sir Thomas Wyatt declared more than four hundred years ago. He was right; he did—and so do we all. Whether the hunting ground be the court of Henry VIII, the Forest of Arden, Broceliande, Estcarp and the Dales, or the deep woods of the far North, the rules are always the same:

You must leave the normal haunts of humankind. Now, as you stand outside the safe, protected places, preparing to enter the forest, beware! Be wise. Here is strangeness. Here is adventure. Take what you must, but no more. Kill cleanly, and abuse neither your prey nor your power. Expect a battle, and fight to win, for the magic here will try to possess you or to kill. You may escape alive. But you will not escape unchanged.

Like Andre Norton, Poul Anderson knows these rules well; his knowledge shows in his many award-winning stories of fantasy and science fiction. Some of Anderson's most electrifying work involves quests, especially mythic ones.

77

For example, the Hugo-winning novella "Goat Song" retells the story of Orpheus in a world of computers and dying mystery, and of one man who dares to go out into the wilderness and bring wonder and danger back inside. His extraordinary *Tau Zero* combines theories of relativity and of an oscillating cosmos with the mythology Anderson has made uniquely his own, that of the far north, where the forests are old and deep and strange, and where the best hunting is.

And as Anderson knows well, the most perilous quarry of all is Man.

Like Andre Norton, Sandra Miesel is both loremistress and storyteller, steeped in the history and legend that permeates her writing. Her novel *Dreamrider,* which earned her a nomination for the 1983 John W. Campbell Award for best new writer, explored the archetype of the Great Tree. That symbol shows up again in "The Shadow Hart," which is dominated by the theme of the hunt. The story itself is drawn from a poem which, intriguingly enough, Poul Anderson puts into *Tau Zero.* The poem is a version of the folktale of King Valdemar who, maddened by grief at the death of his lover, blasphemed and was sentenced, like the Flying Dutchman, to rove the world until Judgment Day. Unlike the Flying Dutchman, Valdemar is not the only person doomed. Here is part of the poem:

> Be greeted, King, here by Gurre Lake!
> Across the island our hunt we take,
> From stringless bow let the arrow fly
> That we have aimed with a sightless eye.
> We chase and strike at the shadow hart
> And dew like blood from the wound will start . . .
> So shall we hunt ev'ry night, they say,
> Until that Hunt on the Judgment Day.

There are worse things than death, this story says. One of them is eternal loneliness, another eternal restlessness. "The Shadow Hart" is a tale of longing, courage, and the desire to rescue a loved one from a fate that is almost unthinkable.

*   *   *

Meredith Ann Pierce's first novel, *The Darkangel*, was a hypnotically evocative story of a quest first to destroy a vampire's power, then to save his soul. Her second in this series, *A Gathering of Gargoyles*, takes that story even further. But in the story printed here, "The Woman Who Loved Reindeer," Meredith Pierce turns her eyes from the somnambulistic beauty of the moon to the far north where strange earth magics coexist with the midnight sun, and the northern lights reveal wonders. This story, part of a novel to be published by the Atlantic Monthly Press in October, 1985, combines many of Andre Norton's themes: the young wise-woman who must make her own way in the world, the struggle against hostile outsiders, and above all, the peculiar understanding that can exist between human and animal.

As befits a writer whose first book transmuted the idea of vampires, Meredith Pierce now turns to the subject of shape-changers, a theme Norton used in *Moon of Three Rings* and *The Jargoon Pard*, and which has long kept people shivering and glancing over their shoulders at dancing shadows or watching the moon and reaching for the silver they keep near to hand.

No one would willingly let a werewolf live. But there are other were-creatures who run on four legs or walk on two. Perhaps the important thing about them isn't the terror they can evoke, but what they reveal of the best—and worst—both of human and animal.

THE FOREST

Poul Anderson

WHERE HILLS CURVED AROUND SOUTHWARD TO MAKE A
vale sheltered and sun-warmed, trees grew thickly. They
were not the birch, aspen, willow, and evergreens that here and
there broke the openness of the Land. These were oak, ash,
elm, hazel, rowan, apple, thorn. In among them were bushes
unlike any elsewhere, tangled together as if to stand off all
outsiders the while that they strangled each other. Stranger
still were the vines that clambered up boles and over boughs,
where in summer their leaves hung like great green raindrops
about to fall. Three brooks ran down from the heights and
burrowed into these depths. Somewhere they joined, for at
the southern end of the vale a single larger stream came forth
and wound its way onward.

That was a long day's walk from the northern end. Men
who had made it said that there the trees finally thinned out.
They did not become as sparse as where the People dwelt,
and the familiar kinds were not very often in sight. However,
at least the horizon was, though on the south a blueness
bespoke the opposite side of a broad bottomland. This was
about as far as anybody ranged in that direction. Few had
done so in living memory, for game had grown even harder
to find yonder than it was at home.

Old folk, harking back to what their grandparents had told
them, said that once the vale belonged to the Land. Then the
first saplings had appeared. Since then, they had grown to

80

mightiness and overwhelmed former habitations. In winter, peering through naked branches, those of the People who dared could still glimpse ancient grave mounds.

None ventured into the wood. It was not forbidden, for there was no reason to forbid it. Underbrush grappled, clawed, bit, rustled, and snapped, hindering bowshot or spearcast, alarming all birds and beasts. A man could not see a stone's throw around him, nor have more than glimpses of sky. Instead, gloom, silence, and rank smells pressed in on him, until he could hardly draw the windless air into a breast where the heart began to gallop. Their graves untended, ancestors lying there surely no longer had strength to come forth and give help against whatever Powers prowled the shadows. No, best leave the place alone.

At most, certain brave women collected deadwood along the fringes for their fires. They did so while wearing amulets of vole skulls, and after getting the Mother She to say a spell. And certain bold youths sought their Manhood Dreams at that same verge, perhaps eating a few of its nuts or berries if the season was ripe, as well as the Ghost Mushroom. Otherwise the wood was shunned.

After all, elsewhere the Land still reached, clean and free. For the most part it rolled gently from worldedge to worldedge, although it grew hillier as you fared east, flatter north and west. Springs made pools and tinkling rills, creeks lazed along over stony beds that seemed to ripple in sunlight, water gathered in hollows to form reedy meres where fowl clamored. Aside from trees, which stood alone or in small coppices but always well apart, the Land bore mosses and berry bushes on its lowest and wettest grounds; grass farther up; heather, gorse, creeping juniper on bleak and thin-soiled heights. In spring the Land was ablaze with flowers; in summer it billowed endlessly green; in fall it went purple and gold; winter turned it white, save for the somber spearheads of spruce and larch. But on a bright day star-fires often glittered there.

Always the Land lay under sky—sun-flame, rain-flood, wind-knife, hail-hammer, snow-hush, breeze-kiss: stars, moon, lowering gray, primrose dawn, wildfire sunset, softness of dusk. It lived with the clouds: dandelion seeds aflight, cliffs dizzyingly tall against blue deeps, vast caverns where lightning danced, smoke-scud on the wind, mists cold and glimmery when maidens went forth on their wedding mornings to wash in the dew—more kinds of clouds than a man could say, but each with its omens for him.

Most times of year the sky was full of wings—sparrow, thrush, rail, plover, partridge, grouse, duck, goose, swan, stork, heron, curlew, crow, raven, hawk—manifold as the clouds. Richly did the land bring forth. Fish swarmed in streams and pools. Hare, fox, ermine, and lesser creatures were everywhere. Herds of horse grazed wildly about. Rare but altogether splendid were the shelk that browsed shrubs and thickets, as tall at the shoulder as a man, their flattened antlers like oak boughs. Before all else were the reindeer, hardily outliving winter, darkening and drumming the earth with their multitudes in summer, life of the People. It did not matter that wolves took some of this game. The Land had ample meat for the needs of every being.

Or so it had been.

There was a man whose Dream at boyhood's end, a Dream he defiantly sought at the wood, had named him Thunder Horse. He became the greatest of hunters. That was well, because in his day the chase began to fail for many others. Even before his birth, the big animals had been vanishing. First the shelk went. Thunder Horse himself never saw anything of them but bones, kept for talismans, nor heard anything but tales. Then horses grew scarce, until years might pass between sightings of a few. Last and worst was when the reindeer dwindled.

The People did not starve. Birds, fish, and small animals remained plentiful, as did roots, berries, pine nuts, and the like. Yet this was not the same as roast steaks and haunches, succulent drippings and brains, savory organs and entrails—food such as gave strength and lasted a good long while in the belly. It broke the spirit of men to come back again and again empty-handed, and eat what their wives and children had caught. Even when successful, their searching had usually been so widespread—they took turns in the nearer and farther grounds—that they could only go to sleep after eating. Seldom did they talk, sing, dance, jape, court, enjoy themselves. Though they could make outdoor magic, the inner caves gaped empty of worshippers, let alone artists to paint fresh pictures, for lamps lacked fat. As vigor and joy went out of the People, fear stole in.

The more thoughtful among them saw worse than that ahead. Hence it was that the Father He finally called a solemn council.

This was in a spring which had, thus far, been more dry and less fruitful than anyone could recall. From end to end of the Land his messengers went, to every household, bidding each send a wise man. He did not call for more, because more could not be spared in this busy season. It was at midsummer and midwinter that the whole People came and camped at the Great Cave for sacrifice, parley, trading, bargaining, and merrymaking—in days when they had had goods to trade, agreements to reach, reasons to celebrate. Otherwise families simply visited each other as the mood struck.

A boy brought the word to Thunder Horse, who lived in hill country near the eastern end of the territory over which the People ranged. It was a day warm and fair, when greenness lately breathed across the slopes was brightening and thickening. Scents of growth steamed from the earth. Wings flashed and flickered overhead. But nowhere in view did a game animal graze.

The hunter sat working on the tent he had taken out of storage, wherein he and his lived during summer. It was amply large and finely made. Yet the paint of its ornamentation had not been retouched these past three years, for that would have required much fat. Despite every precaution, mice always got at the leather; but now, rather than renew whole panels, Thunder Horse had taken to sewing on patches. His flint awl he used freely, since if it broke he could easily chip out a replacement, but he was very careful of his bone needle.

Not far off, the elder of his living children, a girl, kept

watch on the younger, a boy who was still crawling and nursing. Meanwhile she plaited straw for hats against the sun and capes against flies, later this year. At present she and her brother were nude, like their father. Seeing the boy approach, she sprang to her feet and squealed an alarm.

"Quiet, my dear," said Thunder Horse. "It's bad manners to get excited when a newcomer appears, as though he might be dangerous." He smiled to show that he was correcting, not reproaching, and stood up. As he did, his brow drew into a frown. Already he guessed what was afoot.

The boy trotted nigh through the heather, halted, folded arms across breast, and waited, as beseemed one not yet a man. "Welcome and benison," Thunder Horse greeted him. "You come when we cannot offer you such guesting as we would like, but whatever we have is yours." Crinkles radiated from his gray-green eyes as he looked closer. "Are you not a child of Wolfsong and Fireflower on Ptarmigan Ridge?" The boy signed yes. "You've grown fast. That's well done, in years like these."

The boy stared in some awe. Thunder Horse loomed, with the long legs and deep chest to run down a reindeer, the broad shoulders to pack it back after he had slain it. Auburn hair and beard curled around a face whose rockiness was relieved by lively, upward-fluttering lips. The pelt on his chest almost hid the cicatrices made at his initiation into manhood.

He whistled. "Hoy, you in there!" he roared jovially. "Come out and see to our visitor! Also beautify the view," he added as his wife stepped forth.

Laughing Up the Morning had been at work in the sod hut that was winter quarters, making it clean. Although her buttercup-yellow mane was braided and coiled for the task, she wore a bundle of lavender at her throat. It was not really needful, as fair as she indeed was, but she liked to give her man pleasure.

"Welcome and benison," she said. "Are you hungry? We can eat soon if you wish and afterward take our ease." Meanwhile she ruffled the hair of her daughter, who had brought the baby to join them.

Presently she dispatched the girl to a spring nearby, with a tightly woven basket. Having put the water into a hollowed-out stump sunk in the floor of the hut, she used a bent green branch to bring hot stones from the fire and cast them in. When the water was simmering, she added hare, bird, grubs, and dried herbs. This stew she scooped up and served in her best bowls, which were of soapstone, together with swatches of hay to wipe fingers on. Thunder Horse passed around a skin of berry juice which had been working its magic upon itself for a year or two, and everybody should have become cheerful. It was a better meal than most homes could have provided.

Beside the feasts of former times, which Thunder Horse himself could call to mind, it was meager. "I am sorry," he told the boy. "In you I feed your father and mother, of course, and they did better by me when last I saw them. If you had come later, when the reindeer have calved—" he shrugged "—such of them as are left hereabouts—"

"Sir," said the boy, "that is why I am traveling through these parts."

And thus it came to pass that Thunder Horse made ready to go.

"I'm sorry to leave you with all the work," he said to Laughing Up the Morning, "but this is a grave matter, and surely you can cope. If I do not return, or if something else goes wrong, seek the house of Moonlight Walker and Lark." They were her older brother and his wife, who lived not too far off. Though he himself had been summoned, he had a son of hunting age. Thunder Horse grinned. "Fear not. You'll never lack for suitors."

"Whom should I want but you?" she answered.

Grand he looked, attired for his journey. Quills decorated his buckskin tunic, foxtails his breeches, ermine his shoes, blue kingfisher feathers the little bag of magics suspended from his neck. Bone hooks, gracefully carved, secured a horsehide belt on which were charred the totems of his lineage. From it hung, on the right, a bag for hand ax, tinder, and separately wrapped salves; on the left were a waterskin and a keen-chipped, leather-hafted flint knife. His backpack

carried sleeping bag, rain poncho, change of clothes and
footgear, dry food so that he need not pause to hunt, face
paint to don before the meeting, tools and supplies. Strapped
to the pack were bow, quiver of arrows, two javelins, and a
fish spear. A band encircled his head. There in front lifted an
eagle feather, while in back hung a wolf's brush, both given
him for goodly deeds.

So Thunder Horse stood, attired in the pride of the People,
and bade his wife farewell. Thereafter he kissed his children.
Turning, he went away at the long, easy, distance-devouring
pace of a hunter in the Land.

The Great Cave was on the northern slope of the hills
enclosing the vale of the wood. It was said to have been the
ancient home of the People, before waxing numbers caused
them to spread across the country. Many of them still lived
there or close by. Nobody dwelt too far away to come here
for the meetings. That would have been to cease being of the
People.

The holy fire, which must never go out, burned low beside
the crippled man whose duty and honor it was to tend it.
Behind yawned the cave mouth, at the bottom of the over-
hanging cliff which provided actual shelter. In this mild
weather the hides stretched in front had been taken down,
together with their poles. Daylight made vivid the paintings
on the rock, reindeer, horse, fish, hunters, masked wizards,
magical circles and crosses. The ground beneath was cleaned
and smoothed, bare of bedding, cookware, or any sign of
habitation. Such things the women had borne off, together
with their children. The council must be undisturbed.

It must also be aided. Under leadership of the Mother She,
the women had camped on a high place out of sight. There
they danced around a huge, scarred boulder, made offerings,
cast spells, and invoked the help of the landwights for poor
human creatures.

The Father He opened the council with spells of his own.
He wrought these alone, deep in the cave. When he was
done, he emerged chanting; other old men beat drums, a
mutter beneath his high-pitched call. He was not quite the

most aged among those few who had lived long enough for white hair and wrinkled faces, but he it was who gave counsel and healing, held in his head the stories of the ancestors, kept company with the unseen Powers.

Having finished, he sat down by the fire and blinked around the three-layered half-circle of hunters who waited cross-legged and silent. His first son, Hawk Talon, a man grave and gray, rose to take the word.

"Brothers in the People, we are met to ask each other what we shall do. Bad are the times, and long have they been worsening. The dreams of my Father He forebode worse yet. All our rites for the spirits of the game beasts go unheard. Ever more do they seek out of the Land. We know not what we may have done to anger them, for in truth we have done nothing save those things taught us by our forebears. Has any among us had any visions?"

No one answered, until Moonlight Walker, always blunt spoken, raised his hand. When Hawk Talon pointed to him, he said; "I have sought north, farther than ever before, and seen reindeer herds still abundant. Also, living in the eastern part of the Land, I have met strangers, not of us but not very unlike us either. By signs and a few words we had in common, I have learned from them of horses where the hills flatten out to make another great plain. I think it is not the game that is failing us, it is the Land that is failing the game, so it must move elsewhere."

"But why has this happened?" asked Hawk Talon.

Moonlight Walker shrugged.

"I will tell you what I think," said Thunder Horse eagerly. "From old men and women we hear that in their youth the Land was different. It was cool and wet. Forage was rich. Moreover, the Land was open, entirely open. Now warm, dry summers kill off the moss that keeps the reindeer alive in winter. Thus they must needs seek better climes. Meanwhile, trees grow thicker. The shelk do not like this; they fear their huge antlers will catch in the boughs. The horses do not like it; wolves can too easily surprise them, and besides, the grazing is not what it used to be. Therefore they also drift away.

"Why this should happen, I do not know. But I have been thinking that we too should soon move our homes."

A sigh went among the men. Several signed themselves against evil. It would be a terrible thing to forsake the Land, the beloved Land—the graves, the hallowed places, the range where memory clung to every bush and brook.

"Where would we go?" demanded cautious Trout. "Eastward are those strangers. They would not take kindly to invaders of their hunting grounds. Anyhow, that is where the horses went, and we are the Reindeer People. West, say the stories of travelers, it is no different from here, until suddenly the world comes to a stop at the Endless Bitter Water."

"North!" cried Moonlight Walker. "Where else?"

"That is not as easy as it sounds," replied Hawk Talon. "In my youth I was part of a band who wandered far in that direction, seeking dreams and—well—" he smiled a little wistfully "—adventure. It is unpeopled, or nearly so, but that is because it is poor country, set beside the Land as the Land formerly was. The reindeer would not seek it if they had anywhere better to go. This I saw for myself. We all know, as well, ancient songs about heroes who went much farther; tales reach us, carried from mouth to mouth, of hunters who were forced that way by some or other mischance. These accounts agree that beyond the tundra lies a stony waste, and beyond this rises the Everlasting Ice."

Moonlight Walker tugged his beard and frowned. "I did not say we should go that far," he reminded them. "Surely between here and there is some territory where we can live well enough, even if not as well as our ancestors did here."

When White Falcon raised his hand, silence grew so deep that men heard a raven croaking in a distant larch. He was a seasoned hunter, still strong and skillful though his locks were grizzled, and well known for wisdom.

"Whatever we do," he said, "it must be within the next few years. Unless things change, the big game will keep on dwindling—and ever faster, I believe—until it is quite gone from the Land. Without it, we are no longer men and women, but scuttering animals, raiders of birds' nests and rotten logs. For what are we without hides for clothing, tents, packsacks, sleeping bags? How shall we split firewood without antler ax hafts or dig up roots and hedgehogs without antler picks? Can we do without large bones for tools, everything from needles to barbed spearheads? Without grease for paint and lamps, that our artists may work and the rest of us behold, can we perform the magics that keep the goodwill of the landwights? Without the joy of art, the comforts of life, the challenge of the chase, will our spirits not shrivel and blow away like dead leaves? We are hunters, O People, or we are nothing.''

The stillness that followed was long indeed. It was not that anybody had said anything truly new. But now was the first time that men had dared set forth their fears in open council, regardless of whether doing so might prove unlucky. The raven croaked, the wind whispered.

Finally Hawk Talon declared, slowly: "It seems to this person that before we take any step we cannot retrace, we should know more. Let us send bold men north in small parties to cover a big territory between them. Let them find whatever they can find and come back to tell us about it at the midwinter meeting. Then perhaps we can decide.''

A mumble of agreement went through the half-circle.

"Wait!'' exclaimed Thunder Horse. "Are you not forgetting something?''

Hawk Talon overlooked the rudeness of the outburst and asked quietly, "What do you mean?''

"Why must we search only northward? We already know that, at best, nothing lies yonder which is as good as the Land once was. But we have well-nigh no knowledge of the south— save that it nourishes great beasts of its own, as we learned last autumn.''

A certain boastfulness in Thunder Horse's voice was forgivable. He had been the triumphant one then.

Happenings had begun in sinister wise, with a long dry spell. Eventually there appeared a gray pall on the southern horizon. Winds blowing thence carried bits of ash and soot. When rain came at last and cleared the dirt out of the air, the People supposed their rites had brought the landwights in aid.

Soon afterward, strange beasts appeared. It was clear that they had fled the evil in the south and wandered forth across country foreign to them. Thin, exhausted, they knew not how to behave here, and wolves took many of them before men were even aware. After that, the hunters sought eagerly and slew the rest. Most of the animals were a kind of deer, but very different from reindeer, being reddish-coated, sharp-hoofed, slender-muzzled, and with knife-tined antlers—upon the males only.

One creature was terrifying. Beneath horns like a crescent moon, its blunt face peered out of a thicket of dark-brown mane and beard. A great hump at the shoulders did not reach as high as a shelk's, but the whole body was immensely more massive. The tail was long and tufted. Its bellowings were like thunder, come down to an earth that trembled beneath its weight as it charged whatever it saw. Brave men fled, crying that this must be a troll.

Thunder Horse, true to his name, heard the tale and came to see. Laughing, he said the beast left scat, wherefore it must be flesh too and killable. He rallied a few reckless youths to him and they went forth. Skipping clear of the horns when the monster rushed, they danced around its flanks and wielded their spears. Harpoon heads worried away in its guts, blood first trickled and then brawled out, finally the beast stumbled and lay dying. The hunters sang it a death song long unheard, the farewell to the spirit of a shelk, noblest of animals.

Since then, hide and skull rested in the Great Cave. That hide was thick; it would have made wonderful footgear. The meat had been tough, requiring much pounding before it could be chewed, but thereafter delicious; and the hump was gloriously fat.

Meeting silence and dubious looks, Thunder Horse continued: "What game reached us, doubtless fleeing a large fire, must have been a very small part of what lived in its home-land. The south is surely teeming with life. Is that not where the migratory birds go when winter bleakens the Land? *They* know."

"We do not," retorted Trout. "We have sometimes encountered wanderers from the east or the west, but never from the south. Hunters who have ventured a ways across yonder valley tell of nothing but trees becoming more plentiful, while reindeer are soon entirely absent. They have turned back. But what would they find if they went on?" He shuddered. "I think it is a whole country overgrown, like the glen we have here."

Lips tightened, eyes shifted uneasily, fingers traced signs. Thunder Horse raised his hand. "That may be true," he said, "but we cannot be certain until somebody has gone the whole way. Now I have been giving this thought, O brothers in the People. Why is the wood such barren ground for a hunter? Is it accursed? No, I think it is simply unsuited for the big game we know, while the creatures proper to it are absent because they cannot well cross the open country in between."

"Then how did the wood arise?" Moonlight Walker demanded. "It does not belong among us either."

"Perhaps I can answer that," said White Falcon. "How do our own trees grow up, often far apart? Why, winds scatter seeds; birds and ground squirrels carry off nuts, which they are apt to drop. Most of this falls where it cannot flourish, and dies. Some, though, ends in places kind to it. Such is the vale, warm and sheltered. Let only two or three acorns reach it, by whatever set of chances, and presently there will be oak trees making more oak trees. Likewise for other growth. It overshadows native plants and kills them." He paused. "I wonder if the wood may not be the forerunner of something much greater, the Mother Wood moving north."

Hawk Talon himself was appalled. "But then we must indeed flee!" he cried.

"Must we?" Thunder Horse responded. "Can we not hunt the red deer, the moon-horn, whatever roams there? Why stampede north to a life that cannot but be poorer than our forefathers knew—when we might instead trek south into riches whereof they never dreamed?"

"Can you swear that this is right?" Hawk Talon asked.

"Of course not." Thunder Horse tossed his head. "But have I your leave, my brothers, to go and see?"

* * *

He followed the stream that ran out of the glen. As more watercourses emptied into it along the way, it broadened to a river, though remaining shallow enough for a traveler to spy and spear an occasional fish. Other fish he might hope to catch in a weir while he slept, together with small animals in the traps and deadfalls he set. It was indifferent food, but all he could get, aside from the dried meat and berries in his pack. Real game simply did not exist in these parts. At least, it no longer did; bleached bones told of a bygone time when it had prospered.

Day after day Thunder Horse fared. Loneliness began to gnaw at him. He had never before minded being by himself, but that was when hunting, out in the open. On this journey he found stands of the alien trees becoming commoner as he went, closer together, until often whole woods covered the riverbanks and hid the horizon. Rain showers were like the embrace of a friend, doubly precious for their rarity, briefly relieving the sultriness that loured beneath the leaves. When homesickness took him by the throat, he wondered if wisest might not be to quit and return to Laughing Up the Morning.

No, she would think scorn of him, did he yield while any hope remained. Thunder Horse trudged onward.

Strangely, he got back heart when he reached the dead country. That was clear across the valley, where the river turned west, away from hills more high and steep than any in the Land. Having filled his waterskin, he left the water itself behind as he followed his own course south. Beyond the first ridges he found a second valley, much narrower and deeper.

There earth lay ashen. Everywhere the stumps and snags of charred trees reached upward like the fingers of a corpse that has stiffened. A stream flowed muddy and lifeless, poisoned. Nothing stirred save dust and cinders on acrid winds. Seldom did a bird pass by, and then very far overhead. Here must be where the great fire had raged, whence the beasts had fled. Either he turned back—and who could blame him?—or he mustered his entire courage to go on.

It took him a couple of days to get through.

Yet the desolation itself, grimmer than any left by wildfire across the Land, told him how fecund the soil had been, and would someday be again. Hence he was not overly surprised when he found the unscathed realm beyond. Nevertheless he felt an inward shock, for he came upon the sight suddenly. Climbing the southern heights, ashes gritting beneath his shoes and in his nostrils, he topped them where they began a sharp downward plunge. There he halted, drew a gasp, stood a long while trying to understand that which he saw.

The slope before him was too steep and rocky for much plant life. Thus it had acted as a firebreak. An enormous lowland stretched away at the foot of the range; and there reared the Mother Wood.

Right, left, ahead, farther than he could see, trees stood marshalled in their hosts. Low evening light gave a tawniness to the manifold greens of their crowns, and cast mysterious moving shadows where breezes ruffled them. Seen from above, they made a oneness, the hide of a vast, breathing beast crouched upon the world, waiting for he knew not what—for its prey to come to it?

Thunder Horse squared his shoulders, wet his lips, laid hand on knife. "Well," he said aloud, "this is what I hoped for." Was it not? He forced himself to descend.

At the bottom, he spread his sleeping bag under a gnarly giant of an oak and gathered deadwood to burn. When his fire drill had finished its work, the blaze was cheering. He banked it to last overnight; in the morning he might wish to cook. At present, his waterskin emptied, thirst took away appetite for what was left of his rations. Setting traps seemed like more trouble than it was worth.

He slept ill. Night held neither the silence he knew nor the clean sounds of wind and wolf which sometimes pierced it. Here the dark was full of stealthy rustlings, creakings, chitterings, now and then a hoot whose eeriness startled him awake in a sweat.

Morning brought consolation. Dew had fallen heavily. He licked it off stones and sucked it out of moss on boles. Countless different birds trilled and whistled merrily. The rainbow sparkles on a spiderweb held him speechless with delight. Creatures like big red ground squirrels scampered along branches overhead. Tree squirrels? How droll! Thunder

Horse laughed. They should be trappable, until he came upon
big game.

Having eaten, he ventured in among the trees. Underbrush
choked off certain parts, but elsewhere was less thick than in
the vale at home. He supposed that was mainly due to shade,
but dared believe that large grazers helped keep it down. In
any event, he could walk without too much difficulty.

Let him therefore do so. Let him push on as far as was
prudent and see what he could see. How far that was would
depend on how well he did at finding food and water. And
was that not exactly what he had come to learn?

Returning to camp, Thunder Horse stoked up his fire and
made a burnt offering out of his rations. Dancing sunwise
around the gift, he sang the Guardian Song. Facing the
woods, arms upraised, he called: "O landwights of this
realm, I know you not nor what you may want to make you
kindly toward me. Here are no ancestors of mine to intercede
for me. I will try to understand signs you may send me. But I
come a stranger and in need; surely, for your honor, you will
be hospitable to me. It is spoken."

He cast earth upon the fire lest it spread, gathered his gear,
and set forth.

At first the going was easy and wonders everywhere around.
From himself he had dismissed the fear of being enclosed
which made the wood at home dreadful to the People. Here
were spaces indeed, reaches unbounded, but without the
starkness of the Land; rather, these were lush bowers, long
caverns, small flowerful meadows. Above him the branches
came together, often altogether hiding the sky, yet snaring its
light in their leaves and letting flecks of brilliance rain down
over the soft mould beneath. The various greennesses were
beyond telling, from shy foliage of elm to dark moss on
fallen logs. Mushrooms glimmered white from shelter or
craggy on trunks. Air was warm and moist, rich in curious
odors. When he came upon a spring, drank deep, and filled
his waterskins, Thunder Horse believed the landwights were
in truth welcoming him.

Only slowly did he find how mistaken that was.

Time went on, on, on, and still he was amidst the trees and

their shadows. More and more he encountered brush, and must either go far around or else, if it was not too thick, force his way through; withies lashed him, twigs cracked, the racket surely alarmed all game for bowshots about. Otherwise the silence deepened, until at midday no bird sang, no squirrel darted and chattered, nothing was to hear except his clumsy feet and the loudness of the heavy air as he breathed it.

Toward evening he spied a deer and cast a javelin. He missed, as tricky as the light-freckled gloom was, and he had no hope of running it down through the undergrowth. It vanished, leaving him aware more sharply than ever of how alone he was.

Best would be if he returned to the spring while he still had day, made camp, perhaps spent a few sleeps there and got some familiarity with the ways of the beasts. Yes. He grinned ruefully and started back north. . . .

Was he bound north? He could not get a proper sight on the sun.

Long after he should have reached his goal, he realized that every place, every course he took was like every other. Could he even find his way to open country again?

Silence and shadows thickened. He began to have a sense of something that watched him, but when he stopped and peered he could only make out leaves, boles, dimness; holding his breath to listen, he could only hear the knocking of his heart.

Or did a hugeness indeed stir somewhere yonder? In all this strangeness, how could he tell? He forbade himself fear and struggled onward.

That night he made a fireless camp. Whatever punk wood he could scratch together was too wet for tinder. Nor was there anything suitable for a deadfall, and nothing got into the snares he set. They must not be right for catching the lesser animals of these parts. Nonetheless darkness was once more full of noises, low and witchy.

In the morning he blundered ahead once more. When from time to time his skin prickled with a feeling of eyes upon him, he ignored it. His need was too great, to find his way back.

At the end of that day he knew he was in truth lost, quite likely making wild swings to and fro and around when he thought he was pointed steadily. Else he would by now have been free, out beneath unhidden sun and stars. He drained his waterskin, for terror lurked beneath whatever resolution he kept to hammer in his breast and parch his throat. As warm as the nights were in here, he found no dew at dawn, nor did he discover a spring or a brook.

Nor did he see any more of the game he thought must be so plentiful. Trees, brush, and shadows, trees, brush and shadows were all that remained in the world, endless as an evil dream. Toward the close of that day he could no longer comfort himself with memories of friends and of Laughing Up the Morning. Their faces were blurred by the haze of despair that had fallen over him. Blindly he stumbled ahead, because he knew that if he stopped for more than a night's rest, that would be where he left his bones.

Thus it was with Thunder Horse when the Forest Folk came upon him.

They were three hunters, who from afar heard him thrashing about. He did not sound like anything known to them. Moonbeam-quiet themselves, they made their way in his direction—and stopped amazed at sight of the huge man in the outlandish clothes. For his part, he uttered a coughing roar, fell to his knees, and reached empty, trembling hands out to them.

Clearly he was no demon, and he might be a god in disguise. Even if he were a helpless stranger, he should prove interesting. Therefore the hunters were kindly. They assisted the newcomer to his feet, gave him water and food, guided him to their camp, let him recover in the next few days while they completed their mission.

Thunder Horse found more to marvel at than the saving of his life. His rescuers were not quite like men of the People, being less tall, more slender, darker of hair and eyes though fairer of skin—that last, perhaps, because less sun and wind touched them. They braided their hair and haggled their beards off short. Their garb was simpler than his, and without decoration; to breechclout and leggings a man might or might not add a fringed tunic, with perhaps a fur cap on the head. Their weapons were just knives, hand axes, and short, stout spears meant for thrusting rather than casting. The style of stone-knapping was different from his. Later he would learn that they too had bone harpoons and, while they lacked bows, possessed something new to him, fishhooks.

In camp they had raised no tent but, rather, constructed shelters by weaving brush over an uprooted sapling leaned in the crotch of a tree, and chinking any holes with moss. Their fire burned outside the entrance, with rocks behind to help cast the heat inside. It was a snug place to sleep.

In the time that followed, they brought in a couple of red deer. Skinned and dressed, the carcasses were hung well overhead, out of reach of thievish animals. On the last day, exultant, they came in with another creature, the size of a half-grown boy, coarse-haired, with tusks jutting from a long snout. Also they had trapped three short-muzzled, stiff-whiskered beasts of prey, slightly larger than foxes, for the pelts rather than the stringy flesh. Life among the trees was more varied than out upon the Land.

The hunters had no magic bags like Thunder Horse's. However, in a belt pouch each carried a few pebbles on which designs had been painted, zigzags or crisscrosses or more enigmatic patterns. At first he would take out one of these and clutch it in his fist while dealing with the guest. Later, losing suspicion, the group stopped doing this. The pebbles must be their kind of talisman.

Their speech was rapid and singsong, quite unlike the gutturals of the People. Thunder Horse could make nothing of it at first. When he named himself, they seemed startled. None ever tapped his own chest while uttering anything. From hearing them call to each other, he slowly came to associate certain sounds with particular persons—Unyada, Denovado, Zimbarir—though he had no idea what the words meant.

By that time the group were on their way home. Their kills

they carried on their backs, or lashed to a pole between two men in turn. That was less awkward than Thunder Horse had supposed, for they moved with incredible deftness and knew every easiest route to follow. He was the groper and stumbler. At least, now that he had regained his strength, he could help; his shoulders bore twice the burden of anybody else.

Just the same, it was two days of hard travel to their destination. He concluded—righty, as he afterward learned—that they had gone out in a threesome because that many were needed to bring a worthwhile amount of catch home over such a distance, through these narrow and brush-encumbered ways. And, of course, like the People, they must needs often hunt well away from their dwellings, lest they deplete the game closer by.

Their home was a sizeable settlement. Its huts were akin to the camp shelter, but larger and more substantial. They stood not very far apart, among the trees at the front of an over-hanging cliff. It was higher than that of the Great Cave, though it lacked such a deep hole. Here too burned a fire perpetually tended, and was a common meeting ground. Yet no pictures adorned the cliff. Painted pebbles lay about in profusion, but that was all.

Women and children swarmed to meet the arrival, shrilling their welcomes and their astonishment at seeing Thunder Horse. Many crowded around to touch his skin or pluck at his clothes. A shout from an older man, who seemed to be a leader, sent them scurrying back to their tasks. It seemed that they did the work of the village, save for such labor as was too heavy for them. Thunder Horse was soon admiring the skill with which they smoked meat and cured hides. On the other hand, their household wares struck him as poorly made, and they had no sense of blending and flavoring of foods.

His rescuers joined male friends and took their ease. Toward evening men went into their huts, to emerge painted and feather-bonneted for a celebration of success. The women stayed with the simple grass skirts that were their summer garb, and children remained naked. Both sexes bore simple ornaments, necklaces or bracelets of bone, shell, quills, plumes.

The makers of these lacked the art of craftspeople in the Land.

The celebration took place after dark, with feasting, wine, song, drums, dance around a bonfire. The dancers did not stamp out the stately ring-measures of the People, but capered in pairs, man and woman. After a while, such a pair was apt to steal off into the night, coming back looking happy and a bit tired. Thunder Horse could merely stand and watch. Even so, more than one comely young female swayed up to smile invitingly at him. He fought down desire. It would be madness to take advantage of a girl who had gotten drunk, and so court the wrath of her father or husband. Her gaze upon him would grow puzzled, until presently she went elsewhere.

Unyada's family took him into their dwelling. He slept badly on the crowded floor in the stuffy air. He was used to a tent in summer, a solid but spacious sod house in winter. Still, these folk were being generous. Next day several men used hafted axes to slash brush, whereupon their women made him a hut for himself.

Women always worked together to prepare the main meal of the day, which everybody shared. Those were noisy and cheerful occasions. Otherwise a person simply took a handful of whatever was available, as the belly ordered. Besides preserved meat and fruits, this included nuts and roots gathered in the woods. There were also lumps of stuff new to Thunder Horse; women ground dried acorns or seeds between stones, mixed the powder with water or blood, and baked it on heated rocks.

As wonderment wore off, he began to feel himself less than a man, forever taking and never giving. By signs he tried to show that, if nothing else, he would like to help around the village. Women squealed, giggled, fluttered their hands when he tried to carry their burdens or wield their grinding stones.

Luckily, Unyada understood and found a suitable task. Man's work at home was chiefly with wood, felling trees, splitting them into fuel, shaping poles and shafts. Once he got the knack, Thunder Horse's strength made him the best of everybody at this. Already, of course, he could flake new tools and sharpen old ones, though his style was unique here.

He did not work the entire time, or even most of it. Nobody did. He had ample leisure to make acquaintances, get shown around the neighborhood, master such minor skills as line fishing, start haltingly to learn the language.

At first, what he learned was mainly the names of things. He would have had to do this in any case, as strange as most were to him. He found that to the dwellers this immensity of trees was the Forest, and they its Folk. They knew of the open country northward, but feared and avoided it.

Slowly he gained knowledge of beasts. The red deer he had encountered, but not yet the fallow deer—nor the elk, the size of the shelk remembered by the People and likewise possessor of wide, flat antlers, but crooked-nosed and ungainly. In the camp of the hunters he had seen a slain boar and some wildcats. Now, looking at what bones and hides the villagers kept, he learned about lynxes, otters, the terrible bear. A moon-horn such as he had killed was really a wisent. Commoner was the aurochs, not as shaggy or quite as massive but even more formidably beweaponed on the brow. Taken to a nearby stream, he saw his first beavers and their dam. Eventually, guided through the woods by his friends, he glimpsed those other animals of which he had heard.

He would have gained lore much faster if the Forest Folk had drawn pictures. But they did not, and when he tried with a bit of charcoal, they grew so plainly dismayed that he stopped forthwith. Piecemeal it came to him that they lived in dread of . . . of what? The unknown?

The various names that each person used, and frequently changed, were blinds against evil spirits. A true name was kept secret, revealed in private by the mother when a child went through rites of manhood or womanhood, and never thereafter spoken. Ancestral ghosts were not protective but envious of the living, ever seeking revenge for being dead. There seemed to be no landwights whom humans might keep well-disposed by songs and gifts. Instead there were beings remote and implacable, though demanding sacrifices, rulers of sky and earth and underground, of birth and death and luck and misfortune, glimpsed in storm or wildfire or the Forest depths—gods, they were called. And when men whispered of the Horned One, they shuddered.

Was this why they were such indifferent hunters? It was not for lack of skill. The wilderness required more of that than did the Land. In fact, they took deer quite readily. A man would stand in smoke to cover his natural odor and don a fringed tunic so as to resemble a tree; thereafter, step by high and soundless step, freezing into motionlessness whenever the quarry glanced his way, he could work near enough to cast an arm around its neck and stab it in the throat. He could read the subtlest signs of nibbled leaves or bent twigs or dimples in a grassy bank. He could drift like mist down a game trail or through dense growth. Crouched high in a tree, he could drop like a lynx upon his prey. A mat of sedges on his head, he could swim underwater, silent as a pike, until he grabbed a brace of duck from beneath. His snares and traps were marvels of cunning.

Yet save for a rare pig, these men took scarcely any other of the large beasts that flourished everywhere around them. They were not cowards. Was it spirit that was wanting in them?

Withal, they were gentle, helpful, not haughty or covetous as too many among the People were. Thunder Horse gathered that they would not mind if strangers like him moved in. On the contrary, they would be delighted to have more humans nearby. It would relieve the gloom and stillness of the Forest.

True, any newcomers would have a great deal to learn. But that was entirely possible. His hosts being patient teachers, Thunder Horse began to master their arts as the summer wore on. Given a year or two of practice, he should become good enough to make a living. And his sons could be among the best. Besides, instruction would not all be one-sided—far from it. The People had skills unimagined by the Folk, for making of things both beautiful and useful. Above everything else, perhaps, they had the bow. It was too long for handiness among these branches; but surely a man could create a bow short yet powerful.

Aye, what really was most important was the soul in him.

Hunters of the People would seek out elk, aurochs, wisent, the bear himself. That would doubtless be hard at first—they must discover how to do it, and lives might well be lost along the way—but do it they would, because that was in the nature of the People.

No need to fear crowding. The Forest had ample room. It was the Folk who were too few. That might be a reason why they were in such terror of those gods.

Why there were not more was a question that puzzled Thunder Horse. It was not that they made insufficient love. He was slow to recognize their customs and shocked when he did, so alien were these. The trees of the Forest had never witnessed a marriage rite. Men and women lay together as they pleased. After a period of youthful adventuring, they formed couples and shared housing, because partnership was easiest. However, such a union was not necessarily for life, nor did it at any time bind either person to the other alone.

By the time he had become aware of this, the women had given up on him. Handsome and intriguing though the outsider was, either he lay under a geas or there was something wrong with him. For his part, he felt that pursuit would be unseemly. Nevertheless, his wife was afar, and sleeping by himself grew to be very lonesome.

That summer a young girl reached womanhood. The Folk put her in a shelter by herself, brought her the necessities, but kept glance averted and did not speak with her. For one moon she was thus shut in, practicing solitary abasements that would appease the gods. After that she was free and knew her secret name. She continued living with her parents and calling herself Elidir. Thunder Horse thought that meant "Anemone" but was not sure; his command of the language was still feeble. She was pretty, her figure slight but ripening, her tresses crow's-wing black around fine-boned features, huge dark eyes, tip-tilted nose, lips always a little parted over shining teeth.

She took to hanging around him whenever he was at home and she had no immediate duties. As he cut and trimmed his wood, flaked his flints, wrestled or romped with his male friends, there she would be, watching, timidly smiling if his gaze strayed her way. Ofttimes nobody else was at hand; he might be logging or tending his fish lines some distance off.

At first he simply enjoyed her nearness, as sightly as she was. Later he understood what he was free to do if he chose. He refrained, because come autumn he meant to return to Laughing Up the Morning, and Elidir might feel forsaken.

Let them just be comrades. She was never reluctant to talk with this lame-tongued foreigner. From her he could learn more of the language and, perhaps, the soul of her race. To him it remained a mystery.

The end came cruelly fast.

In these canopied, horizonless reaches, Thunder Horse could not keep track of sun, moon, and stars on their paths through the year. However, he knew that summer was drawing to a close. It did so in a last passionate outpouring of warmth, greenness, life. Huge flocks of birds gathered aloft and on the water, making ready for trek. Wolves turned more and more toward hares and voles for food, now that the fawns they had not picked off were grown tall. Antlers waxed and hardened on stags. Elk and wisent bawled, a thunder along the leafy arches. Bears rambled, rooted, raided bees' nests, fattening themselves against winter. Among the Forest Folk, men busied themselves more than ever bringing in venison, and children gathered nuts and berries for the women to preserve. Besides, a sacrificial feast was in preparation. It would take place on the full moon after the first leaves turned yellow, in hopes of winning the mercy of the gods throughout the cold season.

Thunder Horse decided he would go home right after that. His longing was as keen as the winds that must already be sweeping over the Land. He would lift from his wife and children the fear that he was dead. And when the People met, he would have words of hope for them.

Oh, they could not move down here all at once. Next spring he would lead several families back. They would spend an unbroken year or two getting to know the Forest well, what it offered and what it demanded. Thereafter some could return and invite the rest to follow them south. No doubt many would refuse, preferring to follow the reindeer and the old ways—*over the wide ranges, under the starry skies.* . . . Yes, he had been away too long himself. It had become a weasel in his breast, gnawing his heart.

But in the Forest was abundance forever.

From dawn, the morning was sultry. No breeze relieved it; the crowns of trees were like masses of green stone seen against a heaven made wan by pitiless light. Cloud banks swelled in the west, snowy on top, blue-black in their depths, flickery with lightning, but thus far the storm held aloof. Sometimes its mutterings reached the ear, almost the only sound in breathlessness.

Thunder Horse did not see this at the village. There cliff and boughs cut off the sight. Women and children went listlessly about their chores. Able-bodied men were off on the chase, save for him. He wanted to repay kindness as far as possible, and his best service was to cut more firewood. Ax and resharpening stone in hands, waterskin and packet of food at waist, he departed for the clearing.

It was some ways off, because the Folk wanted trees around their dwellings for shelter. It was not large. A man could only fell a young, slender bole; thus a woodlot was nothing more than whatever stand of such could be found within a reasonable distance. This one was nearly exhausted. But human toil made no real wounds on the Forest. The ancient giants stood untouched, and saplings sprang up faster than loggers could work.

At his goal, Thunder Horse saw the sky. Light and heat flooded over him. He stripped to breechclout and shoes before he approached the elm he had in mind. There he murmured an apology to any being who might inhabit it. That was not the way of men hereabouts, they seemed to revere only the gods, but he continued to offer the courtesies he felt were due.

Bracing his legs, he swung. The impact of flint on wood thudded unduly loud in this hush. It ran back through the haft and his arms into his shoulders. Sweat runneled across his ribs and made his lips salty. He would be at this the whole day, and the day after and the day after. It was no pleasure. Far rather would he be padding along a game trail—or, O memories, running down a reindeer through country where cool winds blew! But he might as well get used to the labor. It would be necessary from time to time, once he had settled here, and it was better than starvation.

He had been hewing for a while, and the stormclouds had grown vaster yet, when the corner of his eye caught a movement. Turning, he saw Elidir step out into the rank grass of the clearing. He stopped work and smiled. "Why, greeting," he said.

She advanced shyly, carrying a small basket full of currants and gooseberries. A sweet sight she was, clad in just a loosely woven skirt. Her painted pebble, which had a natural hole in it, hung from a thong between the firm little breasts. She was not as sweaty as he, but her skin had a sheen to it, and when she drew nigh he scented an enticing pungency.

"I thought you would like these," she said low. Her lashes fluttered.

He still must needs guess the meanings of more than half the words he heard, though usually that was easy enough. Harder was to put together speech of his own. "You . . . good. They . . . good. We share?" This last he made clear by pointing and chewing.

She laughed, sat down in a single curling motion, gesturing him to join her. The berries were crisp, tart, refreshing. When he tried to say so, she beamed. "You work too hard," she reproved him. "Nobody else does. Take your ease."

He frowned in his effort to follow. She lay back on an elbow. That made the curve of her hip stand clear against the Forest gloom behind. "You are such a serious man," she went on. "Always you struggle. Why? The gods will do with us as they choose. Enjoy while you can."

His pulse throbbed. She was too beautiful. Otherwise he might better have disentangled what she was saying. He got simply the drift of it. "I . . . work, learn . . . go home." He swept an arm on high, repeatedly, hoping she would see that he meant sunrise. "Five, ten days? Feast. I go home."

She writhed up to crouch on her knees before him. The

dark eyes grew enormous. "You are leaving?" she wailed. "After the feast? No, you mustn't, you mustn't!"

"I . . . come back . . . springtime? . . . Bring woman, children."

Suddenly she was in his lap, surging against him, gasping, "Now, now, now!"

He understood. Fire ran through him. Within his head, an aurochs bellowed. And none would take offense. Men would chuckle and slap his back, while more young women clustered eagerly around.

He had never done a harder thing than to pull her arms off him, push her away, jump to his feet, and shout, "No!"

She rose too, shaken and bewildered. "Why?" she stammered. "I, I, I have lain awake every night wishing—why will you not? I can see you are able. Has a god cursed you?"

Thunder Horse drew a ragged breath. Explaining to her would be like snaring rain. Nonetheless he must try.

He wanted to say, "My dear, you are adorable, and I have had my own sleepless nights, and Laughing Up the Morning would most likely not mind very much. But I cannot harm you, lass, without making a rent in my honor. And this would be to harm you. Oh, you would lose no virtue in the eyes of the Folk. I have come to know that. But I might well leave you with child—and leave you I must—and you would sorrow. You might keep hoping I would return to you, but that is something I could never do, for I will be together with my beloved, and among the People we are one and one as long as both are alive.

"Maybe your feelings are shallow, maybe your spirit would soon rid itself of me. But be that as it may, if you become a mother you would have to find yourself a man, a provider and protector. Should I abandon my own child? Never! A man of the People does not do that.

"Best you go, Elidir. And when hereafter we meet, let us only smile kindly upon each other."

As it was, both their tongues fumbled and stumbled for a long time. The slowness was calming. She scowled charmingly, laid finger to brow, tried these words and that.

And finally she crowed laughter and reached again for

him. "Oh, but that is nothing!" she cried. "I mean, do not fear. It would be wonderful. What better offering could I make the Horned One than a child of Thunder Horse?"

He stepped back. Abruptly the sweat on him felt cold. "What you say? Tell me!"

"You do not know?" She composed herself, though he thought of a wildcat ready to pounce. "Why, the Horned One, the Terrible Stalker, the Forest God—every woman gives him her firstborn at the autumn feast. You will see. We take the little ones to the lake and hold them under. Afterward we leave them in the trees. Oh, it hurts, we weep, but this is what he wants. We do it for the sake of the children who come after, those of them that live. Else he would summon the trees from the earth, and they would come walking on their roots, huge and horrible, to crush us."

Again he must grope for her meaning.

When it came to him, that was like being gored, and hoofs trampling him as he fell.

As if through heat-shimmer, he saw her tremulous smile, he saw her sway toward him. "Then come, let us take what joy we may," she sang. Her fingers closed on his waist.

"No!" he screamed, wrenched loose, and ran.

He felt her look strike his back like arrows, out of the tears that burst forth. "I hate you!" pursued him. "You will never belong here! May you meet the god!"

Somehow he understood every word; and somehow he knew that he understood nothing.

Long and long he wandered about, blind to where he went. It was all the same anyhow, all green and gold, shadowy and silent. Within himself he had a beast to hunt down and slay, unless it killed him first.

They were not trolls, the Forest Folk—not generous Unyada, not loving and innocent Elidir. He must make himself know they were not trolls.

They did what they did because they believed they had no choice. It was why their increase was so slow. Most infants died in any case. Killing the firstborn was like casting one more deadly disease upon the race. Yet the mothers, the young mothers believed they must.

It was a ghastly mistake. The People would move in and show them it was not needful. For the People did not grovel before gods.

Yes. Thus be it.

But he could not remain for that feast.

Nor could he make clear to the Folk why not. They were looking forward to it as a grand send-off for the man who could be bringing them neighbors, allies. He had neither the language nor the heart to tell them what had gone wrong.

No, let him quietly assemble his gear, pack sufficient rations, and be off. By now he was able to find his way northward. When springtime spread hopefulness abroad, he would return; and at his side would be Laughing Up the Morning and her strength.

Thunder Horse sought back to the village. Air had become nearly too hot and wet to breathe. Though the rainclouds had filled half of heaven, earth still yearned for them in vain. Sometimes he heard their drums.

In his hut he made ready to go. Everything he needed was on hand, so packing went quickly.

Several women saw him emerge and depart. They hailed him questioningly. He forced a smile and a wave. It was a blessing that he could not readily talk with them and that they knew it. Doubly a blessing was Elidir's absence. Well, she might grieve for a while, but she was youthful and healthy, she would get over it. How glad he was that he had stood strong against the aurochs in himself.

If they wanted to, the hunters could track him down. He did not expect that. Not only were they busy, they would take for granted that he had his reasons for leaving early, which it was likely best not to inquire about. For in their minds it could be that a god had spoken to him.

Thunder Horse found a game trail bound the way he desired and settled into his stride. That pace was not the long lope which bore him across the Land. This path was too narrow, shut-in, and twisted. However, he moved quickly enough to be out in the open in a couple of days.

Because of the dank heat, he wore just his breechclout. Thorns ripped at his calf. Like a hook and line, the pain drew him back to awareness. He had better pay more heed. Not yet was this country where a man could rove free.

How still it was, how heavy with a sense of something about to be born. His feet whispered on soft, damp earth. On either side, bush, boles, boughs, and entangling vines walled him in. Beyond them reached intricate dimnesses that soon became nights. The roof above was a green dusk where spots of light peered like eyes. He moved as if through a cave underwater, deeper and deeper into weirdness. Each breath he drew was rank with smells of rotting and of relentless growth. The Forest brooded.

The heart knocked within his breast. If only the storm would break and cleanse. If only the least stirring would pass through these leaves and leaves and leaves.

Hark, was that thunder coming close? No, not yet. But something moved. Hoofs?

Was that a raincloud shadowing the sun? No, but something darkened the Forest further.

He halted and stared. What? Were those the branches of a tree that walked on its roots?

No, they were antlers, but enormous. They grew from a head that with its body might have been human, save that it too was gigantic. It grinned with teeth sharp in the beard, it whistled, it droned voicelessly on and on about things too horrible to understand. Hands, clawed like bear paws, wove the rhythm of dance. He, monstrously male, dancing on the legs and cloven hoofs of a deer—he was the stillness and the shadows, the stillness and the shadows. Wind awoke, noiseless dream-wind. The trees bowed low, their leaves lay flat, awaiting the Presence whose hoofs would trample them. He came, he came.

For a handful of pulse beats, Thunder Horse confronted the Horned One. Then he shrieked, whirled, ran and ran and ran, blind, deaf, witless, nothing but terror that fled. The god danced and whistled behind him, before him, around him. The Forest went on in tunnels and caves, leaves and thorns, murks and madnesses, forever.

Men had burst their hearts erenow, run down to their deaths by the Fear they could not escape because it was already within them. Thunder Horse, chaser of reindeer, had strength to stay alive. When at last he fell and oblivion swept through his skull, it was in a glade open to heaven; and the whistling and dancing did not follow. Clouds overwhelmed the sun. An honestly boisterous wind tossed boughs about and stroked at his brow. Lightning flared. Bull-roarings went from end to end of the sky. Then the rain came, *sha-ah, shoo-oo, sha-ah, shoo-oo,* like a messenger out of the Land.

Winter was mild—too mild. Snow lay so thinly strewn that moss dried and died. Wolves found little meat on such herds as had not drifted north.

But at least when the People met before the Great Cave, they could sit comfortably, loosely clad, talk and listen and make their decisions. The holy fire leaped red, yellow, blue. Where it had not blackened the cliff behind it, the paintings stood boldly forth, those creatures that were the life of their hunters. The early dusk was setting in, the first stars glimmered out of utter, blue-violet clarity. A tingling chill was in the breezes that wandered across the range.

After Hawk Talon had called upon him, Thunder Horse went to take stance beside the blaze. He folded his arms and looked over the seated ranks of the People. When his gaze reached Laughing Up the Morning, it lingered.

He drew a long breath, which seemed to carry an odor of distances, before he said: "Some of you have already heard my tale, but I will tell it again for the rest, and for the thinking of us all. You know that I fared south in hopes of finding us a new and better home. I failed. Hear how this was."

In brief words he related what had happened, and saw the horror that had now faded in him break out afresh amidst his listeners. Raising a hand to calm them, he finished: "Aye, it is truth. If we sought to the Forest, we must needs change more than our quarry and our means of taking it. We must become one with its Folk, under its god.

"My venture was not for nothing. Without it, we might

always have wondered whether we were denying something splendid to our children and children's children.

"Now I can tell you, O brothers and sisters, that we will do right to follow the reindeer north. Let us therefore go with whole spirits. We may become poor, but we will remain free."

Author's note:

That set of cultures which we name Magdalenian occupied western and central Europe from perhaps 16,000 to 9500 B.C. Especially in its later phases, it was the culmination of the Old Stone Age, prosperous, artistically creative, technologically progressive. To give a single example, spear-throwers (atlatls) occur in the lower deposits but not the upper, suggesting that the bow had been invented. We can only conjecture how people lived and thought in their daily lives, but it seems plausible that they were individualistic, exploratory, and more rationalistic than superstitious.

What destroyed their societies appears to have been the retreat of the glaciers at the close of the Pleistocene. This took place more rapidly than geologists formerly supposed. As woodland encroached on steppe, Magdalenians must either try to adapt or try to accompany the reindeer—the core of their livelihood, as the bison afterward was to the Plains Indians—northward.

Their successors in their former territories are known as the Azilians. My late friend, the French prehistorian François Bordes, recorded his impression of these as a daunted folk, barely coping with their changed environs. The front of human advancement shifted to the Near East. It would not return to Europe for many centuries.

Those Magdalenians who went north could not maintain their culture for long. Lapps have preserved a mere trace of it, and they are scarcely direct descendants. Tribes moving straight into land which the glaciers had bared perforce developed quite different ways of life. Our discoveries of such innovations as skis and dugout boats, dateable very early, show that the old brave spirit survived.

THE SHADOW HART

Sandra Miesel

AFTER THE HART, THE BIER . . .

She rubbed the crusted pot harder as if to scour that hateful saying from her mind. Hateful saying, fateful saying. Scrub harder. Amaze the cook with the strength still left in these aged arms. Finish before the hearth fire fails.

Back and forth on the whitewashed kitchen wall, her shadow plunged like a wounded beast. But, by the luck of the hunt, no venison graced the good *herremand*'s table this Yuletide, no hated flesh to tear nor bones to shatter. *O God, give me a hart to break as a hart has broken*—Revenge denied, denied, as when she raged to grow black wings and feed on that cursed brute's heart. If only she had the right Words!

Had she all the right Words her kindred knew, her man would not have died while hunting, most surely would not have died unshriven in the wildwood, borne home like bloody meat. Wearily, she tapped out the last of the cleansing sand and wiped the vessel with a greasy rag. Some in this blond country still misliked her dark looks and the Finnish lilt in her speech. Yet if she were in truth the witch they signed against behind her back, she would have cast a better lot for herself. What sorceress culled table leavings for her master's dogs?

But at least she was earning her bread. Better to drag out her days as a wretched serving maid than a beggar. The folk here were decent, the holder of this garth no harsher than needful. She was glad of this shelter this six months past. For scarcely was her lover under the earth when that *beengjerd* wife of his had turned her out to starve. It was a grim blessing that she left no living child to suffer the widow's wrath.

She threw on her cloak and hoisted the bucket of scraps. Since the feasting had gone on so late, the farmyard curs would be hungrier than usual. No sooner was she out the door than the barking began. They smelled the food—and her fear.

Although she had a way with most animals, tame or wild, dogs terrified her. The mere sight of flashing fangs was enough to set old scars aching, for it stirred memories of a half-naked child dodging among the fir trees with a baying pack in hot pursuit. She had been carried off to Estland as a slave and when she tried to escape, her master had set his hounds on her. But for some barely remembered Words from home, the brutes would have torn her apart.

At least the dogs here were stoutly chained tonight. She could see them now beside the byre, leaping blots on the frost-rimed earth. Best to quiet them before someone remarked their frenzy. Ere she spoke, a chill breeze stirred. The dogs cowered in sudden silence, cringing back against the log wall. Brushed by the same terror, she tossed them their scraps with trembling hands. Then as she turned to face the bitter wind, three long notes on a distant horn pierced her to the heart.

She ran. Heedless of her footing, she sped across the rutted yard, skidded on a pool of frozen slops, and slammed into a gatepost near the kitchen door. After catching her breath, she carefully closed the wicket behind her and left the bucket in its proper place. Rubbing her bruises, she limped off to the women's bower in the house yard. She hoped the few roisterers still out and couples seeking private nooks would be too intent on their own pleasures to pay any heed.

But once abed, she could not sleep, either that night or the next. Why should something so faint as that ghostly horn keep her wakeful when the snorings and rustlings of her fellow servants caused scant unease?

She remembered other beds and the sole mate who had shared them with her. Whether in snug wall boxes fragrant with herbs or a saddle blanket spread within some sheltering thicket, she had slept at her darling's side in every district ruled by Denmark's Crown. As sheriff, castellan, counselor, he was ever King Valdemar's loyal man. Did he follow his liege still in the Land of Darkness where the river of poison wends its way and—*Christ have mercy!* Such heathen nightmare should have died decades ago in the ashes of Estland when the Dane lords came to harry that earthly hell. Herself was all she had to give the knight who delivered her from slave yoke and rebel peasant's knife.

She burrowed deeper under covers that could not keep the cold at bay. Her jab at a hungry flea nearly woke the woman next to her. After a moment's pause, she cracked the creature and flicked it away. She used to seek far braver game. In times gone by, she rode to the hounds with her love and joined her strength to his to take the panting hart. Then he would call her his hunt queen and give her the gristly deer-cross cut from the slain beast's heart. Every day seemed summer and dusk stretched eager arms toward dawn, until he was forced to marry a woman hard as Fimbulwinter. *In summer course the hart, but in winter the hind.*

And yet the bond sealed in youth endured though youth itself did not. Years after lust had flickered out they still clung together for warmth. She sobbed for a gray head's weight upon her shriveled breasts. That night and the next, gory antlers haunted her dreams.

Then on the last day of the year, fresh snow fell. Shrouded stillness without made feasting all the merrier within. The heaping platters of pickled fish, pork, and white flour pastries were even heavier than those at Christmas. Her shoulders ached from pouring so many pitchers of beer to wet throats dried out by songs and laughter.

When her stint was done, there was no place left for her at the long plank table flanking the central hearth. Instead, she sat on the opposite wall bench, well away from the other servants, and ate from a wooden plate on her lap. She gazed along a row of ruddy, glistening faces all the way to the

carven high seat where the *herremand* and his lady presided,
little soberer than their household. But if any of these jolly
folk should chance to stare at her, would they see aught save
a smudge of shadow?

She left them to their noisy joy and their New Year's hope.

Afterward, well-muffled and booted against the cold, she
walked up to the main road. The rutted track from the garth
was already trodden but the empty fields alongside it shone
wonderfully white beneath the moonlit sky. From the posi-
tions of the stars, she reckoned the time to be midnight.
Powers were abroad this festive night of time's rebirth, this
miracle season when the sun began her slow return. She
might see alder trees strolling like men or wolves trooping off
to watch the woods' fairy brand their prey for the coming
year. Or else she might meet the Elf-King out seeking his
annual tribute of horseshoes. No, the king she meant to see
was neither of earth nor of heaven. She brushed the snow
from a roadside stump and sat down to wait.

She had scarcely begun her watch when a fierce southwest-
ern wind sprang up. The force of it shook trees free of
clinging snow and rattled bare boughs like bones. As she
pulled her cloak tighter about her, the wind brought the horn
call she expected to hear. She crossed herself, squared her
shoulders, and stepped up to the roadway to challenge the
huntsmen in passage.

At first all she spied in the distance was a roiling blur.
With more than thirty leagues to cover before cockcrow—all
the way to the edge of Sjaelland and back—they had to
course at a furious pace. Then she beheld what few are born
with eyes to see—the Wild Hunt in full career. Men and
mounts alike were pale as mist and followed storm-black
hounds whose eyes were wheels of flame.

She would have fled that horrid belling pack but her
surging panic ebbed once the chief huntsman came into view.
She dared to hail this shade as the liege he used to be. One
wave of his regal hand slowed headlong gallop to dreamy
glide. Clearer sight proved legend true. With a broad hat
clapped on his fur-trimmed hood, King Valdemar Atterdag
looked just as he did when last seen alive. And with the same

crisp courtesy of old, he acknowledged her salute. Among the grim company he led past, she recognized Stig Anderssen, Peder Iron-Beard, and other royal intimates of yesteryear. But if the accursed men in their turn knew her, they gave no sign.

Had the one she sought escaped his comrades' doom? Desire warred with dread as she scanned each somber face. But fate is the hunter no quarry can elude. Last in line—*O merciful God*—rode her lost love.

Her lips froze shut. Still, he heard the name her heart alone could speak. He harkened to her and turned his steed aside. Almost smiling, he bent down as if to bear her away on his saddlebow just as he had a lifetime ago. But his welcoming arm passed straight through her body like a blade of ice.

She fainted under a blizzard of plunging hooves. By the time she came to her senses, the Hunt had gone, leaving not so much as a hoofprint behind.

She rubbed the blood back into her numbed flesh and smeared away tears with her fists. *O God, how can you be so cruel and command us to be kind?* Whyfor did her man deserve this end: for too much faithfulness to a king or too little to a wife? No just lord forced his folk to share in punishment that was solely his nor just judge impose so harsh a sentence for so common a fault. *Stand accused!* Righteous anger flared. She would get justice of both king and God. Whatever the cost, she would wrest her lover free. Wrath warmed her all the way to bed and heavy, dreamless sleep.

The morrow was a Holy Day, to celebrate Christ's first shedding of blood. She and the rest of the household heard Mass in the nearest village. But while neighbors lingered in the churchyard to wish each other New Year's luck, she slipped away unnoticed. Determined to plead her case in the right court, she set out on foot for Sorø Abbey, site of King Valdemar's tomb.

Snow on the road lengthened the short journey. Despite bright sunshine, the cold bit deep through layers of garb. She again had cause to be glad that, when her lover's widow turned her out last summer with only the clothes on her back, she had had the wit to dress beforehand in every warm garment she possessed. Where the woods were thick, she went warily, though the blessed bells of Sorø should suffice to keep the trolls roundabout pent up in their hollow hills.

Before sunset she found refuge in the Abbey's guesthouse. Although she had to share supper with a greedy clutch of paupers and vagabonds, she did not begudge them the chance to eat their fill.

Afterward, she begged leave to enter the monastic church for Compline, the final office of the day. Only a few others availed themselves of this opportunity to stand in the frigid nave while a choir of white-robed monks chanted behind the roodscreen.

As she prayed, she could see her frosty breath—the community did not stint on candles. Banks of huge tapers banished darkness back to the plain brick walls. Above these flickering lights, the wooden Image on the Cross seemed to bleed and writhe. She thought of stags at bay and looked aside. Her gaze kept wandering to the wall niche where the dead king lay. His effigy gleamed icy white atop his huge black tomb.

The service ended. The monks filed out. She lingered alone in the darkened church. Only now did she venture to inspect the object of her quest. The fully armored figure seemed to float on its polished marble slab while watchful rows of pale apostles and prelates stared out of nothingness below. At the west end, figures of the king and his queen knelt with prayerbooks in their hands to receive Christ's benediction. By rights, the other end ought to show Valdemar and a different lady quite otherwise engaged. She laughed bitterly and dared to stroke the stone lion supporting the king's feet. Unearthly chill burnt through her mittened fingers straight to the bone.

She drew back with a cry. Was she a fool to have come? Although others had witnessed the king at chase and gone unscathed, how many dared to trouble him at his rest? She tried to pray but could not. Instead she paced uneasily to and fro, shivering worse with each step. This building held cold as an oven did heat. It might be as long as two hours until midnight. The red sanctuary lamp glowed overhead like the watchful eye of God. If only it hung lower, she would be tempted to warm her stiff fingers over its flame. In happier times she used to carry a hollow metal ball with a hot coal inside for winter comfort. But there were crueller deaths than freezing: Valdemar's queen had roasted his leman alive in the bathhouse.

She pounded her hands together and stamped her feet as she walked her sentry round. The moonlit shadow of the rood crept across her path. She flinched when this shadow touched her own—shades of St. Eustace's cross-bearing hart, the quarry that suffered itself to be hunted to save its hunter's soul.

As twelve o'clock struck, she turned to find the king suddenly there.

"Hear me, Dane-King," she called, and fell to her knees.

"I listen better when petitioners do not fawn—as you whom I knew in life should recall." Valdemar gave a wry smile. "My rank is but an illusion now in all events."

Awkwardly, she faced the ghost of majesty.

"Make haste, woman. The Hunt gathers."

"Why must *he* ride with you, sir—the good lord I loved?"

"One Lord alone is truly good. And was I so very wicked in my day?" Ice crystals sparkled in his thick moustache. "I was a lawgiver, a conquerer, a builder. As pilgrim to Jerusalem, I kept a whole night's vigil at St. Sepulchre's. But I cursed God when my Tovelil was murdered: *'Keep your heaven,'* I cried, *'and leave me the earth that holds her grave.'* I spoke my own doom, and I must serve it."

"And did you condemn your courtiers as well?"

"When sin was shared, so also should expiation be."

"Then share it with your lady and let my love go!"

"Which of the two would I sooner have beside me?" His eyes narrowed, glinting. "That choice lies in other hands. Meanwhile every evening brings another night." He sighed. "Till Doomsday dawns, our company cannot grow less. Our hunting changes not by the season or the century—a chase with never a beast in view."

"No remedy at all?" she screamed. "Where then is justice, on earth or in high heaven?"

"There—or nowhere." He pointed to the rood and took his leave. "Would you have me late to my appointed torment?" His spurred boots made not a sound as he strode away.

She stumbled back to the guesthouse and slept, grateful for the warmth of other human bodies around her. In her dreams, she fled naked through a wintry forest pursued by unseen foes until at the heart of the wood, she reached a fountain of blood that burned. Here was everlasting refuge and healing for all wounds.

She awoke knowing the price to be paid for his freedom: if fate was a hunter, so was love. And what hunts may itself be hunted.

Leaving Sorø Abbey as soon as it was light, she returned to the *herregaard*. Ere her master could scold her for her absence overnight, she gave notice. He railed at her ingratitude and offered blows, but she had heard and felt worse, delivered in hotter rage. Her decision stood. She took the waybread he grudgingly gave and set off the next morning on her eastward journey.

Her strides left deep footprints in snow the Wild Hunt's headlong gallop could not mark. Had King Valdemar built this road he now was doomed to ride? Memory failed. No matter. She had the scent; she knew the trail. There would be no denying the prize she sought.

Three days' trek in deepening cold and rising fever brought her through wildwood and hamlets arranged like shield-rings to shut that selfsame wildwood out. She passed Ringsted Abbey where other Dane-Kings slept in hallowed peace and circled proud Roskilde town with the twin green spires of its cathedral reigning on the heights.

The highroad vanished. But she found a once-familiar track despite encroaching brambles. She could smell the sea and a nearby lake. By Epiphany Eve she reached her goal, the empty royal manor at Gurre. Tove's toy castle stood barred and shuttered. Moss stained its red brick walls. Dark feathers on the snow and piercing cries proclaimed that hawks now roosted in the bower of Tovelil, Valdemar's dove.

She would not have forced entry into the place even if her dwindling strength had permitted. Instead she cut some pine boughs with her belt knife to make herself a rude bed at the foot of a huge birch tree nearby. It had been a gathering point for royal hunts in gladder days when she had ridden with her love behind Tove and the king—black harlot shadowing white. Here she meant to rest until the sky turned round to midnight.

Huddled in her makeshift nest, she pressed her burning cheek against the smooth birchbark and wept for the body she used to clasp. Her tears ebbed, the sobbing passed, and she slept.

Her dream was bitter as her vigil. She saw the summer sky rain swords that stabbed great bleeding wounds into the blooming earth. From that seeding grew a whole steel forest where every leaf and branch was a blade. She fled their clashing, whirring edges over caltrop grass through stands of jabbing spears. The wind's teeth ripped her half-flayed hide, and the chilling torrent that should have hidden her scent washed flesh away from bone.

She awoke sweating and trembling despite the frosty air. Her glazed eyes could not judge the hour from the few stars still visible between scudding clouds. A gale blowing up from the southwest moaned like the baying of hounds. If the pack were already uncoupled, then it must be past midnight.

She was too weary to be brave. Every long year of her age lay heavy upon her. Only her love's sore need held her to the course. She fairly panted for a last sip of water but her flask was empty. And yet the fate she chose promised honor as well as pain. If Christ Himself did not shrink from playing the wounded hart, why should she? *O Lord, once quarry for man's sake, be with me now.*

No drum had she, nor staff, nor fabulous regalia. Let keen desire serve in their stead. Fixing her eyes on the Nail Star overhead, she braced her back against the birch, stretched wide her arms, and summoned the powers that coursed in her blood. She sang. The lost Words came flooding back. In seven steps her spirit climbed the Tree that upholds the heavens like a mighty pillar. She touched the very point on which the sky-roof hangs. . . .

Darkness flowed down the white bark. One heartbreaking

moment later, it shied away from a new-made corpse and sprang into the forest. It wore antlers, hooves, and hide, and woman's form nevermore.

All have faded into shadow—woods and manor, Hunt and prey. They are phantoms faint as drawings on vellum that never felt the colorist's brush. Like an old book read again page by timeworn page, their course runs nightly from Sorø to Gurre, from Unharbouring to Bay. The hart cannot count how many hunters give chase or recall why the number should matter. Its doom is to offer sport until the final stroke that sounds its death.

Alas, how long that horn call echoes . . .

THE WOMAN WHO LOVED REINDEER

Meredith Ann Pierce

1: Branja

CARIBOU WAS NOT YET THIRTEEN SUMMERS WHEN BRANJA brought to her the child. Caribou stood in the doorway of her *ntūla*, or summer hut, gazing out over the mixed forest and tundra just beginning to lose their color and come into fruit as brief summer hurried to its end.

Caribou had known her sister-in-law would come. The night before, she had dreamed a snow bunting alighted on her windowsill with a sprig of bloodthorn in its bill. It had left the berries and flown away, crying its own name: *"Brānja! Brānja!"*

This was always the way of it. Snowbirds were the messengers of the ancestors, and Caribou was a dreamer of dreams.

The figure of her brother's wife emerged from the woods many paces from Caribou and struggled toward her up the barren rise. Branja's progress was slow. She looked weighted with weariness, and was bundled in *lanlāni,* travel furs.

It was two days' journey in summer from Branja's house to Caribou's, and although she was unwed, not yet in womanhood, Caribou lived alone in her father's house—because she could read things in flurries of falling snow, hear words in wind, and sometimes dreamed. The villagers were afraid of her.

No one had offered to take her in when her father had died, last summer's end. Not even Visjna, her brother, for he had been newly married then to a woman outside the Tribe, and his wife had not wanted to share their house with someone little more than a stranger.

Caribou watched Branja struggling up the gentle slope. She was bearing two burdens, Caribou saw now, one a bundle cradled in her arm, the other a deep sack dragging along the ground. Caribou did not go to her. Her dream had not told her what the other would want.

As Branja staggered up to where Caribou stood and dropped her heavy sack upon the ground, Caribou realized that the bundle Branja cradled was a child, just lately come into the world. One bone and leather fastener at the throat of Branja's *lānlan* had come undone, and Caribou glimpsed her sister-in-law's smock stained in two places from the milk in her breasts.

"Caribou," her brother's wife said, panting, not even greeting her, "you take this child."

She held the bundle out. Caribou looked at the tiny thing, golden-haired, fair-skinned and flush-cheeked with cold, but sleeping peacefully. Caribou's hands did not move from her side.

"What child is this?"

"My child," Branja said, dark-haired like Caribou, but with the tan-shaded skin of the river people. "It is mine."

Her sister-in-law did not take it back, held the bundle out still.

"But why do you and Visjna give it to me?" said Caribou.

"No." Branja shook her head, still breathless. "He does not give it. I give it."

Caribou was silent for a while. "It is not his child."

Branja's face crumpled. She blinked, struggling, her voice tight. "It," she said, "it is not his concern what I do with this child."

Caribou studied the infant's fair, well-fashioned features, so unlike her brother's lean, olive ones. "How old is the child?"

"Midsummer," her brother's wife told her. "He was born two months ago."

"While Visjna was away with the caribou at the calving grounds," said Caribou.

Branja chewed her lip, picked the edge of the fur wrapping the child. It sighed in sleep and did not wake.

"I have kept the child as long as I could." Her voice was low, a nervous whisper, "that he might be strong when I brought him to you."

She glanced about quickly, as if fearing somehow to be overheard. Her voice hushed even lower.

"But Visjna will be returning with the herd now, soon. I cannot hide him any longer from the village—I cannot keep this child anymore."

"Did Visjna know you were with child when he went north this spring?" said Caribou.

Branja looked down, shook her head. "No. I do not know. I did not tell him." She looked at Caribou again suddenly, eyes bright, almost pleading. "If he knew, I will tell him I lost the child."

Caribou stood looking at her. She could not bring herself to feel anything for Branja, or the child. She was thinking of her brother Visjna, defying their father and shocking the village to marry this foreigner, this woman from outside the Tribe.

"Why not tell him the child is his?" said Caribou. "How could he know?"

"He would know."

"He would forgive you."

Branja dropped her voice again and shook her head, her whisper growing frantic. "I am afraid."

Caribou drew back from her, blinked once. Those words surprised her. "My brother will not harm you."

Her sister-in-law's eyes implored her. "Not of Visjna," she said. She glanced at the golden infant in her arms. "Of the child's father."

"Who is the father?"

The other hesitated. "A stranger," she said at last. "He . . . came through, passing southward, last fall."

"Southward?" cried Caribou. "Toward the pole—in fall?"
She frowned. Truly, that was strange. Only the wild herds,
the reindeer, ran southward over the Burning Plain toward the
pole in winter. No one knew why they went there or how
they survived the cold. But always they returned in spring,
surging northward toward the warmer lands, to calve.

"Was this . . . *stranger* a lone one," asked Caribou, "a
tracker, following the wild herds?"

Branja shook her head. "No, I . . . He did not say."

She drew breath, gazed at the child, her face contorted
with indecision or grief. Caribou waited. Branja seemed
about to speak again, but then halted, swallowed, shook her
head, and would not look at Caribou.

"Why are you afraid of him?" said Caribou.

"I fear for the child," the other murmured.

"What is the child to him?"

Branja's eyes flashed up. "He said that he would take the
child!"

Caribou felt her lips tighten. "Why give him to me,
then?" she said. "Let the father have him if you do not want
him."

Her sister-in-law's green eyes welled up with tears. Her
full breasts heaved against the clasps of the too-tight *lānlan*.
"You do not . . . you do not understand. This, this stranger—
he is not as we are, Cari."

"*You* are not as we are, Branja," said Caribou.

The woman across from her caught in her breath, as
though she had unwittingly trod on something sharp. The
child in her arms kicked beneath the furs, slept on.

"And how did this stranger know that you would bear a
child?" Caribou added in a moment.

Branja shook her head, her eyes cast down. "I do not
know. He said so afterward—just before he left me."

"Perhaps he will not come back."

"No," cried Branja. Her eyes met Caribou's again. "I
saw him. I saw him in the spring."

When the reindeer herds came back from the pole, thought
Caribou. Surely her sister-in-law's lover must be a hunter,
following the herds.

"Did you speak?" she asked her brother's wife.

The tears in Branja's eyes spilled over now. "No. He stood at a distance. But I saw his eyes." Her glance darted to the child, then back to Caribou. "He knew. And I knew he meant to return and take the child."

Caribou gazed at her sister-in-law. Branja held the bundle out to her again.

"Here, Cari, you take the child—for your brother's sake, not mine."

Caribou felt her heart close up tight then, like a little fist. "What would I do with a child?"

"Raise it," cried Branja. "Care for it."

"For my brother's sake." Branja fell silent. Caribou let anger come into her voice for the first time now. "And how if your lover comes to me, demanding the child?"

Branja shook her head. "He will not come. He will not know I came here. I was careful. I told no one where I was going—I left no trail."

Caribou considered the other's heavy burdens, her staggering steps, her birth among the barge people of the river, not among the woodcrafters and trackers of the wilds—and wondered. Caribou crossed her arms, her patience flayed.

"Why should I ruin myself for you?" she demanded at last. "How do I say to anyone who asks where the infant came from?"

Tears spilled again, streaking Branja's cheeks. "Because you have nothing to lose. You live alone, far from any village."

Yes, alone, thought Caribou. So very alone since her father had died.

"No one cares if you have a child without a man," Branja wept. "Say the child is yours or that you found it. Say that someone gave it to you—only do not say it came from me."

Caribou said nothing then. There was nothing more to say. She uncrossed her arms, gazing off, wondering what thing she might do to make Branja go away. And at that moment's dropping of her guard, her sister-in-law sprang forward and pressed the bundle to her. Caribou closed her arms about the fur-wrapped load reflexively to keep it from falling, and Branja hastily fell back.

Within its furs, the infant sighed and turned toward Caribou, freed one tiny fist from the folds and closed its fingers about one of the long, dark braids falling over her breast. The child slept still.

"Here, Cari, you take this, too," Branja was saying, taking hold of the sack she had set down upon first arriving. She twitched open the neck. "You see, I have brought you *pīsjlak*—how do you say it?—provisions: caribou meat and snow hares, cheese, berries, sweet syrup, and *jaāro* stalk. . . ." She rummaged in the sack, half drawing out packets of this and that.

"I have ample *pīsjlak* of my own," snapped Caribou, struggling to support the heavy child and free her braid. "More than I need. What I do not need is this child."

Branja jerked upright, dropping the sack. She backed away. "But these things will help you, help you with the child."

"How could these things help me feed a child?" demanded Caribou. The infant's grasp upon her braid was like a hawk's. Still he slept. "A child needs milk. I have no goats or caribou. . . ."

Branja backed further away. "Oh, he will be no trouble. He is the perfect child. He sleeps and sleeps and never cries. He will be no burden."

Branja was now paces from the house, still backing away and wringing her hands nervously. Caribou would have followed, but the weight of the child was so awkward in her arms she could only stand clutching it and feared to move lest it slip from her. She had never held a child before.

"And these provisions," her brother's wife was saying. "They are a gift, a little peace offering from me to you." A timid smile flitted now across her lips. "We are sisters-in-law, Cari. We should do such things for one another."

Caribou made to protest but found, all at once, her throat was stopped. She had gotten better hold of the child now. His weight was still and comfortable in her arms, his warm, light breath pleasant against her breast, the tug of his tiny fist against her braid almost . . . agreeable.

"What name does he have?" she managed at last.

Her brother's wife stood watching her.

"No name."

For a moment, it seemed that Branja would speak more, but suddenly she let her breath out as though she had been holding it. It was an outbreath of relief. Caribou lifted the child more upright in her arms and laid its little body against her breast.

Branja whirled then, like a milch goat suddenly untethered, and hurried away, almost running. Caribou stood watching until she disappeared into the woods at the foot of the slope. Then she heard the infant sigh, just as Branja had done, and looking down, she saw the gold-haired infant gazing at her. The child had golden eyes.

He breathed again and closed his eyes, sighing in sleep. Absently, almost without realizing it, Caribou smiled. It had been a long time since she had smiled. His tiny hand released her braid, and Caribou tucked his arm back beneath the fur.

Then she knelt and laid him gently beside the doorsill. Rising, she caught hold of the *pīsjlak* sack and heaved it over the threshold, dragged it in to lean against the wall. Then she returned to the infant and, lifting him, carried him carefully into the house.

2: The Child

So Caribou took the golden-eyed child that had no name into her hut. That evening until dusk, she left him beside the fire and ranged through the woods, covering Branja's tracks and searching the brown, crisp undergrowth for bitter green-leafed *mmōli*, that brings the milk to any woman's breast, even a grandmother aged half a hundred summers or a young maid that has never known a man.

The milk came into Caribou's breasts in three days' time. Until then, she kept the child alive on caribou butter, hare's blood, and a paste of powdered marrow root, which the child laughed and smiled to suck.

Caribou tried to think of a name for him. At first she tried Goldeneye, but he would not answer to it. Yet he laughed and cooed when she called him child, so Child it was with the golden eyes that slept and slept like some tiny sage, dreaming wise little dreams.

He never cried, and when he woke, he smiled and took her long brown braids in his fists. Caribou fashioned for him three *bēla,* sacklike gowns of rabbit fur that could be layered one inside another for warmth, then set him to sleep in a box beside the fire.

He was so quiet in truth that most days she almost forgot he was there, until her breasts grew full and she went to suckle him: first light and midmorning, noon, midafternoon and dusk; then again in the night and just before bed. He never cried in the night for warmth or nourishment, he sleeping in his box beside the fire and Caribou away from him beneath her caribou skins.

Fleeting summer passed away. The autumnal equinox loomed and went, and days grew briefer than the nights. Caribou dreamed of the return of the herders with their caribou from the summer calving grounds. Then laying in the last of her winter stores, she dreamed of the wild deer returning as well, streaming south from the warm northern places where they summered. Soon they would pass poleward in a great thundering train, beyond the Burning Plain, which only they knew how to cross.

It was the morning after her dream of the reindeer that Caribou went to the hot spring in the high country. It was early autumn, and the hard frost already on the ground. Soon, she knew, the heavy snows would begin to fall, shutting the passes and snowing everyone under.

After that, it would be spring again before she might visit the pool, and Caribou wanted to bathe there once more before the snowfall. And because it would be a day's journey there and back, she took the child with her.

The water of the spring was warm and steamy, melting the

crust of frost on the ground nearby. Caribou laid the child upon the banks and stripped her boots and leggings, her shirt and smock of skins and swam naked in the hot mineral water.

Leaning over the half-thawed bank of the pool, she freed the child from his *bēla* and brought him, too, into the water, towing him after her by his little white arms, now flushed pink as a wolf's tongue from warmth. He kicked and splashed in the steaming pool under the pale far sun in the ice-chill air, grinning and gurgling. Then she dried him off with a soft, scraped rabbit skin and laid him among his wrappings again.

At noon, Caribou emerged from the pool, dried herself and dressed. She nursed the child and ate the small packet of pemmican she had brought. Then setting the child on her hip, she wrapped her traveling cloak about them both and started down from the high country.

She had not been traveling more than an hour when she knew by the slope of the ground that she was nearing the narrow glacier trough which rambled north-south between two rills of high country: the Reindeer's Path. She would have to descend and cross, then climb again through sloping woodlands to reach home.

But drawing near the slender valley's lip, she heard a great rushing sound that grew louder the nearer to the rift she came. She began to hurry now, for the sky had clouded over and she feared suddenly some storm.

But emerging from the trees on the slope above the valley, she saw what made the sound—not wind. Below her thundered the reindeer, the vast wild herds sweeping like a river of living silver—all heads and antlers and backs, the tendons in their limbs snapping like whips.

They paced along, faster than human legs could run, southward toward the pole. The ground on which Caribou stood trembled. Gazing south, she glimpsed their thundering train stretching toward the horizon as far as she could see.

They had been passing for hours, she knew, must have come just after she had crossed the valley that morning. She walked along the slope above the herd until she found a narrow place where the hillside was not too steep and sat down. While she waited, Caribou took the child out from beneath her cloak. And the infant cried out with delight, his golden eyes wide and bright, his little mouth agape, laughing. He stretched his tiny hands out to the running deer as they thundered by.

After a little, the rush began to dwindle. When the last of the wild deer, even the stragglers, had passed, Caribou arose and, keeping the child still outside her cloak, began descending toward the valley floor.

She was halfway across the barren, uneven terrain of the narrow trough when she saw two figures on the far slope. One was very tall and long of limb, dark-haired and olive-skinned, a man. The other, a woman in a bright embroidered skirt of the river valley people, had the black hair and tanner complexion of that tribe.

The man waved with his free arm—in his other hand he held a bow, the quiver slung from his hip—and Caribou recognized him as her brother, Visjna. The woman beside him must be Branja, his wife. Caribou halted suddenly, feeling the weight of the child in her arms.

But just as she did so, before she could think what to do or say, she heard a sound: a long, bawling cry like someone in great grief. It came from the north, the direction from which the reindeer had come. Caribou turned with a start, but could see nothing beyond a high rill in the valley floor.

Before her on the slope, she saw Visjna and his wife also turn, heard her brother give a shout of alarm. Her sister-in-law, with a little scream, covered her mouth. The loud lowing sounded again, nearer this time.

Caribou felt the child on her hip waken with a start, his little body against hers suddenly rigid. She looked down, surprised, and the child all at once gave out a high, keening wail like no sound she had ever heard. It echoed the lower, louder cry that had wakened him.

The child began to struggle. His tiny fists thrashed free of the swaddling; his infant legs kicked and churned inside the rabbit's fur bundling. Caribou gripped him tighter, lifted him from her hip.

And all this time, the child's small round face was screwed into a curiously adult expression: not infant's squalling but some deep-felt sorrow, his loud, piercing wail slitting the air.

Caribou shushed at him, tried the soft chattering of lips and tongue her father had used to use to quiet caribou calves—to no avail. The child wailed and struggled on even as Caribou bounced him gently, crooning to him, until his thrashing grew so vigorous she had to clutch to keep from dropping him.

Without warning, his keening halted, so abruptly Caribou knew nothing she had done could have stilled it. The child simply fell silent, half turned in her hands, his eyes cast over one infant shoulder toward the crest of the rise, in the middle of the gorge where they stood. Just then, Caribou heard Branja's second scream.

Suddenly she saw what it was that had caught the child's eye. On the crest of the rise, bright-lit, in sharp relief against the stark hills behind, stood a great reindeer stag of tawny gold.

Larger he was by half a head than even the largest stag she had ever seen. His rack of horns rose from his brow like a nest of golden hands and arms, webbed fingers widespread to the grey-bright sky.

He pawed the earth, stamped once with his great splay hoof, and the tendons clacked. The plumes of breath that shot from his nostrils made little clouds. His great, expressionless eyes as he studied the child in Caribou's arms were deep, pure gold.

The child reached out to him with a delighted cry, so much like one of recognition Caribou was baffled. The great deer circled, pawing the earth again. His breath spurted and steamed.

The child laughed, and the reindeer started forward, then halted suddenly, stiff-legged. His eyes settled on Caribou now, gone dark and dangerous. Caribou clutched the bundled infant tighter and fell back. The golden stag lifted his head and belled: long, deep, a challenge.

Caribou backed away from him toward the sloping hillside of the trough. From the corner of her eye, she saw her brother and his wife start down the slope toward her, Visjna running. The reindeer stared at Caribou, his head high, half turned.

The child began to struggle in her arms again, more violently than before. Caribou was hard-pressed to keep her hold on him. Crying, he twisted toward the deer, opened his tiny hands and reached out to him. The stag let go an answering

cry, strangely mournful, and launched his great golden form
toward them down the rise.

Caribou stumbled into a run. Her breath had frozen in her
throat. Before her she saw her brother coming to a halt as he
neared the bottom of the slope. His wife dashed past him.
She shouted something, interposing herself between Caribou
and the charging deer, but the golden stag only dodged, lowered his horns and feinted toward Branja. The valley woman
threw up her arms, falling back as the great deer sprang by.

Caribou lost her balance, felt her foot skid on a stone. The
child slipped in her hands, and Caribou clutched at him. She
heard the dull smarting of reindeer hooves upon the frozen
turf. Wailing, the child writhed in his padded *bēla*. Caribou
felt her foot skid again on the slick, icebound ground and lost
her grip. The bundled child slipped free.

She lunged to catch him. But before the child could touch
the earth, before her hands could reach the child, a wall of
gold passed before her, almost touching. The reindeer dropped
his head in passing, catching the child safe within his nested
horns.

Caribou heard a whistling, felt an arrow pass over her left
shoulder, and saw it just miss the back ridge of the gold
stag's lowered neck. Whirling, Caribou just glimpsed her
brother reaching for another arrow from the quiver at his hip.

She spun again, back to the reindeer and the child. The
kneeling stag sprang up, snapping the antler-cradle high, out
of her reach. Caribou cried out, her arms outstretched after
the child, but the wild deer was already vaulting away over
the frozen ground.

She heard screaming, thought at first, dazedly, that it
might be her own—until she realized that it came from
behind her: Branja's. Caribou stood unmoving, her lips parted
and the wind blowing into her mouth. Wind blew through the
fingers of her widespread hands.

Visjna was running full tilt after the stag, the child held
safe overhead in his horns. Her brother still clutched his
longbow in his hand, in the other a long, slim arrow, double-
barbed. His narrow quiver banged against his thigh.

Caribou felt her wrist grabbed suddenly, and jerked around

to find herself facing Branja. The valley woman clung to her, her wide green eyes beseeching, her words a breathless shriek.

"He came back, Cari," she panted. "Two nights ago, just as he said he would. Visjna was there. I had told him, told him all of it, just the day before. . . ."

Caribou stared at her sister-in-law.

Her words seemed to be falling from her mouth of their own accord. "He came back." Branja gasped.

"Turn loose," hissed Caribou. "What are you talking of?"

"The father—the father of the child!" the other cried. "But he did not care, my husband, about the child. Cari, it was just as you said. Visjna told him to go away, stood in the door with his longbow. He told him the child was not with us, was far away where he would never find him. . . ."

Sobs choked her. Caribou stared after her brother, the stag, and the child and tried to drag her sleeve from Branja's grasp.

"We spoke; we discussed it," her sister-in-law sobbed. "Visjna said we must bring the child and you to live with us—we were coming to find you—but the stag, the stag . . ."

Caribou tugged her sleeve harder. "Let me go, Branja," she said frantically. "What do you mean? You say your lover returned—what does that matter now?"

But Branja was already speaking. The words ran and tumbled. "Help me, oh, help me, Cari." Branja moaned, then cried aloud, "The stag! The golden stag . . . carrying off my child."

Caribou stared after the shrinking figures, now dwindled finger-small. She had no idea what Branja was trying to say. She cried out, "Let go!" and managed to break free, stumbled into a run.

Branja did not follow: Caribou heard her behind, crying and moaning. A long way ahead, she saw the great stag spring up the side slope of the trough, bolt away into the trees.

Her brother halted for an instant, fitted the arrow he held to the cord of his bow, and shot. He sped on then, upslope behind the shaft, not even waiting to see whether it found its mark.

The arrow fell short, struck slope behind the reindeer's

heels. Caribou was nearly to the slope herself by now. Before her, the stag vanished into the trees, and a moment later, her brother as well.

Caribou struggled up the steep slope, bent, clawing at the frost-caked stubgrass for a better purchase. She reached the wood's edge, and the last that she heard of those she pursued, above the soughing of wind and Branja's bitten-off cries, was the crashing of the golden reindeer and her brother through the brush and occasional cries from the child—no longer wails and screaming now, but laughing gurgles of delight.

3: The Golden Stag

Caribou plunged into the dark woods after her brother, the golden reindeer, and the child. She followed their trail of broken frost, stumbling among the barren trees. But presently the grees grew so thick no frost had formed, and the ground itself was too hard to show any track.

The close-spaced trees threw vague shadows, and the day grew greyer as the clouds thickened overhead. Caribou had long since lost all sound of those she pursued. She had no idea where she was, how late the afternoon had grown.

The black, wind-gnarled trees bent over her. She fell breathless against a blasted treetrunk and leaned there panting; she did not know how long. When her breath came back, she staggered on.

Her limbs felt thick and clumsy, heavy as iron. She struggled over the rough ground, half trotting when she could. A stitch had grown into her side and her breasts felt tight because she had not suckled the child since noon. Thinking of him, she pushed herself on.

The trees gave out, turning to scrub. She came to a rocky place where the ground felt hot underfoot. The frost formed a thin crust, inches above the ground; it broke beneath her step. Here and there plumes of steam rose up through cracks.

She knew she must be nearing the Burning Plain, which her people also called the Land of Broken Snow, beyond which no one knew what lay and over which only the reindeer passed, every autumn at this time, seeking the pole.

Then all at once, the rocky country fell away before her in a graded cliff of steep stair runs and blocks of stone. Caribou saw a vast plain lying below, faulted in places. Great areas lay covered with unfrozen water, while fountains of pale steam spurted and gushed along the fault lines.

The earth, where she could see it through the frost, was in some places greyish brown, in others white as salt. There were pits of what seemed to be bubbling mud. A line of dark, jagged peaks lay on the far horizon.

She heard a rumbling then, felt trembling in the ground. Then she saw, off to her left, the cliffside fissured in a wide groove. And from this trough, suddenly, issued a stream of white and grey, thundering, like a forest of deadwood buoyed along on a torrent.

Her tired vision for a moment refused to focus, and then she realized with a start it was the reindeer. They streamed from the glacier canyon and fanned out over the broken plain, flying south. How had she outrun them? She could not guess, and was too tired to care.

Caribou watched the thundering reindeer, small and far below her, and the weariness in her welled into despair. She thought of the golden stag, lost somewhere in that teeming tide, and the child in his horns. Her breasts ached; her throat felt tight and sore. Her breath came in short, bitten gasps.

She scanned the surging torrent of silver until the afternoon had darkened and the last fleet stragglers bolted from the trough. But not one drop of gold did she glimpse in all that time in all that river of grey.

The vast herd of reindeer dwindled into the southern distance on the plain. Caribou turned from the rocks, back toward the woods. The autumn afternoon was very late, and she was half a day's walking journey from her *ntūla*, at least.

She felt chilled now from long standing, and she had no *grīmmul,* or night cloak, against the cold, no flint for making fire, no food or energy left, and she knew of no one living so near the Burning Plain with whom she might seek shelter.

Caribou gazed at the sky. A thin, bitter breeze had sprung up lately. She spotted cloud banks in the south and west. Dark and heavy, they looked as though they carried snow. Great-moon hung very low over the hills, and Little-moon not yet risen. She quickened her pace as she reached the woods, chafing her arms.

She scanned about her and called out her brother's name, but she saw no one, nothing but lifeless branches and trunks. No answer came. Her legs were aching. She called again, at intervals, until her voice was hoarse.

Caribou wandered through the close, naked trees as briskly as she could for warmth. The dark clouds rolled overhead, and Great-moon slipped away. The afternoon grew greyer still. She skirted the edge of the warm, barren ground she had passed over before, calling her brother's name.

"Visjna!" Even in their fur-lined mitts, the hands she cupped to her mouth were numb. No sound replied. The biting wind lifted her words away.

When she came across her brother's body not far from there, she was too tired even to weep. He lay prone upon the frozen ground and had been dead some hours, she judged, for he was frozen to the ground—she could not budge the body to turn it over.

Her brother's clothes were torn and scuffed across the back and shoulders, bloody there, as though he had been struck several times by something both heavy and sharp. She realized she must have passed within a hundred yards of him earlier. She remembered the huge stag's great, splay hooves.

Numbly, Caribou laid her hands upon her brother's shoulders and sang the dead-song for him then as the long northern twilight began. Then she laid her hands upon her own shoulders and sang again for herself, for she expected to be joining her brother's spirit very soon on its journey to the land of everlasting night.

Visjna's parka was frozen to his body, and even if she could have cut it free, it was too stiff with blood and cold to have given her warmth. She managed to work his *ca'xat* free from its sheath at the side of his belt, and used the blade to cut free the leather food pouch that hung beside it.

She opened it, found it half full of travel fare, all frozen: pemmican, dried berries, nuts. She chipped at them with the *ca'xat,* working off a few slivers. But they were hard and tasteless as bits of bone, chilled her teeth, and gave her no nourishment.

So she spat them out and stared at the body of her brother. His flints and tinder, she knew, would be in a little pouch sewn to his belt near the buckle—no way she could get to them. It hardly seemed to matter now. She would soon be dead.

Caribou eyed the blood frozen brown on her brother's parka. Then she noticed a thing she had not seen before: spatters of something, little smears upon the body and the ground. Some liquid, now frozen dry—it was pale and it was bright, like purest gold.

Caribou stared at it, studied it, could not figure out what it could be. Turning, following the drops of gold with her eyes, she saw they led off through the woods in the direction her brother lay facing, nearly the direction from which she had just come.

If she sat there any longer, she would die. Despite the leaden fatigue, her killing hunger and the bitter cold that clenched her bones, Caribou arose, stiffly, gritting her teeth against the rigor in her joints. She set out to follow the trail of gold.

The trail led her back to the clearing of tumbled rock and warm steam vents, the place she had crossed going toward the cliffs and skirted coming back. The warmth of the earth rose through the soles of her boots. Her toes ached, burning at the gentle heat. She had forgotten the warmth of this place.

Pausing now, Caribou pulled off her mittens in her teeth and put her hands to the hard, barren earth to warm them. After a little, rising, she followed the trail of gold to an outcropping of rock near the center of the clearing. The

tallest stones, reaching twice a woman's height, had thrust up
from the earth in a rough circle, like a fort or crown.

Caribou clambered up over the lower rocks and between
two taller ones where the golden spatters led, into the inte-
rior, and stumbled upon the stag, fallen forward on his knees,
an arrow fletched with Visjna's colors buried in his ribs.

His proud neck lay stretched forward, throat and jaw resting upon the ground, his cradlelike antlers balanced upright
upon his brow, as though he had fallen to earth with the
greatest care to avoid spilling the burden he bore.

And there upon his rack rested the struggling bundle of the
child, crying feebly, as though he had been doing so for hours
and his strength was nearly gone. No breath steamed from the
reindeer's nostrils. His golden blood spattered the ground.

With a cry, Caribou ran to the child and lifted him from
the dead stag's horns. The ground was very much warmer
here, within the rocks. Steam vents, closely spaced, were mist-
ing hot, humid air from their cracks.

The child struggled in her arms, flushed, alive, his spent
voice making more of a hiss than an angry scream. Kneeling,
Caribou dandled him, cooed to him, unfastened her smock
from the shoulder, and gave him the breast.

The child ceased his crying, nursed eagerly. Caribou felt
the pain in her breasts easing now and let him suckle as long
as he liked. He closed his golden eyes at last, drifted sighing
toward sleep. Caribou patted him upon her shoulder until he
gave up his air, then laid him down upon the warm ground.

She refastened her smock then, teeth chattering, for though
the ground was warm, the air was fast chilling and the light
fading with the coming of night. Caribou gazed at the fallen
reindeer, and ran her hands over his heavy winter coat. His
body was still warm, unfrozen with the warmth from the
ground. Caribou set her rattling teeth.

Taking her brother's *ca'xat,* she knelt beside the golden
stag. She slipped the knife through the skin of the chest,
drawing a long slit down the belly. The hide parted easily.
Though heavier and much thicker furred, it was as supple as
rabbit skin. The pelt came away smoothly, bloodless from
the fair white flesh.

She did not stop to wonder at it. Darkness was settling down. She pulled the hide from the carcass and swaddled it about her, furside in, laid the sleeping child upon her lap. Then she cut and ate some of the flank meat from the fallen stag to quiet the tearing hunger in her belly.

The flesh was white as breast of ptarmigan and tasted as though it had been basted in butter, though she knew it had had no heat sufficient to have cooked it, only the faint warmth of the ground, and the deer but lately dead.

Presently, Caribou sensed her spirit returning. She felt strangely rested and well, immensely strong. Then, just before the dark was completely upon them, she cut the reindeer carcass into quarters and dragged each piece beyond the rocks and into the frozen woods near her brother's body, where the heated earth would not spoil the meat.

Returning to the child, she took off her travel clothing, and laid it in layers upon the ground to be her mattress. Darkness had fallen. Little-moon hung hidden behind the clouds. A light snow had begun to fall, she felt the feathery flakes touching her body, heard them hissing to steam when they touched the heated earth.

She unwrapped the child from his rabbit-skin *bēla* and gathered him into her arms. Lying down, she pulled the soft reindeer hide over them both, furside against the skin. That night, she dreamed no child, but a reindeer calf suckled all night at her breast.

4: Reindeer

So Caribou brought the child home with her a second time, and thereafter he no longer slept in the box beside the hearth, but with Caribou in her own bed beneath the golden reindeer hide, turned backside out, furside down.

The next day, after resting, Caribou put on her *bīnnakai*, snowshoes, and returned over the fresh-fallen snow to the wood where she had stowed the quartered stag. There she built a *mūdak*, or drag sled of branches, and brought home as much of the carcass as she could carry in several trips.

The child came with her on the first of these, but he wept and fretted so when they reached the wood and would not be stilled all the long trip back, that afterward she left him in the hut.

Caribou found, to her bafflement, that her brother's arrow that had pierced the golden reindeer's hide had turned itself all a strange golden color. It seemed very heavy now, and hard. She wondered at it, could not make it out. She had never heard of such a thing.

But what surprised her the most, during all that time, was that though she often heard the wild wolves crying in the hills all around, none ever came near the reindeer's body or harassed her in the slightest as she was dragging the carcass back to her lodge.

At the end of a week's time, when she had all the carcass of the wild deer safely stowed in the deep pit cut into the ground beside the house, covered with turf and weighted with stones, she returned a last time to the woods to light a smoldering fire around her brother's body, to thaw the earth to which he lay frozen, and cut him free.

Then she dragged that, too, out onto open ground, and burned him there upon a pyre of deadwood, with the proper laments and offerings of honey and bitternut. Of the ashes of that fire and the fat of the fallen stag, she made funeral soap, golden and smooth.

But of Branja, she never saw anything or heard any word again. She knew not whether her sister-in-law, being ignorant of the ways of the hinterland, might have frozen to death that night in the snow. Or, she reasoned doubtfully, as she washed death from the cabin with the tallow soap, perhaps the green-eyed woman had managed to make her way back to her own people. Caribou shrugged as she swabbed the close-grained wood with clear water, then dried it. She could hardly bring herself to care.

She made many things from the golden stag. The remainder of his fat she rendered into tallow, which formed many long, very thin candles, each of which burned longer than a whole lamp of oil. From the toes of his hooves, she fashioned cups for salt and condiments.

His bones she sawed and ground into buttons and counters and cuff-fastens and fishing-weights, slivered into birks and needles, hollowed into candlesticks, fashioned into the handles of knives and the hafts of other tools.

But none of these things would the child touch. Nor would he consent to be fed from the little hoof bowls. He would not eat the meat of the golden stag when Caribou offered it to him finely ground, well mixed with fat and honey, though he eagerly took cheese and caribou butter, or the flesh of hare and ptarmigan.

Indeed, the only pickings of the wild deer the child would tolerate were the necklace of reindeer teeth Caribou now wore, which the child handled and played with for long stretches, the golden pelt, that was their blanket at night, and the golden stag's antlers, which she had lined with felt and furs to be the child's day cradle beside the fire.

The child grew apace that winter, while Caribou fashioned things beside the fire. He learned to creep and crawl about, well bundled, upon the reindeer hide on Caribou's bed, or the furs upon the floor. Gradually his infant's noises changed to more articulate babbling, though his cries could still sound uncannily like a reindeer lowing, and he was a long time learning the sounds for speech.

His eyes never darkened to anything deeper than yellow gold, nor did his curls turn from their pure, pale blond. Caribou suckled him till he was fully two years old, that he might be well fleshed and strong. And she called him Reindeer, in memory of the golden stag.

It was during the dark of that first, long winter season that Caribou, eating of the reindeer's flesh and sleeping beneath his golden pelt, felt her dreams growing deeper: more vivid and prophetic. She had begun to bleed, in time with the moons, and so counted herself a woman now at thirteen, no longer a girl.

One morning in early spring a drover stopped at her lodge to ask if she had seen his little herd of milch caribou, which had started at the cries of wolves and fled away from him the previous evening. Caribou told him he would find the whole herd safe, grazing on a hillside above the falling stream on the other slope of the mountain with a new calf in their midst, for she had seen it in a dream as she drowsed by the hearth the night before.

After that, people came to her for advice, only a few at first, but gradually more and more until she began to earn for herself the name of wisewoman. When they came, she gave them food and drink, then sat upon the doorstep of her *ntūla,* with the child beside her and the golden arrow on her lap.

After much thinking and running of her fingers along the smooth yellow shaft, she would tell them what they wanted to know: why it was their nannies would not bring forth live kids, or where lost articles were to be found, or which would be the better man to wed.

Then they went away, back to their farms or villages, thanking her with smiles and gifts. And sometimes they came a second time, either for themselves or bringing someone else who needed help. Always those that came again said that Caribou's advice on the other matter had been good and that things had been exactly as she had said.

Sometimes it was things she remembered seeing in her dreams, and other times it was her own weighing of their words which determined what she told them, but always when they went away, they seemed satisfied. Before many months had gone by, there was not a fortnight passed without some traveler footing the new-worn path up to her lonely hut to ask the wisewoman's advice.

Only one thing troubled Caribou, and that was Reindeer. Sometimes she heard the people who came to question her murmuring, with lips only, behind their hands, and looking at him. While still she suckled him, Reindeer usually sat on her lap when she answered the people, or later, when he was older, on the step beside her, listening to her and watching with his great, still, luminous eyes.

They murmured that he was odd, with his yellow hair and fair, white skin, though to her face they said he was a fine boy, strapping and strong, very comely to look at. And Caribou, who knew nothing of beauty that was not in landscape, or livestock, or household things, gazed at the fine-planed features of her growing boy and was not sure.

But when they asked who he was, she answered always, "My brother's child, not mine."

He was a strange child, very solemn now, who neither laughed nor cried anymore, and rarely spoke. He sat beside her in the evening on the hearthstone, listening to some tale she would be telling, half to herself and half to him, and playing with the necklace of reindeer teeth upon her breast: tales of iffs and onts, and halflings that could change their skins.

Sometimes he sat with his hands in his lap and stared into the fire so long, so still she was sure he had fallen asleep with his eyes open. But always when she spoke his name, he turned and answered without starting.

He was restless in spring when the reindeer were running and seemed to know to the moment when they had returned. Caribou often found him, at the end of the day when the outside work was done, standing at wood's edge in the twilight, gazing off toward the chilly southlands until the wild herds had passed north to the warmer calving grounds, and then he gazed northward for the rest of the season.

It was the same in winter, though then he gazed southward again to where the reindeer had passed beyond the Burning Plain. And sometimes, while she gazed at him, Caribou found herself marveling, lost in a dream that he was no human child at all, but some strange other thing that had no human heart.

Yet, for all his strangeness, he was her only joy. Caribou could not say how, before he had come, she had borne the solitude. He was her companion in the day-chores of the lodge: building and mending and splitting wood for the fire, and shared the reindeer coverlet with her at night.

As soon as he was old enough, he accompanied her wood-gathering, or berry-picking, or checking her snares. And before very much longer, she could send him out by himself on one errand while she herself attended to another.

There was no greater happiness for her than to await his homecoming of an evening, or to come home to him at twilight on those days when it had been her turn to check the traps, to find him waiting on the doorsill and have him come out to meet her, put his arms about her waist and gaze up at her with his great gold eyes and ask her solemnly what luck the traps had had that day.

Then one day, when Reindeer was still quite young, a thing happened which troubled Caribou more than she could say. It was springtime, the ice of winter gone and the rush of melting snow now past. The child was four, and Caribou had taken him with her fishing for salmon in the quiet stream that wended past the rise on which her cabin stood.

She had been sitting a long time on the stony bank with her fishing line wrapped around a shuttle that lay in her lap. She was nearly dozing. Reindeer had wandered away, but she felt no alarm. He was a remarkably safe child, seemed never to lose or injure himself. He would be back in his own time, when it suited him. She dreamed a fish had stolen the bait from her line.

Awakening from her dozing suddenly, she knew not why, she sat very still, listening, but heard nothing. Then she noticed in the water before her, beside her own reflection, the image of a reindeer calf.

She made no sound, not wanting to frighten it, and wondered what calf this could be, so well grown so early in the season, and so far south of the calving grounds—unless it were the calf of someone's milch caribou, wandered off from its dam.

The calf was watching her and not its own reflection. She did not move or turn, was just preparing to cluck softly in hope of coaxing it close enough to catch, when Reindeer's voice sounded, so near it startled her.

"There's a fish nibbling your line, Cari."

Caribou caught in her breath, started to her feet and whirled. Reindeer stood upon the bank, and no caribou calf.

"Where is it?" she stammered. "Did you chase it away?"

"Chase what?" the boy replied. "The fish? No, it's still on the line."

"The calf," cried Caribou, glancing into the woods behind him, trying to spot it.

"What calf?" said Reindeer. "You've dropped your framework, and the fish is pulling it into the water."

Caribou gave an exasperated sigh and turned back to the stream to retrieve the line—and halted dead. Beside her own reflection in the water stood that of a reindeer calf. She whirled. Nothing stood there but Reindeer, her boy.

Reindeer moved one hand slightly, scratching his wrist. Caribou felt a gasp stab in her throat as she gazed at the image of the calf in the water, scratching one foreleg with its hoof. She stared at Reindeer.

"What is it?" he murmured, frowning, then gestured beyond her. "You're going to lose it—the fishing line."

Reindeer had no reflection in the water. Where his image should have been stood a reindeer calf. Caribou backed away from him on the bank, bent down to fish the framework from the water without looking at it. The stream was icy on her hand. Reindeer still gazed at her, had taken no notice as yet of his own reflection.

"Get . . . get back from the water," she stammered. "You're standing too near. You might fall."

Reindeer retreated a few paces from the bank. Caribou got hold of the fishing line and straightened, pulling too hard. She felt the fish slip from the hook.

"What *is* it?" said Reindeer, coming a pace closer to her. "Cari, what's frightened you?"

"Nothing," she said, coming toward him lest he draw near enough to the water to see himself. She wound the draggled fishline about the framework nervously. "You came upon me so silently, I didn't know you were there. You startled me. I wasn't awake.''

"I'm sorry," he began, as if by rote—and she had suddenly the feeling that he had no real notion what sorrow meant. "I made you lose your fish.''

"It doesn't matter," said Caribou. "We have enough fish." She knelt to pull the line of caught fish from the water and started past him up the bank. "Let's go home.''

"But it's not yet dark.''

Caribou did not answer, strode on toward the lodge not daring to look behind. Relief flooded her as she heard the boy was following, trotting to keep up. As they cleaned and dried the fish that afternoon, Reindeer was even more silent than usual, and Caribou did not try to draw him out. She stared down at her work and said nothing.

That evening after supper, when the boy sat on the hearthstone staring into the fire, Caribou took out the little disc of silver glass that had been her father's wedding present to her mother, and which she had not looked in for many years.

Holding it aslant so that it showed the hearth across the room, she looked at it. With her own eyes, she saw Reindeer, the boy, but the mirror showed no boy—only a reindeer calf lounging beside the fire.

A tremor passed through her. Her hands shook. Quietly, she put the mirror away, and the next day when she had sent Reindeer off through the woods to a far-off slope to gather medicine-flower, she broke the mirror into a handful of slivers and buried them between two roots of a tree.

Afterward, Caribou told Reindeer no more tales. She herself did all their fishing in the quiet pools, though Reindeer fished the foaming rapids. Caribou painted the bottoms of all her water vessels white with bone enamel so that they would be too pale to show an image.

Her *mar long,* the only blade she had burnished bright enough to reflect images, she kept firmly in its sheath when Reindeer was with her, and she warned him away from still, standing water, telling him it was treacherous. They still went to the hot pool to bathe, as before, but those waters were always milky with steam, so she did not fear.

These changes seemed to sadden Reindeer, as much as his great, unchanging eyes could evidence any mood, but he did not complain. Only once did he reveal that he had noticed any difference: one morning when he was ten summers old and she was warning him for the second time to stay away from clear, dark water while hunting.

"Why is that?" he asked her. "Why are you so afraid? There is something, Cari, that you are not telling me."

And Caribou felt a sudden terror sweeping over her. She shook her head. "No. No, there is nothing," and pretended to be busy with the birchroot she was paring. "It is only . . ."

She looked at him then, feeling an utter helplessness. Her eyes, she knew, beseeched him, though she realized he could not understand.

"Reindeer, I . . ." She almost told him. "It is only that I do not want to lose you."

He gazed at her intently then, for a long several breaths, with his golden eyes. Caribou dropped her eyes. She could not. She could not tell him . . . *what* could she not tell? She had only a terrifying suspicion buried so deep down that she herself scarcely knew what it was she feared.

Reindeer took his bow from the table then and went off into the forest to hunt, while Caribou dropped her face to her hands and wept for a long time, wildly, without understanding why.

5: *Trāngl*

The boy came to her one day in early fall. He had seen his thirteenth summer and was nearly as tall as Caribou now. He had been restless for many days, so she knew the reindeer were running—though they had not yet returned from their summer calving grounds, for still he stared off to the north in the evenings. But they were coming. She could tell from his manner they would pass by soon.

"Cari," he said, "there is a thing I must tell you." His voice was changing, cracked unexpectedly now and again.

Caribou looked up from the candles she was dipping. "What thing, Reindeer?" she asked.

"Cari," he said, quietly, his expression never changing, "I want to go away."

Caribou dropped the wooden candle-frame into the heated kettle, and tallow spattered hot upon her hand, making her wince. Reindeer took the iron tongs from beside the hearth and fished the framework out for her.

"Go away?" she cried. "Go where and why?"

Reindeer handed her the wax-coated frame; she took it gingerly. He gazed off across the room, breathed restlessly.

"Because the reindeer are running. I want to follow them and see what lies beyond the Burning Plain."

"Beyond the Burning Plain?" cried Caribou, gripping the waxy frame till her knuckles whitened and her fingers made impressions in the soft tallow. "There lies only death beyond the Burning Plain."

The boy shook his head, still looking off. "Not for the reindeer and not for me."

Caribou clapped the framework to the hearthstone, shoved it away. "Why do you say that? How do you know?"

He turned to look at her now, his pale eyes burning in the firelight. "Because they have told me, Cari."

Caribou's heart shrank. She drew back from him and was afraid.

"Every year at their running they call to me and tell me of the sweet pastures beyond the Land of Broken Snow, and beg me to come with them."

The breath in Caribou's breast grew still then, and for a long time she could not answer him. "Why do you want to leave me?" she whispered at last.

He shook his head and knelt upon the hearthstone by her. "I do not *want* to leave you. Each year I have refused them, till now."

"Then why now?" she whispered.

His tone had grown gentler. "Because now I am grown tall enough and strong enough to make the trek." He had laid his hands upon her hands. "Cari, I would ask you to come with me, but the reindeer do not want you. Only me."

Caribou's hands curled into fists. "But you cannot go!" she burst out, gazing at him, both angry and beseeching at once. "You are just a boy, not yet a man. . . ."

Reindeer took his hands from hers, stood back, and looked away. "Cari, I will never be a *man*. You and I both know it."

She clenched her teeth against the spasm in her throat. "Why do you say that? What do you mean?"

He looked at her again with his great gold eyes. "Cari, I am not like you. I am not like the others, the people who come to you and ask advice."

"Them!" cried Caribou. "Why do you listen to them, their mutterings—what do they know?"

He looked at her. "More than you, in some things," he said softly.

Caribou caught in her breath. "We . . . we are not different," she stammered, stumbling on the words. "You are not different—not from *me*. I suckled you." Her hands were fists. "We are the same."

But Reindeer shook his head and knelt beside her again, took up her hand in both of his. "How can you say that— why deny it? It is the difference you have been hiding from me since that day beside the stream."

Caribou felt her throat closing tight.

"I have seen my shadow," said the boy. "Have you never noticed it?"

She shook her head, mute, staring at him. His shadow! She had not once thought of it. "It isn't like yours, a human shape. Mine is different."

Caribou closed her eyes and shook her head, leaned back against the mantel stones. Her body felt thin as water.

"And when I listen and talk to the birds and the animals," Reindeer was saying, "you act as though you do not hear it.

So many things are different between us. You laugh and you cry, and I don't understand.''

Caribou felt her breast heave and could get no air.

"And Caribou, look at this," said Reindeer. "Cari, look."

His hands left hers and her fears suddenly sharpened. She sat up quickly, snapped open her eyes, half expecting to find him vanished. But he was still beside her, had drawn his *ca'xat* from his belt and pressed its edge to the fleshy part of his palm. Caribou saw a line of gold well up. He wiped and sheathed the knife again, and held up his hand to her.

"See, Cari; it's not like yours," said Reindeer. "It's gold."

Caribou felt her body slipping away. The room grew dark and distorted. The firelight to the right of her tipped far away and vanished. She felt a brief rush of cooler air. Her left arm and shoulder struck something hard, and then her cheek. She closed her eyes because she did not want to see any more.

"Cari," she heard him saying. "Caribou."

She found herself laid upon the hearth, the wax kettle pushed out of the way on its swinging arm, back over the coals. The heat of the close fire made her sweat. The stones against her back were uneven and hard.

She saw Reindeer above her dimly, bending over her, shaking her. The shaking made her gasp. The air in her throat made things grow sharper and steadier. She pushed away from Reindeer, swung her legs to the floor and sat up. Then she put one hand to her head and leaned against him.

"What happened?" he asked her. "Why did you do that?"

"I don't know," she muttered. Her tongue and lips felt slow. "I don't understand."

"You looked like a hare that has been frightened to death," said Reindeer. His tone, oddly flat, seemed to express neither worry nor distress.

He is like a comet or a running stream, she thought, that has no thought for anything but itself and its own path.

Reindeer said, "You looked like something dead in the snow. I laid you on the hearthstone to warm you."

Caribou straightened and took several quick, deep breaths.

Her head felt clearer. "I fainted," she told him, "because I forgot to breathe."

"Did I make you do that?" he asked her. "Did I frighten you?"

She did not answer, did not look at him. She took his wounded hand that still bled slightly, drops of gold, and stared at it.

"There is something I have not told you," she said quietly. "There is something I have never told you."

She held his hand in her lap and gazed off across the twilit room.

"You are the child of my sister-in-law, but not my brother's child. She brought you to me when you were newly born, just two months old, and gave you to me for safe-keeping. But a great golden stag caught you out of my arms that fall when the reindeer were running, carried you away in his horns. My brother killed the stag, but died himself to do it. When I came upon the two of you, the stag was bleeding drops of gold."

The boy beside her nodded. "Yes, I remember that."

Caribou caught in her breath and turned to stare at him, his fine, fair features catching the firelight. Reindeer nodded again.

"I remember from the time the other, that other woman brought me to you. She was my mother, I think, but she was afraid of me. And I remember when the reindeer came and bore me away. He was my father, he told me, and would carry us beyond the Land of Broken Snow. But then he stumbled, and wheeled about, and struck down the man who had been tracking us. Then we went on a little way, as far as the rocks, before he lay down, saying no more to me. And then you came."

Caribou's fingers slipped from beneath his hand. She gazed at him, unmoving. "Halfling," she whispered. "Wild thing. I don't know what you are."

But she knew; she understood, now—as she let herself understand, for the first time, what it was she had feared so long—that he was a *trāngl*, one of the *traāngol*, the golden deer-men and deer-women that ran with the wild deer.

Reindeer took his hand from her lap. "Cari," he said, "I am going away to follow the reindeer."

She looked at him, drew breath. "Will you come back?" The boy arose, shook his head a little, shrugged. "I do not know."

Oh, he is; he is, she thought, a halfling, a thing I cannot understand. He is beyond my grasp. I can no more hold him than I can halt the running of water, or the turning of stars. She tried to smile, but her face felt crusted, crushed and set like drying clay.

"Come back," she said. "I will use the time you are away to make beautiful things for you."

Reindeer said nothing. He turned from her. He went to the door and opened it, and Caribou saw that outside the twilight was burning down the whole sky into glowing coals.

"Wait," Caribou cried. "You'll take no *pīsjlak*, provisions for the journey?"

The boy stepped over the threshold, did not turn. "The reindeer will show me where good forage lies. I will need no other."

"But wait," cried Caribou again, bolting to her feet. "Take this at least." She ran to their bed, tore off the coverlet of reindeer hide and went to him outside, folded it over his arm. "Against the cold."

"My thanks," the *trāngl* said, that had lived in her house these dozen years and more as a guest, nothing other, and was no kith to her at all. He leaned and kissed her lips.

Caribou drew back, surprised, for all the while his expression never changed. And she had never kissed him before, nor he her. Her people were not like the river valley folk, always kissing each other's mouths.

"I hope that I may see you again," said Reindeer then, and turned away.

Caribou stood by the house door, helpless, watching him go. The sky above was burning gold. She saw him take the reindeer pelt from his arm as he reached the wood's edge and throw it about his shoulders, skinside to him, furside out. Then all the woods for an instant grew bright as fire, and when Caribou could see again, she could no longer find Reindeer among the trees.

She started forward with a cry and darted down the hard, frozen slope to the wood's edge below. But the wood was empty, silent, still, all the trees black and barren, as if burnt. Nothing caught her eye but a wild stag, very far off, bounding through the trees in great strides, a young rack of antlers crowning his head. The setting sun upon his pelt made it shimmer, fire-gold.

PRINCES AND POWER

Much fantasy is written about kings, queens, princes, princesses, and other royalty. One might almost suspect that every writer who's ever made his or her questing hero a noble has read Aristotle's *Poetics,* in which he states that the best tragedies are stories of kings and princes from families with long, tragic, and violent histories.

This isn't to say that fantasy is concerned only with bluebloods. Anyone who's read the Brothers Grimm or Hans Christian Andersen knows that it owes as much to the folktale as to the court, and maybe more. Fantasy is, however, a highly symbolic medium in which kings and queens, princes and princesses, are not just people on quests but quests themselves. Kings and queens have won their power . . . usually; princes and princesses have yet to come to it, whether over their lands or their own minds and hearts. The title and the part usually go hand-in-hand; and when they don't, you've usually got the plot for a good story.

What we've got here is two stories along just those lines. Jayge Carr and Nancy Springer (both readers of Andre Norton for most of their lives) seem to know about kings and princes by instinct. Brancel, the Prince in Carr's "The Price of Lightning," may be familiar to readers of *Hecate's Cauldron* as the wise healer who dares hell to win back his beloved. But how did he become wise and brave?

Here's how—or at least part of the story.

Nancy Springer's Merric is a much younger prince; like Andre Norton, Nancy Springer specializes in writing stories about people who are growing up. He is a child, and needs protection more than power; but yet, since he's a prince, he does need both—and he needs to use both right away. Like the wise children one finds in Andre Norton's books, Merric proves to the adults around him that while he may be just a child, he is at least as wise, at least as noble, as they.

THE PRICE OF LIGHTNING

Jayge Carr

AROUND THE CITY OF BRONZE MARCHED THE GIANT OF
Bronze. His gleaming body was a full five man-heights tall,
and even the wind stirred up by his footsteps was deadly.

"No." Quiet but utterly firm. I-shall-*not*-be-moved.

Vow the Acolyte blinked large brown eyes, ingenious and
eager as a spaniel puppy's. "Bu-bu-but—" he stammered.
Could any man really deny throne and heritage—and a princess so lovely (for a princess) that tales would be told about
her when her very bones were dust? "The Old One says—
any more delay—don't you understand—if we wait until after
the marriage is performed, it will be too late."

The ex-prince shrugged well-knit shoulders. "It's too late
now," he said, his blue eyes bleak, seeing perhaps a betrayed
palace, a slaughtered family—all but one boy, wounded,
unconscious, covered with blood, smuggled out and away to
safety. "It's been too long, too many years. I was still too
young when the time was right, and Drednore the Tyrant has
had too much opportunity to tighten his grip. The people
hate, but rebellion has been ground out of them, and as for
the *nobility*—" A snort of bitter laughter. "If there are any
survivors of the true nobility, they owe allegiance only to
Drednore."

Vow the Acolyte blinked and blinked again. His entire life
revolved around the ancient priest of religion almost forgotten. His life *was* the priest's, ever since a grateful woman

had laid the bawling boy-infant on the time-dulled altar—and that anyone, even a prince, could refuse one of the Old One's pronouncements— "But the Old One *says*—"

"I have heard—too often—what the Old One says. And I know what I and mine owe to him. But the time is not ripe. The time will never be ripe, ever."

Vow was trembling, almost dancing up and down in his fervor. "But *after* the wedding—"

"The wedding, the wedding." The blue-eyed ex-prince who called himself Brancel stalked lithely to the window and stared out at the bleak landscape of his mountain monastery fastness. "What difference can a wedding make? Hasn't Drednore the Tyrant spread his seed among half the women of the City of Bronze, high and low alike? If it is a dynasty of terror the Old One fears, Drednore has already spawned enough images to keep it thriving for a thousand years. . . ."

Vow took a deep breath. It was as if the Old One, too old to travel, stood in his sandals, and the words simply poured out. In truth, they were the ancient priest's words. He was so accustomed to his loyal shadow that he often forgot, or seemed to, that there was a second presence, listening to an old man's soliloquies. "Legitimate heir of royal blood, ancient blood? *That* will gild the seat of his stolen throne with a vengeance, will it not? Once let him dandle heirs of White Jade blood on his knee, and he will have the support of the City of White Jade instead of their disdainful neutrality—"

"What?" Brancel had gone from mild irritation to total fury in a single breath. "Drednore dares to seek a bride from among the nobility of White Jade?"

Vow was remembering something else the Old One had said. "Not merely the nobility," he made his voice a taunt, "but from among the royal family itself."

"But there is only the one princess from White Jade, the Lady Vivyana, she who was once—"

"Promised to the Heir Apparent, the oldest prince of the City of Bronze . . ." Vow watched, satisfied, the anger etched on the proud, clean-cut face opposite, and did not bother to add the obvious: *yourself.* He would not have to report failure to the Old One who owned his life after all.

*   *   *

The priest had been old, his name long forgotten, when the dispossessed prince who called himself Brancel was born. Now he was mere will draped in sagging flesh, though his eyes were still bright and fierce as an eagle's. "You took your time coming," he commented, the young Vow scurrying to settle him more comfortably in the carved ivory chair.

"I'm here now." The young ex-prince sat in the chair opposite the priest's but almost immediately was on his feet again, pacing restlessly up and down. "How many have we that we can trust absolutely?"

The hairless forehead raised slightly, repositioning the map of wrinkles. "Myself. You." He placed a hand wizened as a rooster's claw on the young acolyte's shoulder. "The boy."

Brancel shrugged. "I suspected so. I had hoped for better but—" Another shrug. "A sword is only as sharp as the mind behind it, after all. I have . . . the beginnings of a plan."

"Ahhhh." It was a breathy whisper; then, filling old lungs: "Good. Good. So do I. We will put the best of both together—" Brancel nodded, though it wasn't a question, and a glitter of satisfaction flashed in the deep-set old eyes.

A strange army they formed, the Ancient, an untried princeling, and a boy. But there are more weapons than those that can be held in a strong hand. . . .

Words. The first feint in a strange and subtly fought war. Soon they were spreading from three sources. From the Old One; though for years now he scarcely had stirred from his room, its air laden with must and incense, still he retained the interest of a few who came to consult him. Plus Brancel and Vow wandering the streets, joining groups, crowds, marketplace chafferers, convivial parties in inns and pleasure houses, wherever and whenever an opportunity, an audience beckoned. And sooner or later, usually sooner, the arrival of the lovely princess of White Jade being on everybody's lips, the chance to add another straw to what they hoped would build to a usurper's funeral pyre.

*   *   *

Stories, faces, time blurred together until Brancel was almost acting by rote, his brain numb, his voice hoarse, the words he and the old priest had devised tumbling out almost without his conscious mind's directing them. He was saying, ". . . saw him in practice myself, a mere lad he was then, but no swordsman I've ever seen could touch him . . ." when a hand clamped on his shoulder and a gravelly voice grated, "You speak treason against the mighty Drednore, oily-tongued one."

Brancel's audience, a dozen wine-gay celebrants staggering home after a wedding, froze instantly, sobered by fright.

Brancel turned slowly, both hands carefully visible through the folds of his cloak, to face his accuser.

He breathed an inward sigh of relief—the man was alone, not the head of a troop—and shuddered at the wine-soured breath. Warily he assessed his would-be opponent. And jerked a little at a certain odd shock of recognition, as though suddenly confronted with a mirror and his own face. Not himself, but his opposite, his balance wheel, the one whose peaks matched his valleys, who could be happy when he was sad, who would act while he yet thought. A scarred warrior with the insignia ripped off his military tunic—and just drunk enough to be extremely dangerous.

"Treason, I say," the barrel-chested fighter repeated, eyes gloating.

Brancel could only be grateful it was himself and not Vow facing this tightly strung human weapon. But neither could afford— "Is it treason, then," he asked in a deliberately mild voice, "to tell a pleasant tale, for amusement's sake?"

"Treason to say anyone—most expeck—sheshul some boy— more better swordsman than gread—great lord Drednore."

"What I said was, the lad was the best *I've* ever seen. I've not been privileged to watch m'lord—"

"You never will!" The soldier's hand went to his hilt.

With an inward sigh, Brancel swirled his cloak to get it out of his way and drew his own blade. The soldier's sword clanged against his, low on the foible, and the fight was on.

Brancel was the slighter man, wielding a shorter, lighter sword. His metal-plated shield with its special grips was far away, and he couldn't hold a dagger in his crippled left hand, though he had one strapped in a belt sheath. Worse, he could *not* attract the attention of the guards—or any authorities.

The ex-soldier had a blade in each hand, and considerable skill.

Brancel had more.

He could be useful, thought Brancel, as he lunged and feinted, parried and thrust. If I can take him without killing him—or humiliating him too much . . .

The man closed in, and Brancel warded off his dagger slash with his left forearm. Somehow, the hilt caught on the cuff of the glove and pulled it back. The man's eyes rested on what was revealed—and widened.

Brancel attacked furiously. A thrust, a clever feint, another thrust—and a disarm. The soldier lunged desperately with his dagger, and without quite knowing how it happened, found himself sprawled on his back, a booted foot crushing the wrist of his knife hand, and Brancel's blade at his throat.

The soldier snarled defiance.

Brave as well as skilled, Brancel thought, a pity. But—he's seen The Hand.

With a single sigh for the many shared adventures that would now never be, Brancel cut the soldier's throat.

He shoved his way through the crowd, before any one of them could recover his wits and challenge the victor.

A fair fight, he thought; nonetheless, he was glad to slip into an open courtyard and reverse his cloak, the midnight blue now within, the rich burnt umber showing without.

And the words that were straws continued to pile up.

But Brancel listened to words as well as speaking them, and as the days added up, he began to listen more and more intently for certain words that never came, until his patience ran out and he cornered young Vow.

"I wish the truth," he stated, with the unconscious hauteur of his pampered princely childhood, "and I wish it now. What is amiss with the Lady Vivyana's eyes?"

Vow was the Old One's alter ego; without saying so aloud he conveyed the message that any information of importance should come from the Old One direct. But Brancel had memories of the Old One going back before Vow was even conceived. He cut through the youngster's excuses and praises of Vivyana that he'd heard before: hair like a dark river flowing with amber and crimson lights, delightfully dimpled chin, mouth laughing yet imperious, body—

"What is amiss with her eyes?"

"Amiss, lord? I don't understand. What could be amiss with the eyes of such a lovely princess?" The young brown gaze was clear and placid, except for a slight puzzlement. But he was the Old One's hand, and Brancel knew the Old One well. He persisted. Until—

"They don't match, sir." Brancel drew back, genuinely startled. "Ask the Old One, or anyone who isn't afraid of losing his tongue, if you don't believe me. Her eyes—they are two different colors."

Brancel frowned, trying to remember. A child's eyes *might* change color slightly as they grew older—a little lighter—a little darker—but—two *different* colors? He remembered two sparkling eyes surrounded by thick lashes; light-colored eyes, taking hue and tone from their surroundings.

Light—and matched.

"One's grey, sir, clear light grey. And the other's *green*. Pale green like a new leaf, with a tawny rim."

A pause, then, "The Princess Vivyana will be mistress of this city and all it contains. There is no flaw in her, none."

"Yes, sir. As you say, sir."

The wizard had eyes older than time in a coldly handsome face that would have fitted a man of thirty. Unlike most of his breed, he was smooth-shaven, and men spoke in cautious whispers of the fate of one who dared snicker at the womanish cleft in his chin. " 'Tis naught but rumors, m'lord," he said in emotionless tones.

"Rumors," Drednore exploded, his florid face purpling over the luxuriant auburn beard. "I know they're rumors! What else could they be? That missing prince, he's—he's— you name it! He's blind, he's one-eyed, he has a third eye—no, it's the Lethal Eye. He's lame, he's one-armed—no, he's a brilliant swordsman beyond compare. He's a wizardling, he's been devoted to the Sly One—no, laid on the Wargod's altar—no, the Lady Justice's . . . He's tall, he's short, dark and fair, he's dead, he lives. By the Gory God's dripping blade, they can't even agree on his name!''

"You might," the wizard suggested, "apply to the Princess Vivyana. She of all people would surely know—"

"Wizard"—Drednore stopped his frenzied pacing to fix the other with a glare that had stopped more than one heart—"the woman is mine. I'll not have her disturbed. *You* will discover for me any truth that lies in these tales. And if this princeling yet lives, where he is to be found."

Drednore tossed down the contents of a handsome silver goblet in a single swallow, and his fingers tightened. And tightened. A crunch, and Drednore dropped the shapeless mass of crushed metal to the floor, where its crumpled edges scarred the priceless jade and lapis mosaic. "Find me that princeling, wizard," he said softly.

"There will be . . . the price."

"The usual?"

"Yes. Two unblemished bodies, one of each sex, for my Master."

"Done. Choose them yourself. When will I know?"

"Soon, mighty Drednore. Very soon."

Secure in the ferocity of his punishments, Drednore sadly underestimated the tongues of women. Misdew, Princess Vivyana's bird-cheerful handmaiden, spent hours each day in the marketplace, bringing back cosmetics, ornaments—and gossip. Then, while she brushed her mistress's long, silken hair . . .

"One said that the young prince was a manly paragon beyond price, m'lady, and another that he was hunchbacked and lame, yet a wizard of renown, while a third claimed—"

Vivyana sniffed. "Fools' tongues wag idly. He was a most ordinary child, except for his eyes so deep a blue you could swim in them and that hair brighter than any crown. But—'' She shrugged. "Who can say what changes the years have wrought?"

*   *   *

The wizard's price was prime, a lovely girl with long lustrous hair, and a bright-eyed boy whose grin showed straight white baby teeth. The wizard and his two assistants began, timing all so that the peak of the ceremony would occur at the exact midpoint between dusk and dawn, that magic hour when lost souls howl their way down to the pit.

The lad sensed his fate somehow, and struggled futilely in the grip of Dummox, the wizard's huge mute servant; his thrashing legs disarranged certain carefully positioned objects. The wizard and his apprentice, a sly man called Foxi, meticulously reset everything. Better the climax a trifle later, the spell a hairsbreadth less potent, than the revenge an unbridled elemental could exact.

Afterward, Foxi knelt and howled unashamedly while the gargantuan Dummox striped his back at the wizard's orders for the mistakes he'd made that night. Some, but not all, of the mistakes had been deliberate. Foxi knew the precarious tightrope he walked. He thirsted for the power the wizard's lore could bestow, but once his master decided he'd learned enough to be dangerous . . .

Then it was Dummox's turn: the boy had been his responsibility, and the boy had managed to disrupt the ceremony. The wizard did something to an object kept in a wooden box on a high shelf. The mute writhed on the floor in silent agony until the wizard, after one final gesture that caused the bearlike body to bounce along the floor on shoulders and heels, shut the box. One dispassionate kick in the ribs, one snapped order, and the mute, tears running down his cheeks, dragged himself to his feet and began cleaning up.

Brancel awoke some time after the midwatch of the night, sweat pouring off him in rivulets. With enormous effort, he drew a breath, and it seared as though he sucked in fire. Already the bed was sopping, as the life-fluid poured off him. He broiled in the heat of a giant forge, his bones melting, his eyes blinded by a brightness beyond bearing. He knew that within heartbeats he would be completely helpless. By dawn a corrupted corpse would lie in his bed.

Desperately, he half shoved, half rolled himself off of the narrow cot. The slight *fl-unk* his body made as it landed brought no help, and he lay on the floor, spent, eyes open but unseeing, mouth straining, and felt consciousness—and life— flowing away. Drednore's wizard was mightier than they had thought, that he could send a death geas without a hint of contagion, without hair or blood or spit, without even know- ing his foe's true name—

He twitched, and his fingers brushed against a round ob- ject. Instinctively he grasped, and knew it for the earthen- ware chamber pot. His fingers tightened; he had remembered a counter-spell—but he had no breath to speak the words aloud.

Nonetheless, he formed the words as clearly as he could in his mind—a heart-deep prayer to the Powers—and flung the contents of the pot toward the dying hearth fire. And fainted, not knowing if his desperate ploy had succeeded or failed.

"I said to *find* this princeling, wizard!" Drednore's face was flushed almost maroon. The wizard shrewdly predicted (to himself) apoplexy, and soon; but there would always be, somewhere, a ready market for his skills.

"I did. He is somewhere in the stews. Would you have your army wallow in the cesspits, lord?"

"Not when *you*"—a thick forefinger accused—"could have drawn him hither. Instead you sent him death."

"The omens were auspicious for death, m'lord," soothed the wizard, thinking, *You fool! Without a true piece of the enemy, a drawing-in was impossible; only a wizard as mighty as I could have sent death.*

"But a dead mouth," Drednore howled, "tells me noth- ing, nothing! Suppose he had allies, fellow conspirators! How can I protect myself against the unknown foes, wizard!"

"M'lord, what danger a serpent with its head cut off? Without this princeling to guide them, your enemies will wither into dry dust. And what to you are dust motes on the wind?"

So he calmed the lord, who forgot that a dust mote on the wind, flying into the eye at the wrong moment, could blind a man to his deathstroke.

Misdew brushed her mistress's hair, over and over, until it was a river of light. Tonight was the Fifth Vigil. Soon her mistress would be united with the Red One. Misdew shivered. Tongues had been very busy, and both women knew what the princess could expect, on her wedding night and thereafter, from her lord-to-be.

"Did you find the Shang-cloth, to match the length my father gave me?"

"No, mistress, I searched the market over. There is nothing in this barbaric town one-half so fine as that your father chose."

"Slut!" The whirl, the slap, were so swift, so vicious, that Misdew, kneeling, was thrown backward. She lay, tears jetting from her eyes, her legs doubled painfully under her. Her howled protests of innocence and industry were punctuated by the loud crack of her mistress's slaps, and the gleeful titters of the other maidservants.

Then Vivyana's hand poised, and she hissed almost soundlessly at her hapless maid, "Did you deliver my message?" Louder, "You faithless slut, dallying by the Temple of Fertility, no doubt! How dare you!"

"No, mistress, never, mistress, I swear it! I but searched to your bidding. Please, mistress, I swear it!" Then she whispered, "I waited and waited. He wasn't there!"

Slap!

"You're overfree with your favors, slut. How if I throw you to my lord's soldiers, for their amusement?"

"No, mistress, no. Please, mistress. Naught but your bidding, I swear!"

Slap!

"I am *not* pleased." *Slap!* "I will have what I desire." *Slap! Slap!* "Return to the markets tomorrow!" *Slap!* "And if you *dare* to return empty-handed"—*Slap!*—"my lord and I will wager"—*Slap!*—"how many of his men can abuse

you"—*Sla-aaap!*—"in the space of a glass!" *Slap! Slap!
Sla—*

The other maidservants continued to watch wide-eyed and giggling. The Lady Vivyana angry at her faithful Misdew—it was as good as a masked drama, it was. None of them thought to wonder if it *was* a staged drama after all; for if Misdew was utterly faithful to her mistress, any or all of the others constantly in attendance to the soon-to-be princess-bride of the mighty Drednore might be equally as faithful—to the tyrant himself.

As Vivyana knelt that night for her fifth night-long vigil, her face glowed with innocence and tender piety. Other worshipers were held back by guards; only a robed priest, lighting candle after candle, droning a long prayer, moved within her view. Nonetheless, the sacred hangings could easily conceal watching eyes. She continued to exude piety and grace.

Only when the priest knelt to light the candles at the altar itself did Vivyana get a good look at his cowl-shrouded face. The faintest of whispers floated to his waiting ears. "How dared you . . . !"

A breath on the breeze answered her. "Tomorrow: you, not the maid."

And he moved on.

She would have loved to have stamped her foot, screamed and spit, indulged in a full-fledged temper tantrum. He must know how impossible that was!

The next day, the giggling, heavily painted girl in a slave's costume, her light veil fluttering as she minced along toward the marketplace, had eyes that didn't match.

Four large, brawny guards, in m'lord's uniform, clumped stolidly along behind her, the view of her thinly clad wriggling bottom scant compensation for another dreary search through the markets.

But to the guards' pleased amazement, while she was rejecting every piece that an oily, perspiring merchant could show her, a whip-lean man with eyes bluer than sapphires approached and, after a certain amount of suspicious, pert derision on her part, smooth-talked her into bringing her guards to "examine his wares in comfort."

The merchant was a clever fellow indeed, the guard captain decided over his third mug of mountain-ice-cooled beer. However he had obtained this leaf-shaded, flower-scented courtyard in someone's private villa, with its merry tinkling fountain, away from the heat and bustle of the market, his effort was going to be amply rewarded, judging by the coos and cries of the handmaiden, as slaves unrolled bolt after bolt of fine cloth before her.

Yes, very well rewarded, the guard captain thought, not allowing himself to be distracted—much—from his duty by the warm, merry-eyed slave girl who brought his beer, lingering within easy reach, ripe body a teasing promise. *He's selling her everything. Even what isn't here!*

". . . embroidered by the ladies of piety with a peacock, that proud-crested bird sacred to the Thunder-lord's Consort Herself, a peacock with its glorious tail spread wide, bejeweled with a hundred glowing eyes . . ." he was saying.

"A cloth which I hear praised," the girl in the slave bracelet sniffed, "but which I cannot see for myself."

"Soon. It is being brought overland with the greatest of care," the merchant continued to praise the cloth. "An emperor would be proud to wear it to his coronation . . . peacock is a sign of the Consort's good favor, great good fortune to wear, greater to give."

The girl dressed as a slave looked very thoughtful.

"There will be a price," said the Old One slowly.

His companion pacing restlessly within the small shabby room had eyes blue as a sun-drenched crystalline bay and hair—when it wasn't hidden under a disfiguring dark dye—of a pure amber gold that would flame in sunlight into a fiery red. (Royal red, that hue was called, legacy of a long-ago princess from a distant isle. Though thanks to the proclivities of the royal males, it now cropped up occasionally on nonroyal heads as well.) For now, in the dimly light room, the flame was in the jewel-blue eyes.

"How many times have I said it, flamen. I will reopen your College of Haruspicers and Divinators, I will see you have a place on the Council instead of the priests of the False One, I will—"

"Nay, my son," the priest interrupted, shifting slightly in his chair, pain flashing across his withered features and being instantly suppressed. "I served your father faithfully, and I would now serve you, to my last efforts, not for what you promise, but to see you restored to your rightful place. But I must warn you: when one disturbs the Sleeping Powers, however rightful the cause, there is always a price. A personal price, a price that may be subtly veiled, not paid at once. And since the benefits are yours, that price will be paid by you."

The blue-eyed man frowned. "I am no Drednore. I'll not pay for my desires with innocent blood."

"That is as it should be, Prince. You are a worthy heir to your father. But suppose . . . there is no other choice?" Brancel bit his lip and, slowly, nodded. "I warn you once again, ere you decide to begin. The price must be paid!"

The sun rose higher and higher in a cloudless sky. At its peak would begin that new day that the auspicers had chosen for the start of the joined reign. At noon, then, Drednore and Vivyana would be married. The palace, the citadel, the city were abuzz with preparations. Already, the Processional Way and the public parts of the temple were packed. People were crushed and suffocating, the foresighted ones eating refreshments they had brought, others either careless or preferring to await the promised bounty. Mouth-watering smells swept out from the royal kitchens.

Drednore was conferring with his generals. As soon as his new lady was big—he anticipated he would be sure in about four months—he intended to start a major campaign.

Vivyana was in her suite, her appearance being polished to its ultimate. Her slaves twittered about her, quivering in excitement and fear. All knew that her once-favorite Misdew had somehow offended either her mistress or the lord Drednore himself and now lay in the palace dungeons, tongueless and weeping.

The Temple of the Fertile Goddess was one of the oldest surviving buildings in the city. It was situated on the walled height, in actuality the crushed remains of nameless earlier cities, that the citizens retreated to in times of siege. Indeed, since the altar was open to the sky, one of the guard towers was plainly visible just behind it, a spear thrust defiantly upward. From either side of the altar, two long-roofed colonnades ran, the space between them a marble-slab arena for sacred ceremonies. At the other end, the entrance boasted a cleverly carved archway between the two roofs, and a long series of steps. Despite the crowds that had already gathered, the open rectangular area down the center of the temple, polished marble gleaming in the sun, was empty except for a chorus of rainbow-hue-robed priests, singing respectful prayers to the Goddess. By the altar was the solitary unmoving figure of the sacrifice.

Finally, faint in the distance, could be heard the sounds of procession, rattle of sistrum, beat of tabor, shuffle of feet, and the shrill piping of the double-flutes.

The triumphant sounds could be heard even in the far-off wizard's lair, and the young acolyte Vow, who should not have been there, bit his lip in angry frustration. Timing was crucial, and those cursed, unexpected guards had delayed him. . . . A last turn in the curving staircase and he faced an open archway. Ominous insignia surrounding the opening should have kept him out—and would have sent any servants unlucky enough to have so far mistaken their way fleeing for their very souls—but he calmly removed certain objects from his pouch and began to pray.

Until, holding his breath, he drew aside a heavy drape and stepped through the archway.

At the temple, the long procession including king and bride had reached the sixty-six steps and started up with measured tread. On either side, guards held back the patient throng. It would be over soon; they had only to mount the steps, cross the marble arena, go through the ceremony, and the marriage would be solemnized, the treaty fulfilled.

Except that, as the head of the train approached the top of the steps, a single figure eluded the guards and stalked to the center of the portico, to stand, arms raised heavenward. "Stop, great lord Drednore," his deep voice tolled. "Cease or face the direct anger of the Gods!"

Two guards ran at the man, swords drawn. "Touch me not," he boomed, "on pain of your souls' torment. The Lord of Thunder speaks through me!"

The guards hesitated.

Again he roared. "Thy souls are at stake! Beware, touch me not, and listen!" Green fire seemed to flash from his fingertips; the silence was so intense even the farthest away of the crowd heard him. "Drednore, listen and heed! The God of this city speaks!"

Vivyana, still heavily veiled, her hair spilling unbound down her back, spoke to the man beside her. "Lord, who is this madman?"

"Just that," he grated through clenched teeth, "a madman. An insane old priest who was thrust from his temple for his senseless mouthings. Better his blood had quenched the stones." He marched boldly upward. "Old man . . ." His harsh voice carried as far as the priest's had. "Old man, step aside. This is my wedding day."

"Nay, Drednore, turn thyself about," the priest retorted. "This day is not thine. I have seen omens, I have seen signs. If thee persists, thee will wed only cruel death this day."

"Signs, omens." Drednore sneered, halting a step or two down, but his eyes level with the priest's. "Old man, your mind is withered. The priests have been examining signs and omens these many weeks, and all agree this day is most auspicious for me."

"They forget the old knowledge, ignore the old Gods. They are not of the Ancient Ones, as I am. I know what I know. I say to thee, beware, Drednore. Thee will kiss death if thee crosses this threshold today."

Drednore put up a hand as though to thrust the old priest aside. "Old man, old madman, get you from my path. Go now, and I will spare you, for joy at my wedding and pity on your scant locks and age-clouded mind.''

"Drednore, I will make thee a sign even thee can know; for thee, I will read the lightning!''

"Lightning!'' Involuntarily, Drednore glanced up at the blue sky without a single cloud to mar its pristine clarity. "Old man, old man, will you read the lightning in such a clear sky?''

"Thee would have omens, Lord Drednore, thee would have signs! I will show thee a sign, I will read the lightning—I will *call* the lightning!''

In the wizard's lair, still droning his protective prayers, young Vow built up the fire to a roaring blaze. No time now to pick and choose. A small laden table went onto the fire. A larger table was too heavy to be moved; methodically he consigned its contents to the flames. A crumbling book, a yellowed skull, a ring of strange design, a candle held in a mummified hand. Another book, a cup filled with dark red liquid, a knife, some vials, boxes, a painted egg . . .

In a cage a one-eyed cat awoke and snarled. Vow cut its throat with another knife, threw cat and knife and cage onto the flames. And felt a clammy hand on his shoulder.

"Behold,'' the old flamen thundered. "I will call the lightning! *Look!*'' His outstretched hands thrust upward, the fingers probed the sky; his head fell back, the hood drooping to reveal straggling gray locks. He began a chant, a repetitious droning keen in an unknown language or perhaps no language at all, a strange haunting plaint that made brave men flinch and women wrap themselves tightly, shivering.

"Stop him!'' Drednore looked down. The mismatched eyes of his bride flashed angry fire. "Spit him on your blade if need be. But stop him!''

"No,'' Drednore snorted. "Let him try and fail. No wizard born can call lightning from an empty sky. The mob will tear him to shreds.''

"So be it, then. You have made your decision.'' She smiled, a woman's smile. "*My* lord will be victorious.''

"His heart will adorn the altar of our joining," Drednore promised. "The haruspicers may examine *his* liver for omens." He growled, his eyes catching the wizard's, "An old man's breath can't last too long."

But it did. The crowd, at first fixed into their places by fear, began to stir, to murmur, to mutter. Only the sacrifice, the man whose blood would seal the climax, stood stiffly, eyes staring blindly, at the base of the altar.

Still the howling continued, like the wind whistling about the eaves at night, or lost souls keening their fate.

Until someone screamed, "Look!" and eyes began to turn.

On the horizon was a black spot no bigger than a fingernail.

Two. The size of a man's whole palm.

Then an arrow, a streak of black, growing, spreading, as though a god's hand had gashed the sky to let black blood spurt from the wound.

And the wind, whipping the old man's hair and cloak, playing with the crowd, tugging their clothing, slapping their faces with ungentle hands.

Vivyana screamed as the wind snatched her veil.

Drednore recognized his peril, drew sword, and strode toward the old man.

Too late. *"I will call lightning!"*

The first shaft of light split the sky with the rumble of a thousand drums. It seemed to strike the tower directly behind the altar. Drednore blinked, striving to see through flash-seared eyes. "Wizard," he howled. Another flash. "Kill me this pestilent priest!"

The wizard had already started a muttered spell; but he stopped, frowning. The lair! Something was wrong, missing, hampering him. The spells were not potent, not forming as they should. Foxi, his apprentice, was dispatched on a run.

Again the wizard began his muttering, glaring at his priestly opponent. During his chant, the old priest had moved backward, within the sanctuary, near the altar itself. Now a stinging downpour joined the lightning and thunder, more than rain—harder, sharper, colder. Hail pattered, then pounded on the open floor of the temple, on the surrounding roof. Those who were already under the shelter were crowded by those exposed, pushing and shoving to escape the angry, punishing onslaught.

As it suddenly began, the hail ceased, leaving a wet, cold, bedraggled crowd to view the last act of the drama.

A last flash of lightning speared through the sky, and in the brilliance of its wake—

A woman screamed.

On the height of the tower, glowing fire-bright in the darkness, stood the Giant of Bronze.

"Drednore!" It was the sacrifice who shouted. "Tyrant, usurper! I challenge you. In the name of those whose throne you savaged away, I will fight your metal monster for the right to fight you! Drednore, coward, answer me!"

Drednore glanced down at the wizard, standing slightly behind him. The wizard nodded, smiling a thin smile.

"You are purified to Her Fertility." Drednore's answer reached the furthest of the packed mob. "Your blood will sweeten her stones—one way or the other. Your fate comes, self-proclaimed champion of the dead!"

The tower was a dozen man-lengths high. The giant plunged in an incredible jump, landing in the open area. The floor screamed but held. Under his feet the aged priest was crushed.

Brancel froze in the act of removing the Sacrifice's Cloak. His mind echoed the old priest's words—a price to pay . . .

But the price (oh, bitter!) *had* been paid; the wizard should not have been able to use the monster to kill the Holy One! What had happened in the wizard's lair, where Vow should have been neutralizing the sources of the Evil One's power?

But he could do nothing for the Old One now. He wrapped the cloak around his left arm, smiling wryly at the flesh-colored glove concealing his identifying left hand, and grasped the sacrificial sword lying on the altar.

With a roar like bubbling molten metal, the giant stalked toward him. He heard Drednore say, "Not too quick, wizard. Make him pay for his insolence." Dripping beard and sodden clothes failed to dim Drednore's angry vitality.

The old priest was a lifeless husk, and the giant was coming.

Brancel moved to meet it.

What had happened in the lair?

Vow the young priest whirled when the hand touched his shoulder. Facing him was the human avatar of the Bronze Giant, a hulking, hairless, muscular brute.

And voiceless.

Involuntarily, Vow stepped back. "Avaunt thee!" he squeaked. Frantically, he tried to remember a spell of exorcism.

"Huh-uh-uh-uh," the human giant panted. "Uh-uh, uh-uh-uh!" Again the massive hand clamped on the priest's shoulder.

"I—I—" the youngster stammered. This human monster could hold him, disable him, crack his bones as easily as a cook cracking eggs. Fear blanked his mind, robbed him of the protective spells, his tongue as useless as his opponent's.

"Huh-uh-uh," the giant forced out. "Huh-uh-*uh-uh!*"

"Please—I—I don't—*PLEASE!*"

"*HUH-UH-UH!*" He grabbed and shook, and the slightly built priest dangled from his hands, limbs flapping helplessly, a child pitted against an angry adult. "*HUH-UH-UH!*" He let go, and the young man crumpled to the floor, half-stunned—but with enough spirit left to fumble for the dagger in his belt.

"*HUH-UH-UH-UH!*" A thick finger pointed, jabbing, emphasizing each grunted "*UH!*" Vow's gaze followed that forceful finger.

"Wha—what?"

"*HUH! UH! UH!*" Point! Point! Point!

The priest's eyes widened. "Up *there?* Something up there—*into the fire?*"

Huge hands set him on his feet. "*UH! UH!*" (Nod, nod!)

The young priest was wearing a thigh-length tunic; he held the skirt of it up with one hand and swept everything off the shelf into the pocket thus formed with the other.

The giant shoved him toward the fire.

"Stop!" The priest turned clumsily, holding his burdened tunic with both hands. Framed in the doorway was Foxi, the sly apprentice, his eyes knowing and cynical. "So-oooo . . ."

He smiled, drew his dagger, stepped into the room. "You lazy laggard, Dummox. *Hold* him!"

Vow was hampered by his treasures, still paces away from the all-important fire. Once again, two huge hands clamped on his shoulders.

The strides of the Giant of Bronze were thrice the length of an ordinary man's. His sword crashed down, and Brancel raised the sacrificial sword to guard himself. He felt the shock of those two blades meeting clear to his toes.

Another clash. His head rang, his fingers were numb. The sacrificial sword was meant to be wielded with both hands. He skipped back, clumsily dragging the heavy sword, toward the altar.

With a clang that made his teeth ache, the monster's sword came down a third time—and his own sword was flung away by the force of the blow.

The immense sword poised for the deathstroke.

"*Slowly,* I said, wizard. Let his hideous death be a warning!"

The blade shifted, and a metal hand reached out. Brancel danced aside, the metal fingers missing by a hairsbreadth.

Brancel screamed. Where the fingers had come so near, ferocious pain ate at him. The crowd gasped at the black mark on his side, the stench of burnt meat.

The giant herded the naked man toward the altar. More blackened wounds appeared: shoulder, thigh, chest. Brancel's world was drowning in pain. He stumbled backward, help-less, seeing doom approaching inexorably, hearing the bel-lowing laugh of his enemy. The altar-cloth tangled in his feet, and he fell heavily against the stone.

"Slowly, slowly," gloated a loud voice. "Let's hear him scream some more."

Torment loomed over him. Brancel's fingers fumbled, a weapon, *anything!* His hand closed over a chased goblet.

"The Goddess has been promised *blood,* rash one. Think you Her milk will protect you?" Crude laughter. "Sear his manhood! That should make him bellow!" The metal mon-ster leaned down, fingers reaching.

Brancel flung the contents of the goblet in its face.

*   *   *

At the same time, in the wizard's lair, the young priest
Vow found himself staring down at the fire, not quite sure
how he had arrived there. Behind him a curse, a muffled
cr-rack, a wordless bubbling moan.

He hurled the contents of his tunic into the hungry flames.

Brancel heard a hissing scream, like a molten sword
quenched in water. The monster staggered back.

(Flames ate avidly at a carved box.)

The monster writhed, keening in the center of the arena.
Brancel forced his abused body up against the altar in a
standing position. His arm pointed at the somehow fluid
monster. In the horrified, hiss-broken silence, his weak voice
carried. "I stand on the Goddess's altar. Let Her justice be
done!"

(A wooden box burst into flames, its contents snapping
and crackling as they burned.)

Out of the sky, a flash of lightning smashed down on the
fallen giant with eye-searing fury. The mob surged backward, screaming. When their vision cleared, there was only
an immense pool of frothing, bubbling, burning metal on the
floor.

"Drednore!" Brancel's voice was drowned by the mob's
noise. "Drednore—I won—right—mortal challenge."

Drednore roared with laughter. "You are the Goddess's
meat; the Goddess will have Her blood. Priests! Let the
sacrifice commence!" He whirled in his tracks, strode down
the long length of the arena, avoiding the hissing molten
pool, his cloak swirling behind him. His cloak—that unique
cloth, embroidered in a monastery by knowing, holy hands,
sold to a slave with mismatched eyes, a gift from a princess
to her lord-to-be, that cloak wetted and drying, so that some
of its colors altered, or ran, or smeared together.

In the light of that dreadful, glowing pool, Drednore's
back was plainly visible to the mob. They began to murmur,
to mutter—to shout.

"He on the altar called to the Goddess for justice."

"The Goddess spoke once, the giant is destroyed."

"Look on his back, has the Goddess not spoken a second time?"

"The Goddess will have her blood!"

"Drednore!"

"BLOOD!"

Drednore never realized that he no longer wore a cloak with the Goddess's peacock. Instead, the rain had given him the dark side of the Goddess, a gargoyle face with snakes for hair, a necklace of skulls, and a bloody mouth.

The guards were brushed aside, stunned, trampled, crushed helpless within the mob.

Drednore was skilled and strong and valiant; he sold his life dearly. When it was over, someone tossed the priceless, betraying cloak onto the burning pool, where it crisped and blackened into ashes. Motes on the wind . . .

Brancel saw none of it. Pain had conquered. He lay unconscious on the altar, surrounded by solemn priests.

In the wizard's lair, a numb Vow knelt by the dying survivor of the struggle between the Evil One's two assistants. "He broke my back," the sly Foxi gasped, "*after* I buried my knife in him to the hilt."

"I'll pray for your soul."

"Better—ah, the pain!—speed my passage."

After, the young priest closed the eyes of both corpses—strange, how the silent one had smiled before his face dissolved into death's blankness—and said the proper prayers. Later, he would arrange burial. For now—

The wizard met him halfway down the curving staircase. "Ahhhhhh," breathed the wizard in satisfaction. Some time later, the wizard left tower and city for good, and the lair burst into flames. When the fire burned down to ashes, there was nothing left save a few bits of twisted metal that might once have been a dagger—or a priest's amulet.

Brancel recovered slowly. Many days later, he opened weak eyes onto an opulent palace room. Priests and slaves fluttered anxiously around him. He was fed, bathed, cared for—but no one would speak directly to him.

He was propped on a lounge beside a window, enjoying
the warmth of the sun, when Vivyana finally came, trailing a
retinue of priests and nobles.

"Chosen of the Goddess, I greet you." Her voice was
serene. "I regret that matters of state have up to now prevented me from thanking you properly."

"My Lady Vivyana," he said formally, "I live to serve
you."

"I accept your *homage.*" She smiled.

He was stunned. "But I am . . ."

"You are the Chosen of the Goddess," she interrupted
firmly. "What matter what you *were*—" She raised her hand
imperiously. "Don't speak. I don't want to know. You are
now the Goddess's Chosen Vessel, and great honor will be
yours."

"My Lady Vivyana—" He started angrily.

"My son," quavered a counselor who had been old when
his father reigned, "I know that you are overwhelmed, you
feel you are unworthy. But you have earned all that is to
come, and we must never be remiss in our devoirs to our
Lady Goddess."

"But—" He stared into Vivyana's mismatched eyes. Surely
you recognize me, he wanted to say. I am *Brancel!* But he
couldn't. Because she did know him, and he knew it, and she
knew he knew. Her eyes glittered—triumphantly.

The ancient counselor babbled on. "You will be Consort,
my son, sire of kings. Not ruler yourself, of course; but with
the deaths of all of our royal line and the usurper Drednore—"

Brancel growled, deep in his throat.

"*My* grandmother, you may not be aware"—purring like a
liver-stuffed cat, Vivyana staked her claim—"was sister of
the late king's father."

"So the council has agreed," the oldest went on, "that the
Lady Vivyana, she who would have been our Prince Brancel's
bride, shall rule us as Regina, regent for her children to
come." He bowed to Brancel. "*Your* children, honored Vessel." A querulous, old-man's frown. "We will need to choose
a warlord, a general. Among our nobles—"

"Later." Vivyana's voice rang with hard command. "I

have cousins aplenty, though not sharing the blood of your—
our—royal line.''

Brancel knew how he must appear, weak, scarred, heavily
covered despite the heat of the day. ''My Lady Vivyana,
when I recover—''

''I know what is bothering you!'' She clapped her hands,
her voice a peal of girlish joy. ''Despite my orders, someone
has told you how much you resemble the Prince Brancel, he
who was to have been my liege, how I called *his* name when
I saw you, lying dead it seemed, on the altar.'' She patted his
hand. ''You fear I will look at you and see him, resent you
because you are alive and he''—she squeezed out a tear—''is
dead.'' She patted his hand again, smiling oh-so-sweetly.
''Put it from your thoughts. True, in a dim light, with your
eyes closed, there is some resemblance—but you are not so
very like, you see. Oh, the face, more than a little, but his
hair was burnished gold, and his eyes blue. And while golden
hair may turn lighter or darker with age, blue eyes cannot
turn white, now can they? Do white eyes run in your family,
Chosen One? I confess, I never saw eyes the color of fresh
cream before.''

He could have moaned loudly, or laughed bitterly, at the
lovely, deadly irony. The price paid, for meddling in the
affairs of gods and men. The Sly One's two-edged price. He
had paid, what he thought was the whole, that part of his
masculine beauty he most prized. After the ceremony, when
he had looked in the polished bronze, and seen the hair that
had been spun gold, the eyes that had been blue . . .

If he tried to claim his heritage now, who would uphold
him? The old priest was dead, the younger—missing. Too
young to have known Prince Brancel before the downfall,
though he had witnessed the change. The counselors? Nobles?
Killed by Drednore, or old, blind, faithless. No, without the
priest at his side, without Vivyana's acceptance—faithless
witch! *How came you by your mismatched eyes, Vivyana!*
She smiled again, a smile that told him—much.

She had not been forced unwilling to Drednore's side, not
ambitious, sly, greedy Vivyana. Who could now betray to sit

on her throne instead of beside it. With her prince, too, at her command, her toy, her slave, her—Consort!

Not if he could prevent it!

He put a hand to his forehead. "The temple—I remember—a little. But before—before—" He frowned. "White eyes in my family—my family—my *family*—"

She patted his hand again, but he could sense puzzlement. "No matter. The Goddess chose you. That is sufficient."

"Yes." Now he could be firm. "The Goddess chose me. Lady, you would honor me beyond my wildest dreams, I would have served you until my last breath." *True. I would never have challenged Drednore and his wizard for the throne of my fathers alone.* "But where the Goddess has placed Her mark—and I feel Her brand burned deep within me, deep in my soul as these scars mark my body. I know, have known for days now, I am Hers, I must journey abroad. The Goddess wills it."

Angrily, "You have said naught of any such journey."

"Lady," softly, "I could scarce speak. But it is *so*. I am for the Goddess's shrine at Abana."

"But that—that's months' journey away!"

Exactly! "Yes, lady. Yet as soon as I can travel, I must leave." *Or sooner, ere you decide I am a threat after all, and speed me on a longer journey. And—could the Goddess's Hand be in this in truth? Why did I say Abana, famed for its healing? These scars . . .*

He listened, nodding solemnly, speaking shyly, the picture of an ordinary man overwhelmed by being Chosen, awed by Vivyana, devastated by her loss.

Firm on only one point: Abana.

Perchance, he couldn't help thinking, *I could learn somewhat of the healing art there myself. There's precious little future in being an uncrowned ex-prince.*

It was the Goddess's mercy that Lady Vivyana didn't see his expression following her out the room. *I hope you believe me, witch, so you won't have me slaughtered in my weakness. But living or dead, I'll have my revenge. Your father's a strong king, he'll protect you while he lives. But his sons are paltry, and you're the child of his old age. When he dies . . .*

You've made yourself into a prize worth having. They'll quarrel over you, the warlords, the ambitious nobles, the petty kinglets who would be kings, and tear you to pieces among themselves like a wild dog's prey. . . .

I've never had the gift of prophecy. Lightning, livers, a flock of birds held no hidden meanings for me. I wonder if the Goddess grants me this, this certainty of the ugly fate of she who has betrayed me, in exchange for all I have lost?

There is always a price, that wise old man said, a personal price, a price that may be subtly veiled, paid later and not at once.

You'll pay that price, Vivyana. And pay . . . and pay . . . and pay!

BRIGHT-EYED BLACK PONY

Nancy Springer

WYSTAN SAW THEM COMING FROM AFAR.

Coming through the forest, the tall black horse running
between the twisted trees, so black in the somber shadows,
the rider like a burr entangled in its mane, clinging, curled
small against the assaults of twigs and boughs. Presently, as
they came to a clearing, the rider straightened. He was but a
slim youngster straddling the great war-horse, a lad with
golden hair that flowed down around his shoulders and a long
red cloak that reached nearly to his booted feet. Wearily he
braced himself by his hands against the arch of the steed's
neck as the horse plunged to a shying halt. Before him lay
nothing but water, the wizard's lake, a seemingly endless
expanse dimming into dusk and nothingness within a few
furlongs.

"Forward," the youngster ordered.

The horse danced backward, threatening to rear. Swaying
behind the steed's withers, the rider kicked and shouted,
raising a willow whip. Mastered, the black leaped forward,
splashed through shallows and swam with rolling eyes and
vast nostrils toward an unnatural gloom. Dark mist or midday
dusk—once in it, the horse could see nothing; rider, nothing.
Nothing.

*The steed's breath comes roaring in its chest; how long
can it last? Why do I care, I, the recluse?*

Blaze of bright sunshine and wooded shore. The horse

183

scrambled out of the water and stood, trembling and breathing in great heaves, on the island.

A different sort of place, this of my making. I am a fool to let him set foot on it. But he would have drowned. . . . Such a slip of a lad to come here so boldly on the great horse.

The youngster was staring as the horse caught its breath. Blue trees, slender, graceful as dancers, upreaching, with smooth skin of pearl blue and leaves blue as lapis. Presently he sent his winded steed through them at the slow walk, gazing as if half-frightened. Fear that no longer pursued him, sending him fleeing, but confronted him, slowing his headlong course . . . Forest ended at a sunny tilled clearing.

"Ho," the lad murmured, and the horse stopped willingly.

Amber meadowland, chickens, sheep. A wisp of a rill leading up to a spring. A crazy sod cottage all in turrets and oriels, shapes no sod should take. An ordinary garden: rye, beans, cabbages . . . A man, his strong, bare back turned to the sun, working the earth amidst the plants.

Swallowing, licking his dry lips, the youngster sent the horse forward, and the man straightened and watched intently as the rider approached. Meadow, rill, edge of the garden. The boy slipped down off his big black and covered it with his cloak before he spoke.

"I have come to see the sorcerer," he said, his voice tight but level.

"And who might you be who come to see Wystan?" the laborer asked.

"I'll tell that to Wystan alone," the lad replied, tone hardening into sharp edge. He glanced angrily at his questioner, but the glance stayed and became a stare. The man stood lean, sturdily muscled, his mouth a flat line across the dun mask of his face. And his eyes, beneath brows as flat as his mouth, eyes like polished stone, unreadable.

"I see," the youngster said, his voice still tight and steady. "You are Wystan himself. I beg pardon, but I did not expect to find you planting spinach."

"Parsley," the sorcerer corrected him, unsmiling. He held up a pinch of the fine seed. "And there is more magic in this than in all my spells."

The boy stood at a loss for a reply. "As for my name," he said after a pause, reverting to the former matter, "it is Merric, son of Emaris, prince in Yondria. My father was the ruler until lately. My uncle killed him and killed my older brothers, and now he sits on my father's throne and keeps my mother his prisoner." The lad spoke collectedly, almost coldly.

"Assuming that this is true," said the sorcerer harshly, "what do you want of me? I take no part in the quarrels of princes." Wystan gave the youngster a piercing glance. Merric met his sharp stare unmoved.

Some sort of bitter strength in him. Not grief, perhaps, but certainly desperation.

"I want refuge, nothing more." Merric's shoulders straightened beneath his fine tunic of silk. "No one comes here. They are afraid."

"And are you not afraid?" Wystan asked with a hint of threat.

"Yes. Somewhat." Merric looked straight into the stonelike eyes.

There it is, that odd strength still! Yet the lad is lying; I feel sure of it.

"But I deemed a man of wisdom would feel no need to harm a child."

Wystan's face moved; his mouth twisted ironically. "A child, is it, now, when it suits you? You who make shift to ride the steed of a man, a warrior? Go away."

Merric stood where he was. "This is the horse my father has given me," he said hotly, "and not of my asking."

"So you are a child, then. Am I your nursemaid? I welcome no strangers here." *I dare not.* "Folk do well to fear me. Go."

"You cannot send me away!" the boy blazed. "You are—you are curious about me."

Now how in all the seven kingdoms did he know that? Is the youngster wizard get?

Man and Merric stood glaring at each other. Insects ticked away the moments amidst the grass.

"Very well," said Wystan at last. "Stay, then. But that

great horse must go. This is only an island; there is not sufficient pasturage for him here.''

Merric stiffened, turning his head to look at the black steed which stood sweating and puffing with its head drooping to its knees.

I could provide such pasturage, but I will not. This is a small test for you, my bold one.

"The beast is far too big for you, anyway," the sorcerer added scornfully. "It is as ridiculous to see a child on such a destrier as it is to see a big man on a pony."

"True enough. I had to climb the stall side-bars to get onto him." Merric looked stricken. "But he carried me here bravely."

"Take him down to the shore," said Wystan indifferently, "and let him swim back."

"But no, I cannot do that! He is stable bred; he would come to harm on his own. I will . . ." Merric swallowed, and his thin shoulders sagged. "I will take him back."

True for you, lad. Though now I am certain you lie. Back to what?

Defeated, the boy turned numbly, feet scraping, gathering up the reins.

"Gently, Prince, gently." Wystan took a step closer to Merric and the tall steed. "If it is verily the horse you feel for, and not your own pride in his size and beauty . . ."

"I am no longer a prince," said Merric, "and there is some pride in me, yes, but more chiefly a wish to do no harm."

That is interesting. Harm whom?

The lad was watching the wizard.

"Then see here," Wystan said, and fixing his inscrutable eyes on something in the distance, he laid a hand on the horse's lowered forehead. As Merric watched, the great black steed shuddered, shrank, and changed somewhat in shape, until all in the moment it was a bright-eyed, shaggy black pony. It lifted its head and glanced about curiously. The red cloak dragged by small ebony hooves.

"Bigness is a great burden," said Wystan, "for man and

beast alike.'' His voice was gentler than before, and something had changed in his face, his eyes.

"Many thanks.'' Merric's voice shook, he was surprised by childish tears. Blinking to hide them, he turned away, patted the pony, bent to retrieve his cloak. But Wystan frowned, for the boy had staggered as he moved.

"When have you last eaten, Merric?'' he inquired sharply.

"Some few days ago. I was in haste.''

"And would it have been above you to beg a bite from some peasant, or from me? Come on!'' Wystan took the boy by his arm.

"I—must see to the black—''

"The beast is fine; look!'' The sorcerer was shouting in exasperation. "His weariness is gone with his bulk. Come on!'' He tugged the lad into his cottage, plainly furious.

Hours later Merric was fed, more or less washed, and bedded down in a pile of straw. Wystan sat close to the hearth fire, reading by its ruddy light, and Merric watched him sleepily.

"Your face is completely changed,'' he said when the sorcerer had closed the book.

For a moment Wystan went rigid; then he sighed, softened, and nodded. His eyes were glimmering, deep as the lake on which his island floated, and his lips moved in curves as subtle as its shores.

"I wore a mask earlier, as we all do from time to time.'' Wystan glanced at the boy. "As you still do. Have you not wept for your father and your brothers?''

"There was no time!'' Merric snapped, all his sleepiness gone. "I had to ride or die!''

"But now there is time.''

Merric did not answer. He stirred uneasily.

"I cannot see them in your eyes, your father and your brothers, your mother and uncle,'' the sorcerer said. "Tell me about them. Their names?''

"Some other time,'' Merric muttered. He turned his face away, pretending to sleep, and Wystan smiled.

He will stay here until he has ceased to hide.

The next day Merric rested, for the most part. The cottage

seemed larger than it looked, all in towers and alcoves; he explored it. But a day later he went to look for his host. He took the black pony and hauled water from the spring to the garden, for the season was dry. Wystan had set up a big loom in the sunshine and was weaving a blanket out of wool. Though the cloth was coarse, it was long, tedious work. The sorcerer sat patiently on a tall stool, sending the shuttle back and forth.

"That is woman's work," Merric told him peevishly.

"Very well," Wystan remarked and instantly changed into a muttering crone who puttered about with the warp and weft. Merric stepped back, startled and frightened.

"Which one is you?" he cried.

"Which one is you?" the crone cackled back. "Which is you, the prince or the water-bearer?" Merric fled, and she laughed heartily as he trudged up the dusty hill to the spring.

Time after time, that day and the next, he led the pony down with clay pitchers full of water and poured them in futile-looking patches on the arid earth. The third day he did the same. But when the sun was high, Wystan spoke to him, and he changed his pitchers for baskets and led the pony toward the forest to gather fuel. His legs ached with walking; the way seemed long. The pony plodded and nipped at weeds, as a pony will.

"Come on, damn you!" Merric shouted, for perhaps the dozenth time that day, tugging hard at the strap. This time, being out of sight of the cottage, he lashed the little beast on the belly with the whiplike leather end. The pony gave a frightened leap, showing the whites of its eyes, and Merric turned away from it to lash fervidly at the trees. In a moment his shoulders slumped, his hands went slack. Frightened yet further by this odd and perverse flogging, the pony lunged away from him, snatching the lead from his loosened hands, and it galloped back toward the cottage, its hooves making a sound as of stamping rabbits.

There was still the wood to be gotten in. Hardening his face, Merric followed the black pony.

It had taken refuge with Wystan and was grazing placidly beside his loom when Merric plodded into view. He went to the pony softly and picked up the trailing lead strap. Wystan seemed to take no notice. Merric turned—

"Do not go," said Wystan tonelessly from behind the loom, "if you are going to beat the little black. I can fetch wood myself."

"I do not mean to," Merric said in a muffled voice, but even as he spoke his arms stiffened, his hands clenched into fists. He flung away the lead line, let himself drop to the hard, dry earth, pummeled it.

"Damn the beast," he cried, "it was the power and beauty of it that I loved, to my shame. Now that it is a drudge, like me . . ." His tears sprinkled the sere earth.

"Now I know for certain," said Wystan coldly, "that you are, as you said, a child."

"Damn you too!" Merric shouted at him.

So who is the child here? For all his spleen, I think he is not one to hide himself for long on a mystic isle.

Merric was struggling up, tears spent, turning away, bound away somewhere, anywhere. Wystan got up from his loom and went to stand beside him, stopping him with a touch.

"We are all children," he said far more softly. "And the most part of grief is rage. So weep for your dead."

Merric faced him, unable to hide from his eyes, unable to do otherwise than face the one he had just cursed. "I lied," he told him, hot fury shaking the words. "My father and brothers are not dead. I wish they were! I hate them!"

Wystan nodded, odd glinting lights swimming into his gaze. "Yes . . . and the most part of your rage is grief."

"I hate them, I could kill them, I fled from my own hatred!" Merric shouted, tears starting again. "By my soul, Wizard, what manner of monster am I?"

Wystan snorted. "You'll have to study long to be a monster."

"But . . ."

" 'Twas not I who stayed your hand from flogging yon pony. I or anyone else. You did it yourself."

"But . . ."

"But nothing!" Wystan roared. *Furious. Furious at him*

for making me feel. "It is past noon; would you fetch the wood? There is no fuel for a cooking fire, and I am hungry."

"I—am sorry—"

"Stop whimpering." Wystan glowered darkly. "You are worthy of whatever friendship you can wring from me, and not because you are a prince, either. Because you are here; no better reason. Go fetch wood."

Merric went, afoot and with the baskets over his arms, leaving the pony to graze.

The cottage stood silent that evening, and Merric went early to his bed. Much later, after Wystan was asleep, the prince got up and quietly went out. Wystan was awake instantly upon the soft closing of the door, following Merric anxiously with his mind's eye.

I—had not thought he was of the sort to run away. Not more than once—

Then the sorcerer sighed and smiled, a genuine, warm smile with no one to see it. The prince had gone to the moonlit meadow, searching for a certain dark and shaggy form, and when he had found it, an ungainly, soot-colored lump dozing on the ground, he had curled up beside the warm, furry flank of the black pony. Wystan watched him for a long time as he slept with his face half-buried in the coarse mane.

Merric came in groggily for breakfast the next morning. "You smell of horse," Wystan told him.

Merric said nothing, only made a small face at him over the food.

"I can see them in your eyes now," Wystan remarked after the eggs were gone. "Your father, your brothers. I do not think they intended to be cruel to you."

"Perhaps not." Merric sighed, pushing his plate away. "Perhaps it is just that—they are interested only in power and the usages of power, indifferent to everything else."

"And they assume that your interests are the same."

"I must wear a royal cloak, ride a tall horse—" Merric stopped himself, recalling how he had missed that horse. "I am not so much unlike them," he admitted. "But—they are indifferent to the other things in me, things they do not care to see—"

"Poetry," said Wystan.

And magic too, I think. Though I will not say so at this time.

"I suppose," said Merric in some small surprise. He gave the sorcerer a searching glance. "How did you know?"

"I merely surmised," Wystan hedged, and the boy did not persist, for another thought shadowed his face.

"I daresay I should go back." Reluctance dragged at the words. "They will be looking for me, and they will be angry."

"I think not angry," said the sorcerer, for he knew family. But he had been doing some questing, three days past, and he had seen no sign of searchers in the forest beyond the lake or the meadows beyond the forest, the villages, the strongholds, no one looking for the golden-haired prince. Odd. Sufficiently odd to make him uneasy.

"Stay a few days yet," he told Merric. "If anger there is, it will have passed into fear by then, and they will welcome you home the more ardently."

"I am willing enough to stay," said Merric.

Rain had come to water the garden. They spent the day in the cottage, animals and all. Merric brushed the cockleburrs from the black pony's mane, then turned to Wystan for amusement. Presently the sorcerer found himself showing the boy his books, talking of his craft, telling tales, describing wonders, talking as he had not talked to another mortal in perhaps a decade. They did some small magics at the table, laughing, making a marvelous game of it. Supper was late. Rain darkened into dusk and wind and thunder, fearsome, but the cottage felt snug. Merric slept peacefully on his bed of straw, and that night Wystan slumbered soundly.

Thus it was that he did not sense the stranger's coming.

The man pounded at the door in the darkest of the dark hours before dawn, and Wystan stood rigid, shocked stark awake in consternation. No one had ever come upon him so unawares, not since he had withdrawn to his magical island. No one.

I have let down my defenses, somehow—

Merric merely stirred drowsily on his pallet of straw.

"For the love of mercy!" the man cried in the night, and Wystan stirred up the fire for light, then moved stiffly to the door, his face a mask. The stranger stumbled in, soaking, out of the downpour.

"Sorcerer," he appealed, "I am the most miserable of mortals."

A stocky man, one who was losing the battle with age. Face pulled downward now in long, haggard collops of flesh that looked gray even in the firelight. Wystan let his mask slip for a moment in his astonishment, for this was the man he had seen in Merric—though the fellow's look then had been one of authority.

"I am King Emaris of Yondria." Just a hint, a flash, of the authoritarian in those words, at once gone. "Or, until four days past I was. . . . My sons have turned against me. My sons, my very own blood and get, have turned on me to strike me down." The king spoke in a torrent, tempestuously, glaring all the while intensely at the sorcerer, scarcely noticing the youthful servant or apprentice who stood in the shadows beyond the hearth. "My eldest, Morveran, and the next younger, Emerchion, they who were supposed to be the comfort of my old age, though as of yet scarcely past their passage—they have plotted together and seized my crown and throne. Only by grace of my wits have I escaped with my life. And the youngest, Merric, has gone into hiding somewhere, in league with them to get himself out of the way of their scheme—"

"I have not!"

Merric strode forward to confront his father.

No loving reunion, this.

The prince was full of shock and wrath. "I would never—I have been here all along. I abhor—if you knew how I despise all such schemes of power—"

But Emaris did not answer the anger, for all his passions were lost in astonishment. "Merric!" he whispered. "But—when did you come here? And *how* did you come here?"

"Five days ago. Or six . . ." The youngster stood more quietly before his father. "The black swam me across."

"But—that crossing—" The king shook his head dazedly.

"It is fearsome. The haze, the gloom, unnatural. Only my desperation gave me courage to try it. And my despair gave me no choice. . . . And my dapple-gray carried me through the darkened day and into the tempest of the night, until finally it foundered and sank, and I swam on alone. And only at the limit beyond limits of my strength did I make the shore. So how could you, a youngling . . . ?"

"I am no stranger to despair," said Merric very quietly. But he had never known such despair in his father. King and youngest son stood gazing at each other as if they had never seen each other before, and watching, Wystan forgot to harden his face.

I—have let myself be drawn nearer to that peopled shore. My island floats closer to it, even as I sleep. Else he would never have attained it . . .

"My mother?" Merric asked at last.

"She is in safety on your uncle's estate. In hiding. There is a small cottage in the wood. . . ." Emaris let his words trail away, thinking. But it was the boy who voiced his thought.

"My brothers are not evil youths. They would not have harmed you or my mother, I think. They let you escape."

"Yes. However roughly."

"They are impatient. They think too much of power."

"I have taught them all too much of the usages of power," said Emaris, and for the first time he looked kingly, speaking his regret. He straightened himself, and the haggard look left his face. Wystan stirred uneasily.

"King," he addressed him, not calling him liege, for he gave allegiance to no monarch, "King, what is it that you want of me?"

"Hope."

Food and a warm fire, dry clothing and sleep half answered that, and the wizard bestowed them. Emaris slept past noon of the next day. But Merric was wakeful and troubled, and wandered the woods with the black pony as Wystan sat at his loom.

"What ails you?" the sorcerer asked him curtly as he sat by his father at the evening meal of bread and cold mutton.

Merric did not hesitate, though he had to swallow twice before he spoke. "I feel that what has happened is somehow my fault," he said softly, and Wystan snorted.

"How so?" he demanded. Emaris listened intently.

"My—spleen, my hatred—"

"That is a child's talk. Feelings don't count. Deeds do."

Child's talk, is it? Feelings have made me flinty. Feeling breached, invaded. How long has it been—?

"But," Merric said, words rising on a wind of desperation, "I—thought of something like this, or imagined it, blood shed for the sake of power and the throne. I—and I did not face it, it frightened me. I fled from it."

"So that is what sent you here," said Emaris, wonder in the words.

"I—should have stayed. Perhaps—they would have been ashamed, in front of me."

"It was a cruel time, lad," said his father with fervor. "Far too fearsome for a youngster. You were well out of it."

"And speak no more of fault," Wystan told Merric sternly. "Of foresight, perhaps, but not of fault. The Sight, misunderstood."

Emaris turned to him. "You mean—the boy has—"

"The Sight, and perhaps some powers. Yes. I think so."

"Well." The former king stared at his son. "He was always—different. And I, like a fool, I combatted it."

"If his powers can now be nurtured, he might yet mean your hope."

"We can go to the cottage, join your mother, bide our time." Emaris leaned toward his son. "And when you are ready—the throne. Perhaps not for me. Perhaps for you."

Merric stood up, shaking, his face taut with anger no longer hidden. "I detest such schemes of power," he said in a voice potent with fury. "I will have no part of plots of power, now or ever, power of magic, power of the sword; I do not want them. Nor do I want the throne."

"You've small choice, my son." Emaris stood up as well, but not to intimidate, nor to plead, only, for once, to speak truth. "Your brothers will quarrel—see if your Sight does not tell you the same. There will be turmoil, black times for courtiers and common folk alike. The throne will tremble. Invaders will come, they who always lie in wait. Yondria will fall—unless the rightful king can save her.''

Merric turned and ran outside, into the gathering dusk, fleeing over the meadow to take refuge with the black pony.

"Where has he gone?'' Emaris exclaimed.

"Never mind.'' Wystan stood, keen-eyed, nodding to himself. "He will be back soon enough. He is not one to hide for long.''

Unlike one whom I know. It was not the father so much, the mother—though they did not understand me, they tried to love me, but I would not let them, and I scarcely understand myself, I, the great sorcerer. And it was not the comrades who had their own concerns, or the sweethearts, the ones who spurned my timid courtship, or even that one special beloved, she who loved another. So I swore never to let myself be hurt again. But it was all these things—and no one of them nearly as bad as what has happened to this man, this boy. And they will soon find their way back to the fray.

In the morning the boy was at the door with the pony. The little black had been brushed until its shaggy fur shone; its full mane had been brushed and combed into a silken fall, its ebony hooves polished with oil.

"Is that—your charger?'' Emaris let his jaw drop in astonishment.

"I like him like this.'' Merric hugged the black pony around the neck; its head stood no higher than his. "But if he is to carry my father and me homeward,'' the boy added with a reluctant glance at Wystan, "I suppose he will need to be tall again.''

"Stand back,'' said Wystan. He came forward, caressed the pony under its chin, and it shot up again into a war-horse of eighteen hands' height, powerful and graceful.

"Well.'' Emaris swallowed. "We must both thank you, Sir Sorcerer.''

Wystan said nothing, only brought a packet of food and a blanket, new woven. He glanced at Merric, gave a small, wry smile. There was that between the two of them that went deeper than words, than thanks. The wizard stood by silently as the boy bridled the giant black.

There were no surprises for me, anymore, until these two came.

"You take the reins," Emaris told his son. "He is accustomed to you." The man mounted, helped the boy up before him.

"Come back, someday, and be my apprentice," Wystan said to Merric. "I will send the island to meet you sooner next time."

"You . . ." Merric gaped at him. "You did that?"

"Even as I send it closer to the shore now, for your sake."

"Come with us, rather," Emaris offered, "and be his tutor." But Wystan shook his head.

To leave my longtime refuge? Unthinkable . . .

It was an awkward parting. Father and son rode away, hands half-raised, hesitant, in farewell, and the wizard stood darkly, wrapped in himself. His hands did not move out of the folds of his tunic. Before the black horse had traversed the meadow, the boy chirruped, and it broke into a canter, then passed out of Wystan's eyesight, into the lapis forest.

Nor did he watch it any longer with his inner eye.

Mount, man, and boy found the island shore. Beyond the quiet water of the lake, the mainland showed plainly in the distance, unobscured by any hint of mist or haze. Sunlight rested on the green hilltops.

"Forward," Merric ordered.

The black steed leaped into the water, swam strongly. The mainland soon grew nearer, but the shore just departed seemed to fall no farther behind. Merric glanced back at it, puzzled, and then Emaris. It took the two of them several moments to comprehend.

"By my body," the former king exclaimed at last, "it's following us!"

Black hooves caught on gravel bottom. The horse carried them onto the shore of their homeland. Once on grass, Merric pulled his destrier to a halt, turned. Father and son watched as if spellbound while the island glided up to the main as gracefully as a tall-masted sailing ship coming to port. It joined almost seamlessly to the shore.

Wordlessly they got down off their horse and waited. In a few moments Wystan appeared from between the blue trees, walking fast, with a neatly wrapped bundle on his back and a staff in his hand. He stepped to the mainland. But the feel of that unmagical earth seemed to stagger him for a moment, and Merric and Emaris went quickly to his side. Wystan let his hand rest on the shoulder of the boy.

And as they watched, the island sailed away, into the distances of the nameless lake, into a bright sunlit haze, into oblivion.

I—swam out there, years ago, thinking to drown. The island formed itself out of my dreams as I went under. . . . I climbed back to life by clinging to the roots of it. Now it is gone.

Not even the great black steed could carry three.

"Well," said Emaris gruffly, "let us all walk together, then, and the horse can bear the packs."

"A pack animal," Wystan stated, "ought to be of a more manageable size. Do you not think so?"

Emaris merely smiled, but Merric nodded eagerly, his eyes shining.

Then Wystan turned to the mighty war-horse. It put its head down to greet him, and he laid one hand on the glossy mane between the ears. The steed whinnied gladly, gathering, shifting shape beneath his touch. When he took his hand away, standing on the shore was a small, bright-eyed black pony.

COMMON WOMEN:
UNCOMMON HEROINES

The previous two stories concerned royalty. But not even royalty can go it alone. Fantasy is crowded with "extras"— barmaids, freeholders, hostlers, scholars, companions on the road, a whole constellation of people whom the young, usually royal, and usually beautiful questing hero (or heroine) joins up with for the purpose of getting on with the quest.

In opera such people are called "spear carriers." But what about such spear carriers, or for that matter, broom carriers? What about all those people who are *not* beautiful, not royal, and not brilliant—the harassed, the unattractive, the slightly shady? Haven't they a right to their stories too?

As Andre Norton has shown us, just because a character is plain, scared, or sneaky doesn't mean that he or she can't be the hero of a story. In Sandra Miesel's introduction to the Gregg Press edition of *Witch World,* she points out that Norton tends to even the score: most of her protagonists tend to think of themselves as plain and unwanted. This leaves behind the blond-haired, pink-cheeked heroine of romance to shriek herself into hysterics and laryngitis back at the castle or wherever. In fact, Norton usually employs such "pretty people" as foils: Aldis, mistress of the Duke in *Web of the Witch World,* is contrasted with the tough Loyse; Marimme, timorous and easily thrown into panics, is matched with Gillan, who takes her place in the bargain with the were riders in *Year of the Unicorn,* winning herself a future and

198

her husband a new lease on life. So much beauty can be a trap, as Elys, heroine of several short stories about the Dales, discovers. She rescues her brother from one such trap and is almost tempted by another one herself. She also learns that the "pretty people" of the world may wish her gone when her sister-in-law Brunissende eyes her askance. It isn't looks, perhaps, but integrity that Norton is talking about. Since self-sufficiency is important in her books, it's natural that people who use beauty (which isn't a thing they had to earn) to live off other people are portrayed hostilely.

Certainly, they don't make life any easier for the "extras" and "spear carriers" of the world, or for the stray questing hero or heroine who wanders by, plain and mean as a well-tried knife.

We have two such characters here: the heroines of C. J. Cherryh's "Of Law and Magic" and Anne McCaffrey's "A Flock of Geese." Cherryh's story introduces us to Melot Cassisenen, a barmaid who sold herself to pay a wizard's fee—but didn't get enough money. McCaffrey's story brings us the ominously named Wicca, a pioneer whom desperation forces into ruthlessness and intolerance as she tries to survive time-storms.

These are characters that only a mother—or a master storyteller—could love, at least on first reading: both C. J. Cherryh and Anne McCaffrey are such storytellers.

As we can see in her Morgaine stories (one of which is dedicated to Andre Norton) and her Faded Sun trilogy and Merchanter stories, C. J. Cherryh seems to specialize in losers, loners, and last survivors. In *Gate of Ivrel*, Vanye is a bastard, an oathbreaker, and a kinslayer. Morgaine regards morality as a luxury she can't afford. Sten Duncan is a loner who teams up with the last survivors of a much-reviled mercenary culture. And merchanter Sandor Kreja is a con artist and epic liar with a bad conscience. In her *Thieves' World* stories, Cherryh creates the amoral, vampiric Ischade, with her sinister sense of humor and ironic fondness for fair play—some of the time.

Anne McCaffrey, who dedicated *Dragonsinger* to Andre Norton, uses that book to take the gifted harpergirl Menolly out of cave and weyr to her rightful home. As might be expected from that description, McCaffrey's usually an upbeat writer—but not always. Anyone remembering Lessa as she first appeared in the *Analog*-published "Weyr Search" knows that McCaffrey's characters are quite capable of intrigue, vendetta, and assassination, sustained over long periods of time.

Here we have two unusual stories—McCaffrey's tale of Wicca, an eighteenth-century castaway in time, forced to unscrupulous actions to survive, just like the characters of Norton's Dipple stories who regard the Thieves' Guild as a step up in the world; and Cherryh's story of the most resourceful lowlife to match wits with a man of learning since Eliza Doolittle.

A FLOCK OF GEESE

Anne McCaffrey

THE TIME-STORM SHIFTED AND THAT RESETTLEMENT WAS
enough to rouse Wicca, attuned as she was to the distortion
phenomenon. Awareness returned to her. She fumbled for
light, in her sleepiness uncertain what she was reaching for
until her hand found the slim metal cylinder. She had to
focus her thoughts to remember how to flick on this sort of
beam. Then she angled it to shine on her left wrist as her
fingers sought the digital switch. The display informed her
that the relative elapsed time of the latest shift was four days,
fourteen hours, thirty-two minutes, and ten seconds. Time in
Issaro's society had been exceedingly complex. In her natal
eighteenth century, she had been accustomed to judging the
relative time of day accurately by the sun's position. But the
sun was no longer a reliable timepiece.

From the stone shelf above her pallet, Wicca took the clip-
board and the incredible pen which never needed to be
dipped in ink. When she had added the elapsed time to the
neat columns of figures of time-storm duration, and intervals
between the phenomenon, no sudden insight revealed to her
the secret of the records which she had assiduously kept for
the past three years—elapsed time. Wicca sighed. If only she
could discern the relationship between time-storm and interval, she would be as much in control of her continued
existence as she was of the cave and anyone who resided in
it.

"Damnation take thee, Issaro," she said, ironically aware that Issaro probably had met damnation when he had been caught too far from the cave at the onset of that time-storm. She hadn't meant to lose him until he had unlocked the rhythm of the shifts. If, indeed, there was one, as he had constantly averred. "Be that as it may," she added on a philosophical note.

At some future time, future at least in the sense of her own continuous occupation of the cave, she would probably encounter another man from Issaro's computer-oriented society and, with his help, delve the message of the columns.

Now she prudently turned off the light. It was a useful device, less dangerous than candles or sparks from flint and tinder, and brighter than any lantern. Judicious use would extend the beam's life. One day, when her records had divulged their secret configuration, she might know when she would touch again in or near the time which had produced the compact hand light.

The cold of the time-storm was gone, and Wicca was feeling distinctly warm under her layers of quilts, which she preferred to the lighter-weight blankets and thermal covers the others used. In the earliest days in this cave refuge, there had been freezes of such shocking intensity that her people had bundled together under every available covering to generate enough warmth to keep them alive. Determined never to suffer from such temperatures again, Wicca sewed one patchwork after another from whatever scraps came to hand. The cave had escaped such extremes of weather for a long time, and Wicca had a fleeting moment's anxiety that the balance for such clemency would soon fall due. She folded back her quilts carefully, catching a slight odor from the body-warmed fabric. If it was a good day, an airing would freshen them. Should the river be running clear, and the sun shining, she would have Dorcas launder one or two.

She rose from the thick air mattress. That, like Issaro's digital watch, had been an unexpected treasure, the remnant of camping paraphernalia found discarded by the river. She chided herself for coveting the elegancies when she could not, in all conscience, approve the societies which had pro-

duced them. In truth, the fripperies did make life more
endurable in the cave. The disadvantage was that luxuries,
such as the light beam or the stone-cutters, inevitably lost
their power. Then one had, perforce, to resume the more
primitive ways of accomplishing the same tasks. The tedious,
if reliable, methods caused her people to grumble and be
dissatisfied, forcing her to be unnecessarily stern in order to
achieve her desired ends.

Wicca let her eyes become accustomed to the stygian
darkness of her little alcove. If the stone-cutters had not
depleted their power packs, it would have been a proper
room, instead of a niche opposite the stores. She listened
intently but heard nothing more than the muted breathing of
the sleepers in the main room of the cavern. She inhaled
deeply. The air was still good, though slightly tainted with
the stench of fearful sweat. Wicca thought of those asleep
there: Michael, Destry, elderly Edward, the Indian Fensu,
moaning Rayda, the timorous Malenda, and stolid Dorcas.
Pregnant Dorcas.

Wicca did not dwell on that problem. She pulled her skirts
straight, the fine-textured and durable cloth a product of yet
another culture. She had never been able to bring herself to
wear the more practical but immodest unmentionables fa-
vored by many societies. The sweep of her skirts added a
subtle authority to her slender, erect frame. To have pranced
about in trousers would be to demean herself. Wicca moved
toward the front of the cave complex, one hand on the wall to
steady herself, for the floor of the cavern was uneven. One
day she would have paving stones placed in the worst dips.
She knew the contours of her refuge well and lowered her
head where the ceiling slanted downward. When she acquired
more of the stone-cutters, she would lop off the bumps. Then
she was in the small entrance, an arm's length from the
massive door.

With an involuntary supplication to a God she knew no
longer existed, she hesitated before she put her hands flat
against the wood. She could feel no vibration, pressure, or
extreme of temperature through the wood. She inhaled, smelling neither the acridity of a foul atmosphere nor the damp-

ness of rain or snow, aware only of the preservative in which the wood had been soaked. How well she recalled the jubilation following the discovery of the "railroad ties." It had been the work of most of that interval to transport the bulky pieces of wood to the cave.

"They'll make the best door in the world, and we've found bolts and iron enough to make a frame," Douglas had cried triumphantly. "No more cowering in the back of the cave, praying the elements won't devour us. Nothing in the world, any world, will get through that door when I've hung it!"

Douglas was long gone but his door remained as a tribute to his ingenuity and workmanship. She had rather regretted his exigent departure, but those in the cave must owe their allegiance only to her, not to a jumped-up ne'er-do-well. She was the only person who could discern the ripples that preceded a time-shift.

She felt for Douglas's bolts and eased them back in their well-oiled slots, then tilted the heavy safety bar and drew the latch. She paused once more, though she knew in her bones that this had been a good shift and terror did not lie on the other side. She braced herself to heave open the heavy door.

Spring again! Not a false spring with the mutated horrors growing on the strangely altered ground of three shifts ago. Midafternoon unless this time-shift had changed the sun as well. The fragrances borne on the air were sweetly familiar. Wicca stepped out and turned as she always did, to look up at the mountains, to the everlasting hills. They were all right! The right shape. No help might be forthcoming from their crags and slopes, as the Psalmist had once intimated, but their unchanging aspect formed the one constant from which Wicca could take any reassurance. She feasted her eyes now on their blessedly familiar outlines. Through all the foul and fair forms the land outside the cave assumed after time-shifts, the outline of the hills endured.

"You chose well, good citizen," Douglas had told her his first night in the cave so many years ago. "This is basement rock, solid basalt," and he had affectionately slapped the stony bulwarks beside him. "Part of the bones of this tormented Earth, established millennia ago and not likely to change no matter how these time-storms shift. Until old Earth bounces all the way back to the Archeozoic Age, these rocks will endure. Mark my words!''

She had, until Douglas had tried to turn the then-residents against her and gain dominion over her cave. Ruthlessly she had left him, and them, behind in the next shift. She had missed him sorely for his many skills and his logical solutions to the practical problems of their curious existence. She chose to believe that his theoretical assessments of their condition, such as the durability of the hills, were as accurate as his practical applications.

Once more the hills gave her comfort and assurance. Serenely now, she could turn to see what had transpired around her and in the valley. The rivers, seen through a thin or young forest, were in residence and their banks unmarred by buildings of any description. Those rivers had watered her father's prosperous holding, obtained from the Governor of the Colony, rich farmlands, coveted by his neighbors. Well, she was no longer chattel-goods, unable to guide her own destiny and manage her inheritance. She wondered how those gentlemen, her ardent suitors, had fared the night of the first time-storm when they had chased her into these hills. And fortuitously into the cave which had proved the one sure shelter in this time-heaved world.

A faint breeze ruffled her hair, a breeze wet and clean of unfamiliar taints. She saw no stunted or exceptional trees. In this young forest, she recognized elm, birch, chestnut, oak, ash, and further down the hills, beeches and willows. A comforting undercurrent of noise drifted to her ears, the conversations of birds, animals, and insects. Into what era Earth had passed, Wicca could not guess, for the mountain forests of the American eastern coast had stood undisturbed for centuries before England had established her colonies there. This particular section had been alternately called Upper New York State, Lesser Metropolis, Eastern Sector, Red Region, and had been relatively unscathed by urban development, Douglas had said, until the late twenty-fifth century.

Twenty-five centuries seemed incredible to Wicca, a woman

of the eighteenth. Yet, in some society future to the twenty-fifth, the fabric of time itself had been ruptured, causing the great distortion shift storms during which the planet was flung from one point to another along the fifth dimension. Or so Issaro had asserted. The storm-bedraggled Wicca of the eighteenth century might not have comprehended such a theory, but the Wicca who assessed this new period of relative stability could accept that interpretation after all the marvels she had seen during her twelve years of time-faring.

Wicca moved from the cave's overhang. This would be a welcome stop, though autumn would have been more beneficial in terms of replenishing supplies of herbs, grains, fruits, and nuts. Automatically she bunched her skirt in one hand and began to gather dead branches from the clearing. Firewood and kindling were always in short supply in the cave, and she despised idleness in anyone above any other flaw and would not tolerate it in herself either. It took her no time to gather the first load, which she took back to the cave, stacking it quietly and quickly in the bins. No one was disturbed by her slight noises. They were all exhausted by the rigors of the last shift, though it hadn't been a bad one, and they would sleep until she woke them. That was all to the good. Wicca valued this time of solitude to collect her thoughts and plan how best to use a new shift.

She went back to her alcove and gathered up her quilts. As she spread the patchworks on convenient branches, she hoped there would be game abroad this time. Meat was the most urgent requirement. She would have the able men set snares and hunt. The women could fish and look for spring berries. She had the feeling that they might be here for a goodly while. Time enough to explore and see what other benefits might be derived.

She took a pail from the supply shelves, noting that some of the precious implements had not been stored properly. She'd have a word with Rayda. Born into a high-technology society and loath to dirty her hands or stretch her muscles in honest labor, Rayda had few skills to recommend her to Wicca. She had been in the cave now for five shifts and should be sloughed off as unsuitable. Wicca did not believe in undue benevolence with respect to castaways. She exploited whatever talents they had and generally managed to retain the artifacts with which they came encumbered. Bitter experience had taught her to be ruthless in maintaining her authority and domination. Wisely she had remained silent on the score that she always experienced a warning of the onset of a time-storm. With that unique faculty, she had been able to decide which of her companions of the moment passed the storm in the safety of the cave. Fortunately she had never touched in the same time twice, a mercy of which she was entirely sensible.

So, she would dispense with Rayda at the conclusion of this interval. A simple ruse at the appropriate time would suffice. The woman had no orientation skill at all.

Would it never be possible to have a stable complement in the cave? Wicca wondered. Each occupant possessing skills useful in their transitions and valuable in various of the civilizations in which the time-storms deposited them? Harmonious personalities with no sudden inexplicable ambitions to usurp her prerogatives: a decent assembly of folk all dedicated to surviving decently in this one refuge on a planet utterly abandoned by time's order? The best of all possible worlds?

As Wicca wound her way through the trees in search of early berries she smiled at her conceit. Issaro had suggested, on several occasions, that there had to be other refuges on the planet: other stable areas on the earth's crust or under it. Wicca had scoffed at the notion of trying to contact other survivors, though occasionally the technological equipment to do so had been available to her. Speaking to people she had never met across vast leagues of continent or ocean seemed a futile effort to her. What value would such contact have? How could one possibly pit mere scores of men against this ultimate disaster? She could not envisage that the combined effort of even the most substantial numbers of folk could affect or alter the cataclysm which had overtaken the world. If, as Issaro had maintained, some future scientific experimentation had ruptured time, then all the efforts of the past could not mend that fracture. The wiser course was to endure the phenomenon in reasonable safety and comfort.

Wicca broke from the thin forest into a clearing. Gooseberries grew in profusion on the bushes. Wicca ate greedily of the yellow green ovals, letting the juices moisten tissues dried by the uncertainties of the time-shift.

She had nearly filled her pail when a sudden heavy rustling in the undergrowth alerted her to the presence of some animal. She crouched behind the screen of bushes, observing that she was upwind of the creature. For several fearful moments, she wondered what horrible denizen might emerge. Her relief was double as she recognized the distinctive snout and furry bulk of a bear. Not a large one and, judging by the way it gobbled berries, recently awakened from its hibernation.

Any bear could be dangerous, so Wicca eased her way out of the bushes and walked swiftly back to the cave. Would she rouse the men to chase the bear? No, a thin one with winter-mangy fur would be of little value. And a large predator would provide Michael and Destry with an excuse to use firearms. Still the presence of a bear augured the likelihood of other familiar, and useful, species. Again, she stifled the wish that the season were more advanced and the bear fat enough to be worth hunting. Perhaps they would remain here through the entire summer and be able to garner the autumn's harvest.

The sunlight and fresh air streaming in through the open door had not roused the sleepers. She regarded them with a distaste bordering on contempt. The only really useful one was Fensu, and she could not countenance sharing the cave with the Iroquois, for only the presence of the other three men had inhibited his savage appetites.

Wicca set the pail on the stone floor, the slight grating noise disturbing no one. Michael slept next to Malenda but under separate coverings. Fensu was beyond them, rolled in his lynx furs. Rayda was curled close to the pregnant Dorcas while Edward and Destry, with some curious vestige of chivalry, lay across the entrance to the inner chamber.

Yes, thought Wicca coolly, she would dispense with the pack of them. She had long since gleaned from each what

information and skill could be of use to her. She was bored
with their tales and their long faces. Wasn't it enough to *live*
through the time-storms? With enough to eat and decent
water to drink? Clothes to warm their hides? They had no
courage, no real fortitude, no furnishings in their minds at
all. She had sloughed off far better companions than these.
Indeed, she wondered at her charity in sustaining such a
collection of lazy louts.

"Wake up, you vagrants, you idlers," she cried, prodding
indiscriminately at the sleeping bodies. "Wake up! 'Tis well
past time to be about the business of the day. Fresh meat
must be caught, for I wish to eat a warm meal at supper.
Michael, thee and Destry will help Fensu set traps and
snares . . ."

"We can use the rifles?" Michael threw off sleep quickly
in his excitement.

"What? And drive the game away with unnecessary noise?
I do not have unlimited supplies of powder and shot. . . ."
She paused, seeing the tightening of his face muscles.
"Ammo" was what Michael called powder and shot. "Snares
and traps will be sufficient for our needs."

"Then we are lodged here for a time?" asked Edward and
silence fell for her answer.

"Long enough to profit more by industry and application
than needless questions. Edward, the brook is in full spate.
Fill the big kettle first and then replenish the water butts." It
amused Wicca to make a water boy out of a learned man.
"Dorcas, start the fire. A goodly blaze will rid this chamber
of the chill of time . . . and fear." She glanced around to see
if her jibe rankled. Edward and Destry looked quickly away
and began to fold up their sleeping bags. "Nay, slovens.
Take the bedding out to be aired. Faugh! Malenda! Rayda!
There are ripe gooseberries a short step from here. Strip the
bushes. . . ."

"Then we may not be here long?" asked Michael, catching an inference she hadn't meant.

She gave him a long stare for his impertinent query.

"Why leave ripe berries for birds when they would sweeten
our dry mouths?"

Michael shrugged and moved out of the cave with his sleeping roll.

"Come! I've given you your orders. Do not dally!"

Fensu glided past Wicca, brushing so close that she caught the musky smell of him. Yes, despite his woodcrafts, he was expendable. Rutting animals such as he had forced her from her father's fine farm and into this tenuous existence.

"Days in the dark, and no rest on cold stones . . ." Rayda's sulky voice rehearsed her litany of grievances. Destry caught her arm and gave her a shake to be silent as he pulled her out of the main cavern. Malenda, blankets bundled in her arms, scurried after them.

Perhaps, thought Wicca in malicious hope, the bear might still be in the gooseberries and hungry enough to take a few well-placed nibbles out of Rayda.

She heard the crackling of fire consuming dry wood and looked around approvingly as Dorcas set the kettle tripod in place over the hearth. Too bad the woman had got herself with child and Wicca had not known soon enough to remedy the condition. The docile Dorcas was an excellent, undemanding servant, but not exactly the sort of companion who wore well in the long run, especially if lumbered with an infant.

"I will fetch meal for johnnycake, Dorcas, and herbs while thee pares vegetables. Carrots and onions will probably suit whatever flesh the men snare."

Not a woman to waste breath with unnecessary words, Dorcas nodded acknowledgment and went to the sandbox where the root vegetables were stored.

As Wicca moved down the short corridor to the stores cave, she reached into her copious skirt pocket for the heavy keys.

"It's ridiculous to have locks and keys in this place," Douglas had protested to Wicca when she requested them of him.

"Thee has not yet been through sufficient time-shifts to know how the privations can affect the weak in character. I deem it wisest to keep our stores close guarded."

"What would happen if you didn't make it back to the cave?"

"Ah, but, my dear Douglas, I always shall!"

Wicca had seen no point in explaining to a man of Douglas's time the true significance of the keys. She had received her first set from her father's hand at the age of fifteen and proved herself a careful chatelaine despite the inefficient, slovenly colonial indentured servants. How well that training had stood her through these parlous times.

She selected the heavy key which Douglas had scoffingly forged and slipped it into the heavy lock, hearing the tumblers snick. She supposed that Douglas was much in her thoughts because she was, as ever, grateful for his doors, bolts, locks, and keys. If only the man has been as honest in his dealings with her as he had been as an artisan.

Wicca turned on the diffuse-lamp, noting that its illumination was as bright as ever, and measured meal into the pannikin. She selected herbs from their bags, her fingers pausing over the satisfactory plumpness. Sufficient unto the day! Especially when the demands on her supplies would soon be reduced.

She turned off the lamp, closing and locking the grille behind her. Edward had returned from his first trip to the brook with the big kettle. One glance at Wicca and he made haste to get on with his chore. Dorcas had already set the sheet on the fire for the johnnycake, so Wicca handed her the supplies silently.

Dorcas was carefully mixing water into the meal under Wicca's watchful eye when they both heard the hubble-bubble of excited voices. Michael burst into view, Destry running close behind him.

"The rifle, Wicca! The rifle, quickly! A bear has treed Rayda!"

"A bear?"

"I'd've thought you'd've heard her yelling all the way up here," Michael gasped out. "The rifle!"

Wicca hesitated. The winter-thin bear and his mangy coat were really not worth the powder and shot.

"Or did you know there was a bear when you sent Rayda for berries?"

"I picked there myself a scant hour ago!" Wicca pointed contemptuously at the full pail.

"That tree ain't very big nor strong," Destry added, having caught enough breath to add his argument to Michael's.

Wicca saw Dorcas watching her, hands suspended over the meal bowl. She recognized the anger in Michael's eyes and the anxiety in Destry's. She mustn't seem as if she were eager to be rid of Rayda or she would experience difficulty in discarding any of them at the appropriate moment.

Wicca moved swiftly then, selecting the proper key as she made her way to the gun case. She handed Michael the heaviest of the rifles and two rounds of shot. He gestured impatiently for her to give him more.

"Let thy vaunted skill make the first shot count. The noise will likely frighten the creature away."

Michael gave her a searing look before he turned and pelted out of the cave, Destry behind him. Wicca followed more slowly to the entrance and saw the underbrush flipping back into place after their passage. She sighed with exasperation. That wretched bear! There'd be far too little work got out of any of them today. Perdition take Rayda! Wicca saw that she'd have to contrive cunningly to get the woman out of the cave at all after this "unnerving" experience. All the more reason to see the last of the overtimid Rayda.

Wicca retraced her steps, pausing to be sure Dorcas was busy, the only honest worker of the lot. Both women heard the resounding echo of a shot. Dorcas's hand quickened in the meal, anticipating meat for her stewpot.

"I shouldn't count too heavily on Michael's ability, Dorcas." And her skepticism was punctuated by the second shot.

As she waited to learn the outcome, Wicca turned all the sleeping bags, furs, and blankets on their branches. Malenda led the way, holding back branches as Michael staggered under the burden of a limp Rayda.

"She fainted," Michael said as he laid the unconscious woman down by the fire. "She managed to stay conscious and hang on to the branches until I shot the bear." His eyes met Wicca's in mutually felt contempt.

"Two shots?"

"It did take two. Tough old bugger," said Michael. "Fensu and Destry are dressing the carcass." He unslung the rifle and extended it to Wicca.

"The rifle must now be cleaned," Wicca said, gesturing Michael to that task as she bent to examine Rayda. Dorcas was already beside the woman, sponging away blood.

"Nothing deep. Nothing to swoon over," said Dorcas.

"She's had a terrible shock," murmured Malenda.

Dorcas made one of her noncommittal sounds.

"Thee surely sustained the same shock, I think," Wicca remarked dryly as she began to smooth comfrey paste into the scratches. Blood drops formed on the deeper punctures but most of the gore was due to shallow scratches where Rayda had scrambled through briars and up the tree.

"The bear didn't come straight *at* me," Malenda said in Rayda's defense.

"Did thee manage to pick any berries before this tragic occurrence?"

"Yes, we did . . ." Malenda faltered, looking warily at Wicca.

"Then thee may return to that labor and be sure to return also with Rayda's pail as well. Full, if at all possible. There are several more hours of daylight."

"Oh, you're impossible, Wicca!"

"If I truly were, then all of this"—Wicca's sweeping gesture included the cave, its shelter, and supplies—"would have been unavailable in Rayda's hour of crisis." Rayda groaned. "It will take Fensu and Destry time to dress the bear carcass. You will have their company in the berry patch. Gooseberries will go well with bear stew. Away with thee now!"

In fact the gooseberries and johnnycake were the better parts of the evening meal. The bear had broken its winter's fast on a diet of fish, and its stringy meat was so tainted by that flavor that even Dorcas's fine hand with seasonings could not disguise the taste. Rayda, her hands bandaged and her legs smeared with comfrey paste, moaned from her sleeping bag that she couldn't possibly eat the flesh of the beast that had nearly killed her. A solicitous Malenda fed her pieces of the johnnycake and ripe berries. Fensu was the only one who had eaten heartily of the stew, smacking his lips with a courtesy that Wicca would have preferred he did not practice.

When the men set to scraping the bear hide, Wicca settled herself on her stool outside the cave with the latest patchwork. Sewing did much to tranquilize her after the day's frustrations. Nor did she relish sitting inside on such a bright evening, particularly if she had to listen to Rayda's moans and Malenda's compassionate chirpings.

The current quilt Wicca was working in the Flock of Geese pattern, its patches cut from garments of former occupants of the cave. She had noticed over the years that blues, grays, and browns were the predominant shades of the rural past, while the vivid lighter primaries and curious virulent pastels seemed rampant in most city-futures. Wicca began a new square; the last of Issaro's red tunic triangles and Douglas's plaid patterned shirt were offset by Fanel's gray shirt. The gray was the finer material, to be sure, but of a similar weight to Douglas's and Issaro's. She did have to take care to match textures. She would have preferred good stout linsey-woolsey or calicoes, for the artificial fabrics of the futures puckered and stretched, thus ruining the look of the finished quilt. Still, one had to make do with whatever was to hand. No one complained about the look of the patchworks when they warmed a body during the intense and bitter cold of time-storms.

They had been so lucky these past five shifts, like the triangles of wild geese themselves, all headed in the same direction—spring. The gray intervals had alternated between intense heat and dreadful cold.

Wicca set the final stitch into the square. Then she stopped, looking intently at the pattern, remembering with a sudden clarity the people whose discarded garments had been set to this new purpose. And she discerned an astonishing *order* in that purpose. There was, in truth, a pattern to the time-shifts that had nothing to do with the varying intervals of storm and lull: it had to do with having *been* at each point, of remembering *when* it had been in past or future. She didn't need Issaro's calculations: all she had ever needed was her own recollections, placed in an orderly fashion, like the patchwork pieces, to see the pattern of shifts.

Suppressing her internal excitement, Wicca began to sort through the completed squares, identifying the fabrics, the people who had worn them, the cultures which had produced them. Time was like an enormous circular well. The planet Earth was a plumb weight suspended from a long cord, jerked up and down the well, hitting first one side of the well and then another, jounced up and down by the irresponsible hand that had initiated the time fracture. She was mixing her similes and metaphors but she knew what she meant. And she knew where she was.

First light tomorrow, she could in all conscience send Michael, Destry, and Fensu on a trip down the south river. They would find, she was now certain, a small but not primitive settlement where the south river joined the mightier torrent that flowed southeast to the sea. She would give Michael sufficient ammunition to reassure him. He'd never know. In this time there were few animals left: that poor specimen of a bear proved that to her. There would, however, be those skilled in medical treatments and she could, in conscience, dispatch Rayda to them, once Michael and Destry had returned. She rather thought that Fensu would find this time to his liking and disappear. Savage the man was, but not without cunning and perception. Malenda would go with Rayda. That would seem eminently logical and not the least bit unnatural in Wicca. Michael and Destry could stay on if they behaved, but she could forgo their company. Edward might stay on another shift or two. Physically he had limited usefulness, but his mind was sharp, and she had not yet learned all the wisdom he had spent so much time storing in his head. Dorcas could abide. The babe would not be born for another four months. Wicca smoothed the next patch with careful fingers. The next time-shift would bring them closer to Dorcas's original time. The woman would be more content there and undoubtedly find another husband.

Well pleased with these dispositions, Wicca sorted through the patches in her basket for colors that would combine well in the next Flock of Geese square.

OF LAW AND MAGIC

C. J. Cherryh

BETWEEN PROSPER STREET AND THE AVENUE OF JUSTICE IS a way named Fog; and the houses in this district are old and eclectic. The houses, citizens of Lincester themselves, span centuries; they come slowly to respectability with the weathering of their brick and beams and their new paint into the brown conservatism and eccentricity of this district. Here is a house a mere three hundred years into its age, with the graceful towers that were the style of its day; here is another with the timbered construction of four hundred years ago; and a house of porches which were fashionable a mere one hundred years ago, pierced-wood lace which has weathered to a comfortable silver brown; here is yet another of stone and brick, festooned with vines which try yearly to reach out to the wooden lace: but the owner has bought a spell to keep the peace, and the reaching tendrils continually turn back on themselves. The vines bloom in the spring with blue flowers and perfume the air, but a spell is on them, and the blue is silvered and muted and offends none of the neighbors with unseemly levity. The comfortable house next to the vines on the other side has a tiny yard and a little brick wall: children play there and climb the bricks and play mischievous games, tossing stolen flowers at passersby (and wickedly imagining they are poisoned blooms and that they cast spells instead of flowers. The children on this street are few and fey and very,

very sly, choosing only strangers for their pranks: to trouble adult neighbors would not be wise.)

There is a house of muted red brick; a house of river stone; a house of porches and a house of towers; but there is one house the eye tends to miss.

And near it and across the street by the brick wall the young woman in the cloak fends off a shower of silver-blue blossoms and glances up at the grinning, wolf-faced children. Her hand is calloused. Her dress is nondescript, and her cloak is brown and shows years of wear. She clutches it together tightly about her skirts and shows the fey children a pinched, pale countenance, tangled brown curls within the hood, a long, thin face like theirs, but they are free-running wolves and she is a townbred cur with the habit of being kicked. They are wolves and mercy never occurs to them, only prudence, and they plan wickedness and sport; one of them meditates trying a wee small spell.

But: "The lawyer's house," she says, looking up at them on their wall, all a-row like ornaments, their laps full of stolen vine branches. And their wolfish pupils dilate and contract in perfect time, and one of them tucks his bare knees up and another does, and the third, and the fourth points with a thin, muscled arm.

The house sits withdrawn from the street, a house of brick age-dulled and dark; a narrow house, a house of windows so old and clouded they drink the light in and cast none back; a house so plain and huge and ugly it might be some ware-house. Little sun gets to it in its slight retreat from the street; the alley beside it is bare dirt and dry dust on the few tilted paving stones. The porch is a mere retreat under the slanting eave of a black slate roof hardly blacker than the aged red brick; the front door is set between two age-hazed windows. This is a house without period, without age, without place among such aged finery, but it is large and (perhaps) very old (only perhaps: one could mistake or not remember), but its style is not after all the oldest, though it does suggest that the oldest may be, in comparison to it, far older of their kinds than one had thought. It is in all things vague. And it is a large house and a powerful house, so that in a sudden settling

of things into true perspective, one has to realize that the
lace-house and the vine-house and the house of the wall and
the fey wolfish children are light and this is darkness, this is
age, this is the reclusive house of the neighborhood, the
silence and the mystery which the witch-children fear, the
one house in whose alley they venture only with trepidation.
But casual passersby never notice its dreadfulness. Only the
neighbors and the children know; and now the woman knows,
and clutches her cloak the tighter and leaves the witch-
children silent on their wall.

The wolf-eyed girl who thought of the spell sits by her
playmates and congratulates herself that she was cautious in
her spelling. She is only seven. She knows that she is tal-
ented and hopes to live to become a threat. And this woman
in her poverty disturbs her, because this must be a witch, and
witches ought to be greater and more formidable. The boy
beside her is Sighted and feels a dimming of the day; hugs
his arms about himself without feeling that he does it while
his brother edges closer to him. And the boy from the
towered-house spits at the street below to break the luck
when the woman has gone. None of them go back to their
game. They sit in their row on their fence and watch, and
draw suspicious stares from passing locals who wonder what
mayhem the witch-children are contemplating today, legs
a-dangle as they sit on the wall, not looking at each other but
decidedly looking at something.

It was the nature of the dark house that it never occurred to
the ones who saw the children and looked where they looked,
that it was the dark house they wondered about. Those who
look at the dark house that way cannot be followed in their
thoughts, because they are looking at a different place, an
obscure and difficult place. Their sight has gotten into a maze
that no eye can follow without entering into it as well. The
children's souls have gone colder than they were and they do
not feel the daylight on their backs. They do not feel safe
anymore, but they do not feel any imminent danger either.
The house has been stable for a very long time and time goes
out from here in musty stability. It is the scale of things in
the neighborhood which has been rearranged. A moment is

an hour. A place is the universe. The universe is a street and
a dark house with dirty windows; and they contemplate this
possibility and do not like being so close to it; but they know
it is on every street and that wherever it exists it is always
next door or across the street. It is the most dangerous thing
in the world to stand in its alley or on its porch and the most
fearful thing in the world to think of its door opening.

But it opens for the woman in her shabby cloak. And there
is nothing of the ordinary about her any longer.

The air was musty with the decay of pages and leather.
The light shafted through from the two windows danced with
dustmotes and picked out the subtle hues of books and
yellowed paper in shelves and stacks about the walls, on
tables, chairs—towering stacks about the floor which preserved their own precarious equilibrium against all odds.
Light fell on age-silvered floorboards and on dust; light fell
on a narrow carpet runner which might once have been red
but which was silvered with the dust of time and neglect, and
this carpet marked a trail through the maze of shelves and
stacks, this single faded and dusty aisle of carpet alone
offered a line of sight that led away into a dark corridor
between the stacks of books and between the bookcases and
the laden furniture. Ambush might lurk within the stacks. A
single step, a single shift of weight made the aged boards of
the floor creak and betrayed the visitor. Melot Cassisenen
looked about her, her cloak clutched against her and her body
yearning back toward the daylight. The door had opened
itself. She was not overly surprised. Now, inevitably, it did
the other thing and shut itself; and for a moment the air was
cold. Magic did that, unattended magic: it got its force from
the air and the ground and from whoever was standing by.
Melot shivered: it robbed her as well, leaving her with only
the dusty window-light and that thin red track of carpet, the
color of life all faded, leading into the hall.

"Master Toth," she called out, quaking where she stood.
And again: "Master Toth!"—which sound lost itself in the
maze and drew neither echo nor answer.

Flight urged at her. But the carpet-path beguiled the eye

with its mazy designs, and the fear settled away into a vague and gnawing terror. It seemed logical to go on, since she had come this far; and if there were ambushes, they were likeliest ambushes calculated to frighten and not to harm. She walked the carpeted track and steeled her nerves against bogles and icy touches and whatever sort of whimsy an old man might devise for unwelcome intruders. Her business was certain and she was not a woman to turn when she had made up her mind a thing had to be: she simply told her feet they would go on and never back no matter what her mind was doing. And she told her body not to flinch even if something should run icy fingers down her neck: she was not a proud woman, this Melot, but she was a woman in a hurry, and the fingers of willywisps and goblins were all the same class of nuisance to a woman in her set of mind as fingers of other unwelcome sorts which she well knew how to deal with. She had tactics, did Melot of the *Ram,* and a withering look for man or devil who tried her. It masked a habitual dour despair, like the despair of the conscript soldier who knows tomorrow is like today, and all tomorrows like that one, one more walk and one more fight; and the enemy everywhere. Melot was a conscript of life; to be alive was not what she would have chosen, but by the gods all and several she was too stubborn to retreat once launched.

So she went walking down the dark hall of many doors and called out the name she had called out before, going deeper and deeper into the dark, till the hallway and the carpet ran up against a stack of books and a table with other books and papers. There the carpet and the hall bent to the right with a dim window at the end. This too she followed, past doors and past hanging pictures lost in murk and cobwebs, over the carpet which was her only track and guide, toward what at first seemed only another hall stacked high with books, but which revealed a stair and an ascent lighted by a dim window up at the landing.

"Master Toth," she called up; and: *Toth, Toth, Toth,* the echoes said, but nothing more. So she clenched up her skirts in her fist and climbed, where the faded red carpet led, up and up past the landing to yet another hall all in dark, where crazily leaning stacks of books and papers breathed out a miasma of age and rot. "Master Toth?"

But the carpet went only up the stairs, while the hall floor was bare boards and littered with paper. The stairs promised light above, where by yet another window, dirty-paned daylight streamed into the dust and the neglect.

She chose the stairs and climbed, hard-breathing now, and gathered her skirts past stacks of books. Another turn: a small slit of a window and a door at the top of the stairs.

The air seemed colder here. A prickling ran down her nape. She thought if she turned about at this instant, there would be something black and small and glitter-eyed staring at her from the landing she had left: that was the thing that built itself in her mind. It would grow brave. It would come up the stairs. If she turned around she would see it baring its needle-sharp teeth; and its kingdom was the dark hallway which she had to pass to go down again.

"Master Toth!" She let go her skirts and stepped up to the door and hammered with her fist as her nerve began to fail her. "Master—"

The air chilled and the door opened onto a dusty-windowed loft as mazed with books as all the rest of the house. And before the great windows at the far end of the loft a hunched figure perched on a stool poring over something on a reading stand. This someone turned, a spidery silhouette against the white light; and Melot felt the approach of the black thing at her heels and skipped up that step and inside in haste.

The door closed behind her. The shadow in front of the windows got off its stool, and Melot kept herself close to the door and flight, black thing or no.

"Master Toth," she said in a voice not as bold as her voice in the halls below.

The figure beckoned. She came, closer, closer through the tilting maze of books and papers, and her eyes accepted the light enough to make out this figure, which began to have color—the bottle-green coat and dark hair (white, she had thought) and a lean, smooth face (wrinkled, she had expected) and a fine-boned hand (inkstained) holding a pair of spectacles. Melot's step failed her and her mouth opened for more breath, because he was none of the things she had expected, no crabbed ancient huddled at his bookstand, but a tall young man with the features of a god, except his nose was a bit hooked and his eyes were set too close, so that they stared with a concentration that seemed to focus somewhere in the center of the subject's heart and not at its surface.

"Well?" this young man asked. "Well?" This man looked at her, and Melot Cassisenen felt naked in a way that had nothing to do with clothes, and burned in a way that had everything to do with his handsomeness and the look of those dark eyes which looked straight into her own. No man who looked like that looked that way at Melot's plain face, and all at once she flushed like a thirteen-year-old and felt the floor about to cave in to swallow herself and her purpose, which could not possibly sustain such a stare. The voice so gentle was about to crack like a whip, was about to turn acid with impatience and sting her with wit her wit could not, in its present state, deal with.

It was in such pinches that Melot Cassisenen's mind went blank, and the same blind stubbornness which had just driven her legs up the stairs took over her mouth. "Master Toth, would you be Master Toth?"

"*Dr.* Toth, yes, I am, madam."

She flushed again, hotter than before: and part of the heat was shame and part was rage, since he used a lady's word and hid behind that sober, careful face to laugh at her. "I want a consul-tation." She had practiced this word. She got it out unstammered. She stared him in the eye and refused to give way an inch, though he seemed taller than before and closer. "I haven't got much money. But it's not like you'd have to do more than tell me what to do." She fished at her collar and started to haul up her purse, never turning her back, and the heat burned her face, not from embarrassment of where the purse was, but from what little sum it held and what it had cost her. It was too little, she knew that it was too little, and she preferred his cold contempt to his laughter. Laughter would cut like a razor. Laughter would kill the rest of her soul and she would go away and kill a wizard or two. Or try. And she held the purse out, hating the way her hand shook; and she turned out the money, which was four large silver coins and three small ones. And two coppers.

He left them in her hand and walked away from her to draw up another, smaller stool. "Sit down," he said and went and pulled his own stool out from the table.

Melot came and sat, her left hand clenched on her money; her skirts spread about her on the dusty floor. She reached and swept back the hood of her cloak and stared at the doctor as he sat down on his tall stool. Tremors threatened her. She tried to keep her teeth from chattering, her throat from freezing up. This was a dangerous man, this was a man wizards were afraid of; and he sat there like a boy on a stableyard fence, his long arms about his knees, the spectacles in his fine fingers glinting with gold and glass in the dusty daylight from the window, his books abandoned on his desk.

"I'm listening," he said. "Tell me your name. Tell me anything that seems important. We'll discuss a fee when I know what your case is."

"My n-n-name is Melot Cassisenen." Now, now the stammer threatened in earnest and she fought it back with deliberation. "My brother's Gatan. Same name. He's got this trouble. This wizard got him, this other wizard—well, there's going to be this duel—"

"Be specific. Tell me all the details."

"This wizard—he, well, he was always hanging round the tavern, the *Ram,* over by the Inch—"

"You're a long way from home."

"He—well, I work there, and he was always trouble, I mean, he got drunk and when he got drunk he was trouble. And my brother, well, he'd talk to him sometimes to calm him down—I mean, he was bothering me, he'd try, and my brother, well, he never liked that, but he's got a way about him, my brother does. He can charm the moon out of the sky, and he always knew how to handle this wizard—"

"Tell me his name. I know a good many."

"Othis."

"Ah." The dark, close-set eyes flickered. "*That* one. Yes, I do know him."

Melot looked up at him, sweating; and he gave her no

helpful clues what kind of knowledge this was or how close
or friendly. "Well, when this Othis would give me trouble,
my brother'd go and talk to him and put him off and sometimes Master Othis'd sit and talk at him for hours—well,
maybe he told my brother something, maybe this other
wizard—Hagon, Hagon's his name—" She looked again for
clues and got none. "Well, he took exception, he did, to
something, and somehow maybe this Othis and this Hagon
were old enemies; so Hagon came into the *Ram* and he
grabbed me and he wanted my brother to come with him or
he'd mess me up good, he said, that was what he meant,
anyhow. So's Gatan went with him instead, me yelling after
him and trying to stop him, but this Hagon he knocked me
down, not with his hand, but just like I hit a wall, and he and
Gatan went off in the dark.

"Well, I was scared; and I hadn't got any help—this man I
know, well, he wasn't taking on any wizard, so I went
myself, and I hunted up Othis and tried to talk to him, but he
was all—well, he shoved me off and called Gatan names and
said as how Gatan had made a friend—a *friend!*—he oughtn't,
and said as how he was going to get revenge on this Hagon
and on my brother—" Melot drew breath. Her hands shook.
She clenched them both on her knees and stopped the tremor.
"This Hagon, he set a *binding* on my brother, that's what
Othis said; and Othis put some other kind of spell on him too;
and now they got this problem, because they can't untangle
it, and they've got it set up to have this duel to settle who's
got what, tomorrow, wizard to wizard, Othis said—except—
except—well, where's my brother in this? Who's going to
see he doesn't get hurt? I mean, it's not right—Gatan never
worked for either of them, they got no right, have they? They
can't do that, fight over him, I mean. I figured you'd know it
wasn't right, you'd just sort of like write a letter for me to
these two, and maybe—maybe a letter where it could do
some good. I mean, like you were my lawyer and you were
going to do something, but you don't have to really, I mean,
just the letters, that's all. I got money enough for that; or I
can get more if you tell me what. I mean, just scare 'em a
little. That's all.''

"That's very interesting," the doctor said, and the heat went to Melot's face, a suspicion of condescension. "You're not a witch, then?" the doctor asked.

"I wait tables."

"But you're not a witch."

"Man, there's no one got less talent than me."

"Not born auspiciously."

"My mother coughed me out. Thought I was a stomachache." Melot clenched her fingers on her silver coins. "It was my birthday this Hagon walked in on—I mean, what kind of luck is that?"

"How many days ago?"

"Three."

"How old are you?"

"Thirty-three."

"Interesting. Interesting." The lawyer hopped up from his stool and put his spectacles on, went over to a stack of books, and pulled out the second from the top. He opened it on the table and leafed through it, unfolding pages into untidy charts. "What hour of the day?"

"Third." The numbers came together out of nowhere and coincided, and Melot got off her stool and stood there with her hands clenched on her coins and her heart thumping away. "I got no luck, I never had any luck."

"There are two kinds," the doctor said, and sent the shivers down her back.

"You just write the letters, Master Toth, that's all I want, I mean, it's *Gatan* in trouble, not me."

The doctor looked up over his spectacles, his dark eyes full of surmise and, for the first time, alarm. "Gatan's birthday."

"Same. Same—we always, I mean, we always thought it was funny, like he had all the luck I missed, charming folk was his talent, only he was four years later—"

"The wrong one. Hagon got the wrong one. So did Othis."

"What are you talking about?" The words came out blunt and plain and Melot felt a rush of panic. She laid her fistful of money on the table by the book. "I can't afford you doing all that. Just the letters. I mean, all you have to do is write what right is. They'll listen to you."

The doctor hopped up and pulled out another book. He opened it and stood there riffling through it and reading here and there. "No, no," he said, and: "No, not here, not that, not here—"

"I can't afford a lot!"

The doctor pulled down his spectacles and turned and looked at her. "Melot Cassisenen. I'm not a wizard myself; I'm a specialist whose talent just happens to be keeping track of books and things in books. And that little talent has got me a few others. My clients usually don't come in broad daylight and my fees aren't as straightforward as you offer. The door downstairs, for instance. Hagon himself did that. Othis has contributed a few things about the place. Conveniences. They're very expensive for a wizard. But they pay them. They pay whatever I set, because I have a small talent at research— which means, madam, that no single wizard can master all of them, or many of them: a wizard's investment is too much and too deep in too few books to have any appreciation of interrelated consequences. My investment is shallow, but very, very wide. I am not, precisely, a barrister. I do not plead cases. I'm a consulting lawyer, which is quite another thing. I do not sue nor do I defend or prosecute. I merely advise. Do you understand, Melot Cassisenen? Nor do I practice a law which has to do with justice. I practice the law of nature. I render a simple service to those who meddle in it. I advise of consequences. So I suggest you have a seat, young woman, and wait."

"It's *tomorrow*."

"Yes. Quite. So is sunrise. The question is inevitability. Do sit down, madam, and don't utter a word, if you please."

Melot subsided over to the low stool she had sat on before, sank down, and hugged her arms about her knees, her knees against her chest, watching as Dr. Toth went striding down the long line of shelves against the wall and pulled down one book after another. He carried them back to his desk, dumped them atop the last, pushed his spectacles up his nose, and began leafing through the pages while dust flew up and danced in the light like stormclouds. "No," he said. "No, and no." And slammed the books shut one and the other, got up and dumped them onto the stack beside the desk.

"If—" said Melot, thinking of the letter she had come for.

"Hush!" the master snapped and folded one arm and rested the other hand on his brow, standing there with his head bowed and his eyes squinched shut.

The air chilled, not like a wind, like something had instead leached the warmth and the life out of it. That cold reached into Melot's bones and into her muscles and she could not shiver, she could only sit and sit. Then of a sudden the doctor flung up his head. "Ah!" he said, strode off on his long legs, and whirled about to point a finger at her. "You! Stay on that stool. Touch nothing, hear!"

"Yes, s-sir."

He spun and strode off again, out the magical door, and thump, thump, thump down the stairs before the door had shut, while Melot tucked her cloak about her and shivered and shivered, thinking of the small darkness with the teeth she had imagined on the stairs, in the hall below. It might have been a cat, might have been a dog or even some rat, but it had died here, it had become something awful; it lived here and it could have gotten in when the doctor opened that door, and it hated visitors—oh, gods, gods, gods. Melot sat with her teeth chattering in the shaft of light from the window and with her head spinning and her muscles weakening in their shivers.

At last she ducked her head down against her knees and shut her eyes and tried to get the shivers out, because she was Melot Cassisenen, after all—nobody much, but she walked the streets not with a mince or a flinch, but with a sure, businesslike stride that announced to the world that here walked a woman who wanted no trouble but who was prepared to make it. And *that* for the thing with the teeth, for she had a sharp square heel and a quick foot and a set of lungs that would bring the house down and bring master Toth on the run. So she rested as she could after the cold had taken the strength out of her and she waited and she waited while the sun crawled across the floor and left her in the dark. The beam wandered the length of the hall and lost itself in the stacks of books, so that only one tall mountain of them was alight.

Suddenly a candle lit itself, sending another chill into the air.

Thump, thump-thump, thump—up the stairs. Up and up the stairs, and round the turn, as the magical door opened and Master Toth came in with an armload of books.

Melot started to stand up, started to blurt out a *What now,* then swallowed it and sank down again on her numb backside, because Dr. Toth paid her no more heed than if she had been another stack of books. He set his books down on the stand where the candle was, flung open one and another of them, threw a sheaf of paper onto the lot and sat down on the tall stool, immediately dipping a quill into an inkpot that uncapped itself. Another small chill.

And Melot's stomach growled. She clenched her arms across her belly, trying to silence it. Tried to think of something else. The rumbling came again, loud; and the pen-scratching stopped. Dr. Toth looked at her through his spectacles as if she were something objectionable on his carpet, then pushed his spectacles a degree higher and started writing again, flipping pages and making the candle flame shake and shadows dance.

Another rumble from her stomach. Melot hugged herself and sucked in air and tried to tense her muscles, which only started a shiver. Gods, gods. He would throw her out. He was only interested in his books. He did all this work and there was a fee; and she sold her other dress and Gatan's clothes, and her cooking pots and her mother's ring, and then she sold what she never had sold for money, except once for a doctor for their mother before she died. And it all came to those coins and a dull cold terror that they were not enough, that it was only the books interested Master Toth and he was working on wizard's business never thinking at all about Gatan or herself. She was only a lump sitting here, bothering him in his work. It could not be a letter he was writing. What he had said he would do she could not make out, but it was all as if he was not in the habit really of doing anything beyond handing out advice; and what could she do with advice against a pair of wizards?

Her stomach rumbled again. The pen stopped scratching and she looked up as he looked down his spectacled nose at her.

"In the cupboard there," he said brusquely with a wave of inkstained fingers. "Eat what you like, for the gods' sake, and watch where you're walking."

"Yes, sir." She looked desperately where he pointed and got off her stool onto numb legs, limped over where a small path through the stacks led to a cupboard. A candle lighted there on the counter, blink. She shivered and carefully opened the doors, found a plate of bread and fresh seed-cheese and a bottle of wine. All fresh. All as if they hadn't been lying in a cupboard all day. The air inside was chill, and the wine bottle cold as she poured into a chill cup, and the knife cold as she cut a little bread and cheese.

Then she thought again and put it on a tray and walked timidly, fearfully up to Master Toth; but she knew how to get up to a table and deftly fill a cup with never bothering a gentleman. She set it there on the stack nearest and slipped back to feed herself, a bit of seed-cheese wrapped in bread and wine—gods, such wine, the *Ram* never served the like. It hit her empty stomach and made her head spin as she tidied things and closed the cupboard.

More candles lit. The sun was going. The pen scratched away and stopped as Master Toth took a drink of wine and a left-handed nibble of cheese while he kept reading, all hunched over his books. The cheese slowly disappeared. He took up the pen again. Scratch-scribble, hastily.

Melot crept back to her stool and sat down again, blinking owlishly. She was unbearably sleepy, three days with never but a little sleep and that dreadful, in a shameful bed. The wine sat in her stomach and hummed in her veins and whispered in her skull like bees in a hive.

"We have it," Dr. Toth announced suddenly, "we have it!"—startling her awake, startling her hands to her sides hunting the edges of the stool among her skirts as the doctor held up his paper. "Woman, up, don't dawdle! There's precious little time."

She stood and wobbled. Dr. Toth slid down from his perch and came and seized her by the arm, dragging her with him.

"But," she said.

"Time," he said. "Come along, walk, woman. Melot Cassisenen. Good gods, keep your feet under you, I trust you know where this Othis lodges tonight."

"The Inch—he's got this place he uses—can't you magic it?" She caught her balance as the door opened and left the stairs gaping darkly in front of them, with him dragging her along in the dim light of candles which lit themselves in the stairwell, above the books and the litter. "Can't you—"

"A practical suggestion if I had the wherewithal. I'm not wont to have to race with fools. Tomorrow you say. But which tomorrow, tomorrow of the dawn or tomorrow of the wizards, or tomorrow of the clock? Do you know? No, I thought not." Thump, thump, around the turning and down into the first hall, into the bizarre maze of books, all the candles in the sconces agleam. "Do come *on*, woman."

"Yes, sir. Yes, sir." Melot skipped and ran as best she could being hauled upon in time to his long steps. The door opened for them, and the wind skirled the candles and they went out onto the porch and down, down the steps to the night-bound street.

Melot was staggering when they had reached the Avenue, reeling along with the doctor's fingers clamped upon her wrist and tugging at her to more haste. She ran and ran still, and brought up short against the doctor's side when he stopped and gave a piercing whistle.

More magic? She blinked. There was the least small chill; but it might have been the wind. And there down the Avenue came a public cab, a-rattle on the pavings, one of the wheeled sort, the cabman jogging along at a fair pace—a cabman without a hire, at this hour, just where the doctor needed him. Melot blinked in amazement as the cab rattled up to a stop by the curb. "Wizard's Lane, fast as you can," the doctor said to the cabman, tossed him a coin that made his jaw drop, and opened the door himself and flung Melot in, the third only time in her life she had seen the inside of a cab.

"But—but," she said, smothered in her skirts as the doctor shoved her over against the wall and wedged himself in, "Dr. Toth, that's wrong, it's the Inch, it's—" But the cab was off, rattling along fit to make her teeth clack. "Wizard's Lane," the doctor said firmly. And the cab lurched and jolted. For that coin that had sailed through the moonlight with a wicked golden glint the cabby would run his gut out. He was doing that, and the wheels jolted and bounced. Melot clenched her jaws and clenched her fist on the hanging-strap and swayed this way and that with the doctor as they bounced along, clack, thump, and a missing stone, thud-clack. Her breath refused to come back. Her brain reeled. *But I can't pay, that was gold he threw to a cabby-man, and that's all it is to him, he's rich, rich as a priest and rich as a lord, and I'm nothing, my money's not enough for him and he's young and handsome and I'm not, I'm not, I'm not, can't even pay him that way, nothing I can offer—*

—Does he take souls? Is that what he trades in?

Thud-clack-clack. She heard the cabby panting now, felt the cab steady into that holding pace now the cabby had come to his senses and realized he had to stay alive and stay moving. It was a long, long way; but the man had gold, had gold enough to buy the cab and a soul or two, might be. . . .

Thud-clack. Sway and skid at the corners, jog and jounce. In time Melot heard the cabby panting up ahead as if his gut would burst and his lifeblood spew, but he ran on, and they swayed and bumped one against the other, the doctor in his fine coat and her in her cloak, and outside the windows of the cab the neighborhood changed and changed again. The cab slowed to a walk awhile, picked up: they kept moving, by fits and starts.

And at long, long last they stopped altogether, and the cab tipped, and the cabby came round to their window, panting like a beached fish. "What number was you wanting, milor'?"

The doctor peered out. "Close enough," he said, and flung the door open, and gave the man another something in his hand. The cabby stood there while Melot got out, and tried to help her; but there was dark running from his nose in the moonlight. Melot felt his hand shake and when she stepped clear the cabby just stopped and collapsed there on the curb, head between his knees. And the doctor grabbed Melot's wrist and pulled her along willy-nilly.

Down the street, the peculiar street where more magic was than was comfortable anywhere, and some of the houses with their peculiarities . . . like a face etched on window-glass; like icicles on the eaves of one, or a shimmer of recent rain on its neighbor. Melot quaked in her steps and came on, panting and desperate as the doctor started up long wooden steps to an unpretentious house of beams and towers.

The door-emblem blinked at them and the door swung wide with a gust of chill hardly worse than that all up and down this street, chill to sting the lungs and make a body glad of a cloak. Candles sprang to life inside, and an old man in a blue robe came out of a brighter-lit room.

"Dr. Toth," that one said—a wizard, sure he was a wizard. "What's this?"

"An excellent question," the doctor said and dragged Melot with him as he swept into the lighted room—a library, but ever so much neater and cleaner than his own. Melot goggled at the giltwork and the leather bindings and the lamp in dragon shape and the brass fish that held up a table on which rested an interrupted dinner and an open book.

"Do look lively, woman!" The doctor spun her round by the arm and her startled eyes fell full on the wizard, for wizard he must be, a small gray man in a blue dressing-gown, with sad mustaches and lively blue eyes. "What does she seem like?"

"Why—no one, no one in particular—"

"Ah," said Dr. Toth, and pushed Melot into a chair near the fish-table; he took the divan and helped himself to the wine. "Have some, my dear?"

Melot reached. The goblet he put in her hand weighed ten times what it seemed, and she slopped the wine over in her startlement. Gold, it was gold. She blinked at one and the other of them, and looked doubtfully at the gray wizard as he sat down on the remaining chair.

"Read this," said Dr. Toth, and handed the gray wizard a paper from his pocket. "Does that make sense?"

The gray wizard held it up to his eyes and adjusted it this way and that in myopic concentration. His mouth moved and stopped moving and he looked up with his blue eyes wide. "Who does this describe?"

"Her. It describes *her*, Master Junthin. Two idiots are fighting over her *brother*—"

Gods save me, Melot thought with a mouthful of wine half choking her. Her eyes watered in pain and she swallowed and tried not to sneeze it up, a hand clamped to mouth and nose as she stared at the wizard and the doctor in panic, frozen like a bird between two snakes. "—and one of them has put a hold on *him*, if she can tell a straight story. That's how her luck works, don't you see? They tracked the thing straight so far, and when they got close, their eyes bent right around her and they went for second-best. Her *luck* brought her to me. It had to. She had no choice. It was her *luck* brought the trouble on her in the first place and cozened those fools Othis and Hagon—a luck like that, there's nothing stops it. It rolls downhill and it arranges things—"

"But don't you see?" Junthin said, on his side, "it arranged you and her to be here. And me to be at home. A client canceled. Gods know why—" Owlish eyes blinked at Melot and sent chills down her back before they slid away to blink at the doctor and to glance down at the paper again and up. "If they don't stop this—"

"You *can* find them."

"Yes." The paper shook in Junthin's wrinkled hands. He wiped his face with his sleeve, the paper still trembling and wavering. "O dear gods, dear gods. A nexus. A nexus. O dear gods. How far?"

Melot looked from him to the doctor, whose handsome face was starkly sober. "Master Junthin," said Dr. Toth, "you know that I'm a tolerably important nexus myself. You know I enjoy a certain latitude with the Profession on that account, not mentioning my talent. That my researches per-

sistently turn up a certain set of consequences should I be
. . . eliminated, or bothered, or directly hampered in my
work: do you see? And those consequences are far-reaching.
I consult every wizard's text and put all the prohibitions and
the possible interferences together, and they do assume a
pattern into which I fit rather centrally, I may say, which
assures that of all individuals in all Lincester *not* safe to trifle
with, I am at the head of the list, I in my modest house, my
quiet researches, my inquiries—''

"Yes, yes, we all know that. We pay you handsomely,
extravagantly. *I* pay you. You render a service."

"And keep you from eliminating yourselves or a city street
or perchance Lincester itself by combination of unforeseen
consequences . . . Perhaps, I always considered, that would
be justification enough for what I cast for my horoscope and
my own luck—''

"We never doubt it. But, my dear Dr. Toth, we cannot
stand on—''

"But do you see, Master Junthin, tonight I learned a
different truth about my importance. It wasn't myself had the
importance all along. *She* did. Her luck arranged all of this.
Arranged my birth two hundred years ago. Arranged your
client's cancellation. Arranged all of this and my profession
and our very existence. *Nexus,* man. A big one. *That*'s what
those fools are playing with. They've got her brother. His
luck didn't outmaneuver theirs; they mistake him for some
petty little trinket they can use not knowing that the nexus-
sense they pick up is just the overspill from hers. And I'm
telling you, Master Junthin, if they harm him in their brigandish
behavior, if they run afoul of *her* luck and tie *anything*
important to it—like the welfare of Lincester, do you see? Do
you see what they're meddling with?''

"Oh, dear gods and stars.''

"Wait. Wait.'' Facts and insinuations and promises went
flying this way and that in confusion, like pigeons, and
Melot's head spun. "You promised about my brother . . .''
It was not precisely so, but it was never wasted to try to
convince the other side in a bargain there *was* a bargain. It
was all the wit she had left, with the red wine dizzying her

and the warmth and the profusion of candles and wizard-talk flying past her ears. "You got to get him out, Master Toth. You do got to do that, you took my money—" *O fool! to mention the money, the pitiful money—* She blinked at them and shivered and saw two men and them both magicians staring at her as if she had snakes for hair. "You got to. I got this feeling—I get these feelings—things will go wrong if something happens to him."

"Is she lying?" asked Master Junthin.

"I don't know," said the doctor.

She was. She was lying with a vengeance, because premonitions seemed the only cash these wizard-types understood, premonitions and bad luck and good. She knew how to throw an evil-eye scare into a drunk or to ill-wish a street ruffian and give him the doubts enough to get away; so she did it with a first-class wizard and the wizards' own lawyer— and saw them stare at her and wonder.

"Bless," said the wizard, and the air went a little colder, and the candles dimmed all together and came up again.

"*Do* something. Get the neighbors, can you?"

"Summon? With *her* involved?"

"Have you a countersuggestion, Master Junthin?"

"Oh, gods, oh, gods," Master Junthin murmured. And shut his eyes.

The air went decided chill. A bell began to ring somewhere in the hall. Another rang far away as if it was outside the house. And further and further and further until the air whispered with them.

Melot picked up the goblet and took another sip of wine. She wanted it for her nerves. And she pretended a composure which was the greatest lie yet.

Meanwhile the bells rang and Dr. Toth stood there with his arms folded, looking down at her. With that look on his handsome face that said he had his doubts in both directions.

"Mmmph," she said, and offered the plate of cheese with eyes wide and naive.

He caught the irony. It was dangerous to have done. A meticulous brow lifted. But by the gods, a woman never got anywhere in the world letting the opposition drag her about and tell her sit here and sit there and stare at her like that. Her hair was snarled from running. It fell down around her ears and her eyes, too tangled with itself to stay put; and she sweated, and her best (and only) dress wanted laundering, while he smelled of books and fine soap and even his sweat smelled clean. She was despicable. She was plain and starved and her dress hung about her ribs. And he had talked about him being born—*(two hundred years ago?)*—to satisfy her luck, which rattled around in her brain without a niche to fall into. Two hundred years ago?

Was the way he looked—something he had taken in payment?

The front door opened. Master Junthin went out into the hall and brought in an out-of-breath little man in a dressing gown. . . . "What's toward, what's toward? Good gods, Junthin—" The little man spied Dr. Toth and stopped in mid-word. And even then the front door was opening again. Two women came into the room on their own, like as peas except one had her hair in pins and the other had it dripping wet; and hard on their heels came a fat man with a marmoset on his shoulder. "What is this?" the marmoset piped, falsetto. "What is this?"

There were more arriving. A boy with scales on one cheek. A black woman who cast no shadow. The door kept opening and closing and Melot clutched the wine goblet, aware of the stares no less on her than on Dr. Toth, and hoping—hoping desperately for the sight of two wizards in particular.

But they did not come. And Junthin began to explain the whole affair to the others, using words that slipped in and out of language she knew, till Dr. Toth, unlike himself, stole over to Melot and took the goblet away, took her hand and drew her to her feet like a grand lady, holding her arm locked in his.

"You just have to want your brother," Dr. Toth said. "Mind is very important in this."

"I *want* him."

"Fine, fine. Now you've got to trust Junthin for this. This isn't my kind of affair." He gave her hand a little squeeze and passed her hand grandly to Junthin's reach.

The wizard's skin was cold and damp. "My dear woman, my dear, just stand there, right where you are. Just shut your eyes, hold your eyes shut. Oh, gods, my furniture—"

And from the woman with the wet hair: "A nexus of that size, O ye gods and stars—Junthin, quit babbling about the furniture—"

"But my vases, my vases—" Junthin fled and set one and another of the great ornate vases on the floor, then scurried back to the large rug where others were clearing the tables. The door opened to another arrival—"Never mind," the woman of the pins said to the latecomer, an aged, wizened man, "stand *here*, gaffer Bedizi'n—" And from the old man: "Eh? I was in bed, my cat woke me—eh, Dr. Toth? It is Dr. Toth, 'pon my soul—"

"Be *careful*, gaffer Bedizi'n. For the gods' sweet sake and Lincester's, just stand on that point, *stand there!* Hear?"

Melot looked left and right. Took in her breath, because all of a sudden it started to grow cold; and Junthin began to talk, and all of them to talk. Then the talk became one sound, and that sound rumbled up through her bones like close thunder— "Now, now, now—name him, name him, name him—"

It's Gatan they want, they want me to talk, Gatan, Gatan— *BOOM!* The thunder burst in her face and there was something *there*, while a great fist hit her and she went flying backward into collapsing wizards and the crash of furniture and goblets and trays and vases. She hit the floor on her backside, feet out at angles, and struggled up on her hands to see Gatan sitting there in the center of the carpet without a stitch on and blinking and wobbling back and forth. There were rope burns on him. There was a dazed look on his face. "Gods!" he cried, proving his reality.

"Air displacement." It was Dr. Toth, who was helping up Master Junthin and then gaffer Bedizi'n, who blinked owlishly. "Your cloak, my dear." And he drew Melot to her feet and took her cloak and went and cast it around Gatan, who sat helplessly where he had landed.

"Where *were* you?" Melot cried, clenching her hands to fists and pounding her knees as she gazed into Gatan's bewildered, blinking eyes. "Gatan, Gatan, you great fool, where have you been?"

"In this cellar," he said. "In this cellar." He shivered and hugged the cloak about him; and Melot went and threw her arms about him. He was sometimes a fool, Gatan was; and he looked like one this time, being naked as a hatchling and cold as meat and, gods help him, smelling like a sewer. Weed clung to his hair. She picked at it, patted his unshaved cheek. "Oh, my vases," Junthin moaned at the fringes of things.

"He has a luck," the woman with wet hair said.

"An investment," said the woman with pins, and Melot looked about at her and hugged Gatan fast as the woman rolled her eyes and staggered back against her twin. "An investment . . . O gods, he's carrying something! Do stand up, young man."

Melot applied herself with both hands and Dr. Toth helped and the fat man with the marmoset. "Up, up," the marmoset wailed as the fat man pushed, and Gatan wobbled to his feet and reeled this way and that under Melot's support. Gatan howled, and his face glowed red and changed of a sudden with the shadowed overlay of a man's rough features that were never Gatan's. They changed again, a second face.

"Oh, good gods," Melot cried, stepping back.

"It's Hagon," cried the woman in pins, while the face faded, leaving Gatan with his own; Melot stood there in profoundest shock—Gatan, and suddenly not-Gatan with Hagon's face . . . O gods—what was this they had summoned to the room?

"Not Hagon's choosing," said the marmoset, as Gatan's features glowed blue and changed again. "Now, *that*'s Othis, that was Othis, sure."

"What, what, what?" Melot cried, and grabbed Dr. Toth by the sleeve, but of a sudden it was Gatan again, wobbling there without any glow at all and holding his borrowed cloak about him. "What are they talking about, what's happened to him, what's *wrong* with him?"

"An investment." Dr. Toth took Melot by the arm in turn and by both arms hard and gently, his close-set eyes looking straight into hers. "Hagon evidently intended to transfer some fraction of his power into what he thought was a nexus of considerable intensity. Do you know—no, of course you don't. But with a personal extension into even such a minor nexus, why, Hagon could put the merest portion of his magic into your brother and use your brother's luck to magnify his power, to become a great wizard, not a petty one. And that's exactly what Othis wanted—*that* was the duel. That was what they were set up to do—to wrestle wizardlike for sole possession of this fine young fellow—and, my dear woman, at the worst moment, at the positively worst and most calamitous possible moment in Hagon's procedure or Othis's—your luck brought us to summon him out of their vicinity."

"But—but—can't you help him?"

"Help him, my dear woman?" Dr. Toth straightened back and regarded her down his nose, and flung an expansive gesture toward Gatan, who stood hugging his borrowed cloak about his nakedness. "*Help* him? That's a powerful wizard standing there! Yes, *Gatan!* Your brother's drained them *both* dry; and gods know what else Hagon was up to beyond using him as a catspaw! If your brother has the makings of that linkage in him as well, gods save us all! It was power they were after."

"Gatan?" Melot turned and looked and held her hands to her mouth for fear of something else getting out. But it was truly Gatan. Her own handsome brother stood there blinking and scared-looking. "Melot," he said, "Melot, I'm me, I'm just me is all—O gods, I feel like I could burst, my head, my fingers—"

"Don't!" cried the marmoset. "No, no, no, don't let it loose. Wish it to rain! Quickly, wish for rain!"

"I hope it rains!" Gatan cried desperately. And the air went frosty cold.

"Weather-wish takes time," said the gaffer Bedizi'n, "a great deal of time, young man, I hope you don't expect haste. That's always young folk, always in a hurry. Tomorrow, I make it tomorrow noon, halfish—"

"But Hagon and Othis," cried Gatan. "What will they do to me? They'll come looking for me!"

"Oh, no," said Junthin mournfully. He held one of his vases in his hands and he had a distressed look on his face. "No, I don't think they will." And he came and set the vase on a table that was still upright. It was a flowered urn. It was full to the brim with red liquid.

"Backlash," said Dr. Toth. "Dear me, what an awful mess. The lad got all the useful things out of them in the transfer. But is that one or both in there?"

"Both, I think," said Junthin. "It's the only vase intact."

Gatan sat down where he was, on the rim of an overturned chair. Melot just stood, numb.

"No more Othis," said Junthin. "No more Hagon."

"Good riddance," said the black woman.

"But," said Melot.

"I'd say," said Dr. Toth, "unasked, of course, and unconsulted—that it's going to rain half past noon tomorrow. And everything's going to work out well for this young man. Though I'd say one ought to find him a master right quickly. An untrained talent of his caliber is not comfortable. That advice is free."

Junthin coughed. "My damages—I do have first claim."

"Junthin," cried the fat man's marmoset, "you have no such thing."

"Indeed not," said the black woman without a shadow. "I think we might expect Master Toth to research this matter and tell us the consequences."

"Ah, well. *Now* we come to fees. I'll think of some small thing. The answer may take me a few days and I make no guarantees in this case. And pray, my dear friends, pray earnestly that there were no deeper entanglements. *I'll* take the pair in charge until I have your answer. That should relieve you of some few anxieties. And of, coincidentally, worry about each other." Dr. Toth leaned over the vase, sniffed and stood back with a grimace. "Ugh. A little consultation would have prevented that. I'll have lost my doorspell too. It was Hagon's, and delicate as it is, I'm afraid it's quite done for."

*   *   *

"I don't know," said Gatan, still shivering, though the doctor's study was warmed with a very natural fire, and the doctor had provided a warm bath and a very fine robe once they had gotten in. (It was Melot climbed through the window they jimmied, and let them in among the books and clutter.) Gatan, a mass of nerves on his way home, still grew distraught whenever he talked about his sojourn in that cellar under Hagon's floor. "I don't know *what* they intended to do, I don't know what's to become of me now. What do I know? I can't deal with folk like that!"

"Do have some confidence," Dr. Toth said, looking up from his table and his books. "The solution has to fit all round. And unremarkable as Othis and Hagon may have been separately, *you*'re quite formidable, young man; I daresay we should warn the watch: the storm tomorrow may prove as much. But for the moment I suggest you go off to bed and let me work in peace, ummn? Nice. Nice. Here's an interesting point. Do go. Go, go, go, second door down the hall."

There was no sign of the black thing with teeth out in the hall. Perhaps it was in better humor. Melot saw Gatan to his room and the candles lit themselves for him the moment he entered—"Do be careful about the lights!" the doctor's voice pursued them down the hall.

"I'm scared," Gatan said, though he was a grown man and a half-head taller; he was her little brother and told her such things as she lingered in his doorway. "Melot, I'm *scared.*"

"Hush, trust the doctor, he's very kind."

But she went back down the hall after Gatan had shut the door. She walked into the study with her heart beating hard. And stood there with her hands locked behind her while the doctor pored over a clutter of books and charts as if the night were still young. As if he needed no sleep nor ever would. The way he was two hundred years old and maybe ugly once, but never would be so long as he could bargain with wizards.

And as long as they needed him.

She coughed. Her heart beat doubletime. "You're looking in that book for him—or for me?"

The doctor looked up through his spectacles and took them off. "It does seem to be one case, doesn't it?"

"Like, I mean, my brother's a wizard, isn't he?"

"Your luck made him that way."

"Like you said you were born because I needed you, was that true?"

The doctor blinked at her. "Well—"

"I mean," she said, "when you reckon how much I owe you got to take that into account, like if you charged me too much my luck'd get me clear, wouldn't it?"

"Melot Cassisenen, you are a woman of unparalleled gall."

"Just lucky. Aren't I?"

The doctor stood up. Towered there in his magnificence.

"I reckon," said Melot, "it might be lucky for you if I stayed here, I mean, this place—" She waved a hand about. "It wants dusting. It wants straightening."

The doctor's mouth opened, a very handsome mouth it was, and a very fine face, and him so lordlike and genteel. *"My books—"*

"Fact is," said Melot, hands behind her, rocking anxiously on her heels, "if I was lucky I'd bring luck here, wouldn'I? And if I was lucky, maybe I'd be pretty and have nice clothes like yours and hire me footcabs with goldpieces and have me a brother a very fine and lordly wizard, wouldn'I Master Toth?"

"Wouldn't you? You unmitigated—"

"If I was lucky," she said, and held up a cautioning finger, "only if I was lucky, wouldn't it be, Master Toth? And your books will tell you what's luckiest for you and me and all—won't they?" She smiled at him, a cheerful, believing smile. "I'm what you was born for in the first place—me, Melot Cassisenen—and I'm the luckiest woman alive."

PARTNERS

Anyone who has ever paused by a highway to watch a hawk swoop overhead, played with a dog, or coped with the idiosyncrasies of an autocratic cat shares one of Andre Norton's most noted traits; the love of animals. In her books, they appear not as pets but as friends, companions, and allies. Sometimes, they're more. In *Moon of Three Rings,* the Thassa, especially Moon Singers like Maelen, trade bodies with their friends-in-fur, thus learning the freedom of the wilds as only a keen-nosed, keen-eyed animal can teach it. This can be the making of them—or their destruction. But while it lasts, human and animal form a team, bonded by love, trust, and occasionally telepathy.

Andre Norton will find the human/animal teams described in Jo Clayton's "Team Venture" and Diana Paxson's "Sky Sister" familiar. Jo Clayton, well known for her novels about Aleytys, wearer of the Diadem, lives in New Orleans under the management of her bossy cats, and has created in "Team Venture" a group of companions on a long journey. Some are human, some are animal—and one is neither. This journey is, like most such journeys, a quest. But it's a quest for expiation as well as for knowledge.

Diana Paxson, whose many short stories and several novels (most recent to appear: *Brisingamen,* an adaptation of the story of a necklace fabled in Norse mythology) draw deeply both on archetypes and fine old tales, adapts several themes

from the great storehouse of questing lore in "Sky Sister."
Her Shanna is a princess in search of her rightful place;
Shanna's journey takes her from places she knows well into
lands where mystery and magic are only to be expected. In
the course of such a journey, she goes from inheriting a quest
to making it her own. Nor is Shanna's story the only one we
find here. All of them will appeal to anyone who has ever
wondered at birds in flight—or at how they're going to rise
above their own faults and fears to achieve their goals.

The relationship between partners in Judith Tarr's "Defender of the Faith" is complex, and because the story takes
place in a time and world similar to our own Middle Ages
during the Crusades, it may assume great poignancy. In this
case, the questing hero is neither questing nor a hero—nor
even human. She is Morgiana, one of the Jann, creatures
which, though of a Muslim Otherworld, nevertheless can ally
with the human Faithful against the infidel. In this case, of
course, the "infidels" are the people that we in our Western
chauvinism usually consider the enemy—not just the Muslims
from whom the Crusaders tried to "free" the Holy Lands,
but the ultrasecret, ultrafanatical sect of Assassins. In serving
them, Morgiana runs into a major problem: though she's not
human, she does have a conscience—and she's matched
against an opponent who may well turn out to be a saint.

Judith Tarr, a new writer whose trilogy, *The Hound and
the Falcon,* will begin to appear from Bluejay in 1985, is
ideally suited to telling a tale of scimitars, sorcery, and crises
of faith. A Ph.D. candidate in medieval studies at Yale, she
is equally at home in scholarly research and writing fantasy.
With startling originality, she provides a story about the
theological qualms of a nonhuman that could probably have
caused Richard the Lionhearted to have heart failure.

TEAM VENTURE

Jo Clayton

TURN OFF THE DAMN STORM," ARRYN TOLD HERSELF BUT prodded no answer back, only a wordless sneer and a building fury that echoed the turmoil overhead where storm clouds roiled and moiled and wrung themselves out over the stony hill country. She clucked to Horse, the sound encouragement and apology for hard labor and meager fare. The boxy wagon lurched in and out of ruts which even the inundation soaking her had no chance of softening. Through the curtains laced tight behind her she heard a spitting complaint from Cat as a leak doused her with cold water.

"I wish you'd simmer down," she told herself. Holding the reins in one hand, she scraped water from her face with the other. "It's you calling this misery down on us. I'm sick of storms, you bloody-minded bitch." Herself (mouthless and incorporeal) grinned nastily. The rain fell harder for a while, then began to slacken as the other-within (who called herself Nys the destroyer in moments of megalomania) settled to a measure of calm. Arryn relaxed, sighed, glanced hopefully at the clouds, blinked away the rain blowing into her eyes.

Horse plodded on without comment—up around, down around, up and down—along the unpaved track that passed for a road. Above them on the hillsides, hillmen in layered robes watched over their flocks, watched the gaudy wagon as well, sitting still as the stones about them even when she

246

waved a greeting to them. A warmer wind blew along the hill crowns, teasing at the clouds until swatches of blue showed through the grey along with a clean white light that woke to brilliance slides of orange poppies, clusters of purple lupine, dots and patches of crimson lilies. The sun touched her face, began licking the wet from her clothes and her fine pale hair. She put her feet up on the mudguard, lolled against the backrest, her eyes closed, her face lifted to the warmth.

Nys cobra-reared and snatched at the body, snatched so suddenly that Arryn dropped the reins and nearly rolled off the driver's seat. She fought herself desperately for control of the body, but Nys had simmered to some purpose and it was hard. . . .

Horse stopped walking and curled his head around; he snorted with disgust and flung a call to the sleeping narsit. It wailed distaste, but came scrambling through the curtains, urged on by a vigorous pat from Cat's paw, and clung to the top slat of the backrest with all four handfeet. With another wail, it launched itself and landed on Horse's silken black haunch, sinking tiny scimitar claws through hair and hide. Horse jumped, kicked out reflexively, blasted a mindspeech curse at the narsit, which it ignored. It *changed*.

An oval mirror a foot high stood motionless where the narsit had been, a glimmering mirror that caught Arryn's eye and focused for her a sense of who and what she was, that collected her strength, amplified it and bounced it back to her. Fiber by fiber she detached Nys from the body. Eyes still fixed on her mirrored face, she straightened her body, lifted one hand to the sky where the grey of the clouds was bleaching to a shredded white. The murderous energy and raw force she stripped from herself flowed like water into her hand until her flesh was hot with it, then it discharged in a great ball of white fire that fled upward as if the clouds called it and, when it touched them, exploded with a violence that shook air and earth alike.

The narsit *changed* again and leaped into Arryn's lap, trembling and whistling angrily. She stroked the tan plush on its back until the tremors stopped, then pushed it through the curtains. The handfeet kicked against her palm, then it was

chattering as it turned round and round, resettling itself into
its rag nest. Chuckling, she fished up the reins, slapped them
lightly against Horse's back, part of the game they played to
conceal his more esoteric abilities. —Thanks, old friend—
she mindspoke to him.

—Rather than thanks, stay awake— Horse's mindvoice was
a resonant bass, filled now with acerbic amusement. —Last
time Nys took hold she drove the lot of us off a cliff— He
snorted, twitched his ears.

They'd been togther a dozen years now, the four of them,
Horse, Cat, Hawk, and her. A dozen years and three separate
realities since the Judges of Savastorn sent them into exile.
The narsit was newly come into the Company. When their
travel wagon bounced down in the predawn bustle of Cetanjji
Market, it was sitting on her shoulder, clutching painfully at
her hair, coalesced somehow from the chaos *between*. Little
by little in the two years since then, Arryn was learning what
it could do when her *need* called to it; apart from its malle-
able shape and useful elusiveness, it had another function for
her, providing her with something small and cuddly she
could love.

She fluttered a hand at a bulky striped bundle sitting on a
hill watching her. Maybe watching her. His face was lost in
the shadows of his cowl. Three nights ago, in a place called
Qador's Cut, playing her flute for Cat to dance to, healing
some small hurts, she'd wrung a few pennies and a dinner
from Qador's folk. The Plain below was richer and freer with
its coin, sleepily prosperous from a long period of peace, but
to eyes that knew how to look there were signs of trouble to
come—chains of slaves in the marketplaces, one-handed beg-
gars in the streets, hunger-bloated children in the slums,
haggard sullen looks on peasant faces. She'd moved from
village to village, sachai-house to sachai-house, welcome
until word of her wild arrival at Cetanjji trickled through.
How she popped out of nowhere early one morning in the
middle of Cetanjji Market—a large black horse, a gaudy
box-wagon with iron-tired wheels, a woman dressed in steel
and leather holding the reins, beside her an outsize white cat
with blue green eyes, mask and points of glinting pewter, an

outsized hawk circling overhead, screeching a challenge to them all as the woman shouted the horse into a plunging run that got them out the city gates before the stunned guards recovered enough to sound the alarm.

—I wonder what's on the other side of those mountains? We really should find out, don't you think? But then, why should I ask you, old Horse, when I know you want to know everything. Next village is called Mill Crossing. We're going to spend the night under a roof for once, Horse. A hot meal for me and a bath—gods, I'd kill to sink myself up to my neck in hot water. Fresh oats for you and a good dry stall. Mill Crossing. Sounds prosperous. What was his name—that headman at the Cut? Cludeen, yes, that's it. Cludeen, he said they hold market at Mill Crossing every Hadinday, whatever that is, and a whole hundred families live there and there's a smithy and an Inn. I'm sure I mentioned the Inn already. What is it about this world, Horse, that lets Nys make the weather answer her moods? We've never come across *that* before and I'm sure I don't like it. One thing about this stony ground, water doesn't lie about, we won't have to slog through mud up to the axles, not like what was it—

Horse snorted, curled his head around to look at her.

—You're babbling, Arryn—

—I know, old friend, after one of these bouts it comes out all over me like boils or something—

—Entrancing image, m'dear—

The sun was an orange red half-circle when the travel wagon circled a grove and Arryn saw Mill Crossing laid out before her.

The sturdy small houses with their neat flower plots fronting the main street were blackened and smoldering. Bodies lay everywhere.

Horse stepped over a young woman without hands or head, but stopped—almost as an afterthought—before the front wheels of the wagon rolled over her legs. —Curious—

Arryn dropped the reins and hugged her arms tight across her breasts. The colors were strong in the diminished light, the shadows long and stark, the burnt houses abstractions

divorced from commonplace forms, walls, windows, doors
outlined in black with random red accents, tongues of fire
that flared and died, flared and died, the sprawled bodies
calligraphic images brushed hastily on the pale grey paper of
the street. —What?—

—Wall. There isn't any. Cities on the Plain have walls,
but not Mattibach or Kapnosh or Pullykas or High Tallerkey
or Qador's Cut. Or Mill Crossing—

—I don't . . . Ah! No wall around any of the hill villages
we've visited— She closed her eyes, pressed the heels of her
hands hard against them. —So this has to be new, this
slaughter— She dropped her hands into her lap. —What do
we do now?—

—We get away from here, far and fast as we can— Horse
shook his head, shuddered, shifted his hooves, his iron shoes
ringing against the hard dirt. —Here we are, nice and handy
for a happy lynching. The raiders being long gone, who else
can the hillfolk vent their anger on?—

—We didn't do . . . oh! Scapegoats, scouting for those
butchers—

—Herders up here, should have that custom and that meta-
phor. We've met it often enough, you remember the anhellotti
on . . .—

—Shelve the lecture, Horse. I'm too damn scared and mad
for academic maunderings, however enticing you find them.
Maybe this time we can outrun rumor. Let's get out of . . .
Haridar's tits, too late. Look—

Some distance below the village the road swung round one
of the valley's many groves. (An aside from Horse: —Road
going around the grove again, not through it, either that's a
religious taboo or there's something that scares hillmen in
those groves. Too bad they're all dead here, you could ask
for me, I'd like to know— Interruption from Arryn: —Oh,
thou besotted, this is even less a time for lectures—) A man
had come from behind the grove and was riding toward them,
other men appeared behind him, riding two-by-two like a
troup of soldiers, though they weren't dressed like soldiers.
Horse backed a few steps, setting his hooves down carefully,

not quite callous enough, agitated though he was, to trample
the dead. Or perhaps he thought that wouldn't sit well with
the approaching riders.

—Hold here, old friend. It'll look better if we're not trying
to run. Come in, Hawk, we need you—

Cat came through the curtains, leaped lightly over the
backrest, and posed herself on the seat, excited, eager to flex
the muscles of the meld.

The narsit scrambled onto Arryn's shoulder, tiny black
handfeet once more closing tight about long straight strands
of silver-gilt hair. Going to have to break it of that habit
before it drags me bald, she thought. She untangled the little
creature, settled it in her lap; one hand smoothing again and
again along the narsit's back, she unfocused her eyes and sat
waiting.

Warned by wisps of smoke and the acrid stench carried on
the wind, the an-saich Hathorn vo Cehlt knew his intuition
had been right but late—again too late. By how much this
time? How much the next? For there would be a next, he
knew that with a spreading chill despair; this was the fourth
gutted village, a dozen days' ride from the other three. No
pattern to the attacks: how could you fit a pattern on madness? No special day, no special interval between attacks,
nothing special about the villages, just ordinary hill settle-
ments, the first three in the north, this one in the south.
Behind him his Scrubs went silent when they saw the burnt-
out houses, the scattered dead; but he could taste their individual reactions, the barely disciplined rage, the cool
assessment, the furious and helpless mind-oaths, he could
taste them and put a name to each particular flavor. As
always when he touched them this way, he felt a powerful
surge of affection for them all. He brushed that aside and
turned his attention back to the town ahead.

The woman's stillness hid her from him for a while, but
his eyes lifted finally from the dead and he saw the large
black horse, the gaudy wagon, the cat, and most of all her,
sitting very quiet, waiting for him, moon-silver hair and
double soul, hope where there'd been none before. Fire of
Haaom. The Moonwitch. Mother's Sight was a true seeing.

* * *

The leading rider held up a gloved hand, sunset glinting red off the bands of metal inlaid on the wristlets. He flicked the hand side to side, and the double column split neatly, the riders curving out to circle the village and come round behind her. She stirred, her hands locking together more tightly. (Herself bubbled with silent laughter. Arryn snarled at Nys for stranding them on this world; the solar collectors didn't work worth a damn under a blanket of clouds and the dive device was less than half-charged since they'd had to draw it down several times for same-reality jumps to escape capture on the Plain.)

With his men well on their way, the leader started toward her, holding his horse to a brisk walk, guiding it through the dead with touches of his knees, slight tilts of his body, his anger and frustration visible in the hardened outline of neck and shoulders. He brought his mount to a stop when he came even with Horse. "Who are you? What do you know of this?"

She blinked. "I might ask the same of you. By what right do you question me?"

"Them." He nodded at the men waiting in a wordless circle; he himself sat relaxed, his gloved hands resting lightly before him, the sunset picking out streaks of grey in his dark hair.

With a quick smile she said, "I concede your point. As to who I am, my name is Arryn. I earn my keep as healwoman and musician of sorts. I call no man master and no place home. I . . ."

Hawk's homing scream interrupted her and brought the man's head up, a startled look on his thin, lined face. Hawk came to rest on his home perch, a long heavy rod bolted to the roof peak of the travel wagon. Cat stretched slowly, sensuously, making it obvious that she considered the danger over, knowing she was admired and playing to it to entice more admiration. She yawned with delicate but feigned indifference and began licking her tail. Hawk treaded his rod, giving off bursts of irritation, scolding her in his wordless way for calling him off hunt so needlessly; he could mindspeak as well as the others but usually chose not to. Horse was grumpy and in a mood to be difficult. And that damn man was laughing at them all. When she glared at him, the smile retreated from his lips to his eyes. With a carefully sobered face, he turned his head, called, "Yonar-sul."

One of the men left the encircling line, a stocky, long-armed man with a nose that so overwhelmed the rest of his features that she had to look at him for some minutes before she noticed eyes set deep in smile wrinkles, a generous mouth, and a receding chin inadquately disguised by a short stiff beard. He sketched a casual salute. "An-saich inouk."

"Take Clem and Doro, look out a campsite for us round the bend there"—he pointed up the road beyond the wagon —"so we won't have this butcher's ground under our noses when we eat."

"An-saich." Yonar backed his horse with practiced skill, wheeled, and snapped out commands to the men named, then rode off with them at his heels.

"Manjri-ansul."

A second man kneed his horse from the ring. A small dark man, slim and wiry with eyes black as the burnt-out houses, a gold ring in one ear, a gold chain about the wrist of the hand holding the reins. "An-saich inouk."

"Take the rest of the Scrubs and haul those bodies into the Inn. It's still in fair shape, enough to keep off the wolves and carrion birds." He thought a moment, his head tilted slightly forward, the wind stirring his grey-streaked hair. "Leave one man on guard till you're finished. The raiders haven't returned other times, but there's no use taking chances."

"An-saich." Like Yonar before him, Manjri backed his horse, wheeled, and went off with the other men following silent behind him.

"Most impressive." She let her irritation sound in her voice. She was tired and sore and heartsick and wanted more than anything to get away from this place. "Now that this show is finished, what orders do you have for me?"

He laughed, the sound warm and easy. "Orders for you? I wouldn't dare, Moonwitch."

"What?"

"O fulfiller of dreams, I have reason enough to let you go your way without provoking you to change me into some low things, a frog or a rat or a drift of smoke."

"Fool."

"I don't aspire so high." His smile widened. "Why not turn that thing about and stay the night with us." He touched his forehead in a mock salute. "A most humble request, nothing like an order, Moonwitch. You'll sleep safe in every sense." He dropped his hand on his thigh, turned serious. "In truth, I need your help."

She looked past him, watched shadows lift shadows and carry them away. "Help? With this?"

"Yes."

—Horse?—

—Why not. Better than camping on our own with those killers wandering loose or some hillman out to claim heads—

—If he's a treacherous care for-naught, it's on your head, you quivering jelly— She picked up the reins, clicked her tongue to signal Horse to start himself around. She caught the man watching her, eyes narrowed, as Horse backed the wagon a few paces, then walked it round and started plodding back the way they'd come.

He moved up beside her, riding close to the front wheel. "Interesting collection you've got."

She raised her brows, looked as blank as she could manage. "I don't understand."

He examined Hawk sitting hunched on his rod. "Fresh meat would be a welcome change."

"You do think you're clever."

"Mmm, there's something in what you say."

"You're flying high. Why? It makes me nervous. I don't know your name."

"Over the triple-moon, Moonwitch," he said. "Over the moons, sister of my soul. The an-saich Hathorn vo Cehlt, youngest son of Kerdorn terCehlt vo Tanij, Saich of Cetanjji-Romain. If you must have the whole of it."

"Ah. A prince of sorts."

"Of sorts." His euphoria was gone as suddenly as it had come; when he spoke again there was a brooding bitterness in his voice. "My father lets me play soldier since it keeps me away from Cetanjji where I sharpen my tongue on his parasites." He looked over his shoulder at the men working on their grisly task, swung back to scowl at his mount's ears. "Keeps the Scrubs out of fights too, especially with my half brothers. Dungeon scourings, that's the name they get thrown at them, my Scrubs." He didn't try to keep the pride and affection from his voice. "Best damn fighters on the Plain." He shrugged. "Only problem is no one wants fighters; the Domain has kept its fratchetty peace two hundred years now."

"You sound. . . ."

"Hot to start the killing? Something has to be done, Moonwitch. Privilege, phah! They're parasites, all the saichem, and my father's the worst. You don't think he's going to do anything about this slaughter, do you? They're his, come tax time. Otherwise, it's only hillfolk dying, no one important." His hand closed into a fist and beat on his thigh, one beat for each angry word. "They take and take, these saichem. What's yours is mine, what's mine is mine—and have your hand off if you raise it against me." He passed a gloved palm across his face. "I'm ranting. You're a seductive listener, Moonwitch. Forgive me."

"Nothing to me." She leaned forward, pointed. "A fire. Your camp?"

Horse eased the wagon beneath a huge-limbed ancient oak a short space beyond the edge of the firelight, maneuvering as close as he could to the massive trunk with its surrounding knots of knobbly looping roots. He snorted, kicked at the leaf mold. —Get me out of this sweat web—

—Patience, thou. There's a swim for you later, but no bath for me. Not with this mob of men about— She swung down, using the front wheel as a stepladder, groaning as her muscles complained, then leaned against the wheel, reached back and scratched thoughtfully under Cat's chin. —Fresh meat, the man said. Cat?—

Cat slipped away from her hand, sat up on her haunches, watched Arryn with unblinking eyes.

—So you want to be coaxed, do you? Fetch, my mog. Five coneys at least or I'll let narsit pull your tail all it wants—

Cat lifted a forefoot, examined the extended claws, licked busily between them.

"Narsit."

Cat hissed as the black muzzle thrust past the curtains, leaped from the seat, and prowled off through the trees.

Arryn chuckled and picked up the narsit, cuddling it against her, its small head tucked into the hollow at the base of her throat. Stroking the vibrating body, she stepped away from the wagon, looking up at the perch. —Hawk—

He blinked golden eyes at her, ruffled his feathers. —Meat— There was hungry anticipation in the word.

—Six fine fat birds for us, then you can go play—

Hawk launched himself from the perch with a low swoop and a wild scream that startled the men by the fire and brought Hathorn loping toward her. He stopped beside her and turned to watch Hawk swing round the fire and slant steeply toward the clouds. "What's wrong?"

"Nothing. Hawk's just showing off." She put the narsit on the wagon seat and walked away. The man disturbed her in ways dangerous to her peace of mind since there was no response she could make and keep her conscience whole. Over her shoulder she said, "You expressed a desire for fresh meat. Would you mind unhitching Horse for me? I'm tired."

"At your service, most puissant lady."

"Arryn, please, an-saich."

"Hathorn."

"As you wish."

She settled herself on a root, her back against the trunk, her legs stretched out before her, heels braced against a lower hump. Horse whinnied with pleasure, pranced about a few steps, then trotted off toward the river. Hathorn stepped over the shafts and came round the wagon to stand looking down at her.

"I'm no witch," she said quietly.

"No?" He rested his shoulders against the wagon's side,

his eyes narrowed to slits, deep grooves in his thin cheeks because he was repressing a grin. "And the man-beast familiars?"

"Not of my making. Nor in my service, as you mean it. They're companions in exile, that's all, and that's all I'll say of them. Why Moonwitch?"

"Moon-pale hair."

She pushed wisps of hair off her forehead, drew a long strand through her fingers, wrinkling her nose at the oil on it. "Not much longer if I don't wash it. Mud's more like." She let the hair trickle from her fingers into a heavy web. "That's evasion, Hathorn. I saw plenty of pale blonds on the Plain."

"Blonds that conjure themselves plus impedimenta out of thinnest air? Yonar witnessed your arrival in the market at Cetanjjí; he's been telling me about it." He chuckled. "He was staggering home after a very wet night. Swore off wine for a week after."

"Hah! That's not magic but machine, friend. A bit of business somewhat more complicated than the mill in Mill Crossing but of the same order. Where I was born, magic is not permitted. It doesn't fit their blessed patterns."

"As you didn't fit?"

She made a face at him and he laughed. She pulled at the strand of hair, pulled it apart again, smoothed it down over her breast, dropped her hands into her lap, folding one about the other. "But you didn't know Yonar's story when you first named me Moonwitch."

" 'Know her by her two souls, dark and light.' "

She jerked upright. "No!"

—Yes— His mindspeech voice was a clear tenor. —Moonwitch and Murderess bound in one flesh—

"You . . ." She clamped her teeth on her lip, slapped angrily at her thigh, annoyed by her unthinking acknowledgment that she'd heard him.

"Sister of my soul." He pushed away from the wagon, picked his way through the roots, and settled himself by her feet. "My mother was Dreayl."

"So?"

"The Eddray are said to be power-weavers, moon-linked."

"Said to be. Are they?"

He looked away from her. Moonlight trickled through the hard scalloped leaves of the oak and slid like hot oil down the planes of his face, deepened the black in the lines. "I don't know."

Hawk cried out overhead, a screech of triumph and warning. Two carcasses plummeted through the leaves, plump birds falling like overripe fruit. With sudden laughter Hathorn flung out long arms and caught them before they hit the ground. "Sooquail. It seems we feast." He laughed again as Cat came round the wagon, a white-and-silver ghost with a fat coney dangling from her mouth. She spat it out at Arryn's feet, growled deep in her throat at the birds in Hathorn's hands. With haughty displeasure she stalked off, to reappear a moment later with a second coney. She dropped it and sat on a root to lick busily at a paw. Arryn leaned forward.
—Cat—

Cat pretended not to hear that and contorted herself to lick at the long hair on her belly.

—Three more, my lazy mog, or your life will be a misery—

Oblivious to the threat, Cat continued licking until she was finished. A moment later she sat up, yawned, then walked off with great dignity, her tail held high.

Hathorn dropped the birds onto the coneys. "She's not very pleased with you."

"It's a bit too much like work." Arryn rubbed her shoulders against the trunk, laced her hands behind her head. "This isn't my world. I've got no connection to your moons or anything else. Why Moonwitch?"

He rubbed a thumb over a small spot of blood on one finger. "My mother named you." A long tense silence. He dug his thumbnail into the dry spongy bark, broke a chunk away, crumbled it between his fingers, dug off some more. "True oracles are rare," he said softly, turning the bit of bark over and over in his hands. "Even among the Eddray, so my mother said. The Sight usually comes only to the dying."

The bark crumbled, he brushed it off his legs. "My mother was a slave when my father first saw her, a very young girl with an iron collar about her neck, walking behind a mercenary off a Kalappo ship. One time when he was very drunk, Father told me she was the most beautiful creature he'd ever seen, sun-colored eyes, hair like frozen starlight, skin the bloody brown of mahogany. He bought her and later he married her. People said she witched him into it. I don't think even he knows why he did it. She told me stories of the Eddray, but not where to find them or who her own people were. There was a lot she didn't know, she was stolen from them when she was only eleven. When the mindspeech came on me, she taught me how to endure the pain and confusion. My half brothers were making my life. . . ."

He lifted his head at Hawk's warning screech, caught the second pair of birds and dumped them on the others. "I haven't talked like this for five years, not since my mother died." He began digging again at the bark on the root. "There was no one to tend her but me. My father hadn't spoken to her for years. The Eddray Sight came on her one night. 'The Moonwitch, Hathorn,' she said to me, 'watch for her. She is the sign. The old order falls.' She laughed. It was a hard thing to hear, that laugh. 'Blood and terror, a black tide rising. Bad gives way to worse,' she said. 'She is the sign, Hathorn, moon rising to light the world, Moonwitch and Murderess bound in one flesh. Know her by her two souls: dark and light, death and life.' " His voice dropped until it was little louder than the rustle of oak leaves. "She lingered three days more, but she never spoke again."

"Moonwitch, hah!" Arryn spoke more forcefully than she felt to counter the weight of his expectation. "You've got rocks in your head if you think I'm going to involve myself in politics anywhere on this 'curst world. Push me, friend, and I take a dive into elsewhere. You'll have to find yourself another sign or whatever you think I am."

He smiled at her. "You have nothing to say about it, Moonwitch. The axis of fate is turning, whatever you do will move the destruction on." Voices came floating up the road, muffled hoofbeats, the jingle of metal tapping against metal. "You'll join us?" He got to his feet, reached a hand down to her.

"When the hunting's done." She pulled her hand free as soon as she was on her feet; he went quiet at her quick withdrawal from contact, turned and walked away.

The triple-moon shone silver on the hushed black water rushing past her toes. She stroked the narsit, sharing its contentment, contented herself with the warmth in her belly from Clem's stew and the other warmth from the song and laughter after the meal. She sat on the trunk of a tree knocked down in some storm that whipped along this river before she knew this world existed. Others had sat here before her, maybe lovers come up from the village for the privacy, their bottoms wearing through the bark, polishing the white wood beneath until it gleamed like ivory in the brightening moonglow. The river sang chords and descants past her toes; in the distance Hawk screamed, an eerily lovely paean to freedom; the wind scraped through the stiff leaves of the riveroaks; the trees creaked to their own rhythms; nightshades with black velvet wings swooped and wheeled above the river, their fluting whistles barely audible above the watersong. Through this medley she heard the soft scuff of booted feet, a rattle of brush; because she expected him, because the feel of him came before him, she didn't turn.

"Arryn inek." He stepped over the log and dropped beside her, saying nothing more, reaching for her hand.

She let it rest under his for a moment, then quietly slid it away. "Hathorn inouk." She sighed. "You want to know who attacked the town."

"Yes." He stretched hs legs out, his heels almost in the water. "This is the fourth raid. The Scrubs and I, we ride the hillroads day by day, but we're always too late."

She bent over the narsit, touched fingertips to the round of its skull. —All right, baby, make your mirror and show us what happened this morning—

With a flurry of whistles and squeaks, the narsit *changed*. An oval mirror lay on her knees. With a quick intake of breath, Hathorn reached over to touch the gleaming surface, but Arryn interposed her hand. "No. Look only."

When the mist in the mirror cleared, they saw in miniature

the town waking in the red light of dawn; a horse being shod
at the smithy; a woman emptying slops out a back window of
the Inn; a yawning, scratching hostler leaning against the
stable wall watching a pair of young maids filling tubs at the
pump in the back court. Out in the street women carried
loaves to the communal oven or stopped in the midst of other
chores to exchange gossip. Shadows lay long on the earth.

The viewpoint changed. As if they looked through the eyes
of a low-flying bird, the road slid beneath them, swung round
a wide bend; then they were hovering above a troup of
black-clad horsemen clotted so close it was difficult to judge
how many there were. Each had a long black cloth twisted
about his head with one end pulled across nose and mouth
and tucked into the twist on the other side, hiding the whole
of his lower face.

She touched Hathorn's arm. "Do you know them?"

"No. Not even by rumor."

Horror unfolded in silence. The unprovoked attack, the
hillfolk cut down as the raiders swept along the main street
then came back to spread through the secondary streets. The
blacksmith went down, still clinging to his sledge, wounded
but not out of the fight. He swung the hammer one-handed at
the legs of a horse about to trample him and brought the beast
down, screaming, its foreleg broken. A woman and a boy ran
from the forge and slashed wildly at the downed raider with
hiltless blades from the smithy. The woman fell, feathered
with bolts, but not the boy. Though he killed the raider, they
let him run until one of them caught him by the hair, knocked
him senseless, hauled him across his saddle and rode on.

"Slavers." Hathorn's hand closed on her shoulder, tightened painfully. "I should have known. I should have known."

When most of the townsfolk were dead, the raiders played
with the rest, riding round and round them, swinging their
scimitars in close misses or inflicting nonfatal wounds, taking
their time about these last deaths as if they knew with abso-
lute certainty that they were safe from any interruption.

Arryn watched, chill with disgust (Nys vibrating with
delight), as some of them fired the town while others rounded
up the children and herded them into the empty market

square, boys and girls not younger than five nor older than twelve. The leader of the raiders dismounted and moved through the child-herd, cutting out the fairest, sending them stumbling toward the ring of raiders. Their hands and feet were bound with soft thongs and they were thrown across the saddles in front of the riders. When each horse bore one captive, the leader remounted, lifted an arm over his head, brought it down hard and fast, then sat watching while his men used the remaining children as targets.

The image broke suddenly as the mirror throbbed and waves of darkness rippled across it. It lost form until the narsit lay panting in her lap, shaking, making small whining sounds, eyes dull, pressed beyond its strength. Arryn bent over it, quieting it with fingers that sought and traced the flickering energy lines within the torso and head. She felt a slow trickle of heat leave her and warm the lines, healing its hurts as it had helped her heal the hurts of others. The transfer was slow at first then the draw grew suddenly stronger, so strong in seconds she couldn't break away, she couldn't move, could only sit hunched over the narsit as she was sucked out of her body. (Nys rose, hissing with triumph, extended through the body without opposition, hissed with fear when she found the draw sucking at her too, shrieked in silent rage and clawed at the link, twisted free at last and retreated deep within the body.)

A hand on her shoulder, warm, comforting, giving her the strength to replace the strength leached from her; heat surged into her. She leaned into it, let her head fall over so her cheek rested on the hand. A second hand closed about her wrists, jerking her hands off the narsit. The drain was gone, the link broken. Eyes closed, she lay limp against Hathorn, her limbs flaccid and strengthless.

More cautious than before, Hathorn did not try to touch the narsit. Holding Arryn braced against him, he mindshouted at it —Get off her. You've got enough from her. Get!—

The narsit hissed at him, its plush fur ruffled, its round ears laid flat against its head. It kneaded small black handfeet on Arryn's thighs, black eyes glittering, blasting back at him a stubborn refusal.

—Think on this— Hathorn mindspoke coldly —she could have died—

Squealing, the hair on its body standing stiff, the narsit leaped from Arryn's lap and went lalloping into the shadow under the trees. With a shaky laugh he lifted Arryn onto his knees and held her as she began to regain control of her body. He looked down at the fair head resting on his shoulder, touched it gently with his fingertips. It wasn't quite the frost-white of his mother's, more like pale honey, and it smelled of sunlight rather than night, felt like oiled silk as he smoothed his hand over the round of her skull and down to her waist, over and over.

Arryn sighed with pleasure, nestled against him, startling him into a burst of tenderness and desire. He cupped his hand under her chin and lifted her head so he could see her face. It was round and rather childlike with a deep vulnerability in the large eyes, the trembling lips. He focused on her mouth, wanting her with a sudden urgency that threw him into confusion. Not since adolescence had a woman stirred him like this.

His lips teased hers, finding them soft and responsive. Her hands came round his neck, her fingers played in the short hair curling there. He slipped a hand under the gathers of her blouse, slid it down to cup her breast.

With an anguished sob, she flattened her hands on his chest and thrust him away from her, harder perhaps than she intended, sending him back over the trunk, his head slamming into the hard earth, the breath knocked out of him. Angry and humiliated, he scrambled to his feet, stood plucking at bits of leaf and bark that clung to his hair and clothing. "I wouldn't have forced you."

"I know." Shoulders slumped, her face in shadow, there was a sad resignation about her that touched him despite his anger.

"Why?"

She trembled, he knew that by the tremble of moonlight on her hair, the shiver of moonlight along the edge of the face he couldn't see. "Two souls in one body. You know that. You even named the other. Murderess." She seemed to gather herself, sitting straighter, her head up, though she still would not look at him. "Come sit. Please. I listened to your story. Now hear mine."

"From time's beginning my people have been two. In the dreamtime before we knew ourselves, we were two like horse and rider." She made a gesture of impatience and anger. "Really it was more like a flea on a dog, but the other is what we were taught as children. As time passed the two bodies merged into one until most had one mind, one body, one soul. A certain number of our children were born . . . well . . . different, but our doctors and our . . . hmmh . . . call them sages, our doctors and sages found medicines to help them, and all was well again until the war." She slumped again, pushed at the hair that fell over her face. "I won't try to tell you about that war, you wouldn't understand. How could you understand that the war lasted a day and a night and half another day, then both sides lost? How could you understand that the war lasted a thousand years after that? How could you understand that that war was my father and my mother more surely than the horrified man who sired me, the terrified woman who bore me? I was a pale white worm, Hathorn, with less shape than a cloud until I grew old enough to comprehend shape and desire it, to discover I was a prisoner hidden away where no one would have to look at me and be reminded. I discovered shape, I discovered rage and hate and self-disgust, I discovered the uses of a lie. And when I knew all they could teach me, I escaped."

She wound her hands together. "And I found Nys-within. We took many lovers. We played with them, many games, and the last game was death. At the moment of release we slid a knife into our lover's heart and rode death to our own release. We were very clever and very cautious, but we enjoyed our game too much, we killed too many. The Judges trapped us. We were given choice of mindwipe or permanent exile with others guilty of not pleasing them. We chose exile, thinking it didn't matter much to us where we found our pleasure, but we woke in this form, we woke with Arryn in control, Arryn who was all our gentler, more vulnerable aspects, while Nys the destroyer was left helpless. Or so we thought. Oh she rumbled and she grumbled, but Horse, Cat, Hawk, and I, we mostly ignored her. I was too busy learning to be Arryn." She lifted her head, a bit of a smile back in her eyes. "Not so bad a thing to be, eh, Hathorn?"

He drew his fingers down the side of her face, smiled at the catch in her breathing. "Not so bad."

She put her hand over his a moment, holding it against her cheek, then dropped it and moved a little away from him. "We dived from reality to reality, Horse and I, looking for something we couldn't explain even to ourselves, Cat and Hawk content anywhere as long as there were things to hunt, air to fly in, shadows to prowl. On the last world . . . on the last world there was a man, a poet and a singer of old songs. I loved him. At first I was afraid. But Nys seemed to sleep." Her voice sank so low he had to strain to hear her. "Late one night when he lay beneath me, Nys took our body and changed it. She used the claws she made to rip his throat away." One hand came up to curl around her throat, slide down it, do the same thing over and over until she became aware of what she was doing and dropped the hand into her lap. "After that, she hitched Horse to the travel wagon, called Cat and Hawk, and drove us from that high mountain city. She whipped Horse down the winding road, whipped him till he bled and was blind with pain. Cat yowled and Hawk screeched, but they were bound to the Wagon and bound to go where it went. She drove us off a cliff but in her triumph she was careless and Arryn came forth and used the device to dive us here. Which is how we came to land so suddenly in Cetanjji." She swung around, smiling a little, facing him at last. "I think a touch of unrequited passion is preferable to what else I offer."

"I understand." He got tiredly to his feet. "We'll talk again in the morning."

"Yes," she said, then looked away. "In the morning."

*   *   *

In the crisp cool dawn, Arryn came out of the wagon and sat on the folding steps to comb her hair. She was hurting still and needed Horse's acerbic good sense, but when he ambled up and stood rubbing his flank against a wheel, she would not mindspeak him because Hathorn might hear. Horse snorted his disgust but stayed beside her, his presence comforting without words. Good smells around her. Coffee and frying fish, the strong spicy odor of Horse, wet lacquer and wood from the wagon, bark and leaf and earth. Enough to persuade her that life was, after all, worth waking up for. She was hungry and Clem's cooking was sufficient all by itself to justify existence. She slid the comb into a skirt pocket, poked her blouse down behind the waistband, tugged the tight vest into place, shook out the heavy cloth of her skirt, and went to get her breakfast.

As she ate, she felt Hathorn at the edges of her mind, a comfortable buzz flitting about beyond the clearing. The buzz grew louder near the wagon, not quite separating into words. Mindspeaking Horse. She lifted the fish, crunched at the crisp tail fan. Haridar suck your bones, Nys, she told herself, I wanted him. Ay-my-me-mo, I wasn't meant to wallow in gloom. She licked at her fingers, jumped to her feet, stretched, exuberance sweeping from her toes to the arms stretched high over her head. "*Ohaahh*," she cried, then answered Clem's chuckle with one of her own.

Horse was curried and harnessed, ears flicking idly, eyes focused on distance, his mind turned inward, sorting through yesterday's impressions. Cat sprawled with liquid grace on the seat, staring dreamily at nothing, savoring memories from last night's prowl. Arryn circled the wagon and found Hathorn seated on a root. She waved at the wagon. "Thanks."

He sketched a dismissal. "Can you find the raiders for me?"

"I'll see." She climbed the wheel and swung onto the seat, displacing Cat with a tap on the rump that sent her grumbling through the curtains. "Come, sit beside me and we'll have a look." She swung round and leaned over the backrest, holding one of the curtains aside. —Come, my narsit, I need you—

The narsit yawned, rubbed its handfeet together, scrubbed them over its face. She felt the wagon shift as Hathorn came up and waited until the shaking settled before she called again. —Come, my little one, my friend who answers all my needs, it won't be like last night—

The narsit turned around twice, then sat on its haunches staring at her, or rather, past her at Hathorn. Then it launched itself in a soaring leap at Arryn, flattening itself onto her arm, then her shoulder as she drew it through the curtains, its black muzzle pressed against the curve between neck and shoulder, most of its small body veiled by the sweep of her hair.

Hathorn lifted the hair away from the narsit, tucking the strands behind her ear, his fingertips burning her with their fleeting touch. She felt the heat in her face, the tightness of her skin, cursed the habit of blushing she couldn't seem to break. This will pass, she told herself. I'll stop reacting to him sooner or later. Crooning to the narsit, she settled it in her lap, asking nothing of it till it relaxed into a boneless rug on her knees. —Don't be frightened, my lovely, my little one, it's only for a breath or two. Make the mirror and show me the black riders again, show me where they were just before sundown last night. Find them for me, baby, not now but last night—

The narsit *changed*. Hathorn slid nearer, bent over the mirror, his head close to hers, one hand closed on her shoulder. She blushed again, but knew he wasn't aware right now that he was touching her. He was too intent on the mirror and the scene developing there.

The black riders are moving along at an easy walk, their mounts tired but not laboring; the captive children are still slung across their knees, limp and dead-eyed. They ride between slender white trees with heart-shaped leaves that flutter in the lighter airs, throwing flittery shadows across them.

"Quivering shallon," Hathorn muttered.

The riders emerge suddenly into a small clearing. Rising above the trees ahead is a mountain half again as high as those about it, its glaciated peak bloody in the crimson glow of the setting sun.

"Haaom's Tooth. They're making for the Chute."

The black riders ride clustered together with no urgency to them, as if they know absolutely that no one can follow them or make them answer for the dead. One rides three lengths behind the rest, sitting backward on his horse, hands moving in rhythmic, smoothing gestures, his eyes intent on the ground. As his hands move, the earth boils up and blows smooth behind the riders, fallen leaves scatter themselves carelessly, crushed grasses spring erect. No sign of their passage is left, probably not so much as a dropped horsehair.

Arryn stroked the edge of the mirror. —Enough, baby, you've shown us what we need— When the narsit returned to its usual shape, she gave it a praising pat, then put it back through the curtains.

Hathorn sat staring at his hands. She waited but he didn't speak. When she couldn't bear the silence anymore she said, "You have what you wanted."

He straightened, thrust long brown fingers impatiently through his hair. "Last night. Where are they now?"

"Breaking camp, I imagine," she said tartly. "As you should be. And if you think I'm going to overlook that bunch in the present, you'd better think again. I'm not going anywhere near that . . . that creature. He'd swallow me whole and hardly notice."

"You're coming with us. I need you." His words were clipped, his voice hard.

"Try making me."

"Not I. The children."

"Unfair." She swung around until her knees knocked against his. "You know I can't . . . All right, you win. But don't expect me to go near that witchman."

At sundown on the third day they made a silent camp beside a creek that wound among shallan trees and scattered conifers, not half a mile from the raiders who were settled for the night on the bank of the same creek.

Night is abstract black and white, patterns flat and sharp-edged, with flickers, small sudden movements, imposed on the smoother flow. Cat prowls the patterns, Arryn riding behind her eyes, seeing what she sees, smelling and hearing what she smells and hears. The chords of scent and sound are intoxicating, tempting both hunter and passenger from the purpose of the stalk. Cat grumbles at the restraints that keep her pointed toward the camp of the black riders, but revels in the night and the pleasures of her senses. She lifts her head, dilates her nostrils. Man-scent, a peculiar taint to it. —They are there, just ahead—

A whisper of laughter from Arryn. —You needn't sound so surprised. Hawk told us they were there—

—Hawk, *fft*— Cat threads through the trees, ghosting to the edge of the clearing.

The hairs along her spine stiffen, her back arches, her tail fluffs and points stiffly to the sky, the tip twitching. —I see nothing. I smell and hear them and I see nothing—

The small meadow in front of her is a stretch of moonlit grass and spring flowers with a few deer browsing at shrubs on the far side of the open space. Cat's tail twitches more violently; she can smell the smoke from a fire, the dusty acrid odor of many horses, a powerful man-stink. She can hear, very faintly, a man humming, another walking about, the tiny jingle of spurs, a sudden spitting exclamation in a language she doesn't understand. Puzzled and annoyed, Cat inches closer.

There is a faint buzz an inch or two in front of her nose, a curious foul smell that both frightens and angers her. She reaches out a paw and pats the air before her, feels a barrier like burning glass. Yowling with pain and fear, she leaps back, turns end-for-end, and flees.

Arryn shook loose, rubbed trembling hands down her thighs, then folded them in her lap. Hathorn squatted close beside her, his eyes on her face, one hand resting lightly on her

shoulder. "There's some kind of barrier about their camp,"
she said. "It distorts sight. You see what is not there."

"What about breaking through it?"

"I don't know. It burned Cat, scared her. And she's not
easily frightened."

"How high is it? A dome or just a wall?"

"Not a dome. When Hawk flew over a few moments ago,
he could see them." She tilted her head back. —Hawk—

—No— Hawk's reply was a silent shout of refusal.

—All you have to do is sail down until the camp vanishes.
There's no danger in that— When there was no answer, she
reached out again. —Hawk, if we have to send a man to
look, HE will know—

Hawk swooped toward a tall conifer growing among the
shallons, a twisted tree with a few clumps of long needles at
the ends of gnarled branches. He landed on one of the
branches with a neat explosion of feathers. —HE knows. HE
looked at me the last time I went over, just after you mindspoke
me— He drew his head down until it seemed to rest neckless
on his powerful shoulders. —HE reached for me—

"Haridar! Hathorn . . ."

"I heard. Question is, how much did the witchman get
from his look? Couldn't be that much." —Hawk—

Hawk blinked golden eyes and shifted uneasily on his
branch.

—You won't be over him long enough for him to do you
harm. If you tell me where the witchman is and how high the
barrier is, I can send archers into the trees to take him out.
When he's dead, you're safe. Fly over the camp, drop down
fast like you did a moment ago, then come back here—

Hawk swayed from side to side, releasing one foot then the
other in an agitated dance. His feathers fluffed out and his
head bobbed up and down.

"Arryn, convince him."

"I'll try."—Hawk, you know I can't make you do anything
you don't want to. And I know you don't give half a damn
about the dead or the children, but I need you to do this.
Please?—

Hawk's agitation increased until he was staggering along

the branch. Abruptly he spread his wings wide, screamed and left the tree with powerful wing strokes that carried him high above them in seconds. Arryn watched, wondering what he was going to do. He'd sealed himself against her, retreating into hawk-nature until there was only a fading smell of his other self. He soared toward the thickening clouds, turning and turning in widening circles until he vanished.

"What will he do?" Hathorn's voice had an edge to it; having to depend so much on a reluctant and unreliable agent wore at his temper.

"I'm not sure." She looked around. The Scrubs were sitting or squatting around them, silent shadows nearly lost among the shadows of the trees, watching her and Hathorn; they didn't know quite what to make of her. If she'd been Hathorn's woman, they could have accepted that, put her in one of woman's usual slots and forgot about her. As things were, they were growing jealous of the time he spent with her; soon they'd start trying to protect him from her. She slanted a glance at the dark face so close to hers, saw him smiling, and shook her head.

Hawk plummeted from the clouds, spilled the air from his wings and settled with graceful economy of effort onto the bare branch. Smug with success, he preened his feathers busily until Arryn felt like pulling them out one by one. He lifted his head. If a hawk can be said to grin, he was grinning. —It's not more than two men high. Witchman's alone by the fire, busy at something, don't know what. Others rolled in their blankets, most of them, one or two with the itch or something, can't settle, walking about. Kids are sleeping off to one side. Ain't worried about nothing, that bunch— He spread his wings and screamed, flapped them a few times then tucked them back against his sides, vastly pleased with himself.

Hathorn came swiftly to his feet. "Perrin, Onou, Maccel, your bows. Skewer me that witchman. Yonar, take six, circle round to the far side of the meadow; the rest of you come with me. The barrier will fall when the witchman's dead. That's the signal to hit them."

* * *

Cat came limping into the camp. She jumped into Arryn's lap, curled up, and started licking at her paw. Horse came ambling back from the creek, the narsit curled up on his withers. The shadows under the trees watched them all.

Arryn shivered. —Your thing in the groves, Horse. I think it's waiting for something nasty to happen—

Horse turned his head from side to side, uneasy. —There's nothing there—

—An itchy nothing. What are we doing here, old friend? This is their war— She felt Cat shift under her hands, noted the sudden tension in the long body draped across her thighs. —Why don't I strap on your saddle and get us the sheol out of here?—

—On your feet then, let's go— Horse's burring mindbass sounded amiable and acquiescent, but she wasn't fooled.

—Oh, you do know me, don't you, old friend—

—The conscience the Judges stapled in you is inconvenient at times, but I've learned not to waste my energy arguing with it—

Cat wriggled from under her hands, leaped out of her lap, and stood with back arched, tail bushed, erect and twitching. Eyes fixed on the creek, she hissed threat and warning.

Shadowy feet gliding a handbreadth above the water, the misty image of the witchman came toward her. It halted where the creek smoothed into a deep pool. "Who are you?"

Arryn said nothing. The question the apparition threw at her was no question at all, but a command that she search within herself for everything she was and gift that to him. It. Whatever. Coldness flowed out of the thing and into her, numbing her. That numbness stilled her hands, seized her head so she couldn't look away, though the shadowy gaze sent shudders through her.

Herself struck then, driving outward through the body, taking it without opposition as the mist figure on the water stiffened, convulsed, flicked into nothing. Arryn began struggling to retake the body, but it was too late. Nys was firmly in control.

Vest and blouse were ripped off by hands growing blunt and extruding grey horn-claws like pewter scimitars. The skirt went flying as did her boots. Feet broadened, grew thick pads on the soles and cruel grey claws on the toes. Nys stood in the small clearing, glaring defiance at the Companions as her face changed, thinning, lengthening, jaws heavier, tearing teeth dropping into grooves in her lower lip. With a snarl she wheeled and loped into the shadows, heading for the battle whose first sounds were breaking through the continual rustle of the shallow leaves, the brushing purl of the creek.

The barrier was down. The witchman lay in a loose sprawl beside a dying fire whose coals were scattered but still smoldering, shoulders and torso held off the ground by the dozen or more arrow piercing them. (Helpless in a body lost to her, Arryn felt a measure of satisfaction, knowing she'd contributed to his fall, keeping him too busy to notice the bowmen wriggling up their trees.)

The promise of blood thick in nose and throat, Nys ran from the trees and threw herself on a raider, foot-claws ripping open his back just above the buttocks, hand-claws tearing out his throat. She used his toppling body to launch herself past the gaping Scrub, throwing a snarl at him but leaving him untouched, warned off him by a burst of heat from Arryn. Nys hit the ground and bounded after other raiders, tearing, snarling, mindless in a frenzy of bloodlust, taking cuts and blows as she raged through the battle, howling her pleasure in the pain.

From kill to kill she went, around and around in a spiraling dance of death, power flowing up through her animal feet into her hot, unreasoning brain, around and around until she reached the knot of fighters struggling about the leader of the raiders. With the hunting scream of a great cat, she went leaping up a raider's back, launched herself in a high arching dive that carried her over the weapons of the struggling men toward the man who stood alone within the circle of defenders.

Weapon blurring with the speed of his reaction, he whipped his scimitar up and around, slashing at her. He was too late, too slow. The edge cut into her side, but failed to kill her. Her claws ripped his face away, then she was falling with him, growling deep in her throat, worrying at his. He was dead before their twined bodies hit the ground.

Nys rolled off him and lay on her back, not unconscious but too weak from blood loss and dullness of will to force the body on. Spreading her arms wide, she welcomed wordlessly her lover death.

The raiders still on their feet moaned in unison at the death of their leader. As one they leaped away from the startled Scrubs, tore open their collars, fished out short silver thorns pendant from silver chains. Drawing them between their teeth, they scraped off the wax on their points and drove those points into their throats. The poison was quick. In a breath or two every black-veiled man lay dead.

Hathorn wiped his sword on a torn black cloak and thrust it into its scabbard with a hard clatter loud in the sudden silence. He used the back of a bloody hand to wipe some of the sweat from his face. "Yonar-sul."

"An-saich inouk." Yonar came stepping over bodies, trying to tie a bit of rag about a bleeding arm.

"What's the reckoning?"

"We got a few nicks but every man's standing."

"Good. Break out the medical supplies, take care of the wounded, and you get some powder on that cut before it starts rotting on you." He rubbed wearily at the nape of his neck. "Cut the kids loose, make them help. Do them good to be busy at something."

"What about the healwoman? You brought her for them."

Hathorn looked at Nys lying with open eyes, her blood-soaked chemise barely stirring. "Witchman got to her," he said, after a moment's thought.

"An-saich." Yonar sketched a salute and trotted off, calling out names as he moved, sending men for gear, ordering the children cut loose, dealing with any need that caught his eye.

Hathorn walked slowly over to Nys. He knew she was alive, the mindtouch told him that. It also told him that life in her was ebbing fast. Holding his breath, he knelt beside her, ignoring her weak warning growl, fending off the hand that tried to swipe at him. The blood on her mouth, the fragments of flesh caught in her teeth made him a little queasy; he tried not to think of them as he inspected the oozing slash in her side. He lifted her carefully, carried her to a grassy patch beside the creek. Stripping off the bloody chemise, he pressed it against her side. He clamped his hands down hard, watched anxiously, cursed as the cloth bloomed red almost immediately. Hair straggling into his eyes, sweat dripping from nose and chin, he lifted his head. Cat was licking delicately at the blood on Nys's face, Horse stood beside him. —Horse, you know her, tell me what to do—

—Link with us—

—How?—

—Open your mind to me, I'll draw you in—

Hands locked on the body so tightly they ached, Hathorn fought to let his barriers down. At first the habit of years—a habit nailed in place by pain and humiliation—was too much for him, but his mask had already cracked for Arryn, and at this moment he was battle-weary in many senses, too weary to care what happened to him. The mask dissolved and he was open, defenseless, a boy-child again shuddering at things that walk in the dark. Horsemind was strong and reassuring but strange. He felt Horse's lack of interest in men; they were little to him but hindrances, stupid petty useless obstacles between him and the things he wanted to know. He felt the dark pull of Horse's obsession to acquire information, felt his equally obsessive need for Arryn/Nys and the Companions, a need that stretched now to include Hathorn.

Hawk flew down, stood at Arryn's head, flowed into the meld (sharp jags of crimson and gold stirred into Horse's diamond-hard blue white).

Cat sat back on her haunches and joined herself to them (a touch of cool green with prickings of hot pink).

Hathorn knelt, his hands on Arryn, his eyes on Nys's face, feeling himself pulled into the meld (amber swirling into crimson gold pink green blue).

The narsit scrambled down from Horse and ran onto her bloody breasts, whistling its distress.

Horse gathered the kaleidoscope, aimed it at the narsit-focus.

It *changed.* It floated above her, a burning lens that caught the power from the meld, amplified it, directed it down at the dying woman.

Hathorn felt the body shiver under his hands, felt it burn, felt a flow of force like snowmelt surging up from his knees as if earth herself joined in the healing.

Flesh and bone flowed, unstable as sand, her hands and feet lengthened, narrowed, the claws were absorbed and she had simple nails again, childishly bitten nails, on her square, competent hands. Arryn, not Nys, lay on the grass: slightly overplump, round, guileless face, lips parted over small square teeth.

The meld came apart. Hawk took off into the sky and circled overhead, screaming his triumph to the night and the winds, loosing harmlessly the tensions built up in him. Cat stretched and yawned, leaped lightly to a slab of rock thrusting into the creek where she sat biting at her tail, then licking industriously at the places she bit. The narsit was itself again, whatever that was, sitting on Arryn's breasts, picking unhappily at the blood drying on its fur. Hathorn tried a smile, then laughed aloud.

—Curious— Horse turned his odd eyes on Hathorn, a gleam the man could recognize now lighting the hard brown. —That energy coming up through you. That's never happened before. Do you know what it was? Was it something you did consciously? How . . .—

Sudden mindlaughter. Arryn sat up, blushed a dark red, and held out a demanding hand for the chemise Hathorn was still holding. "So." She wriggled energetically to ease the tail of the ragged garment under her buttocks. "You've met my other half."

"A striking personage."

"One way of putting it."

He pulled her up beside him, strongly aware of the scents and shapes and textures of her body.

She looked around. "So many dead."

The image of Nys suddenly before him, he felt a moment's revulsion, then he stepped behind her, wrapped his arms about her and held her tight against him. "Most by their own hands.'' Arryn was not Nys, nothing like that monstrous killing machine. ''Slavers and murderers. Wasters.''

She rested her hands on his forearms, laid her head against his chest, tilted it so she could see his face. ''Do you have time to walk with me to the other camp?''

''Not much for me to do here. Yonar-sul's a good man. Why?''

''Because I can't bear to be alone for a while and I'm hungry and I should get my drugs.'' She laughed, soundless, exuberant laughter he felt in the bounce of her breasts along his arms, the shift of her ribs. ''And I need some clothes.''

''Arryn-n'mi, I'll come with you.'' He stepped away from her, held out his hand.

She searched his face. ''You mean more than a simple stroll.''

''Horse has adopted me into the Company. You want to argue with him?''

''Haridar, no!''

Sharing laughter, they walked into the friendly dark beneath the trees.

SKY SISTER

Diana Paxson

RAVENS CALLED HOARSELY FROM THE PINE TREES. IT HAD not taken them long to get here, thought Shanna. She could feel rain seeping cold down her back, and her hand slipped on the wet hilt of her sword. She tightened her grip, sent a quick glance up the empty road, and looked back at Hwilos.

"My Lady, you must go now!" His whisper barely stirred the sodden mat of his beard. The cloth she had packed into the wound in his thigh was already reddened.

"What do you mean, go? You got this gash protecting me!"

"I've got my death, trying—" he corrected. His painful smile shook Shanna's hard-won composure. The moist air was raw in her chest and she coughed to cover her emotion. Then she heard a chink of metal from beyond the rockfall and her breath caught. Were the brigands going to attack again? She should have believed the woman at the inn—the road was dangerous, a hunting ground for escaped serfs and slaves. They were too lazy to till the soil, but not too lazy to kill. . . .

"My death will be wasted if they take you!" Hwilos went on.

As Sandy's death had been wasted, and Zan's. Shanna's anguished glance went to the still bodies of the other two men who had come with her from Sharteyn. They had all survived so many dangers! She had been trained as a warrior,

278

and her men were veterans. Who would have thought peasants could fight so cunningly?

But Zan lay in the road before her, felled by a slingstone, and a scythe had made an extra mouth in Sandy's neck as he dismounted to help his friend. The rockfall beyond them blocked the road.

Shanna and Hwilos had already wrenched their horses' heads around to flee when they heard shouts from behind them too. They had compromised by scrambling off their mounts and diving for the illusory protection of a fallen tree. And then Hwilos saw someone move, and as he stood to draw his bow a flung axe had smashed him to the ground.

Pine branches showered them as the ravens sought a closer perch. One of them cawed harshly and was answered from the tree across the road.

"You hear?" breathed Hwilos. "The soldier's friends—I will not lack company. I will throw rocks to make the brigands think we're both here. When they rush me I can meet them with this axe and my sword. I'll have strength enough to make them sorry they took us on, but they are too many for the two of us to get clear. Lady—Shanna—you are kin to the Emperor—you know what they will do if they take you!" The puddle below him was pink with blood now.

"You must go . . . Shanna . . . I will haunt you if you stay here!" The gray eyes held hers.

Shanna shivered and looked away. If she stayed she could only hope to die fighting rather than be captured by men who would avenge upon her all their griefs against the Emperor. Either way, her journey would fail. She had sworn to seek the Emperor—but she had also sworn an oath to her men!

Her grip tightened on Hwilos's cold hand. "I pledged to defend you . . ." she began.

"Nay, lass—" he said softly. "I release you. Only let me die knowing *my* duty's done. See—your mare's waiting there in the thicket, with a clear path across the fields. Lady"—at last his voice showed his agony—"for my sake—go now!"

Shanna coughed again and nodded, incapable of words. She touched his cheek, then, keeping her head low, slipped between the trees. As she reached her horse she heard stones

clattering behind her—Hwilos fulfilling his part of their bargain so that she could fulfill hers. Weeping soundlessly, she
mounted and urged Calur over the muddy ground, urged her
to speed and more speed until the rasp of her breath and the
wind in her ears prevented her from hearing the cries behind
her.

But as darkness fell and the mare faltered, Shanna knew
that Hwilos had lied. She had left him behind, but the
memory of him dying in the rain still haunted her.

Shanna wandered through a wilderness where ravens with
human eyes dove at her on dark shining wings. One of them
looked at her with Hwilos's gray eyes, one had the astonished stare of the man from whom she had won her sword,
and there were others, with the eyes of men she had killed or
who had been killed at her side. *I must be dead too,* she
thought dully, but she could not remember how death had
come.

She remembered a gray road in the rain that turned to a
rutted track that disappeared as darkness fell. She had been
riding, though the coughing tore at her chest and she shook
with chill. There had been no shelter. So she had gone on.

*And now I am in the Otherworld, and no one will ever
know what became of me. . . .* She supposed that thought
should bother her, but the mist was oddly peaceful. Only the
harsh calling of the ravens rasped her awareness. She turned
on them, willing them to go away.

And turning, she saw a light glowing through the gray. It
hurt her eyes. She tried to look away, but it grew, and the
incessant crying of the birds distracted her. Shanna moaned
and lifted her arm to ward off the brilliance, felt pain and
opened her eyes. . . .

For a moment she was not sure whether she had been
asleep and was now waking or had slipped from tormented
waking into a bright dream. She could not understand what
she saw. Her crimson cloak and red leather brigandine hung
from pegs in a wall of weathered boards, and below them
leaned her shield and sword. A second, curved, wall of living
rock was extended to the ceiling by layered stones. The floor

of carefully joined poles was padded with fine rugs from
Menibbe, their colors mellow with age, and richly embroidered hangings decorated the walls. Sunlight streamed through
diamond panes from a cloudless sky.

Indeed, even from the high bed, all that Shanna could see
through that window was sky. If it had not been for the stone
wall, the chamber might have been floating in the air. If this
were the Otherworld, thought Shanna, she liked it better than
the place where she had been. She stretched, testing her long
body, felt the trained muscles weak but functional. Her chest
hurt when she breathed deeply, and her back ached from
immobility. Clearly she had been ill. And before that, there
had been some sorrow . . . her mind shied away from memory.

Pulse pounding from the movement, Shanna lay back again.
Beneath the tangled strands of her black hair, the pillow was
down-filled silk, and the softness beneath her a featherbed.
The silk sheet was worn smooth, soft furs made the coverlet.
Soft . . . it was all soft, like a cloud on which she could float
away.

Shanna's eyes closed and for a little she slept again. When
she woke, the band of sunlight had moved a few feet across
the floor, and she was no longer alone.

A girl was perched on what Shanna had assumed to be a
shelf in the stone wall, her feet tucked under her, her hands
busy with embroidery. Shanna wondered if she were the
artist who had decorated the brown smock she wore and the
wall hangings. Her glossy auburn hair was tied back with an
intricate looping of feathers and beads. The needle caught the
sun in tiny sparks as it darted in and out. She was humming
under her breath as she worked, just the way Hwilos always—

Shanna's breath caught painfully as she remembered. Hwilos
and the others were dead in the mud. She was alone.

She must have made some small sound, for immediately
the girl put down her work and slipped to the floor. Amber
eyes widened; a small mouth smiled.

"You are awake! I am so glad. . . . You were so very ill
when we found you—we were afraid."

Shanna stared at her, unable to keep the easy tears from
welling as she remembered. Glad! How could she be grateful

for her own life when she had lost her men? They were the last survivors of the troop that had escorted her from Sharteyn. With them she could remember who she was, and why she was journeying. But what was she now?

But the bright face before her demanded some acknowledgment. "How did I get here?" she asked hoarsely. Another thought came to her—"Is my horse safe?"

"Oh, yes!" The girl's husky voice was soothing. "Your mare brought you to our valley, and we've stabled her below. Don't worry, please—" a slim, calloused hand lifted the black hair back from Shanna's brow and for a moment rested there. "Your fever is gone, and you will be better soon. I will get you some tea."

Shanna tried to return her smile, but she knew that it would take more than tea to heal the fever of guilt, the chill of loneliness. She watched her nurse disappear downward through a square opening in the floor, a sight odd enough to distract her from her internal dialogue—the place must be built vertically, clinging to some hill.

In a few moments the girl popped up again, balancing a tray with a stoneware pot, a mug, and a basketry platter of grain cakes in one hand.

"I give you good welcome to the Eyrie, Mistress"—she made a half-bow and added, less formally—"and you have my welcome too. I am Chai. . . ." She set the tray on the edge of the bed and looked at Shanna expectantly.

Shanna summoned her strength for an appropriate reply. "Shanna ni Artinor, Royal Daughter of Sharteyn, thanks you for your hospitality and for her life as well." She fell back against the pillows, wondering if the child believed her, for Chai's yellow eyes were widening. Abruptly she stepped back and made an obeisance so deep that she nearly fell.

"My Lady—" she stammered. "You do us honor indeed!"

Shanna frowned. It was normal for her title to bring respect, but not awe.

"Lady, you are of the Imperial kin! Have you come to us from the Emperor?" Chai was on her feet again, dancing with eagerness.

"Oh, my dear, Sharteyn is only one of the northern princedoms. My grandfather married the sister of the Emperor Orein, but now we hardly dare claim kinship! That is why I was journeying—" Shanna added bitterly. "My brother went to do homage to the Emperor when he came of age and has never returned. I was on my way to Bindir to find him. . . ."

"Oh, but soon you will be able to go on—"

Shanna looked at the other girl. "Will I? My escort is lost—" She winced and closed her eyes against the memory of Hwilos's white face wet with rain, but the picture only came more clearly. "It's a long way," she continued with difficulty. "I don't know if I can get there alone."

Chai left her alone then, and she slept out the afternoon and the night again. She awakened to a new day and a great calling of birds, with muscles twitching with the need to be moving despite her weakness. Chai would have brought her a tray, but she insisted she could go down to breakfast—and down it was indeed, with two ladders and a passageway.

She was panting by the time they reached the Hall, built with its back to the cliff like the bedchamber. Shanna stepped to the windows and quickly moved back again, still dizzied by the glimpse she had got of the drop to the valley.

"Now I see why you call this place the Eyrie!" She managed a smile as she took her place on the bench beside Chai. Courtesy forbade her to ask why the place had ever been built this way. Chai looked as if the comment puzzled her, but her mouth was full of porridge and she did not reply.

A young man with a crippled arm was already at the table. He had Chai's eyes. As they ate others entered—two little girls who stared at Shanna like small owls, an older woman with a bitter mouth who shooed them to places down the table and did not return Shanna's tentative smile, a very old man who watched her with bright eyes.

Chai's mother bustled in and out from the kitchen, bringing in sausages, pickled fish, dried fruit, and tea. Finally she set down a last platter of bran-cakes and settled onto the bench, wiping her hands on her apron. She was plump, quick in movement, and Shanna suspected that little escaped her dark eyes.

Chai finished her porridge and turned to Shanna eagerly.

"We can see to your mare when you're finished. She's a fine horse. Did you ride her all the way from Sharteyn? Is Sharn a big city? What sorts of things did you do there?"

"I should hope something better than answering the questions of foolish girls at the breakfast table—"

A new voice, harsh, but not unkind. Shanna looked up quickly and found her gaze held by topaz eyes. This must be Chai's father. He bowed formally.

"My Lady Shanna, I repeat my daughter's welcome. I am Achul Terzel." Sunlight glinted on the silver in his thick, backswept hair as he bent. He straightened, and Shanna lowered her eyes, afraid of his keen glance.

"Thank you," she answered softly. "I would have died." If he sensed her sudden regret that she had not, he was too courteous to give any sign. He nodded again.

"We are honored by your presence here."

He took his seat at the head of the long table and began his meal. Shanna toyed with her sausage while Chai fidgeted beside her. It was very quiet in the big room—too big for the number of people eating there. A dim curiosity stirred.

"Is this all your community?" She asked. Chai opened her mouth to reply, shot a swift glance at her father, and shut it again.

"All there are now—" Achul had heard the question. "We were a proud people once, well known at the Court in Bindir. But time and misfortune have thinned our numbers—"

"Misfortune!" Chai's brother spoke for the first time. "It was malice that left me this way!" He tried to raise his crippled arm. "The bond has been broken. I give *that*"—he gestured rudely—"for the Court at Bindir!"

"Perin!" Chai's mother spoke severely. "Be still! Whatever the rights of it, there is no need to trouble the Lady with our tragedies . . ."

"Yes, but if someone were to *go* to the Emperor—" Chai began.

"We will ask no pardon from *him*." Her father's tone forbade answer.

Shanna looked down at her plate, embarrassed to be the cause of a quarrel she did not understand. But there was

much about this place which was beyond her comprehension—
the mixture of fine workmanship and crude repairs in the
buildings, the worn clothing and the golden medallion bearing the Emperor's crossed wheat sheaves and lightning bolts
set over the hearth. The boy's wild talk of the Court intrigued
her, but she could not imagine what the connection could be.
They finished the meal in constrained silence. The other
woman, the old man, and the children left as quietly as they
had come. Finally Chai swung her feet over the bench and
stood.

"Come on," she said brightly. "I'll show you where
we've sheltered your mare."

As Shanna had feared, it was a long climb to the foot of
the cliff and the stables, but she got a perverse satisfaction
from the realization that Chai found the descent as tiring as
she did. She would have supposed the girl must go up and
down these cliffs a dozen times a week, but perhaps there
was some other, easier way. Clearly the stone stairs were not
the main path to the Eyrie, for Shanna's fingers clutched at
stone that was weathered, rather than worn.

The stables were like the living quarters—an elegant structure of carved stone piers roofed clumsily with woven branches
thatched with straw. Perhaps they had lost their wealth and
could no longer afford to have skilled workers come. But
there was fragrant wild hay in the stall, and Calur lifted her
head alertly as Shanna stepped through the door.

"I know little of horses, but I've tried to care for her."
Chai hesitated behind her.

"Yes," Shanna answered her, "I can see that you have."
She ran her hand along the shining neck, and the mare dipped
her head and butted her gently. "I know, I know. You're
rested now and want exercise," Shanna murmured softly,
moving around her. There were still specks of mud on the
mare's sensitive belly and inner flanks, though the dirt had
been cleaned from her slender legs and the tangles combed
out of her mane and tail.

"Are you going to take her outside?"

Shanna sighed, for the climb down the cliff had tired her.

"I suppose I should, to keep her from getting out of condition. . . ." For a moment she pictured the mare soft and fat in these peaceful pastures, of herself breathing the free wind, safe from the storms of the outside world. Then Calur shoved at her again and she smiled.

"All right, love—we're going now—" She reached for the bridle and the horse dipped her head eagerly. But for a gentle canter around the valley she needed no other gear. Shanna contented herself with strapping the saddle blanket firmly to Calur's back and led the mare into the yard.

A sharp command stilled her long enough for Shanna to vault onto her back, although her heart was pounding uncomfortably when she took up the reins. Chai followed them, watching wistfully. Shanna looked at her, realizing that with her slender bones the horse could carry the two of them easily.

"Would you like to come too?"

Chai nodded eagerly, scrambled up onto the stone wall and hopped to Calur's back as Shanna brought the mare alongside.

"I have never been on the back of a horse before—" Chai confided as they moved down the rough track into the valley. The ground was still muddy, but the sun was warm, and puddles winked blue at the sky. Calur's nostrils widened as she scented the rich grass. She tugged at the rein.

"You're doing very well," said Shanna, reining the mare down firmly to a walk to let her muscles loosen. Only the occasional pressure of small hands at her waist told her the girl was behind her. She added, "You balance well."

Chai giggled. "I like this much better than walking on the ground."

It seemed an odd way of putting it, but the wind was like spring water, and through the saddle blanket she could feel the easy flow of the mare's muscles. It was easy to still her curiosity and simply enjoy the ride.

The track dwindled into a cowpath which was soon lost in the rich grass. Calur tossed her head eagerly, and this time Shanna eased the reins and let her go. The restrained walk became a long, springing trot, then the easy sway of a canter that carried them through the deeply green grass of meadows where sheep grazed like fallen clouds.

The valley twisted through the hills for several miles—a succession of broad meadows strung along the slender silver chain of the stream. To the east, wooded slopes rose steeply to granite crags like the cliff that sheltered the Eyrie, while the western hills were lower, furred with thickets just budding into vivid green. A cool wind funneled up the valley, bearing a liquid twitter of birdsong and the heady scents of opening flowers.

"Go faster, Shanna—let her run now!" cried Chai.

Shanna smiled and shifted her weight forward, loosening the reins. The mare's black ears flicked back and forward again; she stretched her neck and began to run. Wind blurred Shanna's vision as the mare hit her stride. *Run! Yes, run!* her heart echoed. *And leave all my grief behind!*

But at last Calur faltered and she slowed to a racking trot and then an amble, nostrils flaring. Still dizzied with speed, Shanna could feel the mare's flanks heaving as she caught her own breath again.

"So, lass—do you feel better now?" Shanna patted the damp bay neck.

"Oh! It was almost like flying!" exclaimed Chai behind her. There was a plaintive cry from overhead. They looked up and saw a dark shape circling. "Ha! Were you racing us?" Chai grinned and added a harsh call, as if she were imitating the bird.

For a moment it seemed to pause in the sky, then Shanna flinched as it hurtled downward in the long, terrible stoop of the falcon, braked and then glided to a perfect landing on Chai's outstretched arm. Shanna twisted awkwardly to look behind her. The peregrine's wings fluttered as it rebalanced and Chai bent to whisper into its ear. The bird replied with a sound disconcertingly like a soft coo, odd from so fierce looking a creature. The sleek head swiveled and for a moment Shanna met fierce amber eyes. Then Chai nodded, drew back her arm, and launched the falcon upward.

Shanna watched it catch the updraft and spiral lazily heavenward until it was only a speck against the blue. Then she lowered her gaze to catch Chai's. The other girl looked steadily back at her, in her expression an odd mixture of triumph, mischief, and fear.

"I had a goshawk in Sharteyn—" Shanna said when the silence had become too long. "But I never called a wild bird out of the sky."

"Well, I never rode a horse before. . . ." Chai replied, as if that were an answer.

Shanna sighed. It kept happening—this strangeness—just when she was beginning to think of the other girl as a friend. *You are alone*—she told herself. *Just remember that, and you won't be bereaved again. . . .*

"Turn the horse up through those trees—" said Chai after a short silence. "There's a knoll with a lovely view."

Chai had spoken truly. The view was beautiful, but it was the valley on the other side of the hills that one saw most easily, not Chai's home. And when they had dismounted, Chai stood on a rock gazing westward. Calur began to crop eagerly at the new grass and Shanna went to stand beside Chai. Below them stretched the ribbed black velvet of newly plowed fields. Beyond them clustered the buildings of the farmstead. In the distance she could just make out the cluttered outlines of a village, whose smoke stained the sky.

"What's that place called?" asked Shanna, more from a need to break the silence than because she wanted to know.

"Arun . . ."

"Is it a large place? I can barely see it from here."

"It seems large to me," said Chai wistfully. "There are fourteen houses there, clustered around the market square, and in the midst of it, the Shrine."

"And what sort of folk live there?" Shanna went on.

"I do not know. I have never been there."

"Never—" Surprise forced the question from Shanna's lips. "Don't you go on the market days, or for the Festivals? How do you get food?"

The feathers tied into Chai's glossy hair fluttered as she shook her head. "Traders bring their wares to our gates and we barter our embroideries and our carvings and our wool. . . .

We do not go outside the valley anymore.'' She turned her head away so that Shanna saw only her profile carved in silhouette against the brilliant sky.

"But why not? Have they threatened you, or does your father dislike—'' Chai's lips were pressed tightly together, and Shanna could see there was no point in questioning her more. For a few moments she waited, then, angered in spite of herself, Shanna jumped down from the rock and strode across the grass to lie down in the shade of a young ash tree.

After a little while, Chai sat down on the rock, arms clasped around her knees, still gazing out over the valley where she had never been. Shanna noted the dejected droop of her head and found her irritation turning to pity. The problem, whatever it was, was obviously no doing of Chai's, and it was unkind to press her. She thought of going to her to offer some kind of comfort, but the ride had tired her more than she knew. In a moment she would get up—in a moment—Shanna slept.

A small sound woke her. Shanna sat up, blinking, and sensed something sail through the air past Chai. There was a cry. Still struggling to focus, Shanna saw the other girl crumple. Shock jerked her to her feet. Abruptly clearing vision showed her Chai's body blurring into a new shape that fluttered frantically upward as another stone shot through the space where she had been.

Even as her eyes searched the hillside below them Shanna was running forward, drawing the long knife that always hung at her belt and cursing the false sense of safety that had let her come out here with no other arms. She charged over the lip of the hill at a dead run, weaving a little over the uneven footing, and saw someone below—there—a burly man with a sling whose face in that moment was that of the men who had killed Hwilos and Sandy and Zan.

He watched her come, poised as if to throw again, and then, as she passed some invisible point halfway down the hill, his face paled and he ran.

Shanna stopped, panting, at the bottom of the hill. Still weak from her illness, she could not overtake him quickly, and if she followed she might find herself outnumbered and outweaponed as well. She turned and looked back up the hill.

The girl who had tended her and almost become her friend was gone, but above the knoll a brown falcon circled anxiously. Shanna took a deep breath and began to climb back the way she had come.

"You were not supposed to know. . . ." Chai's voice shook so that Shanna could hardly understand her. And Shanna's flesh still stung from the pricking talons of the falcon that had come to her outstretched arm. Her numbed mind strove to reconcile sensory impressions—the warm weight of the bird balanced upon her forearm, the slight body of the girl who sobbed into her shoulder now.

"Father forbids us to go so near the valley, for the people hate and fear us, and we cannot pass our borders in human form. But I did so want to see outside, and I thought that if I was with you . . . and then the stones frightened me and I couldn't help Changing, so now you know! Papa will be so angry with me!"

Things that Shanna had seen and heard began to make sense now. "Did a villager maim your brother?" she asked.

"They think they can get away with anything now that the Emperor favors us no more. When Perin was little an archer shot him in the wing."

"I won't tell your father what happened, Chai—" Shanna said at last, "but you must tell me why your people are in such danger."

"I . . . don't know if I can . . ." stammered Chai. "Once one of my people was oathbound to each Emperor and it was death to harm us. But something happened in my grandfather's time. Now it is only in our own valley that we can take the forms of men. There is only one way—" Her voice faltered, then she began again.

"I'm not supposed to go to the Temple, either, but if you have the courage to come with me, we both may find answers there!"

*   *   *

Shanna's palm scraped rock and for a moment only one toe's balance held her against the cliff; then her other hand found an outcropping of stone and she pulled herself upward, cursing under her breath. She should have known that any shrine held sacred by Chai's family would be somewhere you could only reach with wings! Freed from the need to conceal her nature, Chai had blithely shifted to falcon-form and flown to the top of the cliff. Now she peered downward anxiously.

"It's only a little farther, Shanna—" Her voice fluted down. "Can you make it? Perhaps I can find a rope here!"

"I can make it—" Shanna answered grimly but lacked the breath to say more. When she pulled herself over the top she lay flat for several minutes, breathing hard. Then she turned over and stared, for the Temple of the Winds was like no other building she had seen.

She found her feet and, still staring, followed Chai between the open columns into the space within. Neck craned painfully, she looked up at the round dome whose curved surface was covered with mosaics of men and birds and beings that were neither, veiled by huge, gracious wings. There were no walls; the only connection between the polished white marble columns was the delicately carved balustrade. A square altar of rose-veined marble rose from the center of the floor.

"What Power do you worship here?" Shanna found her voice at last.

"In Bindir men call the Divine One Hoth, but the name we use is Keeper of the Winds—the being who is our ancestor." Chai answered over her shoulder. She was searching the floor around the altar. After a moment she stooped, gripped a silver ring set into the dark marble, and pulled. A slab whose joining had been invisible came up with a scrape of stone, revealing a dark cavity.

"I have only seen my father do this," Chai went on, "but I have the kin-right too. I believe that the Keeper will come. . . ." She gestured to Shanna. "Can you help me? This thing is heavier than I thought."

While Shanna held the stone, Chai lifted from the hold a broad basin of silver, a basket of charcoal, and incense in a curious vessel of blown glass. There was also a fire-drill, but

Shanna's flint and steel were in her belt pouch. They let down the stone again and soon had the charcoal glowing red against the tarnished silver of the bowl. They set it in the midst of the altar, and carefully Chai measured chunks of incense into her narrow palm. The spicy scent prickled Shanna's nostrils even before she scattered them over the coals. A pale ribbon of smoke began to curl upward through the still air.

"This is the only sacrifice Wind Keeper desires," Chai said in a hushed voice. She added more incense to the fire. Shanna looked around her and back at the girl's intent face once more. It was very quiet, and it struck her that this was strange, in such a high place. She shivered involuntarily, realizing that she had not quite believed that Chai could succeed in invoking anything, before. She took a step backward and away from the altar, and then another, and stood waiting, shivering from time to time from something that was not cold.

Chai moved to face the east and lifted her hands. "Wind Keeper—" she whispered, "Hoth, my ancestor, I call Thee, Sovereign of the skies. . . ."

A gust of wind stirred Shanna's hair, blew new life into the coals, sent the sweet smoke billowing around the dome. Again came the wind; great clouds of incense eddied and curled—more smoke than could have come from the number of chunks Chai had placed on the fire.

"Wind Keeper, I summon Thee! Come to me on shining wings! Wind Keeper, by the blood we share I invoke Thy presence here now!" Chai's voice shrilled. Shanna remembered the falcon's harsh cry. Smoke swirled like a veil between them.

And then, as she stared, the smoke thickened and shaped itself into fine features; a slim, androgynous form; and the fringed sweep of mighty wings. The breath caught in her throat and Shanna dropped to a half-crouch upon the cold floor.

But the Presence took no notice of her. It was Chai whom that great arch of wings overshadowed—Chai, white and trembling, but holding her ground.

"You have invoked the kin-bond, Daughter, and I have

come. Are you the last of your line, that you should summon
Me?'' It was as if the air itself had focused to a whisper.
Gooseflesh pebbled the backs of Shanna's arms.

"Not yet, Great One, but without Thy mercy that line will
be ended soon! I plead to you for my people, Wind Keeper—
restore us to our glory again!'' Chai shook back her glossy
locks and stretched out her hands.

"And you, human child. What seek you here?'' Suddenly
the crystal eyes were fixed on Shanna; the whisper probed
her soul. She flinched, then forced herself to stand upright,
swaying in the fitful gusts of wind.

"To learn . . . to help Chai . . .'' She began slowly, then
fell silent, seeking the truth demanded by those pellucid eyes.
"I am lost and alone!'' she blurted suddenly. "I don't know
what to do!''

"Ah—Royal Daughter, I know you now, by the blood you
share with him who rules in Bindir. A child of my blood and
of his together—perhaps there is a purpose here . . .'' the
wind said softly. "Be still, my children, and see, and choose!''

Smoke billowed around them in a choking cloud. Shanna
coughed, breathed in, and coughed again, painfully, for it
was woodsmoke now that seared the lungs and blinded the
eyes. With one arm she tried to shield her face while the other
groped before her. Had some spark from the incense somehow set the Temple on fire? Where was Chai?

But the name that broke from parched lips was "Kraik";
the sleeve with which she wiped her eyes was silk brocade.
Awareness of Shanna and the Temple of the Winds distorted,
wavered, and slipped away as the smoke thinned. The new
consciousness was that of Orein Janufen, the Emperor, trapped
by the fires of treason and despair.

"Kraik, where are you? We must get out—I can't see!'' It
hurt to cry out, but the smoke was thinner here. The Emperor
stared wildly around the room, seeking a weapon, or a way
out. His wife's embroidery lay tumbled on a divan as if she
were about to return and pick it up again. But was she in the
plot too? Who could be trusted?

And where was Kraik—his falcon who was also his friend?
The avian would help him—for generations one of his folk

had been bonded till death to each heir of the Imperial line. Kraik *could not* betray his lord, but where was he now?

He heard shouting from the passageway. They were so close! Must he choose to burn or let them slay him here? Moaning, the Emperor stumbled through a door, smelled the moist pungency of green things and the lush scents of the flowers that opened to the night air. It was the Empress' garden. There was no other exit, but perhaps the bushes would hide him. At least here there was clean air.

He fell to his hands and knees on the velvet moss and crawled toward a tangle of columbine. Something exploded out of the bushes toward him—a flurry of feathers, then limbs. Firelight flaring through the doorway showed him a white, narrow face and dilated amber eyes.

"Oh, my Lord, what is it? Is it the men of Menibbe come at last?" Kraik's whisper was a sibilant hiss.

"Something worse—" the Emperor said harshly. "It is men of Bindir. There is a plot—I don't know who, but the Guard have been corrupted and hunt me now. Find us a way out of here, Kraik! They'll kill me if they find me now—" There was hatred in the voices beyond the garden, and a timbre of excitement he had heard last at the Blood Games. His vision throbbed with the crimson of blood and the bright flicker of swords.

Kraik was trembling beside him. "The only other way from this place is there—" He pointed toward the open skylight above the garden pool. "Let me go, my Lord. I am afraid. . . ."

"No!" Panic distorted Orein's words. "You must not leave me, we can fight them! You must hide me—you are sworn—" A helmed silhouette blocked the firelight and Orein's words died. It paused, then turned away. Frantically the Emperor burrowed into the vines.

"You they will only kill," Kraik whispered. "But they call me demon. They will cage and torture me before my release comes. Oh, my Emperor, my brother, let me go free. I cannot help you here—"

"Here!"—a deep shout—"he must be in here—nowhere else the tyrant could go!" Once more a man's shape bulked against the orange glow in the doorway. Torchlight reddened the little pool.

The Emperor fumbled for the little eating knife that was all the weapon he bore. "I'll defend myself, and you have your beak and talons—if they think you a demon they will fear and flee!" he whispered desperately.

"My Lord—" the answer was a sliver of sound, *"please. . . ."*

Torchlight ignited the air, revealing to Orein's horrified gaze one betraying gold slipper on the moss and the crushed nap marks of his knees. Someone pointed and laughed. Metal clinked as they came toward him.

The Emperor struggled to his feet, the little knife clutched in his hand. "Now, Kraik—*change* and attack them now!"

Eyes gleamed with wicked pleasure from beneath bronze helms. The vines rustled and the eyes flickered sideways as limbs blurred to pinions. A soldier lurched back, swearing, as a brown shape exploded out of the bush in a flurry of feathers and circled, splitting the air with an anguished call.

"Now, now . . . no!" A knife hurtled past the falcon and a frantic beating of wings lifted it higher, higher, until it hovered in the skylight, a dark shape against the stars.

"Death!" chanted the soldiers. "Death to the tyrant . . ." Their line evened; drilled strides brought them nearer and torchlight glared from the blades of their drawn swords.

But Orein scarcely saw them. All his rage and impotent despair were focused on the black shape of the bird.

"Kraik! Come back to me! Kraik, I curse you if you betray our bond! Don't think that shape will save you! I curse you, Kraik—" Now the bird was only a dim flutter against the sky. "As a bird you betray me; a bird you shall remain! May all men's hands be against you, demon-bird! My curse upon you that nowhere in my dominions may you or your kinfolk ever take the shape of a man!"

His gaze was still fixed on the empty sky, his mouth still cursing, when they closed on him, and his blood carried the message through earth and sea and sky. . . .

*   *   *

Shanna shuddered, coughed, and fell back again. Her breast ached where the sword had pierced her, but she was alive—alive—and she would hunt that traitor Kraik to a death beyond the imagination of his fear. . . . She shivered with the backwash of anger and despair. Betrayed! He had left her! He had broken the bond!

But no—she was the one who had turned traitor! She had left Hwilos to die in the rain. She had run away. And he was dead now, and she an accursed wanderer. *Hwilos*—she tried to call, but there was only silence here.

The floor was very cold. She could not stop her shivering. But the palace had been burning—how could it be cold? Shanna opened her eyes, saw stone columns rosy with the last daylight and a golden sky. Smoke curled thinly from the altar. Beyond it a huddled brown shape lay still—Chai . . .

Shanna's teeth chattered. She shut her jaws and pushed herself upright. The wind was soft on her face—it was she who was cold then, and not the air. A dream! The fire and the palace and the agony of the swords had all been some kind of dream. But her veins still tingled with Orein's anger, mingled achingly with her own grief and guilt at having left her men.

I am both betrayer and betrayed. . . .

A movement on the other side of the altar caught her eye. The brown huddle stirred and Chai sat up, face white as the marble, eyes wide.

"Now I understand why the Emperor's curse had such power," she said softly. She looked at Shanna and bowed her head. "My life is yours, Lady, to pay for my ancestor's sin."

Shanna shook her head. The dark weight of her grief was lifting, dissipating as the smoke of the incense was being blown away by the wind.

"No," she spoke aloud, "for I have done the same thing. It is time for forgiving now. And I would do it gladly, but I am only a great-niece of Orein. It is the man who sits upon Orein's throne who must lift the curse from you. . . ."

"Then I will go to him!" Chai leaped to her feet, the

feathers bound into her hair fluttering as if she were already in flight.

"Alone? How will you find the way? How will you tell him what you are and why you have come?" Shanna got stiffly to her feet and took three long paces toward the altar of the winds.

"But I am oathbound myself to go to Bindir—" She set her palms on the edge of the altar. "Orein should have given to Kraik the same freedom that my men gave to me. If you will travel with me, sky sister, perhaps the debts we both owe the dead can be paid."

Chai's eyes were like the stars that were beginning to glow in the evening sky. One swift motion brought her around the altar to lay her hand on Shanna's—a small hand, fine-boned as the claw of the bird.

And then she *was* a bird, whose russet plumage gleamed in the half-light, and Shanna braced to take the falcon's weight on her arm. But the burden on her arm was far less than the weight that had lifted from her heart, and her soul soared with a beating of great wings.

DEFENDER OF THE FAITH

Judith Tarr

1.

NIGHT HAD FALLEN IN THE GARDEN OF ALLAH. STARLIGHT caught and shattered in the fountain which played in its center. Upon its edges, deep in the scented shadows, a nightingale began to sing.

Morgiana slipped from tree to tree, cloaked in darkness. Voices drew her toward the fountain: human voices, harsh and unmusical, drowning out the liquid stream of song.

On a divan beside the fountain reclined the Master of the Garden. A lamp, suspended from a flowering branch, flickered upon his face. His beard was as white as his turban, the skin between them dark, deep-scored with lines of age and care and trouble. His son sat at his feet, a white-clad blur on the edge of the lamp's light.

"No," the younger man said: a deep voice, rough with the effort of holding some strong emotion rigidly in check. "With all due respect, my lord and father—no. There is another way. There must be."

"So you have told me thrice before." The old man's tones were a fainter echo of his son's, thinned and fined with age, but with a core of iron. "Thrice before we have done as you advised, and failed. Six good men have been lost to the Faith by your choosing. And the enemy remains, as strong as ever;

298

and the world comes ever closer to the knowledge of our disgrace.''

''But—*that*.'' The young man's control cracked. Loathing lay beneath, and fear, and contempt for this aged dodderer.

''That,'' his father said. ''Men fail: even our *fida'is,* our faithful ones, with their blessed daggers and their dreams of Paradise. But one being never fails. My father used her, and the great lord before him, Hasan-i Sabbah, the Defender of the Faith, the Living Proof of the true Caliph who is hidden, the Master of Alamut.''

''It is a demon. A creature of Shaitan.''

''One of the Jann, who swore herself in fealty to the first lord of our Brotherhood, and to the second, and to myself who am the third. She has never betrayed us, and she has never failed in any task to which she has been set. And this one is indeed worthy of her. The strongest of the Faithful might quail before such a sorcerer as this one who has risen up under the Prince of Antioch. His power is mighty; and it thwarts us wherever we turn. While that man lives, neither our Faith nor our Mission can be safe. He must die.''

''He can die by more hallowed hands than those of that cat-eyed Afreet. The last man nearly succeeded: he won his way into the sorcerer's confidence and only failed at the last, through his own weakness. Surely, the next—''

''The next will be the one whom I choose.'' The blade had slid from its sheath; old though it was, it was deadly. The younger man opened his mouth and shut it again; his eyes smoldered in a face gone suddenly rigid.

Morgiana stood before them both where a moment before had been only darkness, descending in a deep obeisance. She could feel the young man's hate and fear like a flare of cold fire upon her skin. As she rose, she turned toward his father, whose fear was a saner thing, the just and proper fear of a mortal for a daughter of the Jann. ''My lord has summoned me,'' she said, not quite a question.

''Morgiana,'' he acknowledged her. It was a conceit of his, that by her name he ruled her. ''The Faith has need of you.''

She bowed. "I serve the true Faith and its true Master, in the name of Allah and of Mohammed who is his Prophet."

"Upon his name be peace," murmured the Master. His voice firmed, regained its edge. "There is a sorcerer in the land of Antioch: one of the accursed Giaours, a follower of the false prophet of Nazareth. He lends his aid to Infidel and heretic alike, and breaks the power of Alamut whenever he encounters it. For the Faith and for the Brotherhood, by the oath which you have sworn, I command you to destroy him."

Once more she bowed low. "It shall be done," she said. She drew from her sash a long and wicked blade, written about with holy words; kissed it; and vanished.

2.

Between breath and breath was a time of not-being. Morgiana lowered the dagger from her lips and glanced about. There was no light in this her chamber in the fortress of Alamut, but her eyes needed none. She sat cross-legged in a nest of cushions and carpets, laid the blade before her, and set her chin upon her fist.

Even here, if she chose, she could sense the young lord Hasan's mad mingling of anger and terror. She closed her mind to it, reaching elsewhere, far and far, into the night. A sorcerer would blaze like a beacon in the world of the spirit.

Or be nothing at all.

She laughed softly to herself. So well had he hidden all his magics; the feeblest *peri*-child could find him merely by his absence. She traced the shape of him in the mortal minds about him, centered her power upon the heart of the void, and held it there as she made her preparations.

Upon the stroke of midnight, she sent her body in pursuit of her power.

Pain. Agony. A thousand tiny darts of fire, plunging deep into her flesh, severing the cords that bound it to her will. And all about her, a wall of light.

It was dark. Blessedly dark, and cool, and in her body, no pain. Morgiana huddled upon hardness, gasping.

After a long while she roused, enough to uncoil, to open her eyes. The hardness was earth; a wall rose above her, reaching toward the bitter-bright stars. Her fingers were locked about her dagger hilt. With an effort of will she loosed them. The weapon slid to the ground and lay there, gleaming dully.

Her hand, freed and shaking, explored her body. She was intact save for a bruise or two. When she burst into the solid world, she must have fallen.

With great care she ventured a mind-probe. Her power responded stiffly, with reluctance that was like pain. Yet she gained enough to know that she was no longer in Alamut. The earth was the earth of distant Antioch, and the wall was that of a house in the town of the sorcerer. The name of the town she did not gather, nor did she care to, for mind and body together rose in rebellion.

She was suddenly and violently ill.

The spasm passed as swiftly as it had come. She crouched shaking. Even in her misery, she managed a crooked smile. If Hasan could but see her now, he would forget all his fear of her.

It was well for her reputation that he could not. She groped for her knife, sheathed it with a hand that trembled maddeningly, and dragged herself to her feet. Her legs would hardly hold her. She gritted her teeth and drove herself forward.

The innkeeper cursed the traveler who had driven him out of bed so late and cursed more bitterly when he saw what it was: a slender boy in dark plain clothes, with neither baggage nor servant, and with a face as pale as death. But gold sweetened the man's temper most admirably and gained the intruder a room to himself, away from the common herd of guests.

"Undistrubed," he said in his light husky voice, "and unqestioned."

The innkeeper hastened to agree. Nor was it only the gold that won his respect. "Eyes," he said to himself as he returned to his cold bed. He shivered. "Allah defend me from such eyes." He closed his own, resolutely. But he was long in falling asleep.

<h1 style="text-align:center">3.</h1>

Morgiana opened one eye. Light stabbed it. She gasped and threw up a hand.

It was only sunlight, slanting through a narrow window. Her left hand unclenched from about the hilt of her dagger; her right lowered, and she sat up. She had gone to bed fully clothed, turban and all; somewhere in her tossing, dream-tormented sleep, it had fallen away, freeing her hair: that tumbled about her shoulders, a rare, deep red, like wine in a dark goblet.

She yawned and stretched. She was ravenously hungry. But first—she grimaced with distaste—she had to dispose of the remnants of her sickness. She moved to gather up her hair, to rewind her turban. But she paused.

Her power, flexed, seemed as supple as her body, and wholly healed of its hurts. With it she summoned all she needed.

Bathed and fed and newly clad, she sallied forth. It was a large town in which she found herself, almost a city, centered about a steep rock whereon stood a castle. The white walls shone in the sun; bright banners flew about it, and chief among them a blood-red cross upon a white field. She spat toward it, by instinct. But the castle was not her concern, although it swarmed with Franks. They were no threat to Alamut.

There had been a mosque once. It lay in ruins, defiled with the dung of Frankish cattle and overrun with Frankish dogs. She laid a wishing on it that cleansed away the foulness and put the dogs to flight; and she prayed in the broken court-yard, face toward Mecca, as was proper.

The sorcerer lived not far from the mosque, beside a raw new structure, a church of the Christ. The church held no fear for her. But she approached the house with utmost care, all her power drawn close about her. To those who passed, she was a harmless saunterer, a smooth-faced youth affecting an air of great age and worldly wisdom.

The house seemed a poor dwelling for so mighty an en-chanter. It was small and unassuming; no symbols of power guarded its door, and no demons crouched within to devour any who approached. There was only the barrier she had met before, the wall of nothingness, that turned to searing fire when she touched it with her mind.

She gathered all her courage and firmed her power, and laid her hand upon the gate. No mighty force drove her back. She looked into a dim passage, and a sunlit court with a young tree in its center. A man bent over it, watering it from a wooden bucket. He was a small man, rather plump, with a fringe of colorless hair round a shining bald crown. He wore the coarse black robe of a Frankish priest, knotted at the waist with a cord; a wooden cross lay on his breast.

He looked up, full into her stare, and smiled. His face was soft and smooth-shaven, his eyes round and clear and blue and utterly guileless.

She had never seen a face more innocent, or more terrible.

4.

Morgiana prowled her chamber like a panther in a cage.
Below her, in the common-room of the inn, the nightly
throng waxed hilarious. The innkeeper was a Muslim, but
business was business; if one served Franks, one served
wine. He had not had the temerity to offer her any. *Hajji*, he
was calling her now—rightly enough, if it came to that.
There had been a man in Mecca who had dared to speak ill of
the Lord of Alamut.

There was a man in this town of Alsalam whose very
existence was a threat to the Faith.

In the center of the faded carpet, thrust upright into it,
glittered her dagger. She circled it and sat before it, glaring at
it. "Never," she said to it. "Never have I failed. Never.
And never before now, on the first attempt."

Allahu akbar, said the writing upon the blade: God is
great.

"But," she said. "They have always been mortal men.
Every one. And I . . . I am the Afreet who followed Hasan-i
Sabbah out of the desert, whom he tamed and took for his
own; whom he made into the Blade of Alamut, to strike
when all else fails. He turned me against sorcerers—oh,
many a time! Yet all were charlatans. I slew them all with the
ease of true power."

Inshallah, said the blade: God's will be done.

"This is not a charlatan," she said. "This, truly, is a
sorcerer, a man of power. I am not afraid of him. Allah be
my witness, I am not. Yet he has power. None of the others
has ever had power. I do not know—I do not—"

The blade had nothing to say.

5.

The knights of Alsalam had their own priest and their own chapel; the Christians of the town worshiped their God in the church of Saint Paul of Damascus. The priest there, Father Wilfrid, was a gentle soul—a saint, some would say.

A sorcerer, though Morgiana. Wrapped in a pilgrim's mantle, she knelt and sat and stood with the others as her quarry moved through the ritual of the Mass. The church was very small, and she very close to him; two long strides could have brought her to his side as he bowed upon the altar. So harmless, he seemed, this small fat man with his round blue eyes.

The air sang with power. Her own, she furled close about her like her cloak, lest it betray her. Now and again, her hand would creep beneath the shrouding fabric, to close about her dagger hilt.

Soon now. The people about her shifted and stirred, minds reaching for the outer air; the acolytes measured with their eyes the path of escape. Only the priest had not changed, rapt in his rite.

As it ended, Morgiana's heart thudded against her ribs. Her fingers tightened about the cold smoothness of the hilt. Clouds of incense blurred her sight; figures stirred within them, chanting in sweet alien voices.

Allah! her mind cried. *Allahu akbar!*

The clouds thickened. Shadows passed her, moving slowly, like figures in a dream.

But one was real. A round pale face, and round pale eyes. They smiled at her.

*   *   *

She was alone in the house of the Frankish God. There was no incense, scarcely even its memory. Only the painted walls, and the painted idols; and the Christ upon his cross, erect and triumphant, as if his convict's death had been a victory.

She raised her blade to him. Her eyes blazed, green as a cat's in her white face; her power, freed, crackled about her. "I shall defeat you," she said. "I shall trample you beneath my feet. You, and the demon-spawn who serves you."

She spat in his blank unheeding face, and spun away from him.

6.

Once again, Morgiana set her hand upon the gate of the sorcerer's house. But now it was deep night, and she had laid aside all disguises. She wore the white robes of the Brotherhood of Alamut, whom the men of this land called Hashishayun, and the Franks Assassins.

The gate opened easily. No servant or porter challenged her within. The priest had but two to wait upon him—an ancient Frankish monk and a slave-boy he had bought in Alsalam, whom, people said, he had freed, but who would not leave him. More than they, he did not need. He had the power of his God.

She dared not use her own within these walls, quiet though they seemed. Without it she felt blind and deaf, keen though her senses were, keener than any man's. She advanced like a hunting cat, eyes huge and flaring green in the light of the faint new moon; her ears cocked at every sound, her nostrils flared wide, seeking a single scent. The air reeked of humanity, and of Frankish piety. Of power, there was no tangible sign.

Softly she slipped across the courtyard, round the slender shadow of the tree. Close by, someone snored, a constant, senile wheeze. A childish snuffling played counterpoint. She passed that door without pausing.

Beyond, she heard soft regular breathing. Her own caught; she softened it.

Again, there was no lock, no barrier at all. No storm of fire swept upon her; no sacred terror seized her. She looked upon a tiny cell of a room, a rough cot, a vigil-lamp beneath a crucifix. And her prey.

He slept as a child might sleep, utterly at peace. His shirt was old and threadbare; beneath it she saw another, dark and harsh. Yes; he would wear a hair shirt, would this sorcerer-saint. She eased her dagger from her sash and glided into the cell.

The blue eyes opened. Father Wilfrid smiled, a little puzzled and not at all dismayed that an Assassin's dagger hovered above his throat.

Hovered, only. Morgiana made no move to take the life which lay so placidly in her hand.

The priest blinked and shook his head. "Such dreams I have—and at my age, too. I'd be ashamed of myself. Except," he added in unabashed delight, "that you are so beautiful."

Morgiana cherished the cold fire of wrath which had brought her here, though it hurt almost beyond bearing, a dart of ice, twisting her vitals. "I am your death," she said.

"Indeed? How splendid! So often, I've prayed . . . let it be a good death. Let it be a worthy one. Worthy of God, that is," he said humbly. "Certainly I deserve nothing at all. But I never dreamed that it would be such as you. Are you an angel?"

"I am an Afreet. I serve the Lord of Alamut."

"Even they serve God, then." The priest sighed and smiled. "I'm glad. I'm not a very good priest, you know. I've always been uncomfortable with the thought of damnation. If one *chose* it, certainly . . . but what if one believes that one is choosing salvation? How does God go about solving that?"

"You are damned. You have destroyed six of our Brotherhood."

"But," the priest said, baffled. "Six . . . ?" Suddenly, light dawned. "Ah! All those poor boys who came to kill me. God smote one, not into Hell, I hope; I did pray for him as hard as I knew how. The others stayed to talk to me. They saw the light at last, God be praised. One has even taken the most blessed path of all. That was Hakim. Brother Paul, he is now, for the great Saint. He was my servant for a long while before he confessed all his sins. Poor lad, he truly believed that my death would take him to Paradise."

Morgiana ground her teeth. Her hand shook upon the dagger hilt; she could not control it.

"Child," the priest said, "you must be tired of standing like that. Won't you put your knife away? You can use it later, when you're feeling stronger. Meanwhile, will you eat something? Drink a little? Or don't Afreets . . . ?"

She ventured a stab of power. It met no resistance. Startled, she plunged deep, into a mind like a limpid pool. A peaceful, pious, utterly human mind. He had no power at all. No sorcery, no weapons of light. All his strength was piety, prayers and holy words and a faith which no force of the world could shake.

The crucifix glittered; she forced her eyes away from it, upon the priest. "You are the enemy," she said. "You have thwarted our *da'wa*, our sacred Mission. Through you and your prayers, all of Outremer is closed to us, and far too much of Islam."

"Through me? But how—?"

"They come to you, knight and commoner, emir and *fellah*. They seek your blessing or your counsel. They depart, and no one of us can touch them."

Father Wilfrid sat up, heedless of her dagger. There was a thin line between his brows, a ripple in his mind. He was truly and deeply dismayed. "Oh, no, certainly . . . they come, it's true, but people always seem to come to a priest. Of course I give them my blessing. Even the Infidels seem to want it. How can I refuse them? They're all God's children."

"I am not. You cannot corrupt me as you have corrupted my lost brethren."

"I only talked to them, and told them of the true Faith. Of

course they saw its truth: they were already seekers after God. They had only been distracted by a false path. God has forgiven them. God will forgive you—even you, beautiful demon-child, if you ask Him.''

He needed no weapons, nor any sorcery. He had the purity of his faith. Morgiana threw up her anger as a shield against it. ''Twice I have struck at you. Twice I have failed, for your false God defended you. This time I shall not fail.''

''If my God is false,'' asked Father Wilfrid in honest curiosity, ''then how could He defend me?''

''There is no God but Allah, and Mohammed is his Prophet.'' A second shield, that, a bulwark of belief.

''There is no God but God,'' the priest agreed, crossing himself devoutly. ''How fortunate you are, that you see so much. But how unfortunate, that you're blind to the rest.''

''I see Truth. There is Allah, the Merciful, the Compassionate; there is the Prophet; there is the Book. And there is Alamut, which defends them all.''

''With steel?'' The priest took it from her, easily, and turned it in his plump fingers. ''How lovely. How deadly. How like its owner.'' He looked up at her, smiling. ''My soul will be delighted, to be free at last. Such a burden, a body is. I only wish . . . you should think about things, you know. About God, and truth, and faith. I know He loves you. After all, He made you.''

''He made me the Dagger of Islam.'' She snatched her own from his unresisting hands. She would kill him. For the Faith, and for her own sanity, she would—

He regarded her, head cocked a little to one side. ''Have you killed many people?'' he asked.

''Too many.''

She had not meant to say that. She did not mean it. She obeyed her Master; she served her Brotherhood. The blood on her hands was the blood of sacrifice. She had never killed in anger, never in greed or in hatred. Always in holy zeal.

''Ah, poor child,'' said this latest of her sacrifices. She saw herself reflected in his eyes, a slender child-woman with a white desperate face.

She was not a child. She was not even a woman. She shifted her grip upon the knife.

The priest nodded. "Yes, it's time now. I'll do what I can for you, when I stand in front of my God." He crossed himself and bowed his absurd, bald, saintly head.

Swiftly she struck. The blade pierced his heart; pulsed once, and was still. With a sigh the priest fell back.

"My victory!" cried Morgiana, fierce and high. "*Mine* for Allah!"

Ah, said the priest's smile, and the smile of the figure on its cross above him, *but we allowed it.*

She snatched her dagger from its sheath of flesh and bone and blood, and fled.

7.

The Lord of Alamut walked aimlessly in his Garden, pausing now and then to inspect a rare blossom or to remove a withered leaf. His son followed him in a black cloud of anger and impatience.

At last Hasan stopped short. "She has not come back. She has failed like all the rest. She has deserted us, and turned to the Giaours."

"She faced a very great sorcerer," his father said mildly, "whom she might not have defeated all at once. He was a very holy man."

"Holy!"

"A saint of our enemies." The old man sighed a little. "Sanctity is the most powerful sorcery of all, and the most deadly. But," he added softly, "you will never know that, though they name you Imam in place of the one who is hidden, and make a lie of your ancestry, and worship you as but little less than God."

Steel flashed in the young man's hand.

It never reached its target. The old man smiled into Morgiana's wild green eyes. "Ah, my Afreet. It is done?"

She released Hasan's wrist. He snarled but retreated from them both, glaring at the ground.

Neither heeded him. She bowed low and laid her blade at her Master's feet. "It is done," she said in a strange, flat voice.

He laid his hand upon her head. "Blest be the name of Allah!"

"Whom I serve as best I may." She raised her eyes. They saw the lined and reverend face, the dark steady stare; but her mind saw another altogether. It would be a long, long while before she was free of it. "Have I my lord's leave to go?"

"Go in peace," said the Lord of Alamut.

She laughed, briefly, half in mockery, half in pain, and vanished from the Garden.

But the dagger remained, abandoned at his feet, its bright blade dulled with the blood of the saint.

TALES OF CAT AND FOX

Cats purr, stalk, and prowl through Andre Norton's books, portrayed with such affection that no one can look at them without realizing that she loves cats. At present, she is managed by about seven live cats, and untold glass, china, cloth, plush, ceramic, and painted cats: gifts from friends and well-wishers.

Here is another gift of a cat, this time from Katherine Kurtz, author of a series about the Deryni and of *Lammas Night,* an occult thriller set during World War II. Like Nancy Springer's story, Kurtz's "Catalyst" deals with a young boy—later to grow up into the fabled Healer Rhys Thuryn—who needs to find his path; his foster-family, who already seem to know where their own roads will lie; and, of course, a wise, loving animal.

I think you'll find in Evaine's cat Symber a worthy pack-fellow to Furtig and all the other cats in *Breed to Come,* Simba and Sahiba in *Catseye,* Sinbad of the *Solar Queen,* Bis of *Shadow Hawk,* and all the many, many others.

Jane Yolen's story, "The Foxwife," also combines many of Andre Norton's best-loved themes. First, there are the animals—foxes, whose grace and wiliness Jane Yolen captures (if you'll excuse the phrase) in this story and which were portrayed in Sargon and Sheba in *Catseye.* Second, we see a kind of symbiosis between human and animal which

Norton has captured in *Moon of Three Wings* and her tales of Eet and Murdoc Jern. And third, there is the mythic quality that Andre Norton cherishes in stories from all over the world. Like those stories, "The Foxwife" is a wise and tender story of how an animal—if we can call it that—loves and teaches a human who has much to learn . . . just the sort of story one of America's premier myth-spinners would offer to a sister in the field.

CATALYST

Katherine Kurtz

BITING AT HIS LIP IN CONCENTRATION, ELEVEN-YEAR-OLD RHYS Thuryn stared at the red archer on the board between him and Joram MacRorie and wrapped his mind around it. Smoothly the little painted figure lifted across two squares to menace Joram's blue abbot.

The younger boy had turned to watch rain beginning to spatter against the lights of a tall, grey-glazed window beside them, but at the movement on the board, his blond head jerked back with a start.

"Oh, no! Not *my* Michaeline, you don't!" he cried, nearly overturning the board as he sprang to his feet to see better. "Rhys, that was a sneaky move! Cathan, what'll I do?"

Cathan, a bored and blasé fifteen, looked up from his reading with a forbearing sigh, red-nosed and miserable with the cold that had kept him from going hunting with the rest of the household. The white cat napping against his feet did not stir, even when Rhys chortled with delight and knuckled exuberantly at already unruly red hair.

"Hoo! I've got him on the run! Look, Cathan! My archer's going to take his abbot!"

Cathan only blew his nose and huddled a little closer to the fire before burying himself in his scroll again, and Rhys's glee turned to consternation as Joram's war-duke floated unerringly across the entire board to take the red archer.

"On the run, eh?" Joram crowed, plopping back onto his

314

stool with triumph in his grey eyes. "What are you going to do about *that*?"

Deflated, Rhys huddled down in his fur-lined tunic to reevaluate the board. Where had that war-duke come from? What a stupid game!

He had half expected the outcome, of course. Joram almost always beat him at Cardounet. Even though Rhys was a year older than Joram, and both of them were receiving identical instruction from the Michaelines at St. Liam's, one of the finest abbey schools in all of Gwynedd, it was a fact that Rhys simply did not have the gift for military strategy that his foster-brother did. Joram, at ten, had already announced that he was joining the Michaeline Order when he came of age, to become a Knight of St. Michael and eventually a priest as well—to the dismay of his father, Earl Camber of Culdi.

Nor was it the priesthood Camber objected to—and Jocelyn, Joram's mother, was clearly pleased that one of her sons intended to become a priest. Indeed, Camber had often told the boys of the happy years he himself had spent in Holy Orders in his youth, until the death of his elder brother made him heir to their father's earldom and he was forced to come home and assume his family obligations. Barring further unforeseen tragedy—for a fever had carried off a brother and sister only slightly older than Joram earlier in the year—Joram's brother Cathan would carry on the MacRorie name in this generation, leaving Joram free to pursue the religious vocation that had been denied Camber.

No, it was the Michaeline Order itself that gave Camber cause for concern—the Michaelines, whose militant warrior-priests were sometimes dangerously outspoken about the responsibilities they believed went along with the prerogatives that magic-wielding Deryni enjoyed. Camber, himself a powerful and highly trained Deryni, had no quarrel with the Michaelines' ethical stance in principle; he had always taught his children the duty that went along with privilege.

In practice, however, the Order's sometimes overzealous attempts to enforce that philosophy had led more than once to disaster—for the Royal House of Gwynedd was Deryni, and

sqme of its scions among the worst abusers of Deryni power.
Thus far, royal ire had always been directed against the
offending individuals; but if Joram became a Michaeline, and
the King should one day turn his anger against the entire
Order . . .

Still, Michaeline schools *did* provide the finest primary
training for Deryni children that could be had, outside the
highly specialized instruction given the rare Healer candidate—
and even among the Deryni, a race blessed (or cursed, ac-
cording to some) with a wide assortment of psychic and
magical abilities, the Healing gift did not often appear. It was
the abuse of power, sometimes in mere ignorance, that so
often led to problems between Deryni and humans—or even
Deryni and Deryni.

That was why Camber had sent Joram and the orphaned
Rhys to attend St. Liam's—and allowed them to continue
attending, even when Joram began making starry-eyed plans
to join the Michaelines. After all, the boy could not take even
temporary vows until he turned fourteen. Much might change
in four years. Perhaps Joram would outgrow his infatuation
with the bold and dashing Knights of Saint Michael, and their
distinctive deep blue habits and gleaming white knight's
sashes, and come around to a more moderate choice of
orders, if indeed he felt himself called to be a priest.

Rhys, on the other hand, felt no call to the religious life,
though he was perfectly content taking his training in the
religious atmosphere St. Liam's provided. Nor had he any
idea yet what he *did* want to do with his life.

He had no great prospects. His father, though gentle-born,
had been only a second son, so he had inherited no title or
fortune in his own right. Only his mother's close friendship
with Camber's countess, the Lady Jocelyn, had ensured a
place for the infant Rhys when both parents died in the great
plague the year after he was born. He was clever with his
hands, worked well with animals, like most Deryni, and had
a head for figures—but none of those skills suggested an
occupation for a young gentleman.

One thing was certain, Rhys thought, as he continued to
survey the game board, considering and discarding a succes-

sion of possible but unprofitable moves: he was not cut out to
be a soldier. The military strategy and tactics that were
Joram's passion were like a foreign language to Rhys. With
diligence, and because the subject intrigued Joram, who was
his very closest friend, Rhys had mastered enough to at least
get by in school, and to appreciate that Joram had a natural
flair for such things; but he would never be Joram's match, at
least in this.

Rarely had he been so dismally aware of that fact as he
continued staring at the game board, discarding yet another
futile move. The rain hammering now on the window and the
roof slates above only added to his depression. Even with the
fire and the larger windows here in the solar, it had gotten
colder and gloomier as the storm set in, though it was only
just past noon.

Perversely, he hoped that Camber and Lady Jocelyn and
the rest of the household were getting good and soaked, for
having gone off hunting with the King and left them cooped
up in the castle with only this dumb game to play! Cathan,
who'd been grouchy and irritable all morning with his stupid
cold, should be glad they'd made him stay at home, warm
and dry and curled up with a fur-lined robe, a cat, and a good
book.

As a matter of fact, maybe a book was a good idea. He
was bored with trying to beat Joram. He thought he might go
find something to read, but before he could decide what,
Evaine, the baby of the MacRorie family, came pattering
purposefully into the room, flaxen braids coming undone and
her black cat Symber in her arms. She had the cat just behind
the front legs, its body and tail dangling almost to her knees.
Oddly, the cat did not seem to mind.

"Cathan, Cathan, there's somebody sneaking around downstairs!" she whispered with a six-year-old's urgency, scut-
tling past Rhys and Joram to pause at her older brother's
elbow.

Cathan gave a put-upon sigh and lowered his manuscript
long enough to wipe his nose with a soggy handkerchief.

"I'm sure there is," he croaked hoarsely.

"Cathan, I'm not joking!" she persisted. "I heard them clunking things in the great hall."

"It's probably the dogs."

"The dogs don't make noises like that."

"Then it's the servants."

"It *isn't* the servants!" she replied, stamping a little foot. "Symber came running up the stairs. He was afraid. He doesn't run from the servants."

"He probably got in Cook's way and she booted him with a broom."

"He did *not!*" Evaine insisted, hugging the cat closer. "There's someone down there. Come and see. Cathan, please!"

"Evaine. I'm *not* going downstairs," Cathan snapped. "I don't feel like playing. In case you hadn't noticed, this stupid cold is making me mean and grumpy. Why don't you go pester Joram and Rhys?"

"They're too busy playing their dumb game! Just because I'm little, nobody ever listens to me!"

Rhys, who had been following the exchange with growing amusement, exchanged a conspiratorial wink with Joram, who had also sat back to grin.

"*We'll* listen to you, won't we, Joram?" he said, delighted at the excuse to leave the hopeless game and do something else.

Apparently Joram had also grown bored with the game, for he joined in without missing a beat.

"Of course we will, little sister," he said, rising and adjusting a dagger thrust through the belt of his blue school tunic. "Why don't you show us where you think you heard them? Can't have prowlers carrying off the silver. Do you think they've tied up the servants?"

"Jor-am!"

"All right, all right!" Joram held up both palms and did his best to assume the more serious mien he thought a future Michaeline Knight should wear. "I said we'd go investigate. Why don't you leave Symber here, where he'll be safe?"

"No!"

"Then why don't you let *me* carry him?" Rhys reasoned.

"That way, you can lead the way and show Joram and me where to look."

"All right, you can carry him," she agreed, handing over the cat. "But I think Joram better go first. He's got a knife."

"Good idea," Joram said, though he had to turn away to keep from grinning. As he stealthily pushed the door to the turnpike stair a little wider, holding a finger to his lips for silence, Rhys hefted the cat's front end onto his left shoulder and supported its weight in the crook of his arm. The cat began purring loudly in his ear as it settled, kneading contentedly with its front paws.

Rhys ignored Cathan's bemused and slightly patronizing smile as he followed Joram and Evaine into the winding stairwell. What did *he* care what Cathan thought? If Evaine had judged Joram best suited to lead a military exercise, she was only acknowledging the obvious—and without any of the hint of ridicule Cathan so often heaped upon Rhys for his lesser military acumen. And it was Rhys to whom she had entrusted her precious Symber—which was a far more important responsibility, in her eyes.

On the other hand, Rhys's military training had not been wholly wasted. Trying to place his slippered feet as quietly as Joram or the cat purring in his arms, he sent a tendril of thought questing into the cat's mind—just in case there *was* something going on below stairs that shouldn't be.

And Symber *had* been frightened by something. The big black cat was too wrapped up in the pleasure and security of perching on Rhys's shoulder, purring contentedly as he reveled in that special ecstasy, for Rhys to read any details; but he did manage to catch an impression of *something* Symber did not like, that had scared him enough to send him scooting to Evaine for safety. And somehow Rhys did not think it had been Cook with her broom.

He sent that mental impression off to Joram just before they reached the landing, but only the two MacRories had gotten close enough to even touch the curtains across the entry to the great hall before a pair of hairy arms burst through the split in the middle and grabbed each by an arm, jerking them through.

"I told you I'd seen a kid!" a rough voice bellowed.

"Rhys, Rhys!" Evaine shrieked. And a heavy "Whoof!" exploded from someone far larger and heavier than Joram as Rhys instinctively ducked and hurled himself through the curtained doorway at the side rather than in the middle, burdened by an armful of suddenly startled cat—and found himself right in the middle of a tangle of struggling bodies, both adult and child.

"Cathan!" Joram screamed, sending up a psychic cry as well as he squirmed almost out of the grasp of the man who held him and Evaine and somehow managed to get his dagger free of his belt. "Rhys, look out!"

But Rhys was having his own problems as he tried to duck the clutches of another rough-clad man who suddenly loomed right in front of him. He yelped and lost his footing as Evaine's cat launched itself from his shoulder with all its back claws dug in, but the squawk of horrified surprise from his attacker was worth the pain, for Symber landed on the man's bare forearm with all claws out and clung like a limpet, sinking his teeth into the fleshy part of the man's thumb with a ferocious growl.

Cursing and flailing, the man tried to shake the cat off his arm; Symber only dug in with all four sets of claws and held on more tenaciously. Rhys almost managed to tackle one of the man's legs and trip him, but a vicious kick that only narrowly missed his head changed his mind about that. As he rolled clear, trying frantically to see whether it was only two men or if there were more, and wondering where the dogs were, Evaine wormed out of the grasp of her captor—who was now far more worried about Joram's knife than a child of six—and went for the man molesting her cat, kicking him hard in the shin.

The man howled and whirled around. The reaction cost the cat its grip. As the man grabbed for Evaine and missed, cursing with rage, he made an even more desperate attempt to dislodge the clawing, biting black demon attached to his arm. With a mighty heave, he shook Symber loose and flung him hard against the wall. Evaine wailed as the cat slid to the floor and did not move.

But even worse danger kept Rhys from noticing what happened to cat or girl after that. He was scrambling toward Joram, for Joram was losing the tug-of-war with his attacker for the knife in his hand, when suddenly a third man towered between them, throwing down a bag of booty with a loud clank and seizing Rhys by a bicep with one hand while the other began to draw a sword.

Rhys tried to remember every trick he'd ever practiced or heard about hand-to-hand fighting in the next few seconds, for he was weaponless, and his opponent was probably three times his age and weight. As he ducked under a blow that would have taken off his head if it had connected, he saw Cathan finally careen out of the newel-stair doorway with a sword in his hand, shouting urgently for the servants.

He was too busy staying alive to see what happened as the older boy went after the man who was grabbing for Evaine again. As Evaine dived between Cathan's legs for safety, Rhys's concentration was distracted by even more frantic scuffling between Joram and his opponent. Suddenly fire was searing across the back of Rhys's right leg and it was buckling under him.

The pain was excruciating, the terror worse, as Rhys collapsed and tried to worm out of his assailant's range, clamping a frantic hand to the slash across his calf. His hand came away bloody in the instant he had to look, the thick wool of his grey legging rapidly turning scarlet. He was gasping too hard to utter much physical sound as the man raised a bloody sword to finish him, but his desperate psychic cry reverberated in the hall and beyond as he made a last, determined attempt to fling himself clear of the descending blade—though he was sure he was going to die.

He never knew how Cathan managed to intervene; only that suddenly another sword was flashing upward to block the blow, shattering the attacker's lesser blade, driving on to split the man's skull from jaw to crown. As blood and brains spattered, and before the man even hit the floor, Cathan was whirling to take on Joram's opponent. The man who'd menaced Evaine was already moaning on the floor, clutching a belly wound and trying to crawl out of Cathan's reach.

A handful of male servants finally managed to burst into the hall at that point, quickly helping Cathan subdue and bind the remaining attacker. Only then did Rhys dare to sit up and take another look at his wound.

Oh, God, it was bad!

His breath hissed between his teeth and tears welled in his eyes as he clapped his hand back over the gash and subsided on the floor again.

The great tendon down the back of his calf was cut clean through. Despite the depth of the wound, he did not seem to have bled much after the initial trauma, but the leg was beginning to throb and burn as the first shock wore off. A Healer might be able to repair the injury, but if he could not, Rhys would be a cripple for life.

"I'll send for a Healer!" one of the servants promised, tight-lipped and pale, when he had gotten just a glimpse of Rhys's leg. "Try to stay calm."

Biting back tears, for he was old enough to know that crying was not going to help matters any, Rhys curled into a ball on his left side and closed his eyes, pillowing his head on his left arm and trying to relax while he made himself run through one of the spells he'd been taught to control pain. He was scared, but it was the only thing he knew to do.

It worked, though. When he opened his eyes, the leg was numb and he was no longer quite so afraid. Joram and a still-sniffing Evaine were kneeling at his side, Evaine cradling a motionless but still-breathing Symber in her arms.

"Is it bad?" Joram asked, craning his neck to see. "*Jesu*, he's hamstrung you! You aren't bleeding very much, though. Father will be back soon. Cathan and I have already Called him."

"I think I Called him, too," Rhys whispered, managing a strained little grin for Evaine's sake as he drew a deep breath to keep the pain and despair from rising again. "Him and any Deryni for two counties. I thought they were going to kill us."

"I think they *may* have killed Symber," Evaine murmured around a little sob of grief, ducking her head over the cat's labored breathing. "That horrid man threw him against the wall! He's still breathing, but he's all limp."

As she lifted plaintive eyes to his, begging him to tell her everything would be all right, he caught Joram's faint head-shake. He had to agree the cat did not look good. Wincing as he shifted his good leg to support the injured one, still holding his wound with his right hand, he tried to think how to make it easier for her.

"I'm sorry, little one," he whispered. "Maybe it isn't as bad as you think. Would you—like to put Symber next to me? Maybe a Healer can fix us both, when one gets here. And if I worry about Symber, maybe I won't worry so much about my leg."

With a brave gulp, Evaine laid the injured cat in the curve of Rhys's left arm, closed against his chest and cheek. He could sense how badly the cat was hurt, even though it was unconscious, and he let his fingertips caress one quiet velvet paw as he looked up at Evaine, wishing there were something he could do.

"You—*you're* not going to die, are you, Rhys?" she asked in a very small voice.

He forced himself to give her a reassuring smile. "Don't worry," he said softly. "It's bad, but I'll be all right."

Cathan came and crouched at Rhys's feet to look at the wound, snuffling and wiping futilely at his nose with a bloodstained sleeve, then sat heavily on the floor and let out a forlorn sigh.

"Well, at least Father will be here soon with a Healer. The King's lending him Dom Sereld. He's one of the best. Damn!" He slammed a bloody fist against the flagstones. "I should have gotten to you sooner! I should have come down when Evaine asked me to! They poisoned the dogs with doctored meat while the servants were busy in the cellar. They must've known most of the household were away."

The steward came with questions about the prisoners after that, and Cathan took Joram with him to see to their handling until Camber should arrive. Evaine stayed with Rhys, though, laying her small hands on his forehead and helping him ease into a floating, twilight state that was even more isolated from his pain. It was something Rhys could have done for himself, as most Deryni with any training could have done, but the luxury of not *having* to do it released him to drift off to merciful sleep while he waited for the Healer.

He dreamed about the cat curled in the hollow of his arm—dreamed that the animal snuggled closer and buried a cool, damp nose in his side, purring so hard that the vibration resonated all along his body.

He dreamed of the summer Camber had brought the kitten home: an endearing scrap of plush black fur with eyes like peridots and needle-sharp hooks at the tips of velvet paws. By Christmas, the adorable kitten had turned, as kittens will, into an awkward, gangling catling, all huge bat-ears, over-long legs, and a stringy tail. For months, Lady Jocelyn referred to him as "that damned stringbean."

By the following summer, however, Symber had grown into the promise of his kittenhood and become the sleek, graceful feline Rhys remembered best: friend and comforter and counsel-keeping confidant of all the MacRorie household—though it was Evaine and Rhys he seemed to prefer. It was that Symber who stayed in Rhys's dream, his purr rumbling in Rhys's ear and taking him deeper, deeper. . . .

He started to come up once, but a new presence pushed him gently down. He thought that perhaps he should resist, at least until he found out who it was, but almost immediately he realized that it was a Healer's presence and that it was all right to let go. He sensed the anxious brush of Camber's mind against his own for an instant, and Lady Jocelyn's; but then it seemed far too much effort to even keep wondering what would happen. Drowsily, he returned to the dream of the purring cat.

The next thing he knew, there *was* a cat purring in his ear. As he opened his eyes, still slightly curled on his left side, a svelte black cat body stretched languidly against his chest and kneaded velvet paws against his arm, butting a moist black nose against his cheek before settling back to sleep with a contented purr. A stranger in a rich tunic of Healer's green was kneeling on his right, wiping just-washed hands on a clean towel.

"Well," the Healer said, giving him a pleased smile, "I'm surprised you didn't finish the job yourself. You did fine work on the cat."

"I what?" Rhys said stupidly, for the man's words made no sense whatever.

The man only chuckled and shook his head, tossing the towel aside. Freckles across his nose and cheeks made him look youthful despite his receding hairline, for there was very little grey frosting his reddish brown hair, but Rhys guessed him to be approaching fifty. There were little crinkles at the corners of his dark brown eyes, and his neat little beard and mustache were greyer than his hair. He let Rhys roll onto his back, but he restrained him with a hand on his chest when Rhys would have tried to sit up.

"Not yet, son. I want to make sure I've gotten any clots before you move that leg much. Of course, something like a hamstring's a little tricky to manage on oneself," he went on, bending Rhys's restored leg at the knee and stroking his Healer's hands lightly over the area where the wound had been. "I had to have Lord Camber help me with the physical manipulation. Healing's much easier if you can get injured bits back in the general area where they belong, before you start. Hard to Heal across a handspan of empty space when you're trying to reattach two cut ends.

"But you'll learn all about that when you get some proper training. Did you really not know? By the way, I'm Sereld, the King's Healer."

"I'm—Rhys Thuryn," Rhys managed to whisper, his head reeling with the implications of what Sereld was saying.

"Yes, I know. And a lot of other people are going to know soon, too. It's cause for celebration when we find a Healer we didn't know about." He finished with Rhys's leg and gently straightened it out again, then cocked his head at Rhys more thoughtfully.

"Were either of your parents Healers, son?"

"No. But they died when I was only a baby."

"Hmmm. Any Healers in the rest of the family?"

"Not that I know of," Rhys whispered. "Did I—did I *really* Heal Symber?"

"The cat? Sure looks that way. Controlled most of your own bleeding, too." Sereld chucked Symber under the chin and grinned as the big cat rubbed its whiskers against his hand and purred even louder. "Well, you needn't thank *me,* little friend. You've got your own Healer to take care of you from now on."

Still not quite able to believe what he was hearing, Rhys raised up on his elbows.

"But, if I'm—a *Healer,*" he spoke the word with awe, "why didn't I know?" he whispered. "Why didn't anyone tell me?"

"I suppose no one thought to check," Sereld said, beginning to take instruments out of a basin of water and drying them with a soft cloth. "Those Michaelines of yours don't know everything, you know. And you're not from a Healer family, after all."

Rhys started as the Healer tossed his clean instruments into a green Healer's satchel and they clinked.

"On the other hand, you're just about the right age for the gift to show up, if it's going to," Sereld continued. "Naturally, Healing potential can be spotted earlier, if one has cause to look for it; but unless its manifestation is being deliberately guided by Healer training, the first appearance of the actual gift is often triggered by some great need for it to work." He grinned hugely. "I suppose you could say that your furry friend here was a—*catalyst?*"

Rhys groaned at the play on words, but he could not help joining in with Sereld's hearty laughter. He was grinning ear to ear as he let the Healer help him sit up; and Symber's rumbling purr was an echo of Rhys's own joy as he scooped up the cat and gathered it into his lap.

As Camber and the awed Joram and Evaine and all the others came gathering around to offer their congratulations, Rhys knew that there was no longer any question about what he was going to do with his life.

THE FOXWIFE

Jane Yolen

IT WAS THE SPRING OF THE YEAR. BLOSSOMS SAT LIKE PAINTED butterflies on every tree. But the student Jiro did not enjoy the beauty. He was angry. It seemed he was always angry at something. And he was especially angry because he had just been told by his teachers that the other students feared him and his rages.

"You must go to a far island," said the master of his school.

"Why?" asked Jiro angrily.

"I will tell you if you listen," said his master with great patience.

Jiro shut his mouth and ground his teeth but was otherwise silent.

"You must go to the furthest island you can find. An island where no other person lives. There you must study by yourself. And in the silence of your own heart you may yet find the peace you need."

Raging, Jiro packed his tatami mat, his book, and his brushes. He put them in a basket and tied the basket to his back. Though he was angry—with his master and with all the teachers and students in his school—he really *did* want to learn how to remain calm. And so he set out.

Sometimes he crossed bridges. Sometimes he waded rivers. Sometimes he took boats across the wild water. But at

327

last he came to a small island where, the boatman assured him, no other person lived.

"Come once a week and bring me supplies," said Jiro, handing the boatman a coin. Then Jiro went inland and walked through the sparse woods until he came to a clearing in which he found a deserted temple.

"Odd," thought Jiro. "The boatman did not mention such a thing." He walked up the temple steps and was surprised to find the temple clean. He set his basket down in one corner, pulled out his mat, and spread it on the floor.

"This will be my home," he said. He said it out loud and there was an edge still to his voice.

For many days Jiro stayed on the island, working from first light till last. And though once in a while he became angry—because his brush would not write properly or because a dark cloud dared to hide the sun—for the most part he was content.

One day, when Jiro was in the middle of a particularly complicated text and having much trouble with it, he looked up and saw a girl walking across the clearing toward him.

Every few steps she paused and glanced around. She was not frightened but rather seemed alert, as if ready for flight.

Jiro stood up. "Go away," he called out, waving his arm.

The girl stopped. She put her head to one side as if considering him. Then she continued walking as before.

Jiro did not know what to do. He wondered if she were the boatman's daughter. Perhaps she had not heard him. Perhaps she was stupid. Perhaps she was deaf. She certainly did not belong on *his* island. He called out louder this time: "Go away. I am a student and must not be disturbed." He followed each statement with a movement of his arms.

But the girl did not go away and she did not stop. In fact, at his voice, she picked up her skirts and came toward him at a run.

Jiro was amazed. She ran faster than anyone he had ever seen, her dark russet hair streaming out behind her like a tail. In a moment she was at the steps of the temple.

"Go away!" cried Jiro for the third time.

The girl stopped, stared, and bowed.

Politeness demanded that Jiro return her bow. When he looked up again, she was gone.

Satisfied, Jiro smiled and turned back to his work. But there was the girl, standing stone-still by his scrolls and brushes, her hands folded before her.

"I am Kitsune," she said. "I care for the temple."

Jiro could contain his anger no longer. "Go away," he screamed. "I must work alone. I came to this island because I was assured no other person lived here."

She stood as still as a stone in a river and let the waves of his rage break against her. Then she spoke. "No other person lives here. I am Kitsune. I care for the temple."

After that, storm as he might, there was nothing Jiro could do. The girl simply would not go away.

She did care for the temple—and Jiro as well. Once a week she appeared and swept the floors. She kept a bowl filled with fresh camellias by his bed. And once, when he had gone to get his supplies and tripped and hurt his legs, Kitsune found him and carried him to the temple on her back. After that, she came every day, as if aware Jiro needed constant attention. Yet she never spoke unless he spoke first, and even then her words were few.

Jiro wondered at her. She was little, lithe, and light. She moved with a peculiar grace. Every once in a while, he would see her stop and put her head to one side in that attitude of listening. He never heard what it was she heard, and he never dared ask.

At night she disappeared. One moment she would be there and the next moment gone. But in the morning Jiro would wake to find her curled in sleep at his feet. She would not say where she had been.

So spring passed, and summer, too. Jiro worked well in the quiet world Kitsune helped him maintain, and he found a kind of peace beginning to bud in his heart.

On the first day of fall, with leaves being shaken from the trees by the wind, Jiro looked up from his books. He saw that Kitsune sat on the steps trembling.

"What is it?" he asked.

"The leaves. Aieee, the leaves," she cried. Then she

jumped up and ran down to the trees. She leapt and played with the leaves as they fell about her. They caught in her hair. She blew them off her face. She rolled in them. She put her face to the ground and sniffed the dirt. Then, as if a fever had suddenly left her, she was still. She stood up, brushed off her clothing, smoothed her hair, and came back to sit quietly on the steps again.

Jiro was enchanted. He had never seen any woman like this before. He left his work and sat down on the steps beside her. Taking her hand in his, he stroked it thoughtfully, then brought it to his cheek. Her hand was warm and dry.

"We must be married," he said at last. "I would have you with me always."

"Always? What is always?" asked Kitsune. She tried to pull away.

Jiro held her hand tightly and would not let her go. And after a while she agreed.

The boatman took them across to the mainland, where they found a priest who married them at once, though he smiled behind his hand at their haste. Jiro was supremely happy and he knew that Kitsune must be, too, though all the way in the boat going there and back again, she shuddered and would not look out across the waves.

That night Kitsune shared the tatami mat with Jiro. When the moon was full and the night whispered softly about the temple, Jiro awoke. He turned to look at Kitsune, his bride. She was not there.

"Kitsune," he called out fearfully. He sat up and looked around. He could not see her anywhere. He got up and searched around the temple, but she was not to be found. At last he fell asleep, sitting on the temple steps. When he awoke again at dawn. Kitsune was curled in sleep on the mat.

"Where were you last night?" he demanded.

"Where I should be," she said and would say no more.

Jiro felt anger flowering inside, so he turned sharply from her and went to his books. But he did not try to calm himself. He fed his rage silently. All day he refused to speak. At night, exhausted by his own anger, he fell asleep before dark. He woke at midnight to find Kitsune gone.

Jiro knew he had to stay awake until she returned. A little before dawn he saw her running across the clearing. She ran up the temple steps and did not seem to be out of breath. She came right to the mat, surprised to see Jiro awake.

Jiro waited for her explanation, but instead of speaking she began her morning chores. She had fresh camellias in her hands, which she put in a bowl as if nothing were wrong.

Jiro sat up. "Where do you go at night?" he asked. "What do you do?"

Kitsune did not answer.

Jiro leaped up and came over to her. He took her by the shoulders and began to shake her. "Where? Where do you go?" he cried.

Kitsune dropped the bowl of flowers and it shattered. The water spread out in little islands of puddles on the floor. She looked down and her hair fell around her shoulders, hiding her face.

Jiro could not look at the trembling figure so obviously terrified of him. Instead, he bent to pick up the pieces of the bowl. He saw his own face mirrored a hundred times in the spilled drops. Then he saw something else. Instead of Kitsune's face or her russet hair, he saw the sharp-featured head of a fox reflected there. The fox's little pointed ears were twitching. Out of its dark eyes tears began to fall.

Jiro looked up but there was no fox. Only Kitsune, beginning to weep, trembling at the sight of him, unable to move. And then he knew. She was a *nogitsone,* a were-fox, who could take the shape of a beautiful woman. But the *nogitsone*'s reflection in the water was always that of a beast.

Suddenly Jiro's anger, fueled by his terror, knew no bounds. "You are not human," he cried. "Monster, wild thing, demon, beast. You will rip me or tear me if I let you stay. Some night you will gnaw upon my bones. Go away."

As he spoke, Kitsune fell to her hands and knees. She shook herself once, then twice. Her hair seemed to flow over her body, covering her completely. Then twitching her ears once, the vixen raced down the temple steps, across the meadow, and out of sight.

Jiro stood and watched for a long, long time. He thought he could see the red flag of her tail many hours after she had gone.

The snows came early that year, but the season was no colder than Jiro's heart. Every day he thought he heard the barking of a fox in the woods beyond the meadow, but he would not call it in. Instead he stood on the steps and cried out, "Away. Go away." At night he dreamed of a woman weeping close by his mat. In his sleep he called out, "Away. Go away."

Then when winter was full and the nights bitter cold, the sounds ceased. The island was deadly still. In his heart Jiro knew the fox was gone for good. Even his anger was gone, guttered in the cold like a candle. What had seemed so certain to him, in the heat of his rage, was certain no more. He wondered over and over which had been human and which had been beast. He even composed a haiku on it.

> Pointed ears, red tail,
> Wife covered in fox's skin,
> The beast hides within.

He said it over many times to himself but was never satisfied with it.

Spring came suddenly, a tiny green blade pushing through the snow. And with it came a strange new sound. Jiro woke to it, out of a dream of snow. He followed the sound to the temple steps and saw prints in the dust of white. Sometimes they were fox, sometimes girl, as if the creature who made them could not make up its mind.

"Kitsune," Jiro called out impulsively. Perhaps she had not died after all.

He looked out across the meadow and thought he saw again that flag of red. But the sound that had wakened him came once more, from behind. He turned, hoping to see Kitsune standing again by the mat with the bowl of camellias in her hands. Instead, by his books, he saw a tiny bundle of russet fur. He went over and knelt by it. Huddled together for warmth were two tiny kit foxes.

For a moment Jiro could feel the anger starting inside him. He did not want these two helpless, mewling things. He wanted Kitsune. Then he remembered that he had driven her away. Away. And the memory of that long, cold winter without her put out the budding flames of his new rage.

He reached out and put his hands on the foxlings. At his touch, they sprang apart on wobbly legs, staring up at him with dark, discerning eyes. They trembled so, he was afraid they might fall.

"There, there," he crooned to them. "This big, rough beast will not hurt you. Come. Come to me." He let them sniff both his hands, and when their trembling ceased, he picked them up and cradled them against his body, letting them share his warmth. First one, then the other, licked his fingers. This so moved Jiro that, without meaning to, he began to cry.

The tears dropped onto the muzzles of the foxlings and they looked as if they, too, were weeping. Then, as Jiro watched, the kits began to change. The features of a human child slowly superimposed itself on each fox face. Sighing, they snuggled closer to Jiro, closed their eyes, put their thumbs in their mouths, and slept.

Jiro smiled. Walking very carefully, as if afraid each step might jar the babies awake, he went down the temple steps. He walked across the clearing leaving man-prints in the unmarked snow. Slowly, calmly, all anger gone from him, he moved toward the woods where he knew Kitsune waited. He would find her before evening came again.

CONCLUSION

In her novel *Psion,* Joan D. Vinge created Cat, a brother for Nik Kolherne, Shann Lantee, and Ross Murdock, and for their sisters Simsa (in *Forerunner*) and Ziantha (in *Forerunner Foray*), all the so-called "stack rats," children of ghetto and gutter and casual crime. In our own world, the future of such children is bleak. In the worlds of Andre Norton and Joan Vinge, despite predictions of doom, the story lines elicit from such children incredible capacities for courage and love, which manifest themselves in loyalty and self-sacrifice.

What makes these books so satisfying is that by the time you reluctantly turn the last page, you know that the former thief, vagrant, or menial laborer will be rewarded—and forgiven.

Such books remind us that there is always hope. We too can beat people's expectations—and maybe the system as well. We too can rise above our hardships to become more than we are, maybe even all that we can be. No matter what we've been. And so Vinge's Cat gets a new lease on life. Gundhalinu plans to have the scars from his suicide attempt removed (in *World's End*). And in Vinge's Hugo-winning *The Snow Queen,* Sparks, who had been the brutal Starbuck and almost killed Moon, finds a second chance. It's not that the consequences of an act don't matter, but that almost any act (except the single, irrevocable choice of Darkness) can be turned to good.

Norton does it too. And this degree of forgiveness, this emphasis on being able to start over never fails to remind me of another woman writer, the fourteenth-century mystic Juliana of Norwich whose "showings" T. S. Eliot adapts as "Sin is behovely, but all shall be well, and all manner of thing shall be well."

Once again, in Joan Vinge's "An Open Letter to Andre Norton," she lets us know just how well everything's turned out, closing this book in the most fitting way possible.

AN OPEN LETTER
TO ANDRE NORTON

Dear Andre Norton,

This is kind of a love letter, and I've owed it to you for more than twenty years now—ever since I was in junior high school and I came home from the Mayfair Market one day with your novel *Storm Over Warlock*. When I read the description on the back of the book, I didn't even know what a Terran was . . . but by the time I'd finished the whole novel, I didn't want to read anything else besides science fiction. It was like finding the key to the universe, and although it probably sounds corny, it changed my life.

It wasn't until I'd read several of your books that I found one with a biography that gave away the secret that you were actually a woman. It never occurred to me then to wonder why you needed to use a male pseudonym, but—again without really wondering why—I was thrilled when I learned the truth. Because you were a woman, you were suddenly very real to me: a person, as well as an Author. I lay awake nights composing letters to you in my mind, trying to imagine what you were like.

I knew from the biographical notes in your books that you were a native of Cleveland, Ohio, like my mother; that you had been a children's librarian there and later worked for the Library of Congress; that you had also been an editor of young people's science fiction at Gnome Press, before you became a full-time writer and moved to Florida. I also learned that you had published your first book before you were twenty-one, and that you had written a lot of novels—though at the time I had no idea how many. I used to be afraid that someday I'd have read them all and there would be nothing left to look forward to. But you've been writing for over thirty years now, and I'm still discovering books I never knew about. Just the collection I have contains at least fifty books, including a title for every letter of the alphabet (from *Android at Arms* to *The Zero Stone*). Over the years you've explored (and explained to me) every imaginable science fiction theme, from psionics to parallel worlds, from interstellar to time travel. You've also gradually developed a vast and complicated future history around your science fiction novels, and a fantasy otherworld for your Witch World stories. Almost all your stories beg for a sequel. In many cases you've actually written them, so that I meet old friends again, or sometimes their sons and daughters.

You've used your experience as a librarian to find unusual material on a tremendous range of subjects and make it into stories: not only science fiction novels like *The Time Traders,* which combined extraterrestrials with Bronze Age Britons, but also historical novels like *Scarface* (which strips the glamour from Caribbean piracy and still makes the reader love every minute of it), mystery and spy novels, westerns . . . and more recently, gothics, a large number of adult fantasies, and delightful children's fantasies like *Lavender-Green Magic.*

When I feel fed up with the world, or that people are just no damn good, I like to sit and reread some of my favorites among your novels, because they always end up making me feel better. One of the reasons that they do is your ability to create another world, or time and place, that's so tangible and sense-stimulating I can step into the transporter or through the looking glass and *be* there . . . on Warlock, where the skies are hazy amber and the flora glow with phosphorescence at night; where leather-winged clak-claks drift above the cliffs as I gaze out across the storm-wracked beach toward a chain of ragged islands adrift on sea-fog. . . . Or on Dis, whose sun is infrared and whose seas have boiled away—

where only special cin-goggles can penetrate the suffocating, humid, utter blackness, and reveal to human eyes the degenerate life-forms that survive there, the nightmare creatures that don't disappear when the lights come on. . . . Or in the British Isles, wearing the copper armband of a Beaker trader and singing a song that won't make the charts for four thousand years—meeting a priestess of the Earth Mother, who materializes from the sun-shafted morning mist between menhirs of stone in the quiet forest. . . .

Written in a clean, straightforward prose that never gets in the way of its images, your adventures catch the elusive "sense of wonder" that sets apart good science fiction from all other kinds of fiction and makes a fan into an addict.

But escaping to another world doesn't guarantee a pleasant trip unless the fellow travelers are ones a reader can like and relate to. Science fiction is a field where too often the characters have been cardboard cutouts pushed around the landscape to move the plot along. But you have always tried to make your characters individuals. In your best stories the difficulties they face are not only those of coping with an unknown planet or hostile aliens, but also the overcoming of very real personal and social handicaps. And yet, in the face of all the obstacles that are thrown against them, they retain a basic decency and kindness that makes the reader care about them and *want* things to come out right for them: Shann Lantee, whose life had been a struggle for survival on the bleak mining world of Tyr, who saw his hope of something better—of belonging, even as a menial worker, to a Survey team—destroyed when their camp was wiped out by attacking aliens, leaving him stranded on an unexplored world . . . Holly Wade, a young black girl whose father was missing in action in Vietnam, who was suddenly uprooted from her home in Boston when her mother found a job—one that meant she and her brother and sister had to stay with their grandparents in a town where she was painfully aware of being "different," and where her conflicting emotions drew her into the power struggle between two witch sisters, one good and one evil, who had lived in the town's colonial past . . . Nik Kolherne, who had been an outcast even among outcasts because of his terribly scarred face, who agreed to help the interplanetary Thieves Guild in a kidnapping in return for expensive plastic surgery—and then found that he might lose his new face, or even his life, when he was forced to defy the Guild to save the kidnapped boy's life.

The fact that your protagonists are often life's underdogs—the abandoned, the friendless, the outsiders who are "aliens" among their own kind—is probably a part of what makes your work so popular with young adult readers. At the age when the average person feels the most misunderstood, oppressed, or uncertain about the future, it's a comfort and a relief to meet characters with similar troubles—individuals who are eventually able to surmount not only the situation's physical dangers, but also the painful difficulties of communication, of proving their own worth and independence to a doubting superior or an indifferent universe.

Your obvious compassion for your protagonists, and their humanity toward others, helps reinforce the feeling that the reader too will eventually win through life's trials—and more importantly, that its rewards and goals can be attained by sensible and honorable means. (The encouragement and reassurance that belief gives to a reader are not limited to young adults, either.) The quiet moral values your stories have taught me over the years have always been strong, positive ones, and it's easy to believe that you hold them all yourself.

You also taught me, at an important time in my life, to try to see all people as equals and individuals, no matter what their race (or sex) happened to be. At a time when the average cast of a science fiction story was strictly white Anglo-Saxon Protestant, you followed the unusual course of including important characters who were members of minority groups, in stories like *Star Man's Son: 2250 AD* and the Solar Queen series. And you followed the even more uncommon course of having heroes who were not "All-American" blue-eyed blonds—like Travis Fox, the Native American hero of *Galactic Derelect;* Shann Lantee of *Storm Over Warlock,* a kind of "Heinz 57" of humanity; Kincar S'Rudd of *Star Gate,* who was half-alien. As science fiction writers, and Americans in general, have become more sensitive to the value of the different cultural backgrounds that exist in the United States—and the world—you have made that aspect of your work even stronger.

Your alien characters have been equally varied, ranging from the feline Salarikis and the benign reptilian Zacathans to the vicious insectoid Throgs, whose thought processes seem to have no common ground with humanity's. But your specialty—and probably one of the things my friends and I have always enjoyed the most—is your treatment of relationships between humans and animals, particularly cats. The telepathic rapport between human and animal sensitives in stories like *Catseye* gives the reader, like the protagonist, a chance to experience the world with the heightened senses of a cat, a fox, a wolverine, or an alien creature like Harath in *Forerunner Foray* . . . and a chance to trace the alien windings of nonhuman thought patterns. Their human-animal rapport communicates your own love for animals with a kind of telepathy to anyone who reads your novels.

But for me probably the most important "cause" that you've supported in your writing has been that of the equality of women. Simply by succeeding so well in the "no-woman's-land" of science fiction writing, you've been a role model over the years to my friends and me, even before we ever thought about the significance of having one. (One of the old, tired clichés of science fiction has been that women not only didn't write science fiction, they didn't even read it. And yet all of my closest friends are long-time science fiction readers, who discovered it independently . . . and some of their mothers admit to reading brothers' pulp magazines on the sly when they were girls.)

And in a field where historically the women characters have tended to be Barbie-doll sex objects and witless ninnies, you have never had a single female character who would make a reader ashamed to be a woman. In the 1950s and early '60s, when no publisher would have touched a science fiction story with a female protagonist and readers were reluctant to accept women in nonstereotyped roles, you wrote— consciously or unconsciously—stories with essentilaly all-male casts that avoided demeaning portrayals of women. The women who did appear in the stories were not compromised but were capable and dignified human beings, like the woman chief of the Plainsmen in *Star Man's Son,* and Lady Asgar in *Star Gate.* In *Storm Over Warlock* and its sequel, *Odeal In Otherwhere,* the portrayal of the Wyverns, an alien matriarchy, was both exotic and realisitic without the grotesque pseudo-Amazonian trappings that male interpretations generally gave to female dominance.

Ordeal In Otherwhere had the added distinction of being the first of your books I read to actually have a female protagonist. I had never had any trouble identifying with male characters in science fiction novels, simply because so few women existed (and the men had all the fun anyway). But I'd always treasured the few strong women I ran across, and to have one as a main character—someone I could identify with 100%—was a joy. *Ordeal In Otherwhere* was published in 1964, well before the women's movement had begun to make us all aware of the double standard that weighed down our lives—but Charis Nordholm, the heroine, was a fully liberated woman, who came from a world where sexual equality was the enlightened norm. She was competent, resourceful, brave, and empathic, and she faced dangers with the story's hero and their animal allies as a complete equal. Probably only someone with your popularity as a science fiction writer could have gottenaway with it at that early date.

Since then, men and women have generally shared both the adventure and the center stage in your novels, often taking turns as the viewpoint character for the story. In *Forerunner Foray,* one of your more recent novels, the heroine Ziantha not only lives one life as a human sensitive used by the criminal underworld of the Guild, but shares a mental bond with an unknown male sensitive and becomes two women long dead—Vintra, a humanoid rebel leader, and D'Eyree, an amphibian alien struggling to save her civilization from destruction. Your recent novels written for preteens also feature strong heroines along with, or instead of, boys, giving younger girls someone to identify with as well.

A lot has been written in the last few years about the

importance of providing role models to show girls and women that the only bounds on their future are—or should be—ones they set for themselves. And I realized recently that I could trace the importance of my reading in the way my own life turned out: all of the most important things in my life right now—my writing, my relationships, my interest in science fiction and anthropology—are directly or indirectly the result of how much I loved your stories while I was growing up. Back when I first discovered that you were a woman writer, my own dreams weren't nearly big enough for me to imagine that I'd ever achieve that goal myself . . . but over the years your stories fed my dreams and kept them growing, and in the end I did—

Because of you, I am.

Thank you very much,
Joan Vinge